A
French
Fling

BESTSELLING AUSTRALIAN AUTHOR
MICHELLE DOUGLAS
& RACHAEL STEWART

CONTENTS

Secret Fling

Michelle Douglas

Michelle Douglas has been writing for Harlequin since 2007 and believes she has the best job in the world. She lives in a leafy suburb of Newcastle on Australia's east coast with her own romantic hero, a house full of dust and books, and an eclectic collection of '60s and '70s vinyl. She loves to hear from readers and can be contacted via her website, michelle-douglas.com.

Books by Michelle Douglas

One Summer in Italy

Unbuttoning the Tuscan Tycoon
Cinderella's Secret Fling

One Year to Wed

Claiming His Billion-Dollar Bride

Secret Billionaire on Her Doorstep
Billionaire's Road Trip to Forever
Cinderella and the Brooding Billionaire
Escape with Her Greek Tycoon Wedding
Date in Malaysia
Reclusive Millionaire's Mistletoe Miracle
Waking Up Married to the Billionaire
Tempted by Her Greek Island Bodyguard

Dear Reader,

When an image of a heroine leaping aboard a canalboat begging the hero to hide her popped into my mind, I couldn't help wondering who she was and what she was running from. I also saw the way the hero immediately scowled, and I wanted to know the why of that too. And that's how *Secret Fling with the Billionaire* was born.

Former actress Cleo has been trying to leave her scandalous reputation behind. Unfortunately, a series of disastrous high-profile relationships has kept her in the limelight. After the latest disaster, though, she's sworn off men and is determined to make some serious changes in her life.

Recluse Jude is horrified when Cleo literally crashes through the door of his boat. After a recent tragedy, he's been hiding from the world. But sunny Cleo is exactly what Jude needs, and as they work together to keep her hidden from the paparazzi, they find their assumptions about themselves and each other being challenged.

It was so much fun watching this pair engage and retreat, untangling each other's knots and falling in love. I hope you too love Cleo and Jude's journey to happy-ever-after.

Hugs,

Michelle

To all of my wonderful readers.
To those who leave reviews, who write to tell me
they love my books, and to those who push my
books into the hands of their family and friends and
order them to read them. From the bottom of
my heart, thank you!

Praise for
Michelle Douglas

"Michelle Douglas writes the most beautiful stories,
with heroes and heroines who are real and so
easy to get to know and love.... This is a moving
and wonderful story that left me feeling fabulous....
I do highly recommend this one, Ms. Douglas has
never disappointed me with her stories."

—*Goodreads* on
Redemption of the Maverick Millionaire

CHAPTER ONE

CLEO DUCKED DOWN an alley, her heart pounding and her breath fogging the early-morning January air. How had they tracked her down so quickly?

Because they knew you'd go to Fairfield House.

Seeking shelter in the family home in Maida Vale hadn't worked out the way she'd hoped. Her father had woken her precisely thirty-seven minutes after she'd finally fallen asleep to tell her he was tired of her 'attention-seeking behaviour' and that she'd need to find an alternative hiding place.

Apparently an upcoming election was more important than a daughter in need. Especially one as troublesome as her.

Happy New Year to you too, Dad. Her eyes stung. She told herself it was from the cold.

Footsteps sounded in the chill air and she flattened herself in the alcove of a doorway, holding her breath when they halted at the top of the alley. They moved on and she instantly sped down the alley on silent feet, grateful to be wearing soft-soled ballet flats. Her feet might be freezing, but at least her footsteps were silent.

The alley led down to the canal path in Little Venice. Pulling the brim of her hat down low, she turned left and prayed it was the right choice. Seizing her phone, she started to dial a number…

Thumbs and feet both faltered. Margot wouldn't come to her aid, not this time. In fact, if Cleo messed this up, her sister might never speak to her again.

A lump the size of Fairfield House lodged in her throat. Why hadn't she controlled her temper, why hadn't she…?

Enough.

There'd be time for regrets later. She could whip herself with them then. In the here and now, she needed to focus on not landing on the front pages of the tabloids *again*.

On the path up ahead, another photographer appeared. His back was to her, but he'd turn around any moment. Behind her, she heard the approaching footsteps of the first photographer. Once they reached the path, she'd be cornered. Twisting her hands together, she scoured her surroundings. A wall at least eight feet high towered to her left. She had no hope of scaling it. To her right was the canal. She could swim it. It'd be freezing, but…

Oh, and pictures of you splashed across the front pages of the dailies swimming in the canal in January will make Margot's day, huh?

That'd be worse than today's front page!

Nothing is worse than today's front page.

Her heart pounded in her ears. She needed an escape hatch if she didn't want to ruin her relationship with her sister forever…

She couldn't go forward.

She couldn't go back the way she'd come.

There was an un-scalable fence one way, the canal the other, with canal boats...

She blinked. An open door on a canal boat named *Camelot* beckoned like a bright star.

Not giving herself time to think, Cleo shot across the path and leapt onto its rear deck, the thin soles of her ballet flats slipping on the slick, dew-laden surface, her arms windmilling wildly and her phone flying from her hand to land in the canal with a soft splash.

Don't fall in the water! Don't fall in the water!

Launching herself through the door, she half-slipped down a set of stairs on her backside—not elegant, but certainly efficient.

A lone man glanced up from reading the paper at a dinette. Her picture glared back at her from its front page in silent accusation. Still on her backside, she shuffled to the side behind an arm chair—out of view of anyone who might peer through the door. Lifting a finger, she held it to her lips, then pressed her hands together in a silent plea that he not give her away.

Leaning back, he closed the paper, his gaze briefly resting on the front page. Glancing back, he gestured for her to remove her sunglasses. She did. She had no control over the way her eyes filled, though. Blinking hard, she gritted her teeth, determined to not let a single stupid tear fall. He looked as if he wanted to swear. She wholly sympathised.

Grinding back what sounded like a muttered curse, he eased out from behind the table with remarkable grace for such a large man—not that he was brawny, just tall and rangy. Something inside her give a soft sigh of appreciation. She slapped it hard.

'Hello?' someone called from outside.

Mr Tall, Dark and Scowling started for the door. Praying he wouldn't pick her up on the way and dump her at the waiting journalist's feet, she seized a beanie resting on the arm chair and held it out to him with an apologetic grimace. It was cold out.

He pulled it on over thick dark hair that looked incredibly soft and…

'Hello?' the journalist called out again.

Blue eyes turned winter-frigid. Swallowing, she handed him her sunglasses before he could turn her to ice. He shoved them on his nose and stomped up the steps.

''Scuse me, mate, have you seen a woman come past?'

Her stomach shrivelled to the size of a small, hard walnut. *Please don't let him give me away.* She closed her eyes and crossed everything.

'Look, *mate*, only thing I've seen…'

Her eyes flew open at the thick Geordie accent that emerged from her reluctant rescuer's mouth. Had he travelled by canal boat all the way from Newcastle? Was that even possible? If so, he was a long way from home.

She shook herself. What did any of that matter?

Focus, Cleo.

'What did you see?'

'A lad scaling that wall there.'

'Could it have been a woman?' The hungry greed in the journalist's voice nauseated her.

'Hard to tell. I called the authorities. Seemed dodgy. And, speaking of dodgy, who the hell are you, and what are you doing chasing some woman? Think it's time I called the authorities again.'

Her tensed muscles released and she rested her forehead on her knees. He wasn't going to blow her cover.

Thank you. Thank you. Thank you.

'No, no, I'm just leaving. Not causing any harm. Just an interested bystander.'

Footsteps moved away at a fast clip. Lifting her head, Cleo buried her face in her hands and let out a shaky breath.

Her rescuer closed the door and strode past her to drop the beanie and sunnies onto the table, before filling a kettle and setting it on the hob. Only then did he turn to her, hands on hips, and she had to crane her neck up, up, up to meet his gaze. He gestured to the dinette and she scrambled to her feet, taking a seat.

'You're going to have to wait an hour if you want to give them the slip.'

And then what? They'd be waiting for her at her flat. Her girlfriends' places would all be staked out. 'Thank you for not giving me away.'

He made tea and slid a mug across to her. He didn't ask her how she took it. And he remained standing, leaning against a kitchen bench, one ankle crossed over the other as he blew on his tea.

She took a sip of her tea, welcoming the warmth even if it was strong, black, unsweetened and not what she was used to. The newspaper he'd been reading rested on the table in front of her, a reminder that she'd once again shamed her family. Those days were supposed to be in the past!

Except apparently they weren't. Tears scalded her eyes. She gulped tea and welcomed the burn on her tongue. 'You recognised me.'

He shrugged.

She gestured down at herself. Ditching her usual uniform

of jeans and blazer, she'd raided Margot's wardrobe for a pair of sensible black trousers and a caramel-coloured sweater, before piling her hair up beneath a cloche hat. 'I was hoping this would be enough of a disguise to pass unnoticed until I'd reached…safety.'

Except nowhere was safe, not from the press. If the last eight years had taught her anything, it was that.

'Maybe if you hadn't appeared in the morning paper…'

If.

Guilt, regret and remorse all pressed down on her.

She straightened, registering that his accent had disappeared. Had he assumed it? What an excellent idea!

Glancing up, she caught his scowl, and her shoulders inched towards her ears. 'I'm really sorry I crashed onto your boat like I did. I was cornered…desperate.' She fought the urge to rest her head on her arms. Without meaning to, she spread mayhem and annoyance wherever she went.

'Forget it.'

If anything, his scowl deepened, but the unexpected largesse—gruff though it might be—slipped beneath her guard. She had to blink hard again. She gulped tea as if it might save her.

'Was he worth it?'

'Who?'

Reaching across, he turned the paper over and pointed to her photo. The gesture lifted his rolled-up shirtsleeve to expose a forearm roped with muscle. A tic started up inside her, but she squashed it flat. She'd learned her lesson, thank you very much—men were *off* the agenda.

Turning the paper to face her, she gave a startled laugh. 'Wow, I really did land a good punch, didn't I?'

'I'd have been proud of it.'

For the briefest of moments one corner of his mouth twitched and she held her breath, but it came to nothing, his face settling back into stern lines.

She sobered too. 'He'd just told me he'd been fooling around with someone *close to me.*'

She drained her tea. He filled it again from the teapot.

'I was as angry with myself as I was with him, though. I'd tried breaking up with him a month ago, but he convinced me not to. Told me he loved me.' Something he'd never done before. 'I was trying to be mature—relationships aren't all rainbows and unicorns, blah blah blah—compromise, put the work in...'

'You sound like a self-help manual.'

Her back straightened. 'I've read them all.' She'd done her homework and had put in the hours. She was on Road Straight and Narrow now. 'For all the good it's done me.' She scowled at her tea. 'Men suck.'

'That one does. Though for the next week it'll probably be through a straw.'

She barked out another laugh, immediately clapping a hand over her mouth. Pulling it away, she shook her head. 'I'm through with all of it. Romance is dead.' The sooner she faced that fact, the better.

'Good for you.'

She eyed him over the rim of her mug. 'Are you laughing at me?'

'Nope.' Pushing away from the kitchen bench, he slid onto the seat he'd been occupying earlier. 'I just agree that romance and relationships aren't the be all and end all. Too many people define their worth through them rather than in more stable things. So when things go belly up...' he shrugged '...they don't have the resources to deal with it.'

She didn't know if he meant the comment to be pointed or not but, given her past romantic mistakes, she'd deserve it if he did. And she'd take it on the chin.

She'd thought that she'd drop out of the public eye when she'd stopped acting two and a half years ago. The men she'd dated since, however, had ensured that had never happened. It meant a lot of people who'd never met her and didn't know her made assumptions about her. And she'd take that on the chin too because, in shielding her from those journalists, this man had saved her butt.

She shivered. She really needed to start making better decisions. Whatever she was searching for, it wasn't to be found in any of the places she'd been looking. She'd thought walking away from acting would change everything. It had changed some things, but not all. Her stomach churned: because *she* was the problem. She kept making the same mistakes. How stupid and self-delusional could one person be? She'd honestly thought Clay had been the one.

Don't think about that now.

'In my experience, love is an exercise in deception, disillusion and despair. We'd all be better off without it.'

Whoa. Talk about cynical.

He shrugged at whatever he saw in her face and she shook herself.

Focus on the practicalities.

'So…a quick question.'

He tensed.

'An easy one, I think. If I dropped my phone in the canal…?'

'Gone for good.'

She'd guessed as much.

'Need to ring someone?'

She nodded.

Reaching behind him, he stretched one long arm across the kitchen bench to open a drawer and fish out a mobile phone. He set it in front of her.

Picking it up, she dialled Margot's number and left a message. 'My sister,' she explained, her heart giving a sick kick. 'She won't answer a call from an unknown number. But she'll listen to the message and call me back in under sixty seconds.'

She set the phone on the table and started counting back from sixty. The phone rang when she reached forty-four. She glanced at the man and he gestured for her to answer it.

'Cleo?'

'Hi, Margot.'

'You lost your phone?'

'Afraid so. I was—'

'I don't want to hear about it! Just tell me the press don't have it?'

'The press don't have it.'

'That's something, I suppose. Now listen to me, Cleo, and listen hard, because I'm only going to say this once. If you appear in the papers one more time between now and my wedding, I never want to see you again.'

Cleo would've laughed, except she'd never heard her sister sound so serious. And her sister was the *queen* of serious. Her stomach gave a nauseating roll. 'Margot, listen—'

'No, *you* listen! If you ruin this for me, I will never forgive you. I don't want to see you for the next two and a half weeks. The next time I want to clap eyes on you is the morning of the wedding.'

'But...there are the final dress fittings.' Cleo was Margot's bridesmaid—her *only* bridesmaid.

'We'll make do with your last lot of measurements. Just don't go gorging yourself on cheesecake and crisps for the next seventeen days.'

Cleo held the phone away from her ear to stare at it. She pressed it back again. 'What about your hen night?'

'I don't want you there.'

She sucked in a sharp breath.

'In your current form, you'll ruin it.'

Margot's unspoken 'again' sounded in the spaces between them.

'You will lay low for the next two and a half weeks. I don't want to hear a peep about you, I don't want to see any photos of you, I don't want anything you do ruining my wedding. Do you hear me?'

She tried to swallow the lump in her throat. 'Loud and clear. And, Margot, I swear I won't. I'm sorry…'

But Margot had already hung up.

The expression on Cleo's face had Jude wanting to swear.

'No.' She lifted the newspaper and shook it. 'He wasn't worth it.'

All of the vitality drained from those extraordinary olive-green eyes, and his chest squeezed tight, and then tighter still, as if to make sure he couldn't ignore it. He swore and raged silently, and did what he could to pound it into oblivion.

It didn't work. Cleo's downturned lips, the defeated slope of her shoulders, the way tears had sheened her eyes three times now but hadn't been allowed to fall all caught at him, doing its best to drag him out of his self-imposed exile, his hard-nosed detachment.

Not going to happen. In an hour, after he'd said farewell to Cleo, he and *Camelot* were heading north. He'd settled his grandmother's estate. There was nothing to keep him here now.

'Promise me, you'll do one good thing every day.'

The memory of the promise his grandmother had extracted from him, given reluctantly, plagued him. It'd plagued him for the last week. *Damn it!* If the last nine months had proven anything, it was damsels in distress weren't his forte.

He wrinkled his nose. 'Margot didn't sound best pleased.'

'Understatement much?' She even managed a weak smile.

He stared at it and swallowed.

Slim shoulders lifted. 'It's her wedding in two and a half weeks.'

'She's turned into Bridezilla?'

'No!' Another faint smile appeared. 'Well, maybe a little, but she just wants the day to be perfect.'

As far as he was concerned, anyone who wanted to take the matrimonial plunge needed their head read. 'Perfection is a lot of pressure.'

Cleo blinked and then smiled—really smiled. She had a wide mouth. Her eyes danced, and it was like a sucker punch.

'I don't mean "perfection" in that the sun must shine like it's never shone before, and that there can be no crying babies in the church to break the reverent hush, or that all hell will break loose if the canapés aren't up to scratch—not *that* kind of perfection.'

Okay, she'd lost him.

'Her idea of perfection is that she and Brett will get to stare deep into each other's eyes while they make their vows, that all in attendance will be happy for them and that there's genuine joy at the reception.' She hesitated. 'That all who witness their marriage and celebrate with them will remember the day with fondness—that it'll be a happy memory.'

He ordered his lip not to curl.

'What she doesn't want is for her mess of a sister, who also happens to be her bridesmaid, trailing tabloid photographers in her wake and turning the day into a circus.'

'Are you a mess?'

She held the newspaper beneath her chin. 'I give you Exhibit A.'

Point taken. Cleo Milne was a *total* mess. She might look all sweetness and light, but the media had dubbed her Wild Child for a reason. She'd been an actress on a well-known British sitcom and the kind of woman he avoided like the plague: the kind of woman he'd sworn never to get involved with.

For some reason the front-page spread of Cleo punching her boyfriend—the lead singer of some boy band—reminded him of the look in her eyes when she'd said he'd been cheating on her. His chest drew tight. It didn't matter how famous you were, betrayal hurt.

Reaching across, he plucked the paper from her fingers and threw it face-down on the kitchen bench behind him so she'd stop beating herself up about it. While Cleo might be a mess, her sister wasn't supposed to think that. 'Okay, the timing of that might not have been great, but the berk clearly deserved it.'

'*Do one good thing a day. Promise me.*'

Pulling in a breath, he nodded. 'Right.'

Cleo glanced up expectantly.

'Margot wants you to lie low until the wedding, correct?'

She nodded.

He could help her come up with a plan, and then they could both be on their way. He wouldn't feel like an unsympathetic jerk, she'd have a direction *and* he'd have kept his promise to Gran: win-win.

'Anyway, just wait. This'll all die down in a few days. Once Margot calms down she'll see she's overreacting. She'll want you at the final dress fitting. She'll want you at her hen night.'

Cleo brightened. 'You really think so?'

What the actual hell...?

He didn't know Margot from Adam. Resisting the urge to run a finger beneath the collar of his jumper, he soldiered on. 'Until then, you need to avoid the press. Is there somewhere you can go?'

She chewed at her bottom lip. He stared at the way those small teeth made the lip plumper, deepening the colour to a raspberry blush. A hard hunger flared in his gut. Gritting his teeth, he ignored it. 'Your father?'

She flinched and shook her head.

'Other relatives?'

'It's just Dad, Margot and me.'

Why couldn't her father help her out? He bit back the question. Families could be complicated. He knew that. 'Friends?'

'That's where the press will expect me to go. They'll leap out at me from some shady doorway or corner, frightening the bejeebies out of me and snapping a picture of me looking appalled and terrified.'

And Margot would throw another fit.

'Margot deserves better from me,' she whispered.

'Cleo...' It was the first time he'd said her name. It rolled off his tongue like music and mead.

What the actual hell...? He was a thriller writer, not a poet! It was all he could do not to curl his lip at himself. *You're not a writer any more.* The unwelcome reminder had him clenching his jaw so hard it started to ache.

'Is everything okay?'

He shook himself. 'How's this for a plan? I'm about to head north. I can drop you on the outskirts of London somewhere and you can hole up in some country inn or rental for a fortnight.'

Her face brightened. The hard things inside him unclenched a fraction.

That's two good things, Gran.

He'd chased the journalist away *and* he was helping Cleo come up with a plan for her immediate future.

His lips twisted. *Go him.*

'Or?'

The excited buzz in Cleo's voice had his eyes narrowing. Behind the olive-green of her eyes, her mind was clearly racing. Foreboding gathered behind his breast bone.

'Or I could hide out on a conveniently passing narrow boat for a fortnight. I'd pay you,' she rushed on, as if seeing the refusal in his face.

'No.'

She eased back, chewing on her bottom lip again. His skin drew tight. He resolutely refused to notice that lip.

'I'll be quiet and not make a nuisance of myself, I swear. You'll hardly know I'm here.'

That would be impossible. 'No.'

'Why not?'

'The reason I took to the canals in the first place is because I want peace and quiet.'

'You've been travelling around a while?'

'Seven months.'

Her jaw dropped. 'Surely that's enough peace and quiet for anyone?'

He begged to differ.

Her lips pursed—not in any kind of mean or calculating way, but as if she was joining dots he didn't want her joining. Except she didn't know him, so she couldn't be joining dots.

'I know I'm in complete ignorance of your circumstances, but surely a bit of extra income would come in handy?'

He had to stifle an astonished crack of laughter. Yep, she was in complete and utter ignorance. And that was how he wanted it to stay.

She huffed out a sigh, as she read continued refusal on his face. His grandmother wouldn't be proud of him, but he refused to modify his expression and didn't soften it one iota.

'A week, then. Let me stay for a week and I'll pay you twenty-five thousand pounds.'

He had no hope of hiding his shock. He shot to his feet, whacking his thigh on the edge of the table as he did so. He swore, out loud this time.

She winced and mouthed a silent, 'Ouch.'

He glared his outrage.

She shrugged. 'I'd pay ten times that to save my relationship with my sister.'

Damn it.

'If I had it.' Her lips twisted. 'But I don't.'

He folded his arms. 'Do you actually have twenty-five thousand pounds?' He doubted it. She might've been an actress on a successful sitcom for seven years, but Cleo Milne was the kind of person who'd have long since frittered that money away.

She seized his phone and accessed the Internet, eventually turning it towards him to show him a bank account that bore her name. The balance showed just over twenty-five thousand pounds.

'It's my rainy-day fund.' She paused. 'It's the money my mother left me.'

Her *dead* mother. He dragged a hand down his face.

'And at the moment it's not just raining, it's bucketing down so hard that I'm going to drown unless I do something big. The money is all yours if you let me stay.'

He couldn't utter a single damn word.

'I know everyone thinks I'm rolling in cash. And maybe I will be one day if I ever gain access to my funds.'

What was she talking about now?

'But when I started acting I was a minor. My father signed my contracts. When I came of age, he convinced me to have the majority of my acting income put "in trust" for the future.'

Was he withholding it? 'So this…' He gestured to his phone.

'Like I said, it's my rainy-day fund.'

'What do you live off?'

'The fruits of my current labours.'

Which were…? *None of your business.*

'Fine.' He had no intention of taking her money but he had every intention of calling her bluff. 'One week on board the narrow boat *Camelot* at a cost of twenty-five thousand pounds.' He thrust out a hand. 'It's a deal.'

Squealing, she seized it and pumped it up and down. 'Thank you, thank you! You're a lifesaver.' Her entire body vibrated with relief. 'Give me your bank account details and I'll transfer the money now.'

Hell, she wasn't joking! And he'd just agreed…

'What?' she said when he remained silent.

'No.'

Her whole being fell. 'But I don't have anything else to barter with.'

Her eyes sheened with tears again. *Damn it!*

'The only way to ensure I don't get photographed is to not leave this boat.'

He couldn't kick her off *Camelot*, no matter how much he might want to. He pointed to the phone. 'Check how much it costs to hire a narrow boat for a week.'

She searched the Internet. He made more tea, for himself this time. What the hell was he doing?

His grandmother's voice sounded through him. *'You're doing your one good thing for the day.'*

This had to count for entire week of good deeds! Except he knew Gran wouldn't have seen it like that.

'Okay, here we go.'

She handed him the phone and he handed her another mug of tea before sliding back into his spot at the table to view the information. 'This is for a luxury barge. *Camelot* isn't luxury and it's nowhere near as big.' He fixed her with what he hoped was the steeliest of glares. 'Tell me exactly where you think you're going to sleep.'

'I'm guessing that this—' she tapped the table '—folds down to a bed. Which will do me nicely.' She pointed behind him. 'I can see one corner of your bed from here. I'm not expecting you to give it up for me.'

The narrow boat had a single long corridor, with no internal doors except for the bathroom and toilet.

'There are bunk beds further along.'

She brightened.

'*Not* luxury,' he repeated. The amount showing on her phone was an obscene amount of money. He wouldn't charge that for a month's worth of accommodation. Not that he had any intention of offering anyone a month's worth of accommodation, no matter how much he might sympathise with their plight or how beguiling he found their eyes. He'd charge her a reasonable amount, though. It'd keep things business-like and professional.

'You haven't factored in that I get my own personal narrow-boat captain, though.'

He raised an eyebrow and tried to look as severe as possible.

She grimaced. 'And I'm going to need a few things...'

He rubbed a hand over his face when he realised what she was getting at—he'd have to be the one to get them for her. 'You're going to make me go into a ladies' underwear department, aren't you?'

He'd know what underwear she was wearing. That would be wrong on too many levels.

She winced. 'Sorry, yes. I'm also going to need a tooth-brush, some clothes...and a phone. I'll give you my credit card.'

This woman was too trusting. 'Hasn't it occurred to you that I'm a strange man you don't know from Adam?'

'I know your name is Jude Blackwood.' She picked up some mail on the table to display his personal information.

His hands clenched. She had recognised the name. Did she know...?

She stared back, not a single suspicion lurking in her eyes. He released his breath slowly.

'And I know I can trust you.'

'How?'

'You could've made yourself a pretty penny if you'd made a deal with those journalists and escorted me off your boat. But you didn't.'

She might be a spoiled starlet, but nobody deserved to be hounded like she'd been.

'And I know people. I'm a good judge of character.'

Seizing the newspaper, he slapped a hand on the front page. 'I beg to differ.'

Her eyes dimmed and he felt like an unsympathetic jerk.

'Also, I'm not an idiot.' She thrust out her jaw. 'My sister knows who I'm with and now has your number. She's angry with me, but that doesn't mean she's not going to keep an eye on me.'

Okay, she had him there.

'And, besides the fact that you're all grumpy and growly on the outside, the name of your narrow boat suits you: *Camelot*. I suspect you're more gallant Galahad than misanthrope.'

'You call me that again, and I'll throw you in the canal myself.'

His scowl clearly didn't intimidate her because she bit her lip, as if trying not to laugh. She gestured to the phone. 'Do we have a deal?'

He knocked two grand off the price.

'Oh, but—'

'And I want your sunglasses.'

He added the last because he knew she wanted to feel as if she was paying a fair price. Those sunglasses might be ugly, but they'd provide an excellent disguise. They'd come in handy when he had to return to the real world.

Cleo froze like a deer in the headlights; like a statue; like a lamb to slaughter.

For a brief moment he thought she might hug the stupid ugly things and burst into tears. Instead, she wordlessly pushed them across the table to him. He couldn't say how he knew, but in that moment he knew she'd rather pay twenty-five thousand pounds and keep her sunglasses. He also knew retracting his demand would offend her deeply. He wanted to swear and swear.

Maybe, despite all appearances to contrary, like Cleo he still knew people too.

CHAPTER TWO

CLEO REMAINED HIDDEN below while Jude fired *Camelot*'s motor to life, untied the moorings and started along the canal. He seemed ridiculously capable, single-handedly managing the narrow boat with an ease she envied.

And found ridiculously attractive. *Oh no you don't!* She was making some serious changes to her life. Starting today.

No men. No romance. No making headlines.

Her days of lurching from one mistake to the next, one disaster to another, had to stop. And all the mistakes that had landed her in the papers over the last three years had involved men. The incident with Clay last night had simply been the last in a long line.

A hard burn stretched through her chest. She should've walked away. She'd planned to walk away. But then he said that awful...*thing*...and her 'sensible and dignified' had fled.

She scrubbed her hands over her face. That *didn't* mean she would fall back into old patterns. She *hadn't* been drinking.

She *hadn't* been seeking distraction or diversion. Not that her father would believe her, or Margot. And she had no one to blame but herself. It was what happened when you let people down too many times—they lost trust in you.

A weight slammed down on her shoulders. The room blurred, but she blinked back the tears. She'd honestly thought she and Clay would go the distance. Sure, she'd had the odd wobble, but she'd thought that if she worked hard enough, if she didn't give up, they could create the same sense of security she'd cherished when her mother had been alive. Security she'd been searching for ever since. But obviously she'd been looking for it in all the wrong places.

A lump stretched her throat into a painful ache. How could she have been so wrong? How could she have deluded herself so completely? Was she really so needy? Was she so incomplete—so *emotionally impoverished*—that she needed a man to make her feel fulfilled?

This had to stop. She didn't want to be *that* person.

No men. No romance. No making headlines.

Ewan had dated her to boost his credentials and land a role in drama series. Davide had used her so he could play the victim and gain public sympathy by staging an awful breakup. Austin hadn't cared for anything beyond her looks. He'd been appalled when she'd spent a weekend in her PJs watching old movies and eating popcorn. He'd wanted a trophy to parade in front of his friends.

None of those men had truly known her. None of them had truly cared for her.

And now Clay…

Here was a sobering fact—she was gutted to have been wrong about him, but she wasn't gutted to have lost him. So what on earth had she been doing thinking he was The One?

Pulling in a breath, she let it out slowly.

No men. No romance. No making headlines.

So the one thing she *wasn't* going to do now was develop a thing for her unlikely rescuer. Instead, she'd learn to manage her life with the same ease Jude Blackwood managed his narrow boat.

She glanced around. The life he led was pretty...spartan. The money she was paying him would probably be welcome, though it didn't change the fact that he was as happy about her being on his narrow boat as he would be finding dog dirt on his shoe.

But he *had* let her stay. And he hadn't taken her for a ride, as he could've done; he hadn't cleaned out her bank account. So she'd do all she could to be a model passenger. Maybe then she'd be able to convince him to let her stay for longer.

She glanced around again, taking in the dimensions of the boat. Dear God, how was she going to last even a week hiding out in such a tiny space? She'd go mad!

You'll do whatever you have to, to save your relationship with Margot.

Her hands clenched. Margot had always deserved better from her. She couldn't wreck her sister's big day. Margot had already forgiven her enough unforgivable things. She couldn't cast even the tiniest of dark clouds over her wedding—that *would* be unforgivable.

If that meant Cleo was to be confined to a floating prison for a week or two, so be it.

'Hey, Goldilocks...'

Cleo glanced in the direction of the door and Jude's voice. 'Are you talking to me?'

'Yep.'

'I'm brunette.'

'And yet, just like Goldilocks, you stole into my house.'

'I didn't touch your porridge or sit in your easy chair.'

'But you plan on sleeping in my bed.'

She spluttered and coughed. He didn't mean in the actual bed *he* slept in *with him*. He meant his spare bed.

His head briefly appeared, all dark shaggy hair, piercing blue eyes and a scowl. She wanted to tell him to be careful, that the wind might change, but bit the words back. *Model passenger, remember?*

Part of her wondered, though, if teasing him a little might make her the ideal passenger. Jude Blackwood seemed to carry the weight of the world on his shoulders. It'd be nice to lighten his load, if only for a moment.

'Have you had breakfast?'

'Yes,' she lied. She was already enough of a bother.

Those startling eyes narrowed. She tried not to fidget. He pointed to the kitchen bench. 'Make yourself some toast. That's non-negotiable,' he added, when she opened her mouth. 'I'm not having you faint on me from lack of food. You faint, and the entire deal is off.'

She'd hardly faint from skipping breakfast but nodded, model-passenger-style.

'And, while you're eating, make me a list of what you need. Some time this afternoon, I'll stop and get supplies.'

'Is it okay if I have a look around?'

His voice floated back down to her. 'Surprised you haven't already.'

The kitchen was small and compact. There was an oven, a two-burner hob and a small fridge. A microwave was securely wedged into a corner of the bench, and an electric toaster sat beside it. The contents of the kitchen cupboards told her he lived on tinned soup and toast.

She could do that too, but…

Glancing back towards the door, she tapped a finger against her lips. Everyone enjoyed a home-cooked meal. Wasn't there some saying about the way to a man's heart being through his stomach? She might not want to win his heart, but she did want to win his cooperation. And she'd become rather adept in the kitchen during the last three years.

She found strawberry jam in a cupboard, and a notepad under the newspaper, so she ate toast with jam and set about making two lists: one for the essentials she'd need and the other a grocery list. She checked the pots, pans and utensils. *Camelot* had everything she needed, all in pristine condition, which told a story of its own.

That done, she washed the few dishes, dried and put them away. She made more tea and handed Jude a mug, her arm emerging up the steps and through the door while she managed to keep the rest of herself hidden.

'Thanks.'

She might not be able to see his face, but she heard the surprise in his voice. Well, there had to be a couple of perks to having another person on board. When he was driving the boat he couldn't very well duck down to make tea whenever he wanted. She'd be more than happy to play tea lady.

With mug in hand, she moved along the corridor that opened onto Jude's bedroom with its neat double bed covered with a navy duvet. The room smelled of leather and the sea, like Jude himself.

The corridor narrowed again with two doors opening to her left. The first revealed a tiny toilet, the next a compact shower room. And then the corridor opened into another bedroom with bunk beds. One of the beds was made up with a sky-blue duvet. Cleverly constructed cupboards had been created in the rest of the available space, and several boxes rested along the wall—canned food, toilet paper, long-life milk and a box of yellow legal pads. There was a box of books too. Finally, a set of steps led up to the door leading out to the small deck at the front of the boat.

She mentally measured the space between bed, door and wall. If she moved a couple of boxes, she'd have enough room to do some yoga and other bits and pieces. It'd help keep her sane while confined on board. That was something. She *could* do this.

Back in the living area, she surveyed the space where she'd initially fallen through the door. The sweetest cast-iron wood burner rested in the far corner; the chimney disappearing through the roof was shiny, as if it was regularly scrubbed. A neat stack of wood rested in a box beside it.

Opposite the wood burner was that single arm chair, a foot rest and a small table—a space for one lone traveller. And, of course, more of those cleverly constructed cupboards and shelves. She slid back onto a bench at the dinette, refusing to invade what was clearly *his* space.

The light momentarily dimmed, as if they were travelling under a bridge or through an aqueduct. It would've been insanely interesting to go up and see, except she was currently too scared even to twitch a curtain at the windows. Going up on deck was out of the question. Maybe in a few days' time, when London was far behind. But, then again, maybe not.

She checked over the lists she'd made. She read the paper from cover to cover. She turned to the puzzle page to do the crossword and the sudoku.

Except…what if Jude did the puzzles? She'd stolen onto his boat. She wasn't going to steal his puzzles too. For all she knew, they might be the highlight of his day.

A pile of papers sat on the bench beside her. She seized yesterday's paper and turned to the puzzle page. He *did* do the puzzles—all of them. Of course he did; what else was there to do on a narrow boat?

When lunchtime finally rolled round, she made him thick roast-beef sandwiches and handed them up the steps. Again, she heard surprise in his 'Thanks.'

She ate her sandwich in silence. She resisted the urge to try and make conversation with him, though it settled in her bones like an ache. Jude didn't strike her as the chatty sort, and she'd be a model passenger if it killed her. Dropping her head to the table, she mumbled, 'It's going to kill me.'

She tidied the kitchen again.

An hour later she called up the stairs, 'Would it be okay if I read one of the books in the box in the—' she settled on '—spare bedroom?'

He didn't answer immediately. She swallowed. What was she going to do if he said no? Yoga; she'd do yoga. A lot of yoga.

'Sure.'

'Thank you.'

Racing down to her bedroom before he could change his mind, she carefully prised open one flap and then the other, discovering an almost entire set of 'Jason Diamond' books by Jasper Ballimore—a famously reclusive author who shunned live appearances, television interviews and the public eye. She stared at the books and grinned. A bit of Jason Diamond's kick-ass attitude was exactly what she needed.

Seizing the book on top, she dislodged the receipt and it fluttered to the floor. Reaching to place it back in the box, she glanced at the brief scrawl scratched across the bottom of it in big dark letters.

If you're going to continue in this ridiculous seclusion, Jude, at least drop signed copies into bookshops along your route. Randomly signed Jasper Ballimore books are treasured by fans and will keep interest alive.

There was a PS.

When can I expect the next book? It was due three months ago!!! Give me something to work with here, Jude.

She dropped the note back into the box as if it had burned her. *Jude* was Jasper Ballimore? Oh, my God, that wasn't a secret he'd want her knowing! Her heart thundered. *Okay, all right, get a grip.* She was an actress, wasn't she?

Except she hadn't trained as an actress. Playing a part in front of a camera was very different from pretending to be something she wasn't in front of real people about real things in real life.

Fine! Hauling in a breath, she closed her eyes. She'd simply wipe this moment from her mind, never think about it again.

Folding the note, she tucked it down the side of the box before settling on the surprisingly comfortable bunk bed and cracking open the cover. She lost herself to the story for a happy hour, before once again chafing at the enforced inactivity. She wasn't used to being so *still* and it meant the same ugly thoughts kept circling her mind like sharks. Had she tested Margot's patience too far? Did Margot now hate her? Could she fix this?

She always came back to the same conclusion: lie low for the next two and a half weeks and allow the media speculation to die down. That way, Margot's big day wouldn't be marred by the paparazzi wanting to snap pictures of Cleo.

They'd want to snap pictures of the bride instead, and the proud father of the bride, prominent politician Michael Milne. The bridesmaid would remain firmly in the background. Cleo crossed her fingers.

Mid-afternoon, Jude moored *Camelot*. She heard him tying off and, well, whatever else one did when mooring in a canal. She pulled herself into immediate straight lines.

Don't talk his ear off. Don't ask him for anything unnecessary. Don't be a pain. And definitely don't remember that he's Jasper Ballimore!

When he appeared, she sent him the smallest of smiles and slid out from behind the table. Rookie mistake, because space on the narrow boat was at a premium, and it shrank alarmingly when she and Jude were both standing in the galley.

She moistened her lips. 'Is there anything I can do?'

'Nope.'

'More tea or...?'

She broke off eyeing the flask he had tucked under one arm and the lunch box he held in his hand. As if in a dream, she reached for them. The lunch box held untouched sandwiches and a couple of biscuits. The flask was full of tea.

'It doesn't matter, Cleo.'

Oh, God, had her face fallen? She wrinkled her nose. 'And here I was congratulating myself on being helpful.'

He took the lunch box, removed the biscuits and set the sandwiches in the fridge. 'No harm done. They'll keep till tomorrow.'

Clutching the flask, she slid back behind the table. 'This won't.' She poured herself a mug. It was still steaming hot. He slid his mug across and she filled it too.

He didn't sit. 'If it's any consolation, your sandwiches taste better than mine.'

She stared down her nose at him.

'You put hot English mustard on them.'

She'd found some in the cupboard.

'I forgot what a good combination that was. Who knew hot English mustard could make such a difference?'

Her heart gave a funny little twist. What else had he forgotten during his *ridiculous seclusion*?

None of your business.

She gestured to the door. 'Where are we?'

'Uxbridge.'

Uxbridge? *Uxbridge?* She could get from Maida Vale to Uxbridge in an hour on the tube; she could probably cycle it in under two hours. She made herself smile. 'Great.'

He leaned back against the bench, crossing his legs at the ankles. 'You're a terrible liar.'

She grimaced. 'I had no idea cruising the canal was so leisurely. I thought we'd at least be in Oxford by now.'

His lips twitched. She thought it'd be kind of nice to see them break into a full-blown smile.

'There's been a bit of traffic in the canal.'

On New Year's Day?

'Slows things up.' He sipped his tea. 'You were hoping to be out of London by now.'

It was a statement, not a question. She shrugged. 'I suppose so, in an ideal world. But, as long as I stay below and out of sight, it doesn't really matter where I am, does it?'

Jude eyed Cleo over his mug, trying to work her out. She was doing her best to be low maintenance—not to make a fuss or be a bother—but she was keyed up tighter than an anchor winch.

Think it might have something to do with the fact her pic-

ture appeared on the front page of the newspaper today? Or that her lying scumbag of a boyfriend cheated on her? Or that her Bridezilla of a sister was throwing hissy fits?

Even he had to admit the woman had a lot going on. And, in spite of it all, she was holding up pretty well. *And* she'd gone to the trouble of putting hot English mustard on his sandwich. He didn't know why that caught at him, only that it did.

'If it's any consolation—' he shrugged '—I hate London too.'

She waved both arms towards the door. 'What on earth are you doing here, then, when you've a whole network of canals at your fingertips.'

He tried not to scowl. 'My grandmother's funeral.'

She froze, a stricken expression in her eyes, and he immediately wished the stark words unsaid. Cleo might be a total mess, but she didn't deserve his bitterness. 'Don't look like that. You weren't to know.' He tried to shrug, but the movement was jerky. 'As executor of her will, I've had to remain and settle her estate.'

Her eyes filled. 'Oh, Jude, I'm so very sorry.'

Her sincerity almost undid him. He needed a change of topic…fast.

'You check out your sleeping quarters yet?' The boat was a reverse configuration, with the sleeping quarters in the bow rather than the stern.

She nodded. 'Your boat is amazing.'

His cup halted halfway to his mouth.

'I mean, it's not very wide.'

He lowered his mug. 'Less than seven feet.' Six feet ten inches, to be precise. Reaching up, he touched the ceiling. 'Six feet six inches high.'

For a moment her gaze rested on him, weighted with something that had an invisible hand reaching out to squeeze the air from his body. Shaking herself, she glanced away. Air rushed back into his lungs.

'The design is clever, each nook and cranny designed for maximum storage. Like I said—amazing.'

'And your bed?'

'Comfortable.'

She really wasn't going to be a prima donna about this? 'It's tiny and cramped.'

'I might not manage a full yoga routine in there but, as you promised me a bed and not a yoga studio...'

Her eyes danced. He resisted the urge to smile back and wondered how long her good behaviour would last. 'You'll have more privacy down there. I'll pin a sheet up in the doorway of your bedroom later.'

'I don't want you going to any trouble.'

'No trouble.' It was as much for his peace of mind as hers. He didn't want to catch a glimpse of a naked leg or...

He shook away the images that flicked through his mind, but not fast enough. His skin tightened as if it had grown too small for him. A throb started up deep inside. *This* was why he didn't want her—or anyone—on board *Camelot*. He wanted peace and quiet...

'You're hiding from life.'

He straightened as his grandmother's words sounded through him, glaring at his feet. 'Did you make a list of the things I need to get you?'

She wordlessly handed him a sheet of paper. His brows shot up at the first item on her list. 'A tape measure?'

'If I'm not going to my final bridesmaid fitting, then I need to make sure my measurements don't change too much. If they do, I can send the dress maker the new measurements.'

He stared.

She rolled her shoulders. 'A bridesmaid has certain responsibilities. I've let Margot down enough. From now on, nothing but perfection will do.'

He opened his mouth. He closed it again.

'I'm not going to starve myself, if that's what you're worried about, but nor am I going to gorge myself on doughnuts.'

She liked doughnuts?

He went back to her list: toothbrush, yoga pants, T-shirts... underwear. His nose curled.

'What? It's the phone, isn't it? I know it's a hassle, but I put all the details there and—'

'The phone is a piece of cake.' He pointed to the offending item. 'I've never bought ladies' underwear in my life. How am I going to find the...?'

She gazed at him blankly.

'The right kind?' He'd walked past the women's lingerie section in department stores. It was bigger than the entire men's clothing section!

She pressed her lips together, as if trying not to laugh. 'It's easy-peasy. I only wear silk and lace.'

What the hell...?

'They're about this big.' She held her finger and thumb about two inches apart. 'And they come in a colour called rose blush—'

He choked and she broke off, laughing. 'I'm pulling your leg, Jude. I didn't think you'd take me seriously.' Her grin widened. 'You should've seen your face.'

I'd rather not, thanks all the same. Joke or no joke, he now couldn't get the image of Cleo wearing nothing more than a scrap of silk and lace the same colour as her lips out of his mind. He shouldn't be imagining Cleo practically naked. And he sure as hell shouldn't be thinking about her lips.

Intellectually, he'd known that Cleo was attractive—he'd seen a few episodes of the show she'd starred in and had seen the headlines of her many scandals. But in the flesh Cleo was more beguiling than he'd have credited. She vibrated with life. *She sparkled.*

None of it changed the fact that she was the last person he'd ever get involved with. He didn't court scandal. He preferred to live his life out of the limelight, thank you very much.

'You can get all the things on my list at a department store, or even a supermarket.'

He glanced back at her list.

'You don't need to go anywhere fancy. The underwear will come in a pack of five.' She reached across and pointed. The scent of pears filled his nostrils—fresh, sweet and oddly innocent.

'I've written the details here—bikini briefs, a hundred percent cotton. But full brief, boy leg, trunks will all do too.'

She'd written all of that down, as if aware the ladies' underwear department might bamboozle him. He needed to stop making mountains out of molehills. 'Colour preferences?'

'Don't care two jots.'

Obviously she was determined to keep up the low-maintenance masquerade.

He tapped the final item on her list. 'Puzzle book?'

'It's important to keep the mind active.'

His gaze slid to the paper.

'I didn't do your puzzles. I checked the papers from earlier in the week and saw that you did them.'

Her thoughtfulness slid under his guard. 'You could've done the puzzles, Cleo. I wouldn't have minded.'

'Seemed presumptuous—not my paper. And puzzles can be a routine thing. You might settle in after dinner with a nice cup of cocoa and unwind by doing the puzzles.'

She had him nailed.

I know people.

Maybe she did. 'Substitute that mug of cocoa for a dram of whisky, and you just about hit the nail on the head.'

She bit her lip. 'I made another list. I hope it's not presumptuous but, Jude, I love to cook.'

She handed him another sheet of paper—a shopping list!

'I thought I'd make a lasagne for dinner tonight, if that's okay with you.'

'Lasagne?' he parroted stupidly. The papers always made out that Cleo was a high-maintenance, spoiled starlet. And, while he appreciated the lack of foot-stomping about the size of her bedroom, he found it a stretch too far that she was now offering to cook. Next she'd be offering to knit him a scarf!

She's an actress. She's probably buttering you up so you'll let her stay for another week.

'I know it's not diet food, but it'll only be a small one. You can have the leftovers for lunch tomorrow, if you want.' She wrinkled her nose. 'I'm in the mood for comfort food.'

Her expression had his chest clenching.

Actress, remember?

'And I've made a list of ingredients for a stir fry for tomorrow night. I checked the size of your fridge and we should be able to fit that lot in.'

'You don't need to cook, Cleo.'

'I want to, honestly.'

More likely a case of seeing his cupboards were stacked

with nothing but tinned food. He rolled his shoulders. There was nothing wrong with tinned food. And yet the thought of home-cooked lasagne had his mouth watering. *If* she could cook…

'Besides, it'll give me something to do.'

She held her credit card out to him, but he raised both hands, warding her off.

'But—'

'Getting caught with your credit card and going down for credit card fraud?' He shook his head. 'No thanks. Besides, that could blow your cover.'

She swore. 'Then I want an itemised account. You need to bring all the receipts back with you.' She pointed a surprisingly fierce finger at him. 'I want to see *all* the receipts.'

It was novel not to be expected to pick up the bill—a fact that would undoubtedly change if she found out who he was. 'Deal,' he said, seizing his phone and keys.

Her hands twisted together and she suddenly looked young and vulnerable, as if he were her only friend in the world and she was about to lose him. He bit back something short and succinct. At the moment, he *was* the only person who knew where she was; the only person who seemed to care about the plight she was in. She might be a celebrity, but that didn't make her invulnerable. It didn't shield her from grief or heartache.

'Will you be okay while I'm gone?'

She pasted on a too-bright smile that made his eyes ache. 'Absolutely! Is there anything I need to know, or do?'

He shook his head. 'We're tied up safe and sound, but there are narrow boats moored either end of us. Don't answer if anyone knocks. And keep the noise down.'

'Roger.'

It took him off-guard, how much he hated leaving her on her own. *Crazy.* She'd be as safe as houses, provided she stayed put and out of sight.

'Look, provided I can negotiate the ladies' underwear department without too many hassles, I shouldn't be gone longer than an hour.'

Her eyes danced then. 'Good luck with that. And don't worry about me; I'll be fine.'

Of course she would. He nodded at the paper. 'Do the puzzles. I'll grab another paper while I'm out.'

It took Jude two hours. When he clattered back on board, Cleo jumped up and rushed across to take bags from him.

'What on earth…? Did you leave anything in the shops for the rest of the people?'

'Very funny.' He shoved a bag of fresh doughnuts at her.

She stared at them, then back at him. Her eyes grew suspiciously bright. 'You bought me doughnuts?'

'Comfort food. Won't happen again. Dieting again after today,' he muttered, easing past to set the shopping on the kitchen bench.

She slid into the bench seat, facing him. She stared at the doughnuts as if they were diamonds. He rolled his shoulders. They were just doughnuts. Didn't the people in her life do nice things for her?

Her boyfriend cheated on her. Her sister is making ridiculous demands of her. And her father…? Who knew what the deal was with her father?

'Why are you scowling?'

He jumped, making the scowl comical. 'I have three words for you, Cleo: ladies'…underwear…department.'

She laughed. In this light, her eyes were the colour of sea

mist—*really* pretty. And when they danced they could steal a man's breath.

'Was it dire?'

'The sales lady thought me a pervert. She didn't believe me when I said the underwear was for my little sister.'

'Do you have a little sister?'

'Well…no.'

'If you had the same expression on your face then as you do now, then she'd have known you were lying.'

'See?' He lifted his hands. 'I told you she thought me a pervert!'

Another laugh gurgled out of her. It made him feel good, as if he'd done a good thing. He nodded at the bags in front of her. 'Phone, yoga pants, T-shirts, hoody, PJs. Check and make sure they're all okay.'

He upended a bag of pears he'd bought into a bowl. Lifting one to his nose, he inhaled its scent. *Heaven.*

'What's this?'

Damn. He dropped the pear to reach across and pluck the boutique bag from her fingers. 'I…uh…it was supposed to be a joke—make you laugh.' He rolled his shoulders. 'But now it feels pervy.'

Her brows shot up. She eased out from behind the table to stand in front of him. 'Intrigued now.'

With a curse, he shoved the bag into her hands, scowling. 'Joke, remember?'

She pulled out a package wrapped in tissue paper and unfolded it. He winced at the tiny rose silk-and-cream lace panties that dangled from her fingers.

God, what would she think of him…?

Clutching them to her chest, Cleo roared. She bent at the waist as if unable to contain her mirth and literally *roared* with laughter. Tears poured down her face. Straightening, she tried to speak, but one glance at him sent her into fresh gales. She had to hold onto the table to stop from falling to the floor. Collapsing on her back on the bench seat of the dinette, her feet kicked the air, her entire body convulsing and her face crinkling.

With laughter. Something in his chest wrenched free and he found himself grinning.

'You braved a Victoria's Secret store?' Pushing upright, she stood again, mopping at her eyes. 'I can't believe you did that. I wish I could've seen your face.'

'I should've gone there in the first place. The staff just took it in their stride—proper professionals.'

She hiccupped another laugh. 'I didn't think anything would be able to make me laugh today.'

His heart pounded against his ribs too hard.

'Best joke present ever, Jude.'

Really?

'You're a gem. Thank you.'

Reaching across, she hugged him. She was all soft, warm woman, and she hugged him as if she really meant it. He couldn't remember the last time… Everything inside him started to ache.

Letting him go, she slid back into her seat and pulled the doughnuts towards her. 'Doughnut?'

He dragged air into cramped lungs. 'No thanks; I'm having a pear.'

CHAPTER THREE

CLEO WATCHED JUDE fork the tiniest amount of lasagne into his mouth, as if he didn't trust that she could actually cook. One bite, and his face cleared, and then he tucked in as if he hadn't eaten in a week.

Something stupid caught low in her belly. He looked as if he hadn't had a home-cooked meal in *forever*. She was suddenly and fiercely glad she'd offered to cook, and beyond the fact that it had given her something to do.

He glanced up, his gaze pinning her to her seat. 'Everything okay?'

'No.' The word blurted out before she could stop it. The joke panties were to blame, and the doughnuts. They'd changed everything. She didn't want to lie to him. He deserved better.

'I know you're Jasper Ballimore.'

He froze.

'There was a note from your publisher in the box of books.'

He set his cutlery down with one succinct and very rude word.

'Your secret is safe with me—I promise. But it's a big secret, and you'll want to protect yourself. Have your lawyer send me something—a non-disclosure or confidentiality agreement—and I'll sign it. I won't tell a soul.' *Please don't throw me off your narrow boat.* 'It's just—'

'What?'

The word was barked from him and she could feel herself shrivel. 'It just seemed wrong to feign ignorance.'

His glare didn't ease.

She closed her eyes. 'Do you want me to leave?'

'So you can run off to the press?'

Her eyes snapped open. 'You think that's what I'd do?'

He remained silent.

Her sinuses burned. 'Oh, that's right—I'm *that* girl. The train wreck, the car crash, the wild child who'll do *anything* for attention. The kind of person who takes delight in wrecking lives for the fun of it.'

Their gazes clashed. He grimaced. 'That's not what I meant.'

'That's exactly what you meant!' Her hand clenched, but she didn't slam it on the table as she wanted to. 'I thought you of all people would understand.'

'Me?'

'Yes, *you!*' She lowered her voice and spoke in a whisper. 'As Jasper B you guard your identity jealously, do everything you can to avoid publicity. I thought that meant you understood the half-truths and lies the media feed on—the twisted version of reality they peddle. I thought you were safeguarding yourself against it so you could focus on the writing rather than the celebrity. And I thought that meant you'd be able to see beneath the lies they printed about people like me.'

All the good things inside her—the things that had kept her going for the day, the tiny threads of hope and optimism— all dissolved.

'You're a writer. I thought you'd have more *imagination*.' Seizing her fork, she stabbed a piece of rocket. 'But you're just like everyone else.'

'Cleo…'

She sent him a tight smile. 'Silly me.'

Jude's hands clenched and unclenched on either side of his plate. 'Everything you just said is true. I'm sorry.'

She stared back stonily.

'*Really* sorry.'

She swallowed and glanced away.

'I've been operating under too many mistaken assumptions where you're concerned, which isn't only unfair but stupid,' he said. 'I should never have made that crack about you going to the press. If that had been your plan, you wouldn't have told me about your discovery in the first place.'

He looked haggard, as if he loathed himself. It was a hundred times worse than his previous scowl.

'I've no defence other than the fact you caught me off-guard. I panicked. My unmasking was the last thing I expected today.'

She suspected *she* was the last thing he'd expected today. He'd made an error of judgement, but he wasn't the only one. He didn't deserve to go to the gallows over it. 'Forget about it,' she mumbled. 'I can get on a bit of a soapbox about it.'

'With some cause.'

She shook her head. 'I've not always made good decisions. I can't blame the press for that. Besides, you don't know me. For all you knew, I could've been about to try and extort money from you.'

He stared.

'It happened to me once.'

'How? Who?'

'An ex-boyfriend. He'd taken photos of me without my permission.' Naked photos.

His Adam's apple bobbed. 'And those photos were published, weren't they?'

'Well, I refused to be blackmailed.' It was also the moment she'd decided she was done with the whole celebrity scene. 'I did sue, however.' And the money she'd been awarded had paid for her website development training. She rolled her eyes; and more therapy.

'Cleo...'

'Apology accepted, Jude.'

He opened his mouth and then closed it; nodded.

'So...' Picking up her cutlery again, she tried for light-hearted and breezy. 'Jason Diamond is your creation, huh? That's pretty amazing.'

Jason Diamond was one of the most beloved fictional characters of modern times. One of the good guys—ex-law enforcement and reluctant hero, he stood on the side of the weak and underprivileged, fighting for those who couldn't fight for themselves. Justice could be his middle name.

He glanced up and shook his head. 'Don't make that particular mistake. I'm nothing like JD.'

She went back to her lasagne and salad. 'JD is always helping damsels and dudes in distress—just like you helped me.'

'I didn't jump in front of a bullet for you.'

He shrugged, as if saving her from the press hadn't been particularly noteworthy. She stopped eating and frowned. Had his shoulders been that broad earlier? Dragging her gaze away, she focussed on cutting her food, lifting it to her mouth and chewing.

Keep things light.

'You might be asked to take that bullet if I screw up again and ruin Margot's wedding.'

A corner of his mouth twitched. 'You're not going to ruin Margot's wedding. She's just stressed. Brides get stressed. It's a thing.'

'A...*thing*?' She raised an eyebrow. 'You have experience?'

'I'm a writer.'

He shrugged again and she could've groaned. Every time he did that it drew her attention to the breadth of those annoyingly *broad* shoulders. Her fingers tightened around her cutlery.

'I do my due diligence; squirrel odd snippets of information away. Believe me, stressed brides are a thing.'

She leaned towards him. 'Are you going to have a stressed bride in your next book? That could...'

She gulped back the rest of her words, recalling his publisher's note. He obviously wasn't writing. And reminding him of that wasn't in the spirit of model-passenger behaviour.

'Thank you for letting me cook tonight.'

He frowned. 'Why are you thanking me? I should be thanking you.'

She sliced a cherry tomato in half. 'I really do like to cook.' It was one of the two things that kept her on the straight and narrow—exercise and cooking. 'And cooking dinner made me feel as if...'

'What?'

'As if I was pulling my weight a bit. Making up in a small way for thrusting my presence on you.'

He pointed his knife at her. 'You're paying me, remember? *And* you traded your sunnies.'

She tried to look casual, or at least not stricken. 'Oh, in that case, you got a bargain.'

'Did you see I grabbed you another pair while I was out?'

Had he? Abandoning her food, she rifled through the bags still sitting on the bench, her hand eventually emerging with the sunglasses. She put them on. They felt wrong, but they covered her eyes at the front and sides—great disguise sunglasses. 'How do they look?'

'Very chic.'

Smiling, she took them off and set them on the table. 'Thank you.'

'You want to tell me why you're so attached to those ugly things you were wearing earlier?'

'You want to talk about the next JD book?'

He pursed his lips. *'Touché.'* Then he pinned her to her seat with a ferocious glare. 'Is Margot worth it—all the sacrifices you're making?'

She went hot all over and then cold. When she realised she clutched her cutlery as if it was a weapon, she forced herself to loosen her grip. 'Yes.'

They ate in silence after that.

A short while later, Jude shook himself. 'I bought a bottle of wine. Would you like a glass?'

'No, thank you.' She eyed him carefully, moistening her lips. 'I don't drink.'

He held her gaze. 'Alcoholic?'

'No. At least, I don't think so. It's just, when I drink, my guard lowers and I'm more likely to do something impulsive.'

'Something you'll regret?'

'Usually something that will cause my family pain and, or, maximum embarrassment.' Such as appearing on the front page of the newspaper having an altercation with her jerk of a boyfriend. *Ex-boyfriend.*

'And, before you ask, I wasn't drinking last night. Clayton just…'

'Got under your skin?'

She should've walked away. But then he'd said that dreadful thing and she'd seen red.

'Stop beating yourself up about it, Cleo.'

Easier said than done.

Jude finished his lasagne. She stood and reached for his plate. 'You want more?'

'Is there more?' He eyed the leftovers, watching as she cut him another generous slice. 'There's enough left for dinner tomorrow night.'

'I don't like having the same thing two nights running,' she informed him. If his expression was anything to go by, that wasn't an issue for him. 'Breakfast and lunch, I don't care. Dinner, I like to mix up. Which means there's enough here for you to have seconds now and for lunch tomorrow too if you want.'

'I want,' he said as she slid the plate in front of him. 'It's great.'

'May I?' She held up a pear.

'Knock yourself out. Help yourself to anything you want. It's part of the deal.'

She sat again, sliced and cored the pear, her mind going over the question Jude had asked—was Margot worth the sacrifices she was making? She suspected he was more like his fictional creation than he cared to admit. He saw her as a damsel in distress and Margot as a villain. That couldn't be further from the truth and she needed to disabuse him of the notion. She didn't want him concocting some Jason Diamond scheme to win her justice. He'd be fighting for the wrong side.

'You think Margot is the bad guy in all of this, but you couldn't be more mistaken if you tried.'

He stopped mid-chew.

'Margot is worth ten of me. And I owe her.'

He finished his mouthful slowly. 'You sure you don't want that glass of wine?'

'Positive, but don't let that stop you.'

He rose and poured himself a glass of red. 'Look...' He slid back into his seat. 'Just because you were a little wild when you were younger...'

'I was charged with being drunk and disorderly twice. I was photographed dancing half-naked in the fountain in Trafalgar Square!'

'Not your finest hour.' He pointed his fork at her. 'But it doesn't make you a bad person.'

'And that's before we throw in the series of disastrous relationships I've had with high-profile men.' With last night's fiasco being her crowning glory.

'Again, it doesn't make you a bad person.'

But it did make her a delusional one—or maybe she was just a slow learner. She dreamed of creating the warm, family environment her mother had. To date, though, she could never have made that dream a reality with the men she'd sought to find it with. She'd just been too blind to see it.

Swearing off men for the foreseeable future wasn't only her wisest course of action, it was the *only* course of action that made sense. Until she could make better decisions where men were concerned, she was avoiding all romance, full-stop.

No men. No romance. No making headlines.

She took her time eating a slice of pear. 'Do you know

what Margot's dream was, before she decided to follow my father into politics?'

He rolled his shoulders. 'This isn't any of my business, Cleo.'

'She wanted to work for the United Nations. She made it through the first and second rounds of testing, and the first lot of interviews. The next hurdle was another interview. The powers that be decided at six p.m. the night before that it'd take place in the family home at seven-thirty a.m.—apparently they like to take you off-guard and make things stressful to see how you perform under pressure.'

Jude rubbed a hand over his face, as if sensing this story didn't have a happy ending.

'I stumbled in at seven forty-five after a night out, still drunk.' For God's sake, who stumbled home drunk at practically eight in the morning? 'And I proceeded to tell all assembled that Margot was a saint, and that perhaps she'd missed her calling as a nun.' Acid burned her throat. She'd been so angry at the world. 'I said her perfection was annoying and called them all a bunch of smug do-gooders who deserved each other.'

Jude swirled the wine in his glass. 'I'm guessing she didn't get the job.'

'No.' She couldn't look at him. 'It's the worst thing I've ever done.' She'd *never* forgive herself for it, not for as long as she lived. 'I was so bitter. So lost after our mother died.'

Their mother had been the machine that had kept the family running. Cleo had only been seventeen when she'd died. Margot had been twenty-two. Cleo had been twenty-two when she'd ruined Margot's dream.

'Apparently, I wanted to make everyone as miserable as I was.' And in that instance she'd succeeded. 'I resented Margot for being so seemingly perfect and doing no wrong, even while all the time she was hauling me out of trouble time after time.' She forced herself to meet his gaze. 'She didn't deserve that.'

'And yet she forgave you.'

For which she'd always be grateful. 'When I sobered up, I was appalled at what I'd done. I grovelled for days, begged her to forgive me.'

She'd been so ashamed. She still was.

'Margot laid down the law—said I had to go to rehab. I agreed. I wasn't doing drugs, but nobody believed that at the time, and I *was* drinking too much. So off to rehab I went. She also said I had to get counselling. I did, and it helped. That's the point when I started turning my life around.'

'And maybe she thinks losing that job is a small sacrifice to pay to have her sister well and healthy.'

'She probably does. She's a good soul. But you have to see, after all of that, I can't ruin her wedding too. I can't cast *any* shadow over it. All eyes should be on her, not me. Her focus should be on marrying the man of her dreams, not getting me out of another mess.'

Was Brett the man of Margot's dreams, though? As Margot's bridesmaid, not to mention her sister, it was her duty to make sure of that, wasn't it? And how could she do that when she was stuck on a narrow boat in the middle of nowhere? Her lips twisted. Unlike her, though, Margot was smart.

Be more like Margot.

'It's not too much for her to ask me to keep a low profile for the next two and a half weeks.'

He blew out a breath and nodded. 'I guess not.'

'You asked me if she's worth it—she's worth my every best effort.'

He leaned back, his shoulders sagging as if he'd just lost a fight. Except they hadn't been fighting, had they?

He tapped a fist to his mouth. He had firm, lean lips and she found her gaze riveted to them. A woman could weave fantasies around a mouth like that...

She tore her gaze away. *For God's sake!* She had to stop this. She had to stop making such terrible mistakes. She would *not* start fantasising about a man she barely knew.

'If we're going to successfully hide you for a fortnight...'

She blinked, and then her every muscle electrified. 'A fortnight? Did you just say...?'

His lips twisted, as if he were mocking himself. 'I think we both know I'm going to let you stay for as long as you need to.'

She could hug him! Except, she'd already done that and it had been a huge mistake. Plus, she was only making *good* decisions from hereon in. 'I'll pay you.'

He was a successful writer—*really* successful—but she'd read somewhere that writers didn't actually make all that much money.

'You'll pay me what we've already agreed and take over the cooking for the duration of the trip.'

She opened her mouth to argue.

'That's the deal—take it or leave it.'

Snapping her mouth shut, she dragged in a breath. She'd have to find some other way to repay him. 'I'll take it. And, Jude, thank you.'

He scowled and shrugged.

'I mean it. You're a lifesaver.'

'I'm a moron,' he muttered, making her laugh.

'Why?' Cleo fixed Jude with a gaze he couldn't read. 'Why are you helping me? I know you're a decent guy and all, but I also know you wish me a million miles away.'

She looked so alone and his heart gave a sick kick. She was used to everyone expecting something from her, wanting a piece of her. He suspected Cleo didn't get favours for free; they'd always come with a price tag attached. Was it any wonder she wanted to know what price she'd be asked to pay for the privilege of remaining aboard *Camelot*?

Exhaustion pounded at him. He uttered words he'd have not expected to say to her in a million years. 'Nine months ago, I lost my brother—car accident.'

Her quick intake of breath speared into his chest. 'Oh, God... Jude.'

'If I could do anything to bring him back, I would.'

She scrubbed both hands over her face.

'If you cry, I'm kicking you off *Camelot*.'

It was an idle threat, but she buried her head in her hands and took a ragged breath before pulling them away again, her eyes dry. 'You know how important Margot is to me because that's how important your brother was to you.'

Something like that. His nostrils flared as the familiar grief rose through him. He glared. 'We're not talking about this any more.'

'Okay.'

There'd just been too much loss. He didn't want to face any more, not even as a bystander.

Jude rose early the next day. He'd not slept well, too aware of another person occupying space on his boat, finding sanctuary on *Camelot*, just as he had. And he was still reeling from the fact that he'd allowed it to happen at all. He might not have been hard-nosed enough to escort Cleo off *Camelot* into the waiting arms of the journalists, but to let her stay for longer than an hour...

His hands fisted. Coming face to face with Elodie, his late brother's wife, at his grandmother's funeral had opened wounds that had barely had the chance to heal. God only knew why, but it had thrown him and left him feeling bruised. When Cleo had crashed onto his boat, his defences had been down.

He cast off at first light. Peering into the mild early-morning light, he could admit to himself that he didn't regret letting her stay, not really. What he'd started to doubt were his motives. Helping Cleo wouldn't erase the events of the past. It wouldn't give him absolution. It would, however, provide him with distraction.

And yesterday morning, sitting at the table, trying to read the paper, distraction was exactly what he'd craved. He'd wanted to drive Elodie's bitter words from his mind, if only for an hour.

And now Cleo was here, all warm, lovely woman, trying her best not to be a nuisance, and that had slid beneath his guard in ways he hadn't expected. Her sparkly chatter, her easy frankness and irrepressible humour were balm to a starving soul.

Which was stupid, and wrong. Because, first, he didn't deserve balm; and, second, unlike his fictional creation Jason Diamond—who in Jude's more optimistic moments he'd once considered his shadow soul—his motives weren't pure. In searching for distraction, he was in danger of using Cleo.

When he added his growing attraction to her—because, damn, Cleo was pretty with her dark hair, that classic English rose complexion and those extraordinary green eyes—it had the potential to lead him to places he had no right to go to.

She was a woman in need. She was vulnerable. His hand tightened on the tiller. He would *not* take advantage of her.

'Good morning.'

Cleo peered up at him blearily from the bottom of the steps, blinking sleep from her eyes.

'Do you know what time it is?'

'Sorry, I wanted to get an early start. I want to put some distance between us and London today.'

She smothered a yawn. 'Good idea. Do you have your flask with you or would you like a coffee?'

'No flask. I was hoping to rely on your good nature. I'd kill for a coffee.'

A few minutes later, she handed him up a steaming mug and sat in his easy chair to sip her own. From there, if she ducked down a little she could peer up at him, and if he ducked a little he could glance down at her. She looked ridiculously cute in her flannel pyjamas—deliberately chosen by him to cover her from head to toe. She wasn't supposed to look sexy in them.

He ground his teeth together. She *didn't* look sexy in them. 'Sleep well?' He didn't glance down. He didn't want to see those generous lips curve into a smile if she answered in the affirmative or that cute nose crinkle in a grimace if she answered in the negative.

'I never sleep well the first night in a new place.'

Had her nose crinkled? He glanced down. Nope, her face was smooth. She'd drawn her feet up onto the chair, a pair of his socks on her feet, because he'd realised last night that she'd forgotten to put socks on her list of things for him to buy. He'd hunted her out a pair of his own. They looked better on her than they did on him.

They're just socks.

'What can you see?'

Her words dragged him from his thoughts. He glanced

around. 'There aren't many people around. Why don't you pull on my mac and a beanie and come up to see for your-self?' Nobody would recognise her in that get-up.

She shuddered and shook her head. 'Too risky.'

The story she'd confided to him last night—her guilt over ruining her sister's chance at a dream job—still chafed at him. He understood guilt. He understood wanting to make amends. He might never find redemption for himself, but he'd help Cleo keep her promise to Margot. Family meant everything—a fact he'd only discovered after losing his own.

He shook the sombre reflection away to focus on paint-ing a picture for her with words. 'It's still and pretty. There's a fine mist rising from the water and the canal looks like a mirror. It's the colour of mercury tinged with a rosy glow at the edges.'

He fancied he heard her sigh.

'In summer, the plane trees are a bright green, but at the moment the branches are bare. And, while the sun is mild, it's sparkling off the dew, which makes the city look gilded... washed clean.'

'How pretty you make it sound.'

Speaking of sound... 'The morning is meeting with the birds' approval.'

'Oh, yes! They're singing their hearts out.'

Her smile... He forced his gaze back to the canal. 'There are a few narrow boats moored to our left, which is port. Starboard is to the right.'

She repeated that as it fixing it in her mind.

'Bow refers to the front, and the back—' he patted the rail-ing behind him '—is the stern.'

She repeated that too.

'There's a canal path that runs both sides. To the left there's a brick wall, probably houses and shops behind it.'

He continued describing what he could see. She listened as if mesmerised. But he suspected that was a symptom of a lack of sleep and not enough caffeine in her system yet. He hadn't spoken for this length of time, uninterrupted, in an age. He found he didn't hate it.

'That was perfect!'

He blinked to find her beaming up at him. His pulse stuttered.

'You ought to be a writer.'

He knew she'd said it to make him laugh, but a black cloud threatened to descend.

'Also, I wasn't dissing your boat when I said I didn't sleep well. I'll sleep like a log tonight. I'll probably snore and keep you awake.'

He couldn't resist teasing her. 'You did that last night.'

'I did not!'

He bit back a grin. 'How'd you know?'

'Because, if I had, I'd have a sore throat now.'

'When *do* you snore?'

'When I have a cold, have had too much to drink or am over-tired.'

'Forewarned is forearmed. I have earplugs.'

She laughed and it blew away the threads of that black cloud. He wasn't entirely sure that was a good thing.

She made scrambled eggs for breakfast. He told her she didn't have to cook his breakfast. She said she was making it for herself and it was just as easy to make enough for two, which was hard to argue with. He ate it standing at the tiller.

Afterwards she disappeared for a while. He heard the shower running. He heard her wash the dishes, and then moving about, as if tidying up. She made tea—which he declined—and sat at the dinette doing things on her phone, probably sending texts and reading emails. And checking the newspaper sites to make sure she'd not appeared in any of them.

She did some stretches in the space beside the dinette, a few yoga poses and sit-ups. She walked the length of the narrow boat a few times. More than a few times… A lot of times…

After lunch—*damn that lasagne was good*—she sat in his chair with the crossword book he'd bought for her.

'Jude,' she called up, 'I'm looking for a five-letter word that means "to push forward". It ends in an L.'

'Impel?'

'Yes!'

They did three crosswords. At this rate, he'd need to stop somewhere and buy her another puzzle book. She disappeared again for a while; he thought she was taking a nap, but thumping vibrated from the front of the boat—something unfamiliar. 'Are you okay?' he called down the stairs.

No answer. Damn it! Was Cleo okay?

Easing into the bank, he threw the middle mooring rope over a bollard and tied off, before racing through the boat's very narrow corridor. The thumping hadn't stopped. He halted in the doorway to her bedroom and then rested his hands on his knees, relief pouring through him.

Cleo had her back to him, her phone in one hand, earbuds in her ears, dancing—in a head-banging style—to some playlist or other. Easing upright, he grinned. She gave a silly little shimmy before jumping and turning on the spot. She still didn't see him, though, as she had her eyes closed, her mouth moving silently to the words of the song. Then she froze and opened one eye, as if sensing him there.

Scrunching both eyes shut on a groan, she covered her face with her hands. Straightening, she pulled the earbuds from her ears and glared. 'I know this is your boat, but you're not allowed to sneak up on me.' She gestured around. 'Privacy, remember?'

'I called out but you didn't answer. I felt thumping. I was worried.'

Her cheeks went bright-pink.

'I thought you were stuck somewhere or had fallen or something.'

She groaned again, even louder.

His grin widened. 'It was quite a dance.'

'Hey!' She thumped his arm. 'I didn't know I had an audience. And I'm sorry if I worried you...made you pull over...'

'No probs.' It was time for a toilet break anyway. There were a lot of pros to his solitary cruising, but tying up whenever he needed to pee was not one of them.

'How do you do this?' She thumped down onto her bunk bed. 'How do you not go stir crazy?' She gestured. 'How do you keep so *fit*?'

'I go running, first thing in the morning and then again in the evening.'

'You didn't go running last night.'

'I had unexpected company.'

She blew out a breath and nodded.

She was bored and it was only day two. She'd be climbing walls by the end of two weeks. 'What do you do, Cleo?'

She stared at him blankly.

'During the day, when you're at home—what do you do?'

Her face cleared. 'I'm a freelance website designer. I've

several jobs on the go at the moment. If I were at home, I'd be working on those.'

'What equipment do you need to do your work?'

'Just my laptop. It's got everything on it: the software I use, all of my clients' details, all the work I've done on the projects so far...'

'Is there someone who could have your laptop couriered somewhere for you?'

'My flatmate Jenna. We've been friends since... well... rehab days.'

'Do you trust her?'

'With my life.'

Cleo, he suspected, was far too trusting.

'Right, have her courier it to this address.'

Turning, he walked back to the galley, jotted an address down on a scrap of paper and handed it to her.

She stared at it and then at him. 'You're a life saver, you know that?'

His lips twisted. Yeah, he was a real knight in shining armour.

CHAPTER FOUR

CLEO ARRANGED FOR her laptop to be sent to the address Jude had provided.

'All done,' she called up the steps.

'Excellent.'

That was it. He said nothing more. Of course he said nothing more—the man was a recluse. He enjoyed his solitude, solitude she'd so rudely disturbed. Her stomach churned.

Don't bug him. Don't pester him with a thousand questions. Don't give him a reason to retract his offer.

Nobody would think to look for her on Jude's narrow boat. *Camelot* was the perfect place to hide. She couldn't give him any reason to abandon her on the side of the canal.

Zipping her mouth very firmly closed, she reached for her Jason Diamond book and lost herself in its pages. She came to with a little bump a couple of hours later when they moored. Voices carried over the water, along with the low hum of traffic. Water lapped against the hull and somewhere nearby a lark sang. The lapping water and bird song was soothing. The sounds of traffic and people not so much.

'Where are we?' she asked when Jude descended inside.

'About quarter of a mile from Hemel Hempstead's town centre. Normally I'd moor at Apsley, but we made good time today.'

No doubt due to the early hour they'd set off this morning, and the cracking pace he'd kept up all day.

Those broad shoulders lifted. 'It's not far for me to duck out and grab a few things.'

She bit her tongue to stop from asking what *things*—none of her business.

'Need anything?'

She shook her head. He stared at her for a long moment and it made her fidget.

Don't frown at the poor man. Instead, she pasted on a bright smile that made him blink. Too much? Ugh. Why could she never get that balance right?

'Thanks for checking, but I've everything I need. We've all the ingredients for dinner. And, if we're stopping in Berkhamsted tomorrow, I'm guessing I can grab a few additional things then if I need to.'

'What shoe size are you?'

She frowned, even though she wasn't supposed to frown. *Why?*

He merely raised an eyebrow and she threw up her hands. 'A four, but—'

'Can I get you to do me a favour while I'm gone?'

'Absolutely. Anything,' she replied, shoe sizes promptly forgotten. She'd do anything she could to repay his kindness and make sure he didn't kick her off his boat. 'What do you need done?'

'I want the names of five charities to donate a thousand pounds to.'

Five thousand pounds was how much she was paying him to keep her hidden onboard *Camelot*. She swallowed. 'You're donating five thousand pounds to charity?'

He remained silent.

She forced herself to ask a different question. 'The search parameters...?'

He shrugged and her mouth went dry. His shoulders were *the best*. She could imagine dancing her hands across them, glorying in their breadth, testing their strength...watching his eyes darken with desire as she did so. A bit like they were doing now...

Fingers clicking under her nose had her blinking. 'Earth to Cleo!'

She jerked and blinked. 'Sorry! Off with the fairies.' Heat flooded her cheeks. 'Parameters...?' she croaked.

'Local would be preferable, and I'd like some proof of efficacy.'

'Consider it done.'

He turned and started up the steps. 'Same rules as before—keep the door locked, don't answer if anyone knocks and...' He held a finger to his lips.

'I'll be as quiet as a church mouse,' she promised.

'No dancing,' he said with a grin, closing the door behind him.

She stared at that closed door, feeling oddly bereft. Jude might not be chatty, but his presence was oddly reassuring. Shaking herself, she pulled out her phone and started researching local charities. What on earth would he be into, though? What would he like to support—be *proud* to support? Where on earth should she start?

Abandoning her phone, she reached for pen and paper and jotted down all the things she knew about Jude. He was a writer. He lived on a narrow boat. She tapped the pen against her chin. He'd been in London to attend his grandmother's funeral. He'd lost his brother in a car accident nine months ago. No wonder he rarely smiled. She couldn't begin to imagine how awful it would be to lose Margot like that, so suddenly.

What on earth...? Losing Margot in *any* fashion would completely and utterly gut her. Her chest clenched and her breathing grew rapid. If she didn't succeed in lying low for the next fortnight...

'Stop it!' she hissed, forcing herself to take deep breaths, releasing them in slow, controlled measures as her therapist had taught her. She needed to stop imagining worst-case scenarios. It wouldn't do anyone any good. She needed to conserve her energy for keeping her promise to Margot and not being too much of a nuisance to Jude.

She stared at her list. Seizing the Jason Diamond book, she read Jasper's bio and added 'cricket lover' to the list. Pulling her phone towards her, she started madly searching the Internet, losing herself in the research. She made lists of lists, eventually narrowing the selected charities down to five local—or at least local-ish—options for him.

She froze when someone jumped onto the stern deck and went cold all over. Was someone going to knock, try to break in?

The door opened...

And Jude appeared. Sagging, she glanced at her phone to find an hour and twenty minutes had passed in a flash, just like that.

His brows rose. 'Expecting someone else?'

'What?' She blinked. 'No! I've only just finished coming up with your five charities and I...'

'You?'

She surreptitiously covered the notepad with her hand. 'I got caught up in the research and hadn't realised so much time had passed.' She sent him a weak smile. 'For a moment there, I thought I might have to fight off a robber.'

He stared at where her hand rested on the pad and her stomach scrunched up tight. She nodded at the bags he held, hoping to distract him. 'What have you got there?'

When his attention turned to the bags, she pulled the pad onto her lap and pushed it down between the dinette seat and the wall.

'One pair of running shoes, size four.'

He set them on the seat beside her. She stared at them and then at him. He couldn't mean...? 'I can't go running with you, Jude.'

'Sure you can.'

'If someone recognises me...' She rubbed her hands over her face. It'd be an absolute disaster. 'I can't risk it. I...'

'And in this bag are two wigs. Now, I know they'll probably itch, but it's better than you staying on board and climbing walls.'

She bit her lip. To be able to go for a run... But if she was seen... If she was seen *with a man* it'd be splashed across the front pages in an instant: *Cleo the serial dater.* And what if the press then dug deeper to find out who Jude was? What if they discovered he was Jasper Ballimore? He'd be unmasked. The scandal would explode! Margot would be devastated. And Cleo would've let everyone down—*again.*

'Cleo!'

She snapped to at the command in Jude's voice.

'Try the wigs on.'

He'd gone to so much trouble. The least she could do was try on the wigs. *Model passenger, remember?* She pulled the first box towards her and lifted the lid. Oh, wow. These were proper wigs, not cheap knock-offs bought for fancy dress. The first one was honey-blonde with long plaits and a fringe. She couldn't help grinning. 'Did you also get me denim overalls and a piece of straw to chew?'

Maybe Jude had a cowgirl fantasy. And maybe that would be kind of fun...

Gah! Stop it.

'The other one is, in my opinion, the real *pièce de résistance.*'

He uttered the phrase with the most deliciously perfect French accent and leaned back against the kitchen bench, the picture of relaxed ease, but she sensed an alertness, or perhaps an anticipation, in him that piqued her curiosity.

Pulling the second box towards her, she lifted the lid and her eyes went wide. The wig was a riot of light-brown curls that would hang down past her shoulders. She ran a light finger over a curl. 'This is really lovely.'

'The sales lady said you'd need to be careful with it if you wanted to maintain the curls, but nobody in real life has hair that perfect unless they've just come from the hairdresser. Messing it up would make the disguise all the more perfect.'

He reached out as if to do exactly that, but she held it out of reach. 'Let me try it on first. Then we can mess it up.' Racing into the bathroom, she tried it on and stared at her reflection. *Oh, wow.*

'Well?' Jude called out.

She moved back into the main cabin. Jude's jaw dropped. 'I wouldn't think you the same woman.'

His gaze travelled over her face in a way that had her nerves pulling tight and a pulse at her throat thrashing. Her breath caught as an expression akin to hunger stretched through his eyes, but then his lips thinned and he shook his head.

'It's all wrong with what you're wearing. This—' he gestured to her new mane of hair '—is too perfect, too formal. While this—' he gestured to the rest of her '—is casual and...'

And what?

'It doesn't work together.'

She wanted the floor to open up and swallow her. The only way Jude had been looking at her was as a problem he needed to fix. He wasn't looking at her as a woman he found attractive. She didn't *want* him looking at her that way either!

Lifting her chin and pasting on a smile, she said, 'That's easily fixed. Do you have an elastic band?'

Turning, he searched in a drawer and handed her one.

She gestured to the beanie sitting on the bench. 'And that.'

He handed it to her.

She tied the wig into a low pony tail and jammed the beanie onto her head.

He cocked his head to the side. 'With all of that hair pulled back, we can see more of your face now.'

Meaning someone might recognise her.

'You have another elastic band?'

He handed her a second one.

She shook out the wig and ran her fingers through the curls to frizz them up a bit, before fashioning the hair into two low bunches, pulling out wisps of hair to frame her face. 'How's that?'

He nodded slowly. 'That could work.'

His expression, though, told her that it was still a little too perfect. 'Wait until I do this.' Pulling the bands free, she grabbed his hairbrush from the bathroom and reefed it through the wig. When she was done, she held it out at arm's length. 'Now it's suitably frizzy.'

Without a word he handed her the blonde plaits. She pulled it on, the fringe tickling her forehead. He didn't say anything. Her hands went to her hips. 'Well?'

'I wouldn't have known it was you,' he finally said. He pointed at the fringe. 'It changes the shape of your face.'

Moving back to stare in the bathroom mirror, she frowned. 'Fringes don't do me any favours. Which, in this instance, is perfect. With a bucket hat and sunnies, no one will recognise me.' Even Margot would be hard pressed to recognise her in this wig.

'Except you can't run in hat and sunnies—not at night.'

She pulled off the wig. 'I'm not running with you, Jude. I can't risk it.'

'You're going stir crazy.'

Oh, God. 'Have I been bothering you?'

He rolled his shoulders. 'No.'

That clearly was a lie.

'The thing is—' he rubbed a hand over his hair '—you're going to have to sign for your laptop tomorrow. I should've told you to address the package to me. I don't suppose you did, by any chance?'

Her stomach plummeted. She shook her head.

'But with a wig, a pair of sunnies and a beaten-up bucket hat…' Rifling in a top cupboard, he turned and tossed her a navy number. 'No one will recognise you.'

What if he was wrong?

'Same with the jogging, even without hat and sunglasses.

Plus, there won't be many people about, not at this time of year. The canal path is lit, but the light is dim. And you'll be jogging behind me.'

To get out and expend some pent-up energy would be heaven.

'And I don't want you getting sick on my boat. Nor can I imagine Margot being thrilled if you turn up on the day of her wedding looking like a ghost.'

She shifted her weight from one foot to the other.

'We'll have an early dinner, give it time to settle and then go running when most people are already tucked up inside.'

He made it sound easy. He made it sound doable. Ever since she'd screwed up three years ago, exercise had been her crutch. It had helped her deal with *everything*. It gave her the resources to cope.

'The fresh air will do you good.'

Hadn't she told herself earlier not to keep imagining worst-case scenarios? Jude wouldn't lie to her. 'Okay.' She gave a short nod. 'In that case, I guess I should get dinner on now.'

He moved aside to let her slide out of the dinette and then slid in to where she'd been sitting while she gathered up the wigs and shoes and dumped them on her bed. Returning to the galley, she began pulling ingredients from the fridge.

'Cleo?'

'Hmm...?'

'What's this?'

Something in his tone had her swinging round. He sat with his back to her. Between his fingers he held up the list she'd made. She froze: the list of the things she knew about him.

Something had gone cold inside him. He turned and what-ever she saw in his face had her paling.

'Are you keeping some kind of a dossier on me?' Had she figured out *who* he was? Beyond Jasper Ballimore, that was.

Giving a nod that held a world of fate, she set the red pepper she was holding on the bench and pressed her hands together. 'Turn the page over and read it…and the one after as well.'

Turning his back to her, he did as she said. He closed his eyes as he joined the dots.

'I wrote down what I knew about you so I could…'

'Choose five charities…' That would have a connection to him.

'That you'd be happy and proud to support.'

He'd set her the mission, wanting to give her something to do—to keep her occupied and stop her from surfing news sites, or constantly checking her phone, hoping to hear from Margot. If she didn't stop that soon, she'd drive herself batty.

'You startled me when you returned from your shopping trip. I'd become so wrapped up in the search I'd lost track of time. You were upon me before I realised. I didn't have a chance to get rid of my notes. I know it doesn't look good, but the motive was innocent.'

He nodded. Behind him, she started slicing and chopping. He ought to make conversation, move them on from this awkward moment, but he couldn't manage it. Not when the facts of his life were written in black and white in front of him, stated so baldly and starkly.

'So…' The strain in her voice made him wince. 'Do you approve of said charities?'

Pulling in a breath, he stared at the final list she'd compiled. It included a literacy programme for adults, home help for the elderly, the UK Canal Trust, a charity that paid for deprived local young people to learn to drive safely and a struggling cricket club. When was the last time anyone had taken this much trouble for him over such a simple task? Anyone else would've simply listed the things *they* thought worthy.

'Of course, those aren't the only things I know about you.' The sound of spitting oil and the scent of frying onions filled the air.

Why did the fact that she'd taken so much trouble touch him so deeply?

'That's the thing when you ask yourself a question like that, isn't it? Other answers bombard you for days afterwards.'

More hissing and spitting sounded. More delicious scents rose in the air.

'I know that you're kind to damsels in distress, which means you'd probably approve of a donation to a women's shelter.'

He added it to the list.

'You have a sense of humour—the joke knickers are proof of that.'

He didn't know whether to wince or laugh.

'So maybe a donation to a comedy festival? It's a good thing to do, to make people laugh.'

He jotted that down too, then held his breath as he waited to hear what else she thought she knew about him.

'You're ridiculously reclusive, but I don't think there's a hermits' association you can donate to—though maybe funding a writers' retreat would suffice. Peace and quiet for writers is something you'd approve of.'

Absolutely.

'Also, you can't cook, so donating to some kind of life skills programme might also be a worthwhile pursuit.'

Her observations were disconcertingly perceptive.

'And you understand the importance of exercise,' she finished. 'So in all likelihood an exercise education programme would appeal to you too.'

He stared at the fourth item on her list again. Sliding out from the dinette, he moved to the other bench so he was facing her. 'Matt was a good driver.' He didn't want her thinking Matt hadn't been a a good driver. Or a good person.

She met his gaze and nodded once, before turning back to the stir-fry, wielding her wooden spoon like a wand. 'I'm sorry you lost your brother, Jude. I can't even begin to imagine.'

Her quiet sympathy, its sincerity, lodged in his throat, making it impossible to speak.

'And I'm sorry that it was stated there on my list like that. As if...'

He raised an eyebrow, doing his best to look unmoved.

'As if it wasn't the biggest and worst thing that's ever happened to you.'

The edges of the room blurred. *The biggest and worst thing.* That summed it up exactly. A laugh scraped out of him. 'Want to hear the crazy thing? I was in the car when it happened, and basically walked away without a scratch. How wrong is that?'

He'd walked away while Matt...

Dead—in a split second—from hitting his head the wrong way. The world had gone dark after that night. The light had never come back.

Warm hands sliding into his brought him back to the present. He stared into eyes tempered with concern. 'What happened, Jude?'

He lifted a shoulder and let it drop. 'A deer. It raced out of the woods and onto the road.' He answered because he didn't know what else to do; he didn't want to lose the comfort of her touch. 'Matt swerved to avoid it.'

Her lips parted and a sigh escaped, low and sympathetic.

'We'd been at the pub.' It had been Matt's turn to drive. 'I was the one who called time.' His heart gave a sick kick. 'I thought he was drinking low-alcohol beer.'

She swallowed. 'He was over the limit?'

'Only just. If I'd waited half an hour longer...'

Her hands tightened in his. 'It wasn't your fault.'

Forget waiting half an hour; ten minutes, two minutes, would've made all the difference. Even sixty seconds! Then they'd have avoided that deer. And Matt wouldn't have ploughed the driver's side of the car into a giant oak.

He flinched as that moment played through his mind. If only he'd known Matt had been drinking full-strength beer. If only...

'It wasn't your fault, Jude.' Cleo shook his hands and leaned closer. 'It wasn't!'

Tell Elodie that.

He slid his hands from hers. He didn't deserve her comfort. 'He left behind a grieving widow and a three-year-old son.'

She rubbed a hand across her chest, as if trying to ease an ache there. 'Such a terrible tragedy.'

A tragedy he should've prevented.

'Jude...'

'Enough, Cleo. You asked what happened and I told you.' Realising how brutal that sounded, he added, 'But I thank you for your condolences.'

She bit her lips, her eyes throbbing into his.

'I just don't have the heart to keep going over it.'

With a nod, she rose and went back to their dinner. A short time later, she set a plate of chicken stir-fry and rice in front of him. Considering the subject they'd been discussing, he shouldn't have had an appetite, but the sight of the food—colourful and glistening—and the scented steam that lifted into his face had him ravenous.

He forked food into his mouth and closed his eyes to savour it. 'I wish I'd lied to the coroner.' The words left him unbidden, making him blink.

She acted as if his confession was wholly normal, spearing a piece of broccoli on her fork, popping it into her mouth and chewing thoughtfully. 'Which bit would you lie about?'

He tried to eat slowly, but the food was insanely good. 'The bit where I said he lied to me about what he was drinking.'

'I'd lie to keep Margot out of trouble. I'd help her hide a body.'

He huffed out a laugh. Her lack of judgement was unexpected, and unexpectedly welcome. It eased some tightness inside him.

'Keeping schtum about that wouldn't have changed a thing.' His fingers tightened around his cutlery. 'All it's done is mar everyone's memory of Matt.'

'Nonsense!' Chicken and rice slid off her fork to splat back to her plate. 'Is that your enduring memory of your brother?' She pointed her fork at him and proceeded to answer her own question. 'Of course it isn't. You think of the time you were both at the crease in a county cricket match and won the day on the last ball of the final over.'

That had never happened, but he'd once fed Matt a perfect pass in a football game. Matt had drilled the ball into the top-left corner of the net for a stunner of a goal. It had been a thing of beauty.

'And the day you were his best man at his wedding.'

His lips twitched. He'd never seen Matt so nervous; he

would never forget the look on his face when Elodie had appeared at the end of the aisle.

'And your grandmother would've remembered the day he graduated from university and…the time he burned down the back shed.'

Ha! That had actually happened.

'And his wife will remember the first time she met him and setting up house with him and the birth of your nephew.'

His chest clenched. To her dying day, Elodie would hold him responsible for Matt's death.

'You should've known he was drinking. You knew how much stress he was under at work. You should've taken on some of the responsibility. You should've been helping him.'

She was right on every count—he should've.

He pushed his plate away.

Cleo pushed it back. 'You'll offend me if you don't finish it.'

He glared. She shrugged. 'You want to know why I'm such a Jasper Ballimore fan?'

No. Yes.

'Why?'

She scooped up more of the deliciousness on her plate and ate it, chewing slowly, as if savouring it. He picked up his fork with a scowl. The food was too good to waste, damn it.

'Jason Diamond helped get me through the worst of my therapy. You, or rather your pseudonym, appeared on my radar after a particularly…rough session.' She wrinkled her nose. 'It's hideous, coming face to face with one's own failings.'

She could say that again.

'Anyway, there was a book my therapist suggested I read, so on my way home I dropped into the big book shop on Piccadilly. Your publicist was there and you had dialled in to talk with her about your latest book. I couldn't believe how many people had come to listen to you speak. I mean, it's not like you were there in person signing books.'

She spiked a piece of chicken with her fork, followed by a slice of pepper, a bit of carrot and a broccoli floret. He doubted she'd fit it all in her mouth. Setting down her fork, she rested her chin on her hands and stared at him. 'You spoke about your inspiration for Jason Diamond—how you'd always loved writing, how hard it could be but how satisfying too. And I thought to myself, here's a person who's living life on their terms, forging ahead with their dreams. And a tiny voice inside me whispered, *if he can do it, so can you.*'

He stared.

'It felt like serendipity—a tough therapy session and then stumbling into your inspiring talk.'

Inspiring? *Him?*

'So I bought the book my therapist recommended and your book too. I alternated reading a chapter of my therapy book with chapters of Jason Diamond. I swear his adventures kept me sane.'

That made him laugh.

He slowly sobered. 'I didn't give you enough credit when we first met. But, other than New Year's Eve, you hadn't appeared in the papers for…'

'Eight months. When Davide orchestrated that scene at the premier of a new movie and prostrated himself at my feet on the red carpet.'

His lip curled. 'That's right. He cried, claimed you'd destroyed all his dreams, or some such nonsense.'

'All news to me. We'd already parted ways, but I'd agreed

to honour the public commitments we'd made. He did it for the publicity, to get his name in the papers.'

Men like Davide and Clay had preyed on Cleo, taking advantage of her kindness and good nature. And in return the world had pointed an accusatory finger and condemned her—himself included. She wasn't perfect—her terrible dating record proved that—but he'd written her off as a vapid starlet based on what? The media write-up? There was *so* much more to this woman. Cleo had hidden depths he suspected he'd barely scratched.

Not only that, she'd made significant changes to her life. She'd turned her back on the celebrity scene. Cleo wanted to move on; it was just the rest of the world wouldn't let her. She had, in fact, done an amazing job at turning her life around, at no longer being the 'wild child'. She ought to be proud of herself. Her *family* ought to be proud of her.

'I just wanted you to know I'll always feel grateful to you for Jason Diamond and his kick-ass attitude.'

She pushed her plate away. As she'd finished most of her food, he asked, 'You done?'

At her nod, he seized his fork and polished it off. The brightening of her eyes was his reward. 'Seriously good,' he told her, sitting back and patting his stomach. 'And, for the record, I think you've done a great job at turning your life around. I expect Margot recognises that too. We're not going to let anything ruin that, I promise.'

It was a rash promise. But all this woman wanted to do was to save her relationship with her sister. She deserved the opportunity to do that.

Rising, he took their plates to the sink. She followed and butted him away with her hip. 'I'll do the dishes.'

The heat from her hip burned against his thigh. He edged

away, the scent of pears filling his nostrils. 'You don't have to wait on me.'

'But you're doing all of the boat driving and stuff. This is me pulling my weight where I can.'

He snorted. 'The difference is that you're paying me an absolute fortune to do "the boat driving and stuff".'

'Money which you're giving away.'

She pointed down towards his easy chair. 'Go and do your puzzles.'

'And then in an hour we're going for a run,' he reminded her.

Her eyes shadowed. Reaching out, he touched her cheek. 'It'll be fine, I promise.'

She moistened her lips and his gut clenched.

Her gaze fluttered to his lips. Her chest rose and fell... It'd be so easy to reach across and press his lips to hers. To...

They both snapped away at the same moment.

She busied herself with the dishes. Rather than grab a tea towel as he'd planned to, he retreated to the other end of the cabin and hid behind the newspaper. Nothing was going to happen between him and Cleo. He wouldn't let it. He might not be a hero, but she was alone and vulnerable. And he refused to be her next big mistake.

CHAPTER FIVE

'OH, MY GOD!'

Cleo clapped her hands and danced on the spot while Jude locked the door behind them. When he turned, she took a plait in each hand and twirled them, beaming up at him. He shook his head, but one side of his mouth hooked up.

'Not a single person recognised me!'

'There weren't enough people out there to recognise you.'

There'd been a dog walker and three other joggers, and no one had given her a second glance. She danced on the spot again.

Jude braced his hands on his knees, his chest rising and falling from the exertion of their run. She took the opportunity to admire the powerful lines of his body. He wasn't built like the musclebound cover model that graced the covers of his Jason Diamond books, but he was strong and lean without a spare ounce of flesh. And those shoulders...

He glanced up and froze at whatever he saw in her face. He straightened slowly, his gaze pinning her to the spot. 'What?'

'Nothing.' The word squeaked out of her.

A dark brow rose. It made her heart hammer harder.

'It's just that this—' she pulled off the wig and beanie '—was inspired, and I so needed that run, and I feel so much better for it—euphoric, you know? And for a moment there I was tempted to hug you.' *And more.*

She gripped her hands in front of her. 'But that's not a good idea, because we're all sweaty, and hugging you wouldn't be a good idea anyway, because…' *Oh, God, shut up now, Cleo.* 'You know…' *Floor, open up and swallow me.* 'I don't want to send mixed messages or give you the wrong idea…'

Jude closed his eyes. His lips turned white. She zipped her mouth shut.

'I'm in no danger of getting the wrong idea.' Those eyes snapped open. 'I've no intention of…' His hands made vague gestures, filling in the blanks. 'But no hugging is an excellent rule.'

She straightened. A rule now, was it? 'I couldn't agree more.'

She glanced at the ceiling, the floor and the wall—everywhere but at him. 'D'you want the first shower?'

He gestured her towards the bathroom. 'Knock yourself out.'

She showered, dressed in her cute though far from sexy pyjamas, bustled back into the main cabin and set about making hot chocolate. 'All yours,' she shot over shoulder, barely looking at him, sucking herself in as he eased past. Setting two steaming mugs on the table, she slid onto one of the bench seats—the one that ensured her back would be to the bathroom and Jude's bedroom. She didn't want to risk even the briefest glimpse of him emerging from the shower in nothing more than a low-slung towel, his skin gleaming...

Stop it.

What was wrong with her? Did she mean to spend her life lurching from mistake to mistake? Two days ago, she'd had a boyfriend!

Yeah, but he was a bad boyfriend.

Oh, right, so that means it's okay to immediately jump into bed with another man to soothe your hurt pride, for revenge sex?

She sipped her hot chocolate, letting its warmth filter into her. She didn't want to be the kind of person who did that. Given the circumstances, jumping into bed with any man was a bad idea. Besides the fact the media would have a field day if they found out, she'd had enough therapy to recognise a negative pattern when it slapped her on the head. The short-term satisfaction of sleeping with Jude wouldn't outweigh the damage she'd be doing to herself.

Where men were concerned, she was a disaster. She needed to work out why. And, once she'd done that, she'd work out what to do about it. If she'd been looking for love in all the wrong places, then she needed to start looking for it in the right places, or in different ways.

Besides, Jude wasn't interested in her like that. And who could blame him? He craved the quiet life. A woman like her—one who landed herself on the front pages of the newspapers with remarkable regularity—had to be his worst nightmare. And yet he *had* let her stay. Because he knew what it was like to lose a brother and he didn't want her losing her sister.

She picked up the notepad with the list of charities she'd collated. Behind his stern appearance and reserve, Jude was a bit of a softy. He didn't need to be messed with by the likes of her. Setting the notepad back down, she pressed her hands together. She'd abide by his rules. She'd be the easiest and best of boat roomies. She'd prove to Jude, her father and Margot—especially Margot—that she wasn't a hot mess. She'd prove that they could trust her. And maybe one day they'd even be proud of her.

Jude appeared wearing an old pair of tracksuit bottoms and a baggy, long-sleeve T-shirt that didn't plaster itself against his body like a second skin. Not that she'd have noticed if it had.

She gestured. 'I made you a hot chocolate. You don't have to drink it if you don't want, but as I was making one for myself...'

Eyeing the mug as if it might bite him, he lifted it and took a sip. His brows shot up and something in his face lightened. 'This is good.'

She stuck her nose in the air. 'I'm an excellent hot-chocolate maker.'

It earned her a chuckle that made her breathe a little easier.

'You're also an excellent runner.'

He leaned against the bench; he *didn't* take the seat opposite, where their knees and feet might accidentally touch. She wished she hadn't mentioned hugging earlier. This was his boat, *his home*. He should be able to relax here. She needed to make things comfortable again.

'You'll find I'm excellent at many things.' That earned her one of those rare half-smiles. 'Therapy taught me the benefits of positive self-talk.'

'I think we can safely tick that KPI off the list for the day.'

She laughed. He could be funny when he wasn't concentrating on frowning all over the place. 'Running keeps me on an even keel—gives me an outlet for my excess energy, and the exercise endorphins are good for my brain. It's my number one strategy for staying on the straight and narrow.'

He crossed his legs at the ankles and stared at her over the rim of his mug, his eyes gratifyingly going glassy as he took another sip. 'You keep yourself on a tight leash.'

She didn't want to spiral out of control again. 'Thank you for making tonight possible, Jude. To be able to run is... It's everything.'

'I know.'

Something told her he understood exactly. What demons was Jude wrestling with? Did he really hold himself responsible for his brother's death?

She shook the thought away. It was none of her business. It didn't take a rocket scientist to see that Jude Blackwood was a private man—a *very* private man.

He took another sip of his drink and a low hum sounded from his throat. It vibrated through her in an utterly delicious way. 'How long since you had a hot chocolate?'

'I honestly can't remember. If you'd asked me, I'd have said not to bother making me one.'

'And look what you'd have missed.'

'And look what I'd have missed,' he echoed, his gaze stilling as it rested on her...darkening when it lowered to her lips. Two beats passed. He jerked upright and reached for the list of charities.

Cleo tried to catch her breath, trying to calm the crazy racing of her pulse. The way he'd looked at her... No, no, he wasn't interested in her *that* way.

He slid into the seat opposite, careful to angle his knees away from hers. 'Which charity should I donate to first?'

'I'd start at the top and work my way down.'

'The literacy programme it is.' Pulling out his phone, his fingers flew over the screen. 'There, done.' He set it down again.

'What's the deal with that?' She nodded at the list. 'Why not choose your favourite from the list and give all the money to that one?'

He immediately removed his gaze from hers, and she wished she could retract the question. She was supposed to make things easy and light, be an undemanding travelling companion, not some nosy parker.

She opened her mouth to change the topic, but he spoke first. 'One of the last things my grandmother asked of me— made me promise—was, for the next year, to do one good thing every day.'

She stared at him. Her heart started to pound.

'And I reckon giving a thousand pounds to a worthy charity is a good thing to do. So, for the next five days, that's what I'm going to do.'

Her eyes burned. *Oh, Jude.* That would not have been what his grandmother meant; she was certain of it. He'd taken his grandmother's words entirely the wrong way.

A new thought slammed into her. *Oh.* Clasping her hands in her lap, she fought against the sudden burn of tears. 'That's why you let me stay.'

He hesitated, then shrugged. 'You needed help. You asked for help. And it's not like you were interrupting me doing anything important. Having a passenger might be inconvenient, but not unworkable.'

There you have it, Cleo: you're an inconvenience. Let that be lesson to you.

In her lap, her hands gripped each other so hard they

started to ache. She was simply part of a to-do list he needed to tick off.

What were you hoping for?

She fought the urge to rest her head on folded arms. 'You hid me, you agreed to let me stay, you bought me the essentials and today you made it possible for me to go for a run. *And* for the next five days you're giving a thousand pounds to charity.' As she named each event, she flipped out another finger. 'Are you trying to get ahead or are you simply a high achiever?'

He scowled at the contents in his mug. 'I broke my promise. Between my grandmother's death and her funeral—five days—I did *nothing* good.'

'You were grieving. Your grandmother would've understood.'

'A promise is a promise.'

The haunted expression in his eyes caught at her. 'Jude...'

He stood abruptly. 'Thanks for the hot chocolate. Crossword and whisky time.'

She watched him settle in his chair by the wood burner, her heart aching, burning and bleeding a little. But she kept her mouth zipped tight. Every instinct she had told her he wouldn't welcome her opinion.

You're a smart and resourceful woman. Find a way to show him instead.

Smart and resourceful women didn't have their photos snapped throwing punches at their boyfriends. Smart and resourceful women didn't let their sisters down.

Swallowing, she seized her Jason Diamond book and lost herself in a comforting world of heroics, where right and wrong were easy to identify; where injustices were righted and the good guys always prevailed.

* * *

Cleo strode into the main cabin and lifted her hands. 'What do you think?'

Jude stared at her for several long *fraught* moments. Finally, he nodded. 'If I were a photographer on the lookout for Cleo Milne, I wouldn't glance at you twice.'

She let out a breath. She had on the curly wig, which after her ministrations now sported a realistic and somewhat unattractive amount of frizz. She wore yoga pants, a sweatshirt and had twined an old scarf of Jude's around her throat. Grabbing the new sunglasses, she perched them on her nose. It was a far cry from her usual attire of jeans and wool blazer.

'We are just nipping out to get the laptop and coming straight back?' she checked, trying to stop the panic from choking her.

He nodded.

Going out in the broad light of day was a far cry from jogging the canal path at night. She'd felt safe last night, with the darkness hiding her and Jude's back shielding her. But this felt risky.

He settled his hands on her shoulders. 'No one is expecting to find you in Berkhamsted.'

'There's plenty of speculation in the papers about where I could be, though. It's like a game of *Where's Wally?* Any journalist worth their salt will be keeping their eyes peeled.'

'You spend too much time on those damn news sites.'

He gave her shoulders a gentle squeeze. It put the heart back into her, and had her straightening her spine.

'You worry too much.'

True on both counts. But as soon as she had her laptop she could get back to work and stop fretting so much.

'Okay, let's do this.'

Standing on the towpath moments later, she tried not to fidget, but her stomach clenched so tight it almost cramped. Jude turned from locking *Camelot*'s door and frowned.

'Tell me a story.' The words blurted from her.

'A story?'

She nodded, keeping her gaze on the ground in case anyone should be around… lying in wait and watching for her. Her pulse sky-rocketed. 'God, Jude, please take my mind off impending disasters.'

He stepped onto the path beside her and she nudged him. 'You're a master storyteller. I had to force myself to put your book down last night and get some sleep. It's the second time I've read this book. I know what happens, yet it's still so compelling. So *once upon a time*…'

A hollow laugh sounded through Jude. A master storyteller? Not likely. A master storyteller could pick up a pen or drag a keyboard towards them and words would pour from their fingertips. A master storyteller could lose themselves in a story for hours at a time, could wrestle with a plot problem for days and then feel ridiculously victorious when they found the answer.

None of this applied to him, not any more. Where once there'd been creativity and an intriguing swirl of ideas, a burning fire to pick up a pen, there was now a black hole. He might not have been physically injured the night of the accident that had claimed Matt's life, but he hadn't been able to write since.

At first he'd thought it a symptom of his grief. After Elodie had made it clear how bitterly she held Jude responsible for Matt's death, though, guilt had stifled all inspiration and had laid a rotting blanket over the first tentative buds of his reawakening creativity. He'd found himself utterly incapable of writing a story of honour and courage for an upright hero like Jason Diamond.

He now doubted he'd ever write again. Despair threatened to descend in a smothering black cloud. The thought of never again experiencing the rush and joy, the challenges and frustrations, of writing a story... To have that door now barred against him...

What right did he have to such consolation, though? If he hadn't been so selfish, he'd have noticed how much pressure Matt was under. He'd have noticed that Matt had started to drink more. He'd have noticed *something*. Then he could've done something to help. But he hadn't noticed anything. He hadn't *done* anything, too engrossed with his own selfish needs and wants.

And the worst of it was that he wondered now if it was because he hadn't *wanted* to notice anything, hadn't wanted to be dragged into working for his family's firm, Giroux Holdings. Because he'd wanted to lead the life *he'd* wanted.

And now it was too late, all too late. And Cleo wanted him to tell her a story? He knew she was nervous. He knew she sought distraction. He knew she had no idea what she asked of him but...

'Did you always know you wanted to write thrillers with a good guy hero?'

He forced himself to focus on the question rather than the chaotic blast of emotions roiling through him. He mightn't manage a story, but he could probably answer the odd question or two. 'In the early days, I had no idea what I wanted to write.' He frowned. 'Actually, that isn't exactly true. I wrote whatever took my fancy, no rhyme or reason. I must have at least a dozen manuscripts that aren't JD books in various stages of completion—from entire first drafts to just a few opening pages.'

'A dozen!' She halted to stare up at him, her eyes wide, as if she thought a dozen a particularly amazing number. Despite everything, he found himself fighting a smile. Maybe it was her wide-eyed awe, maybe it was the hair that fizzed around her face, completely messing with her normal tidy lines.... Those eyes, though, were the same compelling green. And those lips...

With an effort, he dragged his gaze from her lips and forced his legs forward again, only slowing his pace when he realised she had to rush to keep up. 'And, if we counted actual ideas for books, we'd be talking three or four times that number.' Talking about writing was much safer than focussing on his reactions to this woman.

She heaved a sigh as if his words had evoked the happiest of thoughts. He worked hard at keeping his gaze on the path in front of them.

'What kind of trees are those?' She pointed to the tall stand of trees bordering the towpath.

'Beech—very common. Harder to tell with no leaves on them, though.'

She made a noise in the back of her throat. 'I'm terrible at anything botanical. I've never had a garden. But it'd be lovely to have one.'

It seemed a small enough wish, and an achievable one. 'You'd need a big garden for those.'

'But don't they look pretty? Actually, not so much pretty as grand.'

She turned, hands on hips, to stare back the way they'd come, and he realised someone was coming along the path towards them. *Right...* 'Your name for the rest of the day is Fran.'

Her lips twitched, but she didn't look away from the beech trees. 'Look at the way the light is filtering through the branches. It'd make a really nice image.'

'For what?'

Pulling out her phone, she snapped a couple of pictures. 'In my spare time, I muck around with creating website headers. Much like you do with story ideas.'

Did, not *do*. *Past tense*.

But he tried to see what she saw in the beeches, tried to see what had captured her imagination. 'It's…peaceful.' His shoulders loosened a fraction. 'A little bleak, but kind of timeless.'

She smiled up at him, as if he'd given her the right answer. Turning, she started walking again, mumbling a greeting to the couple as they passed, but keeping her gaze lowered.

'So, back to our conversation…'

What conversation?

'If you hadn't written the JD books—or if they hadn't been picked up by a publisher—which of your many projects would you have pursued instead?'

Her knuckles had turned white where her hand gripped the strap of her handbag. The couple hadn't recognised them—had barely looked at them—but her fear of being unmasked overrode what logic should have told her. If he couldn't find a way to help her relax, her tension would give the game away. So he told her what he hadn't told anyone. 'A young adult fantasy trilogy.'

Her hand abruptly unclenched. 'Like *Lord of the Rings*?'

Lord of the Rings was one of his favourite books. Did she like it too?

'It takes place in a kingdom called Ostana. No elves or orcs, but there are dragons and—'

'Are the dragons good or evil?'

'Generally good, but they're like people, in that they can be a bit of both.'

'Tell me more.'

'There's a mysterious dark force threatening the world, a boy who doesn't know he's a king, and a girl who doesn't realise she's a dragon rider.'

She did a funny little skip and clapped her hands. 'Tell me they fall in love.'

'Yep.'

'And that together they save the world.'

'Ah, but it's not that simple, is it?'

He led the way off the towpath and into the town of Berkhamsted. It was eleven-thirty, and the town was bustling. From the corner of his eye he saw Cleo swallow. 'Eventually they save the world, but there are a lot of ups and downs first.'

'Tell me more!'

'Well, he's timid and runs away at the smallest sign of danger, while she's too cynical to believe in happy-ever-afters. Plus, she's bossy. They hate each other on sight.'

'Of course they do. But fate forces them together?'

He couldn't *not* smile. Her eyes had lost their hunted expression, replaced instead with the avid interest of a true reader. 'Something like that.'

'Tell me this trilogy is written.'

Was she actually holding her breath? 'Books one and two are. The third has been started.'

'Tell me I can read it.'

'And here we are at the delivery place,' he announced, pulling them to a halt.

She tensed. Her hand clutched the scarf she'd wound around her throat.

'*Look... Fran*, you're an actor. Think of this as a role.'

'Did you see me act?' she snapped. 'I was terrible.'

His head rocked back. 'No, you weren't. Your character was troubled, but you brought out her vulnerability beautifully. You made her sympathetic. She did some awful things, but the audience wanted her to find her happy-ever-after all the same.'

Her jaw dropped. 'You watched?'

He wasn't admitting anything. 'I caught a couple of episodes. And in today's drama series you're an ordinary person with slightly frizzy hair collecting a parcel. You need this particular parcel for an assignment because you're a mature student at the local community college.'

'What am I studying?'

'Horticulture.'

Her lips twitched. Her death grip on her scarf eased.

'I'll make a deal with you, Fran.'

Her lips twitched again.

'You do yoga, right?'

She nodded.

'If you relax your shoulders—ease them down from around your ears, unlock your jaw and unclench your hands—I'll let you read the first chapter of my trilogy this afternoon.'

She immediately did everything he asked. 'You *so* have yourself a deal... Brian.'

Brian? He nearly tripped up the first step.

Chuckling, she leapt up them lightly and reached the door before him. For the briefest of moments he wondered if he could write a similar scenario into one of his books. It could be fun at some stage during the third instalment of

The Crown and the Fire Wielder if Clement and Ruby had to don disguises—Clement having to pull on a mantle of command while Ruby had to act meek and downtrodden.

Cleo opened the door and the thought slipped away as they waited together in line. It took a while for the assistant to locate Cleo's parcel and he snapped into hyper-vigilance mode.

Like JD? Ha! He was no hero. But he had no intention of letting anyone blow Cleo's cover.

Eventually the parcel was located, signed for and handed over. Keeping his steps steady, he moved towards the exit and gestured for Cleo to precede him through the door.

Except she grabbed his arm and tugged him to the side; maps of the local area were lined up in neat rows in front of them. The pulse in her throat raced. 'Impending disaster!'

What the hell?

'Across the road. The man in the blue jeans and grey woollen jumper...'

'Journo?'

'Yes.'

Glancing towards the counter, his jaw clenched. The assistant stared at them, her phone to her ear. Cleo followed his gaze and swore softly. They'd been rumbled. And they needed to move fast.

Seizing Cleo's hand, he tugged her to the side door, shot out of it and set off down the street and into the bustling heart of the town. A shout sounded behind them and they broke into a run. Rounding a corner, he pulled her inside a huge discount fashion store, ones with racks of clothes everywhere.

Cleo took the lead and towed him to the back of the shop. They half-crouched when the journalist halted in front of the plate-glass window, ducking down when he turned to peer in their direction. Keeping low, Cleo led him to the fitting rooms. She collapsed onto a bench seat. He locked the door behind them and gestured for her to lift her feet onto the bench—in case anyone happened to look beneath the door.

Maybe he'd grown used to narrowboat living, but the room didn't feel too cramped. What he wouldn't give to be safely tucked away on *Camelot* right now, feeling cramped and unable to escape the mouth-watering scent of pears.

'What are we going to do?' she whispered. 'That witch of a sales assistant will have given him our descriptions. And he knows what we're wearing.'

Setting his backpack on the bench beside her, he rummaged round, emerging triumphantly with her blonde wig.

Her jaw dropped. 'You wonderful man!'

She immediately pulled off the frizzy wig and donned the plaits. The difference it made was remarkable.

'Here, put this on.'

He blinked when she shoved the curly wig at him.

'Hurry up.' She pulled the backpack towards her to check its contents. Grinning, she pulled out a battered beanie he'd forgotten was in there. 'Truly wonderful,' she murmured, pointing at him.

He didn't tell her the beanie was an oversight. It had been ages since anyone had thought he'd done anything wonderful. He pulled on the wig. He looked ridiculous, but she pulled a hair-tie from her handbag, gestured for him to turn around and made some kind of low bun at his nape. The touch of her fingers had hard darts of electricity zapping across his scalp. He had to clench his teeth and silently recite his eight-times table.

Once she was done, she pulled the beanie over the wig until it covered his ears, curls spilling out to frame his face. He blinked at his reflection. He no longer looked like a man wearing a woman's wig. He looked like a hippy...and that could work.

'D'you have a shirt on under your jumper?'

He pulled the jumper over his head, careful not to disturb her handiwork. She stowed the jumper in the backpack. 'I hate to ask you...'

He was already ahead of her. 'I'll go out there and get you a completely different outfit.'

'Then I'll do the same for you.'

He came back with oversized denim overalls, a multi-striped jumper in some kind of fuzzy fabric and chunky, dangly earrings. She grinned when she saw the ensemble. Taking the backpack, he moved to the dressing room next door. A few minutes later, she tapped on the door. He took one look and gave her a thumbs-up.

She blew out a breath. 'Okay, give me your sizes.'

He told her, taking her clothes to stow in the backpack. She returned with super-baggy black cargo pants, a tight long-sleeved T-shirt with a 'peace' sign emblazoned on the front... and a cardigan! He nearly snorted with laughter.

Her eyes danced as she pushed a big tote bag into his hands. 'That should be big enough to stow the backpack.' Which was when he noticed the wicker basket she held over one arm. *Perfect.*

'Give us a cover story,' she ordered.

'We're a couple who are into sustainable living. We have a stall at the local market where we sell handmade crafts, though we've both part-time jobs to help pay the rent. You work at a nursery while I'm a night-time shelf-stacker at a grocery store. And today we're...' he glanced at her wicker basket '...going on a picnic.'

Ten minutes later, they sauntered out of the shop as two

completely different people. Cleo stopped at a deli and bought a loaf of sourdough, cheese, bananas and a bottle of sparkling water. She took his arm and they made their way back to the boat, looking like a pair of young lovers.

Back onboard *Camelot*, he ushered her down the steps, pushed the door closed and slid the lock into place, before swinging to face her. She had to be frantic. She...

His mind blanked. She'd bent at the waist, both hands clapped over her mouth to stifle her laughter. 'Oh, my God, Jude. I should be beside myself, but that was so much fun.'

She said the words as if they ought to start with capital letters, so in his mind he gave them capitals: *So Much Fun*.

She was right. Which made no sense...

Her eyes danced and her lips curved upward, and it woke something deep inside him, shaking it free and making him glad to be alive. He could no more stop from leaning across and pressing his lips to hers then he could have stopped the tide.

CHAPTER SIX

CLEO SMELLED LIKE pears and tasted like freedom.

And she froze, as if taken totally unawares.

What the hell...?

Jude started to move away, but her fingers tangled in the ridiculous cardigan he wore, dragging him back, her mouth opening under his...

And he was gone. Cupping her face in his hands, he devoured her, learning the shape of her mouth, learning what made her shiver or brought a low hum to life in the back of her throat. Every time she sighed, moaned and deepened the kiss something inside him loosened and unfurled, forming an entirely new shape where before there'd been nothing but a hard, dark lump. Desire, need and the invigorating thrum of blood coursed through his veins.

Curling her fingers into his cardigan all the more securely, as if anchoring herself there, she devoured him back and all thought fled as things fizzed and sparked with an urgency that ought to have shocked him—that might have shocked him if he'd been able to think straight.

Growling with hunger and heat, he tried to temper the inferno that gripped him, tried to temper his strength, afraid of holding her too tight. As if she had no such concerns, she lifted up on tiptoe and flung her arms around his neck. The full length of her body pressed against his.

He backed her up until they reached the table, lifted her onto it and settled between her thighs. He caught her soft cry inside his mouth and a rainbow of colour arced behind his eyelids as their bodies strained towards each other.

Her fingers dug into his buttocks as if to drag him nearer. His fingers dug into her hips as he pulled her as close to him as he could, air hissing between his teeth when small, seeking hands slid beneath his shirt to explore the contours of his stomach and chest, her palms grazing against his nipples and making him jerk.

It was too much too soon. He couldn't breathe.

Dragging his mouth from hers, he pulled in gulping breaths of much-needed air as they stared at each other, their chests rising and falling, air sawing in and out of their bodies.

Cleo couldn't pull her gaze from Jude's. The blue of his eyes was piercing and bright, and it sent a thrill circling through her.

How could a simple kiss be so *consuming*?

She touched fingers to her lips. It hadn't been simple, though, had it? That kiss had reverberated through her in a way a kiss never had before. His hands cupping her face had made her feel safe. They'd been gentle but strong—their strength had become her strength. And the kiss had sunk deep, the echoes of it imprinting onto muscle and bone. That had to mean something…

She blinked. It couldn't mean *anything*!

Planting her hand in the middle of his chest, she pushed him away, slid off the table and backed up a step. 'You said no hugging. It was a rule.'

She didn't recognise the voice that scraped out of her throat. She recognised the self-loathing that immediately smothered all the sparkling blue brightness in Jude's eyes, though.

Oh, no, Jude. Don't do that to yourself.

Kissing was a bad idea, but it didn't have to mean the end of the world. He shouldn't hate himself for it. Rather than focus on the confusion raging inside her, or the desire coiling through her, she focussed on finding a way to rid that expression from his eyes.

Sliding in at the dinette before her legs gave way, she dragged off her wig and slanted a smile in his direction. She couldn't let him take the blame for what had just happened. That wouldn't be fair. *She* was the train wreck, remember?

'However, as we didn't hug—not really—I guess we didn't technically break any rules. So that's okay.'

He backed up to his easy chair, reaching behind to swivel it round before collapsing into it—as if he didn't trust himself to sit at the table so close to her. He was probably worried she'd jump him and kiss him again.

Her fingernails dug into her palms. He might have a point. It was exactly what her body was demanding she do. Except…she wasn't that person any more.

Don't ruin everything. Don't revert to type.

She *needed* to be better. She swallowed. *He* deserved better. And she needed him to not feel bad about this or it'd be another item on the long list of things to feel guilty about.

Sending him the tiniest of smiles, she shrugged. 'It was a hell of a kiss, though.'

He rubbed his hands over his face. 'I'm sorry, Cleo. I…'

'Don't.' Her smile faded. 'I was as into that as you were.'

'But I promised to look after you.'

'No, you didn't!' Her every muscle stiffened. 'You promised to give me a place to hide—*nothing* more. Jeez, Louise, you just went above and beyond in helping keep my identity secret, and I'm *really* grateful for that. But it is *not* your job to look after me.'

Pursing his lips, he stared at her. 'Is that why you kissed me back—because you were grateful?'

Her laugh might've held an edge of hysteria. She did her best to rein it in. 'That was *not* a pity kiss, Jude.' *Nuh-uh.* 'That little adventure of ours, managing to avoid detection and giving that journalist the slip… I haven't felt…'

Resting elbows on his knees, he leaned towards her. 'What?'

'It made me feel more alive than I have in…' *Seven years.* 'In a long time.' She moistened her lips. 'It went to my head and I felt like…' She swallowed, clearing her throat. 'Celebrating.'

But that had been entirely the wrong way to celebrate. Though now she had to wonder if, in keeping herself on such a tight leash for the last few years, had she chased all joy from her life? She pushed the thought away to deal with later.

'Also.' She pinned him with a glare. 'I don't give you permission to look after me.'

He straightened.

'By all means help me out if, like today, my cover is threatened, but I *can* look after myself. That whole calling myself a damsel in distress was supposed to be a joke.'

Delicious frown lines deepened. Everything about this man was delicious. It was enough to make a grown woman weep.

'You're going through a lot at the moment, though, Cleo.'

'So are you.'

The frown became a scowl. 'You just broke up with your cheating boyfriend.'

She folded her arms. 'You just lost your grandmother.'

He paled and her heart went out to him. He'd been dealing with the weight of the world.

'In my world, losing grandmas trumps cheating boyfriends every single time.'

He blinked. Colour rushed back into his face.

She clapped a hand to her mouth. 'I'm sorry, that sounded so much better in my head than it did out loud.' This wasn't some kind of contest and she hadn't meant to make it sound like one. 'I'm sorry,' she repeated. 'Don't ever put that in the book. I don't think readers would like it.'

He laughed, as if he couldn't help it. It wasn't a particularly joyful laugh, but she'd take what she could get. 'If you get to look after me. I get to look after you.'

Blue fire flashed from his eyes. 'I don't need looking after!'

She spread her hands, as if to say, 'I rest my case'. 'I'm starving. You want some lunch?'

He glanced at his watch and looked to be doing some kind of calculation in his head. 'I want to set off ASAP.'

An excellent idea; she wanted to put as much distance between them and that ruddy journalist as possible.

'But I'd appreciate it if you could hand me up a sandwich in half an hour.'

'Deal.'

Cleo spent the rest of the day working. Not on one of her many paid projects, but on an odd and sudden inspiration. Rather than stamp it out or ignore it, as had become her habit in recent years, she decided to indulge it. Because seven years of not having any real joy in her life…that was awful!

At seventeen, the acting out and partying had been an attempt to outrun the grief of losing her mother. It hadn't worked; therapy had helped her see that. But it now seemed she'd gone too far the other way, viewing fun, laughter and joy as things she ought to avoid.

She didn't want to live a joyless life. She could experience fun and gladness without descending into those old damaging patterns of behaviour. She needed to make room to let joy back in.

Late afternoon, Jude called down that they were docking in a marina and for her to stay out of sight.

A marina? Why? Was everything okay? Was there an issue with *Camelot*'s engine or…?

Oh.

Her heart dropped to her feet. He wanted to be rid of her, didn't he? He was going to ask her to leave. Because of that kiss. And because they'd nearly been unmasked. Because she was a mess, and he didn't want a mess like her in his life.

And she couldn't blame him, because if he was seen with her it would lead to speculation, and speculation could unmask his secret identity. 'You look like you've lost your best friend,' Jude said, coming below deck. 'Everything okay?'

She made herself smile and nod. A marina made sense.

Jude was a decent guy; he wasn't just going to dump her on the side of the canal. He'd find her passage on another boat first. *Then* he could wash his hands of her with a clear conscience.

She had a crazy urge to yell and throw things, stamp her feet and cry.

'Cleo?'

Jude didn't deserve a temper tantrum. She'd be a model passenger if it killed her. 'A marina? Is all well?'

He frowned. 'Do you trust me?'

She might only have known him for three days, but in that time he'd kept her secret, had kept her hidden and he hadn't betrayed her when it would've been in his financial interests to do so. She nodded. 'Yes.'

If he thought now was the right time to part company, she'd accept it with all the grace she could muster.

'Here's the thing… After the incident in Berkhamsted, I think the media will start scouring the canals for you again.'

Oh! She should've thought of that. If that kiss hadn't completely befuddled her, maybe she would have.

Don't think about the kiss.

Letting out a slow breath, she straightened. 'D'you have a plan?' One that didn't include dumping her on someone else's narrow boat.

He opened his mouth then frowned. 'What smells so good?'

She gestured to the kitchen bench. 'Banana bread. I baked some earlier.' *For joy.* 'I found some flour. I didn't think you'd mind.'

'Of course I don't mind. I…' He shook himself.

'The plan…?'

He straightened. 'As long as you're in agreement, I thought

of organising a car to get us as far away from here as possible.'

'*Excellent* plan.'

Her relief was due to the excellent plan and not the fact he didn't want to be rid of her. 'When?'

'We'll leave under the cover of darkness.'

Jason Diamond style? She grinned. 'You've always wanted to say that, haven't you?'

One corner of his mouth twitched, but then he sobered. 'I need to go out for a bit and make the arrangements. In the meantime...' he stalked into his bedroom and returned with the tote bag they'd bought earlier '...you'll need to pack.'

'Roger that.'

He headed for the door. 'Same drill.'

She nodded. 'Don't answer the door. Don't make any noise.'

'I'll be as quick as I can.'

Packing took no time at all. What else ought she do? They'd bought food for dinner. Was 'under the cover of darkness' before or after dinner? She paced for a while before pulling out her laptop and working on her fun project again to give her mind something different to focus on.

It was dark when Jude returned. 'A car will collect us at ten.'

That answered the dinner question. 'Where are we headed?' North was her guess—a remote farmhouse in Yorkshire or Northumberland would be perfect.

'Still being decided. Things are in motion, though. I'm just waiting to hear back.'

From whom? She didn't ask as he moved into his bedroom, presumably to pack his own things. And probably to avoid her. He'd barely looked her in the eye since that kiss.

* * *

They ate crumbed steak with mash and veg for dinner. She didn't pester him with questions about *the plan*. He seemed oddly keyed up, so she remained on her best model-passenger behaviour.

She also did her best not to notice the way his eyes half-closed on each mouthful, as if relishing every bite. It did strange things to her insides—made her stomach soften and her chest clench. It made her want to cook her entire repertoire of meals to discover his favourite.

He glanced up and caught her stare. 'What?'

She forced herself back to the mechanics of eating. 'Do you ever treat yourself to a pub lunch?' Wasn't that one of the things people did when cruising the canals—stop to enjoy the delights of a canal-side pub? Because Jude quite clearly enjoyed his food.

'Nope.'

'Why not?'

He didn't answer, just shrugged. Talk about excluding joy from one's life. He made her look like an amateur.

'I'll sometimes grab a pie from a village bakery.'

That was as much as he allowed himself? The admission had her wanting to cry.

Afterwards, they cleaned up and did the dishes. There was still nearly three hours before the car was due to collect them, though. And, while they didn't speak about it, now that night had fallen the memory of their kiss burned in all the spaces between them.

Jude retreated to his chair with the paper. She cut banana bread and made them hot chocolate, which they sipped in their individual corners. Her mind worked overtime. She waited until the contents in her mug had reached the halfway point before speaking. 'When I was in therapy, I had to keep a gratitude journal.'

He glanced up, watchful...silent.

'I scoffed at the time, thought it silly and gimmicky, but it really did help.'

He looked torn between saying something unfriendly such as, *So what?* or something supportive, such as *Good to hear.* In the end, he opted for silence—no surprises there.

'I think we should do that for as long as we're on this... adventure. I'll go first.'

The newspaper rustled in his lap. 'Why do *I* have to do it?'

Because it would help him focus on the positive things in his life. Because it would help him realise what his grandmother had meant. 'You don't. Not if you don't want to.'

His shoulders unhitched.

'But it would keep me company and make me feel less vulnerable and alone.'

Those glorious shoulders tensed again. 'I believe that's what they call emotional blackmail.'

She wrinkled her nose. 'I feel as if I've ruined your life.' His jaw dropped and she added, 'Not your whole life, just these couple of weeks where I'll be invading your privacy.'

'Cleo...'

'And knowing that there are some things in your life every day that you feel happy about and grateful for would help ease my guilt.'

He set his mug and the newspaper onto the small table beside him. 'You're making banana bread and real food. You've nothing to feel guilty about.'

'Hey, I said I'd go first!'

She stared at him in mock exasperation and he huffed out a laugh. 'You're incorrigible, you know that?'

She stuck her nose in the air, but her insides had started a little tap dance. 'I've been called worse.'

He shook his head, gesturing for her to continue.

'Okay, so we need to name three things each. First on my list: I'm ridiculously grateful we managed to avoid detection in town this morning. And this is going to sound a bit twisted, but it was also fun—edge of your seat stuff, like watching your football team surge forward in the last seconds of extra time and scoring a goal just as the final whistle sounds.' She folded her hands on the table. 'Incredibly exhilarating...but I really don't want to go through it again.'

'Noted.' Jude had no intention of letting anything like that happen again. 'First on my list is the banana bread and dinner—both delicious.'

She pursed lips that were pure temptation. The continuous effort to resist them left him exhausted. Leaving *Camelot*'s close confines would be a relief. His lips twisted; even if it did come with problems of its own.

'There are lots of things to feel grateful for, or that were good about my day, but there are two in particular—'

'Like what?' he cut in. Other than the amazing food she'd served up to him, he was struggling to think of anything else to put on his list.

She nibbled a corner of her banana bread. 'There are always the old chestnuts to fall back on—like, I have my health, my family have their health, I have somewhere safe to sleep, have food in my belly, clothes on my back, blah blah. And don't get me wrong; I *am* grateful for all of those things.'

He nodded. Not everyone was so fortunate.

'And there are more besides that might usually make my list—like our run last night. The air was crisp, it didn't rain, there weren't many people about and that stretch of the river was really pretty.'

It was why he'd stopped there.

'I'm glad I have my laptop, that I had a good night's sleep and that I made banana bread. That I'm no longer climbing the walls.'

She rattled them all off with such ease. He fought a scowl; it wasn't a contest.

'And I'm *really* glad my face wasn't plastered on the front pages of any newspapers today,' she added with a roll of her eyes.

Her name had appeared, though. That 'where's Cleo?' version of *Where's Wally?* continued to create speculation. It had to be playing on her mind.

'But none of those things made it onto your list?'

'Nope.'

He tried to not sound grudging. 'What's your number two, then?'

'I had an epiphany.'

He shuffled up a little higher in his seat. 'Which was…?'

She cupped her hands around her mug, though he suspected her hot chocolate had been drunk long ago. 'Our adventure today…'

'Some people would call it a misadventure.'

'Meh…potato potahto. It ended well, so I think we can drop the *mis*.'

He acknowledged the hit and gestured for her to continue.

'Getting away with it gave me a weird high and I suddenly realised that whenever I feel like that—'

'Like what, exactly?'

'Excited, jumping up and down with… I don't know.' She chewed on her bottom lip. He did his best to not notice. 'Glee, laughter, a sense of fun, delight… I realised I try to stamp those things out, try not to feel them.'

He leaned towards her and fancied he could smell pears. 'Why the hell would you do that?'

She stared at her hands. 'The first four years after my mother died, I was trying to hide from what I was feeling—the grief. I felt lost and I tried to hide that beneath a veneer of fun and partying hard. We already know how that played out and how I've since tried to turn over a new leaf.'

He nodded.

'For the last three years, though, I've equated things like glee and flights of fancy and lots of laughter with losing control. I've been so focused on keeping on the straight and narrow—trying not to do anything that would horrify and disappoint Margot and my father—that, basically, I've been murdering all and any high emotion that's bubbled to the surface.'

She mimed the stabbing knife from the shower scene of *Psycho*, her eyes rueful but with a hint of laughter in their depths, and he couldn't entirely smother a laugh.

'I hadn't realised that until today. And it struck me as kind of dense.'

'Only kind of?' He raised an eyebrow.

She poked out her tongue. 'Anyway, I'm through with doing that. Your turn.'

Cleo had let herself fully indulge in a moment of stress-relieving laughter, had gloried in her close escape, had let herself be wild and free—and what had he done? He'd gone and kissed her.

'No, no!'

Her voice broke into his thoughts.

'You're not supposed to look like that when we're making our gratitude lists.'

'Like what?'

'Angry...scowly.'

'Can we list regrets?' The words growled from him.

'Absolutely not! This is a gratitude list—things to feel good about, not beat ourselves up for.' Her eyes narrowed. 'And, for the record, that kiss shouldn't be a regret.'

'It sure as hell didn't make your list of things to feel grateful for.'

'Only because I was being tactful,' she shot back.

He stabbed a finger on the arm of his chair. 'It shouldn't have happened.'

'Maybe not, but it was a damn fine kiss all the same. One I'm not going to forget in a hurry.' Her lips curved. 'I bet I'll still remember it when I'm eighty. And, when I do, I bet I happy-sigh.'

His stomach clenched; *everything* clenched. The kiss had been hell-on-wheels spectacular. It had blown him open, and to deny that he wanted to kiss her again would be a lie. But it didn't change the fact that it shouldn't have happened.

He shouldn't play with that kind of fire. He'd had his heart shredded by a woman once before. He wasn't going to allow that to happen again. And even if Cleo was nothing like Nicole, his ex, she was still a hot mess. He had no desire whatsoever to be her next big mistake. He'd witnessed what loving and then losing his brother had done to Elodie. He wasn't going to open himself up to that kind of pain.

Cleo had boarded his boat and had promptly sworn off men. Given her situation, it was a smart move. He wouldn't mess that up for her.

'I refuse to regret something that has the potential to be

a happy memory.' Cleo held her head high. 'It was just…a moment. We stopped when we should've, called a halt when we should've. It's only if I follow up on it now that it would become self-destructive. And we've already agreed we're not going to do that.'

Her words brought no comfort because he wanted to, with his every fibre. But by this time tomorrow she'd know exactly who he was and…

No. Just…no.

'I don't think you ought to regret it either. And if you do then I don't want to hear about it.'

Her candour, delivered with sledgehammer bluntness, startled a laugh from him.

She raised an eyebrow. 'Okay, what's your number two?'

'I saw an otter.'

Her eyes widened. 'When?'

'Just before we pulled into Berkhamsted this morning.'

'And you didn't call me? Why not?'

Because he'd thought she was trying to stay out of sight. 'It was there one moment and then it was gone. It all happened too quickly.'

Her face turned wistful and he nodded. 'It's one of the best things about cruising the canals—catching sight of a kingfisher or watching swans glide by. And, when I'm very lucky I occasionally see an otter. I saw a badger once.'

'What about hedgehogs?' She gave a gusty sigh. 'I love hedgehogs.'

'From time to time. They're endangered now.' His plan meant otters and hedgehogs wouldn't be featuring on the agenda for the foreseeable future, though. His stomach churned again at how close he'd come to blowing her cover.

After promising to keep her safe, he'd almost handed her to the media on a platter! If they'd been caught…

But they hadn't been. He let out a slow breath. They were still safe. Soon, though, this section of the canal would be crawling with journalists. It was time to get her well and truly out of their reach. He should discuss the plan with her, except it'd change her focus from her epiphany to her fears. And, once she knew the truth, everything would change.

'What's third on your list?' he asked instead.

A slow smile spread across her lips.

Don't focus on her mouth. Hmm, look—delicious banana bread, see? He shoved the last bite into his mouth in an attempt to distract himself, but all it did was stick in his throat.

'I did a fun thing. A fun work thing—only it wasn't work because it wasn't an actual job. It was a bit of play—for joy, you know? I had a ball. Want to see?'

Before he could answer, she lifted her laptop from the spot on the seat beside her where it was charging and lifted the lid. Retrieving a file, she turned the computer to face him. His jaw dropped when he realised what was facing him: a website home page…for *him*.

His Jasper Ballimore author headshot was a cartoon of an archetypal musclebound hero, and she'd clearly grabbed it from his current website, as it sat to the left below a header. This header was all swirling black shadows and golden fire, which managed to look both threatening and beautiful at the same time. Rather than Jasper Ballimore, the name Jay Ballimore emerged in various shades of teal and sapphire from the shadow and flame.

'Jay Ballimore?' he murmured.

'I thought, if you were writing a young adult fantasy series, you'd need to write under a different name than the one you use for your thrillers.'

She scrolled down. There was a paragraph beside the author photo that he couldn't read from this distance, and beneath that she'd created three mock-up covers for the trilogy he'd told her about as they'd walked into Berkhamsted.

'I thought "Jay Ballimore" sounded suitably fantasy-ish. Not all your thriller readers will follow you here—' she tapped the screen '—or vice versa, but you will get some crossover readers who adore the way you write.'

Was she one of them? He shook off the thought and gestured to her computer, his mind a tumble of confusion. *'Why...?'* Why would she go to so much trouble? Why would she invest so much time in something that would never become a reality? Things inside him bucked at that thought, as if they hadn't given up hope of finishing the series. Which was odd, and not entirely welcome.

He rose. 'May I?'

At her nod, he took the laptop, retreated to his seat and read the paragraph beside his photo.

Let Jay Ballimore take you into a world of stolen thrones, ancient fire magic, cursed swords and majestic dragons in this brand-new fantasy series where a pair of seventeen-year-olds, who hate each other on sight and on principle, need to learn to work together if they want to save all that they love from destruction.

She made it sound like a done deal!

Well...? The inner voice sounded a lot like his agent's. He ignored it.

He glanced up and she shrugged. 'Like I said—it was fun. I love doodling around like this.'

Doodling? This wasn't doodling…

'And, while I love Jason Diamond, thrillers aren't my usual jam. Fantasies are, though. My fave authors are Naomi Novik, Tolkien, Sarah J Maas… Oh, and so many others!'

She rattled off names—his favourites featured among them; he'd never heard of the others, but made a mental note to check them out. It had been too long since he'd read a book, too long since he'd wanted to, but the urge swept through him now.

He clenched his jaw so hard it started to ache. He'd been as guilty as Cleo in cutting joy from his life, but he wasn't giving up reading for anyone. A man was allowed one comfort.

'That wasn't supposed to make you mad.'

He glanced up to find Cleo biting her lip, dismay etching lines into her lovely face. 'I'm not mad at you, I'm mad at myself,' he said.

Before she could ask why, he rushed on. 'This is amazing, Cleo. You're very talented.'

'Thank you. Like I said, it was fun. Though, of course, my ulterior motive is to spur you on to write the last book. I *so* want to read this series!'

He knew she said it to lighten the moment, but he couldn't laugh; he couldn't even smile. Write the last book? Impossible.

You sure?

She clapped her hands. 'Your turn.'

He dragged his mind back to the gratitude list. What the hell was the last item on his list? He contemplated using one of her old chestnuts and saying he was grateful he had his health and a place to sleep. But, no matter how much he wanted to, he couldn't do it. She'd given so much of herself. It wouldn't be fair.

'After I say it, there's to be no questions, no discussion...
nothing.'

'Okay.'

He dragged in a breath. 'For the first time in nine months,
it didn't hurt to talk about writing.' He still couldn't get his
head around it. 'I'm grateful for that.'

Her jaw dropped, her eyes widening with a hundred questions, but true to her word she didn't utter a single one. And
then she smiled, a beaming light of a smile that felt like the
beginning of a fairy tale.

His phone buzzed. Picking it up, he read the message and,
rising, he handed her the laptop. 'The car is here early.'

CHAPTER SEVEN

NERVES JANGLED IN Cleo's stomach. 'It's an hour early.'

Jude's phone buzzed again. He read the message and shrugged. 'Things are moving more quickly than expected.'

Um...okay. Trying to look composed, she stowed her laptop into the tote bag, donned the blonde wig and settled a beanie over it.

'What are we going to do with the perishables?' She gestured to the fridge and the pears on the kitchen bench.

'Leave them.'

'Which means you'll come back to—'

'There's not much left and I've a caretaker coming in to look after things.'

He did?

'Though we're not leaving the banana bread.'

Reaching across, he seized the banana bread and wrapped it in wax-proof paper and a clean tea towel.

'Here, put this on.'

She caught the mac he tossed to her and shrugged it on. He swung her tote bag over his shoulder, picked up the small case he'd packed for himself and stowed the banana bread under his arm.

'We're in luck. It's started to rain.' He pushed an umbrella into her hands. 'As soon as we reach the top of the stairs, open it and keep as much of your face behind it as you can. I'll go first. Just keep your eyes on my feet and follow.'

'Is there something you're not telling me?'

He swung back.

'Am I about to be greeted with the flashes of a hundred cameras?' If she was, she'd rather know that now.

'There aren't any journalists waiting to pounce on us, but after what happened earlier I'm taking every precaution; that's all this is about.'

Right.

'Ready?'

'Yes.'

They exited *Camelot*, and she followed him along a dock and across a small yard to a waiting car—big, black with tinted windows. Not that she got a good look at it. Jude ushered her before him, taking the still open umbrella and shielding her as she slid inside the car's luxurious interior, before following her.

She stared at him as the car pulled away on silent wheels. 'Have you worked as a bouncer or bodyguard? Because you did that like a professional.' It reminded her of her acting days when she'd been filming on location.

He sent her a wry smile. 'No.'

'Where are we going?'

His phone buzzed with an incoming text. He read it and

grimaced. 'At the moment we're heading to the airport. The rest I'm still trying to sort out.'

The airport? Oh, God. He was going full Jason Diamond heroic on her. This had to be costing him a fortune. Reaching across, she squeezed his forearm. 'I want you to know that my rainy-day fund is at your full disposal.' She'd cover whatever costs she could.

Glancing up from his phone, something in his face softened. 'Cleo...'

The phone rang and he blew out a breath. 'I have to answer this.'

When they reached the airport she was ushered onto a private jet. Before she could splutter out a single question, Jude disappeared into the cockpit. From then, for all intents and purposes, they travelled separately. When the jet set down in Nice, two bodyguards ushered her to another car with tinted windows, drove her down to the harbour and escorted her onto a super-yacht.

A super-yacht!

She was shown into a saloon and the yacht immediately headed out of the harbour. She had no idea if Jude was on board or not.

Half an hour later, he strode into the saloon wearing an exquisitely tailored suit that fitted him to perfection, highlighting his broad shoulders and strong thighs. It was so unexpected, her jaw dropped.

Grimacing, he shrugged out of his jacket and irritably flicked open the top two buttons of the crisp white business shirt, like some kind of movie star. Her mouth dried while her pulse surged in giddy appreciation.

Don't.

She dragged her gaze away. She couldn't afford to indulge

a single carnal thought where this man was concerned. As previous experience had proved, she was a terrible judge when it came to romantic partners. And he was just too *tempting*. Just... *No*.

He poured himself a Scotch from the polished blond-wood bar at the far end of the room, before sauntering down to sit directly across from her on the semicircular sofa—a bespoke white leather indulgence that fitted the curve of the room.

An acre of space spread between them—literally *and* figuratively. She lifted her hands. 'Who are you?'

Hooded eyes stared back. 'You didn't look me up on the Internet?'

It hadn't occurred to her to do any such thing. 'Is Jude Blackwood another pseudonym?'

Seizing his glass, he moved to sit beside her. Not too close, but close enough that she could see the exhausted lines fanning out from his eyes. Something in her chest clenched.

'Not a pseudonym, but my name isn't well known in England.' He sipped his drink. 'You've heard of Cesar Giroux?'

Everyone had heard of the Giroux family, though Cesar had died four years ago. 'What does he have to do with you?'

He stared into his Scotch. 'Cesar was my grandfather.'

Her eyes bugged. *No way.*

'*You're* the Giroux heir?'

The Giroux family were French industrialists who'd made their fortune several generations ago, and had been adding to it ever since. They were one of the richest families in France, feted wherever they went. Cesar had been nicknamed 'Midas', because everything he'd touched had turned to gold.

Random snippets of news reports came to her: Cesar's state funeral; the shocking death of the older brother, Matthew—Jude's brother; his mother, Cesar's only child, dying of a drug overdose when Jude had been a young boy; one of Cesar's nieces marrying a Scandinavian royal. The family was wealthy, powerful and influential, and their fortune legendary.

Her cheeks burned. 'I offered the *Giroux heir* the use of my rainy-day fund to help finance our escape? *Seriously?*'

'Cleo—'

'And when I crashed onto your boat and inferred you were living frugally and that some extra money might come in handy...' As if he'd been living a hand-to-mouth existence—how he must've laughed.

Floor, swallow me now.

Reaching out, he took her hand. 'You treated me like a real person. You judged me on our interactions rather than my family's fortune. You treated me like you would anyone else. I treasured that.'

The expression in his eyes had her heart flipping. She carefully reclaimed her hand and eased back a fraction, things inside her becoming too heated and needy.

'I wasn't trying to deceive you. I was just...enjoying my anonymity. I'm sorry I didn't tell you who I was sooner.'

She waved that away. 'Totally understandable.' She'd have done the same in his place.

'So...you don't want to throw your drink in my face or punch me?'

She tried to glare but failed. 'It should be too soon for that joke.'

He gave one of those crooked half-smiles that never failed to send her insides into a spin. She recalled that moment earlier when his lips had found hers...

She jerked back, horror dawning through her. 'You're *seriously* famous.' He was ten times the news story she was.

'You have to be one of Europe's most eligible bachelors. You—' she gestured at him and then to herself '—and me. If we're photographed together…' It would create a sensation of *monumental* proportions.

'I know.' Tilting his head back, he drained the contents of his glass. 'But you forget I've also the kind of wealth that can shield you from the media. And I'm going to use every tool at my disposal to do exactly that. I assure you, Cleo, no one is going to discover where you are and who you're with. You have my word.'

The yacht was amazing. When Jude took her for the grand tour the following morning, Cleo spent most of it trying to haul her jaw off the floor. Besides the spacious saloon with its opulent white leather sofa and blond-wood bar, there was an oak panelled dining room, a galley kitchen that was thrice the size of *Camelot*'s, and eight bedrooms, all with *en suites*. There was an office-cum-library and a gym.

There were staff quarters on a lower deck. There was a magnificent pool at the stern. There was a hot tub on the main deck, and the upper deck had a sky lounge—all clear glass and marvellous light. There were myriad outdoor seating and dining areas. As soon as the first helicopter flew overhead, though, she avoided all of those, along with the sky lounge. She couldn't get the image of a telescopic lens out of her mind.

She and Jude fell into a kind of rhythm. Because the yacht was operating on a skeleton staff, she continued to cook while he ate with the same relish he'd shown on *Camelot*. They worked out in the gym, and they set up their laptops in the yacht's generous office.

They danced around each other trying to act normal, *very*

careful not to touch. Yet every now and again she'd glance up and catch an expression in his eyes—an expression of heat and yearning, sweetened with a strange tenderness. And her reaction was always instant and totally out of proportion— her skin would prickle with a heat that made her fidget, made her antsy. And it wasn't the kind of antsy that a hard session in the gym could ease.

No men. No romance. No making headlines.

She kept repeating it silently, like a mantra. She wasn't going to let herself down. She wasn't going to let her family down. And she wasn't going to let Jude down either. *Nothing* could happen between them.

'You don't have a French accent.'

It was their fourth morning on the yacht and Cleo was pounding the treadmill while Jude's legs furiously pumped the stationary bicycle.

'Didn't you grow up in France?'

He wore shorts and his thigh muscles bunched and flexed. Her mouth went dry. With an effort, she dragged her gaze away. She had no idea how to mitigate the intensity of her *want*. She wanted him, with a fierceness that made no sense. She did her best not to think about it and tried to focus her mind on other things. Yet she'd constantly jerk back into the moment, realising she'd been indulging in flagrantly detailed fantasies of making love with him: slow sensual love-making; fast, furious love-making. Intense love-making...

She couldn't remember ever wanting anyone with this kind of intensity.

In perfectly accented French, Jude now said, 'My French is flawless.'

'*Oui,*' she agreed.

'My parents divorced when I was six and my British father insisted that Matt and I be educated in England. We spent most of our school holidays at the Château Giroux, though.'

She'd seen photographs of the château, located on the outskirts of Paris. It took grandeur to a whole new level.

'I was close to my maternal grandparents before they passed.'

She kept her gaze to the front. 'And you were close to your paternal grandmother too.' The one who'd made him promise to do one good thing a day. 'When did you get to spend time with her?'

She couldn't resist a quick glance in his direction to find her question had surprised a smile from him, which made her breath catch.

No, no, that was the exercise. She slowed her pace to ensure oxygen could still reach her bloodstream.

'When my father dumped me and Matt in boarding school, we barely saw him—or my mother. Gran upped sticks from London and moved to the town where the school was located. She insisted we spend every weekend with her.'

'Oh, what a lovely thing to do! She sounds wonderful.'

He nodded. 'She took two rowdy boys, who were pretty angry at the world at the time, in her stride.'

Of course they'd have been angry. They'd been ripped from all they'd known and abandoned.

'She made us into a family,' he finished simply.

Her eyes filled.

'If you start crying, Cleo, I'm throwing you overboard.'

'I'm not crying!' She picked up her pace again. 'You make me jealous. I've no memories of my grandparents.' She sent him a sidelong glance. 'I'm sorry, Jude. You must miss her enormously.'

'I believe you already gave me your condolences.'

The timer dinged and they both stopped, both breathing hard from the exertion. 'But now I know more about her, which means my condolences are more.'

'More what?'

'Just…more.'

Climbing off the treadmill, she reached for her towel and pressed it to her face and neck. Glancing across, she found Jude's hungry gaze glued to where she'd blotted the towel to her throat. The racing of her pulse nearly brought her to her knees. She deliberately turned away.

'What about your dad?' *Breathe, Cleo, breathe.* 'Do you ever see him?'

'He died when I was sixteen. A lorry blew a tyre on the motorway and slammed into his car.'

She swung back, her heart sinking. 'Oh, Jude, how awful.'

He rolled his shoulders. 'We weren't close.'

'That doesn't make any difference. It's worse in some ways, because now you'll never know what the future could've held.'

He stared, and for a moment she thought he might say more, but then he shook his head and ushered her through the door. 'I need a cold drink before hitting the shower. You?'

She nodded.

'It must be time for you to answer a few questions for a change. What about you? Were you close to your mum?'

Oh, God. Had she been asking too many questions? Of course she had. She needed to stop doing that…

'Cleo?'

Jude's eyes narrowed at the way Cleo had started frown.

She shook herself. 'Yes, really close.'

Hence the reason Cleo had gone off the rails so spectacularly after she'd died, he supposed. He handed her a bottle of water from the bar in the saloon and sprawled on the sofa. 'What was she like?'

'Smart, vibrant, fun. We didn't know what to do after we lost her.'

She paced around the room, her gaze fixed on the view outside. 'She brought out the best in us. She made Dad talkative, when he's not the most communicative of men. Margot has a tendency to be a bit too serious, and she got her to laugh and be a bit silly. She made them relax and have fun.'

She smiled, remembering, but she was still too keyed up, too tense. This woman needed to learn to relax. 'Cleo, sit. You've just spent an hour pounding away in the gym.'

She shook her head. 'I'm not sweating my dirty sweat all over your white sofa.'

'Why not?'

'Respect.'

'It's hard-wearing and easy to clean,' he shot back. 'And I insist.'

After the briefest of hesitations, she perched on the very edge of a seat. But he suspected she'd only done it to humour him. Maybe talking more about her mum would help her unwind. 'How did your mum bring out the best in you?'

She sent him a sidelong glance. 'You might not believe it, but I was a shy teenager. Mum brought me out of my shell. Acting was her idea; she thought me joining a drama group would help me gain confidence.'

Confidence she'd lost when her mother had died. His heart went out to her.

She tapped a finger against her water bottle. 'You know, we've never really functioned properly as a family since.'

She stood again, strode across to the bank of windows and stared out at the view—at the hills of Nice rising up behind the terracotta tiles of the city. The sun glittered off a sea that sparkled silver and blue. 'I can't believe how beautiful it is here.'

'Come up on deck.' It was January, so it was cold, but not like in London or Paris. She'd been cooped up for too long. The fresh air would do her good.

She shook her head.

'Why not?'

'There are other yachts.' She pointed.

They were miles away!

She then pointed skywards. 'And haven't you heard the helicopters passing overhead?'

Was she worried they might be news helicopters?

'Anyway, I'm content inside.' She gave an excited wiggle. 'Do you know how amazing this is?' She turned on the spot, her eyes filled with a mix of awe and delight, and something in his chest softened. Some silly thing he did his best to ignore.

'I feel as if I've been rewarded for my bad behaviour— land myself on the front pages and get whisked away to the French Riviera.'

'Or maybe you were rewarded for sticking up for yourself. Clay deserved everything he got.' Reaching out, he gently squeezed her shoulders, her warmth flooding every pore. 'You deserve every drop of good fortune that comes your way, Cleo.'

She stared at him as if his words had momentarily immobilised her. Her gaze lowered to his mouth. Full lips parted, as if parched.

Hunger roared in his ears. To taste those lips one more time…

Cleo tugged herself free, leaving his hands empty. She backed up a step, and then another one, her eyes not meeting his. She pointed behind her. 'I…uh…shower.' Turning, she fled.

He clenched his hands at his sides and counted to twenty until he was certain she'd reached her cabin before heading to his own. His punishing cold shower should've left him blue, but barely took the edge off the heat banked just below the surface of his skin. He needed to tread carefully—very carefully. He'd sworn to himself that he wouldn't get involved with Cleo. It was just too…dangerous. There was a warmth beneath his desire that instinct told him would lead to trouble of the heartache variety. He wasn't opening himself up to that, no matter how much he wanted her, or how much he liked her.

He'd been burned before, and he wasn't interested in repeating the experience. Nor was he interested in opening himself up to the agonies Elodie now suffered.

While Cleo was doing her best to get her act together, what would happen the next time life dealt her a blow? Would she act with maturity, or not? What if he unintentionally provided that life blow? A bad taste coated his tongue. Their attraction had the potential to be monumentally destructive, materially and emotionally. His body might burn for her, but he'd burn in hell if he gave into the temptation.

'Okay.' Cleo put down her book—the third in the Jason Diamond series—and clapped her hands. 'Gratitude time.'

He held up his puzzle book. 'I finished the cryptic crossword.'

He'd had his staff grab a host of puzzle books from the airport. Just as they had on *Camelot*, he and Cleo continued to do identical puzzles and compared notes at the end of the day.

'No way! I need a clue for three down. It completely bamboozled me.'

She was a novice when it came to puzzles, but was smart and quick. Given enough time, he suspected she'd overtake him. Not that they'd be here long enough for that.

Stretching, he shifted on his seat. 'Go on, then, hit me with your gratitude list.' He wouldn't say he looked forward to doing this gratitude thing, but he'd started to find it easier. And the way her eyes lit up when she listed her items was a definite consolation.

'My beef stew was perfection.'

His mouth watered at the memory. 'It was.'

'I don't always get it right, but I did tonight, which was satisfying.'

He searched his mind for something to add to his list. 'I fixed an engine problem. It was a bit tricky, but it worked.'

She stared. He half-scowled. 'What? If you can have beef stew, then there's nothing wrong with me putting engine repairs on my list.'

'Absolutely *nothing* wrong with it. I thought you'd have an engineer for that.'

He did, but engines were another kind of puzzle, and he liked to tinker.

'It's just, you're so…*capable.*'

Their gazes locked and the air between them shimmered. It took all his strength to wrench his away and lift his glass of whisky to his lips.

'I added a book page to the Jay Ballimore website.'

He glanced back.

'It was fun. Want me to send it to you?'

He stalked across to the bar and poured himself another finger of whisky. 'Sure, why not?'

'Say please.'

Her teasing made it hard not to grin. 'Cleo, could you please send me the new website page that you made today? I'm curious to see it.'

She wriggled in her seat. 'That acknowledgement almost makes my list, but I'm afraid it's trumped by Margot.'

He started to walk back to his seat but froze at her words. With an effort of will, he made his legs move again. 'That sounds...' *Promising? Ominous?* He sat. He had no idea.

'I've been emailing her every day with my gratitude list. Today she emailed back with hers. Nothing else, no other message, but it's a start.'

He swore.

She blinked. 'Did you just say *a very rude word*?'

He glared. 'Must you always over-share?'

She crossed her arms, her shoulders inching up towards her ears. 'It feels safe to share here. I...'

'It's not a criticism.' Her confidences made him feel privileged. He scowled: and beholden.

'I'm in awe, that's all,' he grouched. 'You seem to find it easy.'

She sent him the smallest of smiles. 'What happens on a super-yacht remains on a super-yacht. Same goes for narrow boats.'

Dragging in a breath, he nodded. 'I'm pleased you're making progress with Margot.' That was huge news.

'Thank you.'

She stared at him expectantly. His scowl deepened. 'Okay, there's to be no response to what I'm about to say, got it?'

'Okay.'

'I started the first chapter in book three of my fantasy series.'

Her eyes widened. Her hands slapped to her thighs. She leaned towards him...

He pointed. 'Not a single word.'

Her mouth snapped shut. Without uttering a word, she happy-danced, then she picked up her Jason Diamond book and opened it to the bookmarked page.

He couldn't have said why, but it made him smile. 'That's great news about Margot, Cleo.'

She didn't look up. 'Thank you.'

'The website page...?'

'Already sent.'

Margot was talking to Cleo again. He had to double every effort and ensure nobody discovered where she was. He wouldn't let anyone ruin this for her.

As for the writing... What the hell did he think he was doing? When he took his place as head of the Giroux family, there'd be no time for writing. There'd be only duty and responsibility. Duty and responsibility he had no intention of shirking ever again.

CHAPTER EIGHT

'THE POOL IS HEATED, Cleo. You can go for a swim if you want.'

Cleo turned away from the window with its view of the pool. It wasn't a plunge pool, but a proper pool—one any resort would be proud of. She suspected she'd been staring at it a little too wistfully. 'It's just hard to not keep admiring the view. I mean, the Côte d'Azur! I have to keep pinching myself.'

No matter how much she might want to, she couldn't go for a swim, even though there was a wardrobe of clothes in her cabin, including swimsuits. The pool was on the open deck, and helicopters continued to pass overhead with monotonous regularity.

She was Cleo Milne. Jude was the Giroux heir. And together they'd be tabloid gold. Margot deserved better from her. *Jude* deserved better from her.

He stood. 'Come on.'

'I'm not swimming, Jude.' It was too risky.

'I'm not talking about the pool.'

Another session in the gym? Excellent idea! Powering down her computer, she followed him. But he didn't lead her to the gym; instead, he led her to... *The hot tub? No way!*

Turning on the jets, he took her hand and plunged it into the water. 'Feel how warm that is.'

She nearly swooned. It was heaven.

Releasing her, he pointed to the awning above. 'This area is covered.' He pressed a button on the wall and shade screens lowered. 'A telescopic lens isn't getting through that lot.'

Still, she hesitated. It was hard enough being in the same room as Jude, working at different ends of the huge table in the yacht's office or sitting on opposite sides of the curved white sofa in the saloon, let alone jumping into a hot tub with him.

'You said you wanted more joy in your life. And yet here you are, still turning your back on it.'

'No, I'm not!'

'And I can't help wondering why.'

She rubbed both hands over her face. 'Because I don't want to keep making the same mistakes.'

He blinked.

'Surely you understand that? I want to find joy responsibly. I don't want to keep looking for it in the wrong places.' Especially not in the lead up to Margot's wedding. She couldn't afford to be reckless or rash.

He folded his arms. 'It's just a hot tub, Cleo.'

Which of course made her feel like a fool.

'And there's no chance of the paparazzi snapping a picture of you here.'

Even to her paranoid eyes, all looked safe.

'And I dare you.'

'You...*what*?'

He raised an eyebrow.

The hot tub was huge. Hitching up her chin, she pointed to it. 'I'll meet you here in ten.'

He was already in the tub when she returned, a cocktail glass in one hand, the picture of relaxed, and *potent*, masculinity. An identical glass rested nearby for her. 'But I don't...'

'Mocktail,' he said.

He'd made her a mocktail? That was kind of...sweet. Self-consciousness had her momentarily clutching her towelling robe to her chest, which was crazy. She'd worn swimsuits on her TV show. Thousands of people had seen her wearing a bikini. But she'd bet Jude hadn't been one of them.

Stop it. Get in the hot tub. Gritting her teeth, she dropped the robe onto a nearby chair and climbed in. Jude studiously glanced away, as if doing his best not to notice. She did her best to not notice him in turn.

Seizing her mocktail, she sipped it, tasting pineapple juice, coconut milk and a hint of lime.

'Delicious.' Setting it to the side and sliding up to her neck in the water, she closed her eyes and let the heat and bubble jets work their magic.

She didn't open her eyes. 'Okay, I'll admit it—this was an inspired idea.'

'I think we've earned it.'

She opened an eye and peeked at him. The hot tub was built on generous lines, but even from this opposite corner— as far away from him as she could get—the breadth of his shoulders and the golden perfection of his skin beckoned.

His jaw clenched, as if he'd sensed her gaze. Heat of a different kind gathered in all the places she didn't want it to.

Gritting her teeth, she forced her eye shut. She wouldn't do anything stupid. She wouldn't do anything reckless or self-defeating. She'd caused enough havoc in Margot's life. Her sister deserved to have the wedding of her dreams. Cleo would hate herself forever if she cast the smallest shadow on the day.

A helicopter passed overhead and she forced herself to imagine worst-case scenarios—such as what would happen if she and Jude were snapped in a hot tub and the photograph plastered across the front pages of the newspapers. A slavering horde of paparazzi would then trail in her wake, catcalling and disrupting everything with their pointing cameras and impertinent questions. She imagined the hurt and betrayal stretching through Margot's eyes, the way her father's mouth would tighten as if he'd been stupid to expect better from her, and died a little inside. Was a brief fling worth that price? *Hard no*.

Anyway, what was it Jude had called love—an exercise in deception, disillusion and despair? She shuddered. No way was she getting involved with someone with a world-view that bleak.

Which begged its own question. She stared up at the awning. 'Can I ask you something?'

'Hasn't stopped you in the past.'

Her stomach clenched. Had she been bothering him?

'Ask your question, Cleo.'

'It might be considered invasive.'

'I can't wait.'

His assumed nonchalance made her smile. Something had lightened inside him during the last few days and she was glad of it.

'How has your Jasper Ballimore identity remained a secret? How has one of your girlfriends not spilled the beans?'

When he remained silent, she lifted her head to glance at him. 'I told you it was invasive. It's just, girlfriends always have a way of finding things out.'

Turning his head, he raised a wry eyebrow. She forced herself to settle back again. 'Though, unlike me, you probably haven't had a series of disastrous relationships.'

'The problem, Cleo, is when your family is as wealthy as mine you never know if someone wants you for yourself.'

'Or whether you're a status symbol and a meal ticket.'

'Exactly.'

'Are you saying you've run shy of romantic relationships all your life?'

'It's my MO now.'

Which meant it hadn't been his MO once.

'I've no interest in marrying and being made a fool of.'

Overhead, another helicopter passed by. She couldn't see it, but glared in its direction. 'Was Matt disillusioned in love too?'

'Matt and Elodie were very much in love. But Elodie has been in hell since Matt died. It seems to me that love extracts a price, and it's not one I want to pay.'

It took every effort to not look at him. Someone had hurt him, and had hurt him badly.

'I did contemplate marriage once.'

She swallowed her surprise.

'However, the woman I considered proposing to...'

Had she cheated on him, betrayed him? Her heart clenched. Jude deserved better, and if she got her hands on the woman...

'She discovered my Jasper Ballimore secret and proceeded to name a price to keep it. I got my lawyers on it immediately.'

'The witch!'

'It was a small price to pay to get her out of my life. I'm grateful I didn't make the mistake of marrying her.'

She glanced across. 'I hope she rots in hell.'

He met her gaze and shrugged. 'It was a long time ago.'

The glance grew heated. She dragged hers away and resumed resting back and gazing upwards. That kind of betrayal would have left a mark. No wonder he'd become so cynical. 'I'm sorry you were treated so badly.' She swallowed. 'And thank you for not throwing me immediately off *Camelot* when I told you I'd discovered the secret too.'

'You're nothing like Nicole, Cleo. *You* have a good heart.'

She refused to let his words warm her. Reaching for her glass, she raised it in his direction. 'To a train wreck with a good heart.'

He raised his glass too. 'To good hearts.'

She sipped then set her drink aside. 'What I don't understand is why it's so important for Jasper Ballimore to remain a secret.'

He was quiet for a moment. 'I don't need the money from book sales, which has freed me from the pressures of publicity. I've been fortunate to enjoy the best about being an author without the downsides.'

Some people would have seen the fame as the best part.

'Also, Jasper Ballimore isn't on brand for the Giroux name.'

Not 'on brand'? Did he mean not serious enough? She straightened. 'Says who?' Had this come from his family? 'Your family should be proud of you.'

'They are—those who know about it.'

'So...this is a decision you took on your own?'

'Look.' He sat up. 'With great wealth and privilege comes great responsibility.' He recited it like a lecture. 'I need to carry on my grandfather's legacy. There's no room now for frivolous things like writing. Giroux Holdings is a family corporation. The head of the family needs to work hard to maintain that for the sake of future generations.'

'What? While everyone else suns themselves on a super-yacht?'

He stared, then grinned, as if her outrage tickled him. Her heart did a silly pitter-patter thing. 'Everyone pulls their weight, Cleo. There are no shirkers.'

She mulled that over. 'Being head of the family sounds like a big responsibility.'

'And one I left entirely on Matt's shoulders.' His mouth turned grim. 'The problem is, I inherited my grandfather's Midas touch. When it comes to business, I have his knack for making money.'

But it didn't feed his soul the way writing did. He didn't have to say the words out loud. She could see it for herself.

'Matt, though, encouraged me to pursue what made me happy.' His jaw clenched. 'But in doing that I left him alone to deal with everything. I could've helped him. I *should've* helped him.'

Oh, Jude. He held himself responsible for so much.

'That's all nonsense, you know.' She kept her tone conversational, but his glare turned glacial.

'You're not responsible for what happened to Matt. And being head of Giroux Holdings doesn't mean you can't write. You're the boss now, you can arrange things however you want. You don't have to play the martyr.'

His jaw dropped.

'If Matt had asked for your help, would you have denied him?'

'Of course not. I—'

'Did Matt hate being the head of the family?'

'That's beside the point.'

It so wasn't. 'Don't make the same mistakes your brother did, Jude. Change things so your nephew never feels as hemmed in and restricted as you now do.'

His lips twisted. 'Ah, but that's not the traditional way things are done. We're a family who values its traditions.'

'Just because something is traditional doesn't mean it's good. Innovation has its place.' She flicked water at him. 'You want your nephew to be happy, don't you?'

'What the hell kind of question is that?'

She spread her hands. 'So change things to suit you all. You could establish a family committee to share the load. I bet you have uncles and cousins who have the necessary skills and would love more responsibility.'

She could see him mulling that over for two-tenths of a second. 'That would bring its own problems.'

'There will always be problems. No system is perfect.'

He glared. 'What else do you see in this utopia of yours?'

But the heat had left his voice and she bit back a smile. 'You might have to remain the titular head, but you can delegate, delegate, delegate.'

He rolled his eyes.

'You'd work part-time for Giroux Holdings and spend the other half writing. That way, you wouldn't be neglecting your responsibilities *or* what feeds your soul.' He'd be abdicating neither duty nor joy. 'In keeping the latter, you'll be better at the former.'

'That doesn't necessarily follow, you know?'

'I think it does. Anyway… *I dare you.*'

He rolled his eyes. 'Some people will hate the idea.'

'But I bet your nephew's generation will thank you.'

They were both sitting rather than reclining. It gave her the most spectacular view of his shoulders and chest—his *naked* shoulders and chest. Her bikini-clad breasts were visible above the water line too, and she noted the way he carefully averted his gaze. Her skin drew tight and fire raced through her veins. She forced herself back into a reclining position, sinking her entire body below the waterline. *Breathe.* 'What would Matt have thought of the idea?'

He didn't answer, not that she expected him to.

Overhead yet another helicopter passed. She glared. It was better than focussing on thoughts of hurling herself at Jude. She pointed skyward. 'What do you think they're hoping to find?'

Without warning, Jude rose and stepped out of the hot tub in a single lithe movement. Water sluiced down his body, his trunks plastered to the most glorious pair of glutes she'd ever seen. Her mouth went dry. She'd never wanted with the kind of want she now did. The man was *beautiful*.

'Out of the hot tub, Cleo.'

Her heart lurched into her throat. Had he seen…?

'We're leaving.'

Her heart settled back to beat erratically in her chest. 'Leaving?'

He gestured at the helicopter. 'It was a mistake coming here. I thought you'd be able to relax.'

'I am! Jude, you don't need to—'

'We're leaving for the Château Giroux. It's where I should've taken you in the first place.'

CHAPTER NINE

THEY DROVE THROUGH the iron gates of Château Giroux at seven o'clock that evening. Clean lines graced the palatial four-storey façade and four elegant towers rose at each corner. Cleo stared at the fairy-tale elegance and had no words.

Outside it was all white stone walls and black slate roof. Inside it was white marble and soaring ceilings, the walls lined with works of art intermingled with what she assumed were family portraits. There was elegant furniture, exquisite Aubusson rugs and antiques stretched for as far as the eye could see.

'It's beautiful.' She breathed, staring around, trying to take it all in.

The housekeeper sent her a smile as she led them up the grand staircase to a room at the top of the stairs, an enormous drawing room. A fire crackled in the fireplace and the furniture, while grand, had clearly been chosen for comfort.

A little boy, maybe three or four years old, leapt to his feet, shouting, 'Uncle Jude!'

Racing across the room, he launched himself at the man beside her. Jude caught him easily and swung him into the air. The childish giggles made her smile.

After a hug and more tossing, Jude set the boy on his feet and turned him to Cleo. 'Oliver, this is my friend Cleo.'

Cleo held out her hand. 'I'm very pleased to meet you, Oliver.'

Oliver shook it. 'Are you going to marry Uncle Jude?'

She choked back a laugh, but for the life of her couldn't meet Jude's eyes. She fought to keep her tone light. 'Well, Oliver, as much as I like your uncle, I expect not. We're just very good friends.'

'Would you like to see my truck?'

'Yes, please, very much.'

Before he could haul Cleo across the other side of the room, though, a woman rose from one of the sofas arranged near the fire. 'Oliver, come here.' Her voice was sharp. 'Do not bother the lady.'

'It's no bother,' Cleo assured her. 'I like trucks almost as much as I like boats.'

The little boy grinned at her. The woman did not.

The touch of Jude's hand at the small of her back urged her forward and had warmth curling in her abdomen and circling lower in ever more concentrated circles. It took all her concentration to make her legs work. The burning, the need and want remained long after he'd removed his hand.

'Cleo, this is my sister-in-law, Elodie.'

'Pleased to meet you.'

'Delighted,' said the other woman, though her frosty gaze declared otherwise.

Cleo glanced at Jude. His clenched jaw and flared nostrils told their own story. A woman, presumably a nanny, entered to take Oliver to bed. The little boy kissed his mother, hugged his uncle and promised to show Cleo his truck in the morning.

'You're looking well, Elodie.'

'What are you doing here, Jude? You know I don't want you here. You're not welcome.'

Not welcome? But this was his home.

Cleo stepped forward. 'I needed a bolthole. Jude has very kindly played the hero and brought me here to hide from the paparazzi.'

At Elodie's questioning eyebrow, Cleo explained how Jude had helped her to hide from the paparazzi when they'd been chasing her.

'And how long are you planning to stay?'

Elodie directed the question at Jude, but Cleo pretended it had been meant for her. Lifting her arms, she turned on the spot. 'Now that I've seen the Château Giroux, I'm thinking forever.'

The light-hearted words were meant to dispel the tension, but they fell disappointingly flat. Elodie turned burning dark eyes in Cleo's direction. 'As for Jude playing hero? I find that unlikely.' And then she was gone.

Cleo's stomach dropped to her feet as pieces of the puzzle fell into place. It wasn't just Jude who blamed himself for Matt's death—Elodie did too. And the expression on Jude's face made her want to weep.

Don't hug him. Don't hug him. Don't hug him.

But not hugging him with the hardest thing she'd ever done. Swallowing, she kept her chin high. 'Aren't families grand? This reminds me of Christmas four years ago. It was a real barrel of laughs.'

A huff of a laugh left him. 'You're...'

'Let's settle on "incorrigible". It's more endearing than "irresponsible" or "irreverent"—which happen to be two of my father's favourite words when referring to me. Oliver is a sweetheart,' she added. 'He adores you.'

'It's mutual. Elodie, though...not so much.'

'Who'd have guessed your family would be so much like mine?'

'Let's not compare war wounds, Cleo.'

She was a guest in his house. She'd do whatever she could to make their time here as comfortable for him as possible.

'Let's eat.'

As if he'd magicked them from the woodwork, staff entered and set a table at the far end of the room with steaming bowls of French onion soup and slices of French bread topped with bubbling cheese.

Her stomach rumbled its approval, and one of those beguiling chuckles rumbled from Jude's throat to trace a tempting finger down her spine. She did her very best to ignore it. Instead, she chattered about mundane things until some of the darkness had receded from his eyes.

As had become their habit, they retired early. She'd never slept in such a luxurious room. She should've slept like a log, and yet she tossed and turned, yearning for the sound of lapping water and the slight rocking of a boat.

Jude's and her bedrooms shared a sitting room. On *Camelot* they'd been physically closer—they'd been able to hear each other moving about and talking in their sleep—and yet the knowledge that he was only two doors away...shouldn't be more tempting, more intimate. But that was exactly what it felt like.

Don't think about it. Instead, she replayed that moment when Jude had leapt out of the hot tub with the decision to bring her here to the Château Giroux. Because he wanted her to relax, to let down her guard, to feel completely safe.

She could see now why he'd stayed away. And yet he'd come here anyway...*for her.* It was one of the kindest, most stupidly unselfish things anyone had ever done for her, an act of open-handed generosity that created a warm glow at her very centre.

He was the most amazing man.

And he was only two doors away.

Don't think about it.

After another hour of tossing and turning, she gave up. Grabbing a throw and her book, she padded out to the living room. She pulled up short when she found Jude staring moodily into the embers that were dying down in the small grate.

He glanced across. 'Can't sleep?'

Dropping her book onto the coffee table, she arranged herself at the other end of the sofa, drawing her feet up, careful not to touch him. 'The bed is exceptionally comfortable, and I should be dead to the world, but...'

'You never sleep well the first night in a new place.'

She stared. He remembered...

He shrugged. 'It's an interesting character trait.'

She tried not to read anything into it. 'So what's your excuse?'

He turned back to the fire. 'Too many ghosts.'

'Matt,' she murmured softly.

'He and Elodie made their home here after they married.'

'And you?'

'My grandmother moved back to London when Matt and

I finished school. I split my time between here and my flat in London.'

He hadn't wanted to abandon his grandmother. Her stomach softened.

'I have an apartment overlooking the Thames.'

Of course he did. They both stared into the fire. 'And yet you banished yourself to *Camelot* for the last seven months.'

'Not banished—I wanted peace and quiet. Wanted room to breathe.'

She understood that he'd needed to adjust to the new reality of life without his brother, but in his grief and misplaced guilt it seemed he'd shut himself away from everyone.

She turned to face him more fully. Inside her were things with jagged edges. 'When was the last time you were at the Château Giroux?'

'The day we buried Matt.'

She wanted to weep. 'Have you stayed away because of Elodie?'

He nodded. 'It's hard for her to see me.'

And then she was on her knees and so close the heat from his body beat at her. 'It's not fair of her to blame you for your brother's death, Jude. Or to punish you like this.'

'She has every right!' His eyes flashed. 'I should've realised Matt had been drinking. I should've taken the car keys from him. I should've insisted we take a cab home. I—'

'None of it was your fault!'

Her words rang around the room. Surely his grandmother had told him this, his cousins and friends? But maybe he hadn't been ready to listen.

'Jude, it was an *accident*.' He opened his mouth but she rode on over the top of him. 'It wasn't your fault Matt had been drinking. Of course you believed him when he told you he hadn't been. He probably thought he was fine to drive.'

He stared at her.

'And it wasn't either your or Matt's fault a deer raced across the road when it did. An *accident*,' she repeated. '*Nobody's* fault.'

His lips twisted. It took all of her strength not to reach out and touch him.

'And, as for feeling guilty about not having helped out more with the family business… Matt had a tongue in his head. If he'd needed help, he could've asked.'

'That doesn't change the fact—'

'Maybe not, but beating yourself up about it changes nothing. Nor is it fair of Elodie to blame you for it. You miss Matt too.'

'Yes, but…'

She pressed a finger to his lips. 'You can help now, though. There are some things you can do. For one, you owe it to Matt to have a relationship with Oliver.'

Eyes the colour of a turbulent sea throbbed into hers.

'And you can help Elodie move past this, Jude. Her hurt and bitterness are understandable, but it's hurting her. She clings to it because she's scared, because it's easier to be angry than to be heartbroken, but it'll eat her alive.'

He gripped her hand like a lifeline. 'How do you know this?'

Sitting back on her heels, she pulled in a breath. 'They didn't call me Wild Child for nothing. All of those late-night parties, all of the drinking and acting out—that was me trying to run away from my grief for my mother. Therapy helped me see that, helped me realise how self-destructive I was being. When I stopped doing those things and faced my emotions…'

He leaned towards her. Their faces were so close she could feel his breath on her lips and her heart stuttered in her chest.

'What?'

She had to swallow before she could speak. 'It let the good stuff back in. I began to remember the good memories. I started to feel hopeful.' She let out a shaky breath. 'I found a purpose, something to work towards, and I found a way to live with the grief.'

'You think I can help Elodie overcome her anger, and her resentment of me?' He shook his head. 'That's impossible.'

'It's not impossible, not for you. I know you don't see it, but you're amazing. Seems to me you can achieve just about anything you put your mind to.'

His jaw sagged. He hauled it back into place, his gaze throbbing into hers. Oh, so slowly, his gaze lowered to her lips. Hunger blazed in his eyes and things inside her throbbed to life.

She broke all the rules. Leaning forward, she kissed him.

The warm magic of Cleo's lips had heat filling Jude's every pore. He wondered now if this had been inevitable.

Sitting in the hot tub with her had been torture. Trying to look unmoved had taken all his strength. He'd been aware of her tension. Aware of the heat in her gaze when it had rested on him; her curiosity; her interest; her restraint.

And the way she'd tensed every time a helicopter had passed overhead… He'd focused on *that* rather than everything else. It had been the one thing he *could* act upon.

He'd hoped coming here would diminish what was happening between them. But he wondered now if they'd been building to this from the first moment she'd clattered onto his narrowboat.

He sank into the kiss like a starving man. Threading his fingers through her hair, he kissed her with an intensity he had no hope of tempering, and with a thoroughness he hoped told her what an extraordinary woman he thought her. Cleo gave so much of herself with no expectation of anything in return. With her silly, light-hearted teasing, her gratitude lists and her frank confessions, she'd felled all of his barriers. *And* she'd given him hope.

Her fingers tangled in his hair, pulling him closer, and fire blazed in his veins. Pulling her onto his lap, he pressed a series of kisses along her jaw and down her neck, her skin satin-soft, and she hummed her approval, the sound arcing straight to his groin.

Slow hands traced a path along his shoulders and down his chest, sparking heat and intensifying need. Cupping her breast in his hand, relishing its weight, he stroked his thumb across it and her nipple beaded to hardness with flattering speed. It had him hungry to draw it into his mouth, to touch her with his tongue. To taste her…to have her naked beneath him and arching into his touch, crying out his name…

He froze.

What was he doing?

'Oh, no, you don't.'

Cleo's ragged whisper scraped across his raw nerve endings. She straddled his lap and he had to force back a groan at the way her body slid against his with an intimacy that left him dry mouthed. His fingers dug into the soft flesh of her hips, though whether it was to anchor her there or to put her away from him when he found the strength to do so he had no idea.

Seizing his face in her hands, pale green eyes stared into his. 'Why are you hesitating? I know you want me, Jude. As much as I want you.'

He couldn't deny it, not with the evidence of his desire throbbing against her. He clenched his teeth and forced himself to breathe through the red heat. 'You came to me for help.'

'And you don't want to take advantage of me?' A dimple appeared in her right cheek.

'You said sleeping with anyone at the moment would be self-destructive. I don't want to do something that will have you hating yourself in the morning.'

Her smile faded. 'I don't leap into bed with men I barely know any more, Jude. I no longer use sex—or alcohol—as a way to hide from my problems. And you're not just *anyone*.'

His heart gave a kick that knocked the breath from his body.

'I know we only met a bit over a week ago, but we've spent every waking hour of that time together.'

True enough. He'd shared things with her he'd never shared with anyone.

'I know you better than some guys I've dated for months.' *Like that jerk Clayton Carruthers?*

'What's more, I like you. And I think you like me.'

'Of course I like you!' Meeting this woman had changed his life. He was writing again. Whatever decision he made in regard to it, it was still a consolation of sorts. His heart kicked again—hard. She made him think it might be possible to fix things between Elodie and him.

'This thing—' she gestured between them '—isn't about me forgetting my troubles for a night or two.'

'What is it, then, Cleo?'

She braced her hands on his shoulders, smoothing the material of his soft cotton T-shirt over his arms. 'I like you and I want you. Neither one of us is in a relationship. We're free to indulge in a fling. I know you're not interested in a long-term relationship, so don't think I'll be mistaking this for anything more than what it is.'

He wasn't interested in anything long-term. He felt too broken at the moment; his life was going through too much change. Besides, parading any kind of coupledom happiness in front of a still grieving Elodie... It was out of the question. But a short-term fling...?

'This will be fun and pleasure and tenderness...' A smile trembled on her lips. 'And a happy memory.'

He would be a happy memory for this extraordinary woman! A fault line opened in his chest, letting in light and warmth.

She patted his chest with soft hands. 'Now, you may not feel the same, of course.'

She made as if to move off his lap, but his fingers tightened about her hips. 'I think you're the most amazing woman I've ever met. I burn for you, Cleo.'

She stared at him, her lips parting as if his words had taken her off-guard. Tilting up her chin, he slanted his mouth over hers in a scorching kiss that had her fingers digging into his biceps, before wrapping around his neck. She kissed him back with a fiery enthusiasm that had him breathing hard.

Lifting her in his arms, he strode into his bedroom, kicking the door shut with his heel. Tonight he would be the one to give *to her*. He'd give her body all the pleasure that was in his power to provide. He'd make sure it was a night she'd remember when she was eighty—a memory that would make her smile whenever she thought of it. A good memory she could pull out and hold close whenever she needed to.

He followed her down onto the bed and kissed her deeply, slowly… Restless hands moved across his body, but he tried to ignore them.

'Jude…' She panted. 'I need you.'

'And you're going to have me, sweetheart—in all the ways you want me. But first…'

He flicked open a button on the satin pyjamas the staff had found for her and then another…slowly…until he had the shirt spread out and her beautiful breasts exposed to the air and his gaze. Need roared in his ears but he tamped it down.

A sigh left her as his fingers danced across her skin. 'But first I'm going to savour every delectable inch of you.'

A cry left her lips as his mouth closed over one nipple. He sucked, lathed and traced the shape of her with his mouth and tongue. She arched into his touch, the inarticulate noises in her throat making him hard and hot, yet he refused to rush. Her pyjama top fluttered to the floor as he kissed his way down her body.

He ran his fingers through the damp curls at the juncture of her thighs, teasing and tempting, deliberately avoiding where she most wanted to be touched as he divested her of her pyjama bottoms before kissing his way back up her body—ankles, knees, thighs… When he traced his tongue along the seam of her and circled the most sensitive part of her in slow, lazy strokes, her shocked cry, the way her body lifted, almost undid him.

But the sweet scent of her…the taste of her…the feel of her against his mouth and tongue and arms…

'Jude, I need…'

He slid a finger inside her, her silken flesh tightening

around it. 'I have you, sweetheart.' He lapped at her with his tongue, slowly, rhythmically, hypnotically, until, with a cry and his name on her lips, she came.

Once the fluttering of her body had subsided, he eased away, rolled on a condom and lowered himself over her, bearing his weight on his forearms. He brushed the hair from her face. Heavy-lidded eyes opened and a sultry smile spread across delectable lips. 'I think I just died and went to heaven.'

He grinned down at her. This woman made him feel like Superman. 'I aim to please.'

Her fingers danced down his body, her fingers wrapping around him. 'You certainly do that.'

That wicked hand moved up and down with a gentle strength and purpose that had air hissing between his teeth. Seizing first her right hand and then the left, he trapped them beside her head.

She pouted up at him. 'Why can't I play too?'

His erection nudged her entrance, she lifted her hips to greet him and they slid together in a single smooth motion.

'Oh!'

Her whimper made him tense. 'Did I hurt you? I—'

'No.' Her head moved restlessly against the pillow. Tugging her hands free from his, she ran them down his body to dig surprisingly strong fingers into his buttocks and haul him even closer, her legs wrapping around his waist.

'It's just…' Her breathing grew ragged, sawing in and out of her lungs. 'I've never wanted someone so soon again… after…'

He couldn't not move then. The sensations built between them hard and fast. Her warmth and energy, her very essence, surrounded him like a blessing. She gave a final cry, her muscles clenching around him and then his body followed with a will of its own. His hoarse cry filled the room as a golden heat flooded him and stars burst behind his eyelids. Wave after wave of sensation spiralled through him—deep, intense pleasure—and finally peace.

Jude lay in bed and stared at the ceiling, Cleo a warm bundle curled against his side, and watched the early-morning light filter into the room, appreciating the soft-focus gentleness of it after a night of love-making that had left him feeling remade.

It wasn't just the love-making, though—it was the words Cleo had spoken to him. Words that had hope stirring in his heart.

He might feel guilty that he was alive when his brother was dead, but Cleo was right—the event that had claimed his brother's life had been an accident. He couldn't change it, no matter how much he wanted to. But he remembered the look in Elodie's eyes whenever they'd rested on him...

He felt the searing ache of missing his brother that refused to subside...and his regret that he hadn't helped more with the running of Giroux Holdings, that he hadn't taken some of the responsibility from Matt's shoulders. His lips twisted. Being a scapegoat had given him a role to play. But that didn't help anyone. It was no healthier than all the younger Cleo's drunken partying.

Matt would want you to have a relationship with Oliver. He knew the truth of that on a bone-deep level. He needed to be an admirable role model for his nephew; emotional cowardice wasn't admirable on any level. He also knew Matt would want him to give Elodie all and any support he could.

Cleo had made him see it was time to stop hiding. It was

time to fight—to fight for his family in the same way that Cleo fought for hers.

Cleo stirred and a smile curved her lips as she blinked sleep from her eyes. A warm arm slid across his chest and she made a sound of approval. He immediately grew hard.

'Did I mention you have a great body?' she murmured.

'You might've mentioned it once or twice.'

He grinned. She grinned.

'I vote that this thing goes for longer than one night.'

He rolled her over and kissed her. 'I second that vote.'

CHAPTER TEN

JUDE TAPPED ON the open door of Elodie's private sitting room. Elodie's faced hardened when she turned. 'I don't want to see you. I don't want to speak to you.'

A hard knot formed in his stomach. He had to fight the instinct to turn and leave. Recalling the expression in Cleo's eyes last night, he pushed his shoulders back and nodded. 'I know.'

She blinked.

'The thing is, Elodie, your anger at me and your wish to avoid me don't seem to be helping. You're just as unhappy now as you were nine months ago.'

'Unhappy?' she spat. 'How can I be anything other than *unhappy* when my husband is dead?'

'You're no more *at peace*, then.'

Her eyes flashed. Jude rubbed a hand over his face. 'Running away hasn't worked out so well for me either.'

Striding across, she stabbed a finger at him. 'You don't deserve peace.'

Everything inside him burned. It took all his reserves of strength to remain where he stood rather than removing himself from her presence. When he spoke, his voice emerged low, the strain stretching it thin. 'I know you think blaming me is a way to remain strong, but I'm starting to think the opposite is true. Blaming me is stopping you from moving on. You're using all of your resources to remain angry at me, instead of using them to come to terms with your grief.'

She stared back stonily.

'What I've started to realise is that the truth is preferable to continuing in a lie, even when it isn't palatable.'

He ached to reach out and take her hands or hug her, but she held herself so aloof, he dared not. He could not force her to hear his words, *really* hear them, no matter how much he wanted her to. But he had at least to try.

'I'd do whatever I could to make your life easier, Elodie, but continuing in this lie isn't helping any of us. The fact is, I'm *not* responsible for Matt's death. I didn't know he'd been drinking.'

'The alcohol *had* to have affected him. You should've seen that!'

'I wish it had been evident, but it wasn't. The fact I didn't notice, that I didn't pay more attention, is something I will regret till my dying day.' He swallowed hard. 'But it doesn't change the fact that the accident wasn't my fault.'

She took a step back, her eyes widening.

'I've played it over in my mind so many times. Everything happened so fast—*so fast*. Matt's reaction was pure instinct. I don't know if he'd have done any differently if he hadn't had anything to drink. I don't know if I'd have done anything differently if I'd been behind the wheel.'

He dug his fingers into the hard knot of muscle at his nape. 'I wish he'd told me how much pressure he'd been under at work. I wish he'd asked for my help. I wish even more that he hadn't had to ask. I wish I'd seen it and leaped in to do what I could.' *That* would be the biggest regret of his life.

'What I do know, though, is that Matt wouldn't want me beating myself up and blaming myself for any of it. Even if I had been at fault, he wouldn't want me beating up on myself. He was always generous like that.'

For a fraction of a second something in Elodie's eyes lightened. In a heartbeat, it was gone again. He despaired that anything he said would touch her.

'He wouldn't want you miring yourself in all of this bitterness and anger either.'

'You have no idea what he'd want!'

'Not true,' he said slowly. And in some fundamental way that gave him back his brother. 'Matt would want me to support you in any and every way I could. He'd want me to have a good relationship with Oliver. And this will sound harsh when I don't want it to but, Elodie, Oliver deserves better.'

Her quick intake of breath speared into his heart. 'How dare you?' Her whisper was hoarse. 'I love my son.'

'I know you do, but Oliver deserves to have all of you, not half of you.'

She backed away from him, shaking her head.

'Do you want to know what it's like beyond the anger and bitterness?'

She stared, swallowed and glanced away. 'How?'

'It's not much different in some ways. I miss Matt every

single day. So much, sometimes it's like there's a hole inside me.'

She pressed a hand to her mouth.

'But letting go of my guilt and anger—at myself and the universe—has forced me to accept that Matt is really gone for good.'

She stiffened.

'It doesn't matter how much I don't want that to be true. It's a fact. Matt isn't coming back.'

Her bottom lip wobbled.

'In its place I've been remembering some of the good times we had—some big, some small. They pop into my mind when I'm least expecting it. Like the week Gran took us on a yachting holiday to the Lake District. We were ten and twelve. It was magic.' He couldn't help smiling at the memory. 'Matt's excitement when he got into his dream college at Cambridge.' He waited for her to meet his eyes. 'The tone of his voice when he told me he'd met the girl he was going to marry.'

Elodie's shoulders started to shake and he did what he should've done nine months ago. He pulled her against his chest and held her as she cried out her grief and her pain.

Cleo stared at Jude sleeping. His face at rest looked more youthful, more at peace. She resisted the urge to reach across and press her lips to his. These last few days had been idyllic. She still couldn't believe that from so much disaster she'd found so much *joy*.

The thought had her swallowing. This was a temporary refuge. She couldn't forget that. She and Jude were finding temporary consolation in each other, nothing more. They'd become friends and then lovers. The former would hopefully endure, but the latter had an end date. In six days' time, she'd return to London and be the model of propriety at her sister's wedding.

Six days? She glanced at Jude again. Would she get her fill of this man in that time? Together they'd scaled heights she hadn't known existed. And yet it hadn't taken the edge off her hunger, or his.

The thought of leaving him... An ache gripped her chest. Slipping out of bed, she padded through to her own bedroom and changed into a pair of jogging bottoms. Jude considered love an exercise in *deception, disillusion and despair*. He had no interest in anything long-term. She had to respect that.

And anything beyond a clandestine affair was out of the question. For pity's sake, he was a hundred times more high-profile than any of her previous boyfriends. Think of the media frenzy. If their names were linked, it would create *so* much tabloid speculation. Exhaustion swept through her. She was tired of being in the limelight, tired of the derogatory innuendos, tired of no one taking her seriously.

She dragged on her trainers and pulled the laces tight. She'd sworn to Margot she'd fly under the radar. She *would* keep her promise. She simply needed a moment to get her scattered emotions back under control. They were running high today, which was to be expected. Letting herself outside, she set off around the massive gardens at a fast clip, the air icy in her lungs.

Jude met her on the terrace on her return. He smiled, but his gaze searched her face. 'You had the energy for a run?'

She shrugged. 'A necessity. Your chef is a gem, and I've been indulging a little too much.'

'Come and have breakfast. You can shower later. Elodie won't mind.'

He'd told her about his conversation with Elodie. His courage in baring himself to the other woman had left her speechless. The gulf had been breached, though, and both Jude and Elodie were doing their best to mend their relationship. She didn't doubt there'd be rocky times ahead, but nor did she doubt their ability to get through them. She'd been so happy for him.

'It's due to you,' he'd told her.

'Nonsense!'

'I've seen how fearless you've been in mending your relationship with Margot. I've seen how determined you are to not let her down—the lengths you've gone to and the sacrifices you've made.'

'She's my sister,' she'd said, as if that explained it all.

'*Exactly*. You refuse to let your own hurt or resentment or guilt stop you from doing what you can to fix things. Even when that turns your life upside down. Even when the demands made on you aren't reasonable. You've done it gladly, without complaint. Me? I just went into hiding.'

'You were grieving.' In his shoes, she'd have travelled those same depths of despair. 'You needed time, and now you've had it you're seeing what you need to do, and you're doing it. You should be proud of yourself.'

She'd kissed him then and there hadn't been talking for a very long time.

Afterwards, when she'd been luxuriating in a golden glow of contentment, Jude had turned his head on the pillow. 'Meeting you has changed my life, Cleo. For the better.'

She'd had to blink away tears. She'd nestled against his side and pressed a hand over his heart. 'Ditto, Jude.'

She followed him through to the dining room now, and Elodie's brows shot up when she saw Cleo's running gear.

'A run? Is it not freezing outside? Did not you and Jude use the indoor gym earlier in the week?'

'It was *bracing*. And I like the fresh air.' She grinned. 'I'm also aware I'll be walking down the aisle in a bridesmaid's dress in a week and I want to fit into it.'

Elodie laughed, but was it Cleo's imagination or had Jude's eyes clouded over at the reminder she wouldn't be here this time next week? She shook off the thought—definitely her imagination.

She glanced up a short while later to find him frowning at the way she picked at an omelette. She forced herself to lift a morsel to her lips and make noises of approval.

His frown deepened. 'Is something wrong?'

Elodie became instantly alert then too. Cleo abandoned her cutlery and willed the tears away. 'It's Saturday.'

They both nodded.

She tried to smile, but the sudden concern that flickered across Elodie's face, and the way Jude's brows lowered, made her think she hadn't succeeded. 'It's Margot's hen night tonight and…' She trailed off with a shrug. She ought to be there.

Jude and Elodie threw her a party. Jude surprised her with a designer dress in hot pink that he'd had specially delivered. Fun and flirty, it fitted like a dream and made her feel like a princess. And the relatives who'd travelled to the château for the weekend joined in the festivities with gusto.

The château's chef excelled herself. There were delicious platters of canapés—clever things made with prawns, bacon and asparagus—exotic salads and cold meats. Sweets included tiny crème brûlées in shot glasses and mini chocolate eclairs. There was non-alcoholic fizz to wash it all down.

There were party games that had everyone laughing, and dancing under the lights of a disco ball. Everyone wanted to dance with her, and made the most delicious fuss. Jude's family were warm and loving with the same bone-deep decency that ran in Jude's veins. Their enjoyment wasn't feigned, and it made Cleo realise what she lacked in her own life—a sense of belonging, a place where she could be herself and not always be so guarded and on her best behaviour.

'Would you like to record a message for the bride?' Jude asked later in the evening.

'Yes, please!' She handed him her phone to do the recording.

The volume of the music was turned down, though the disco ball continued to flash, and she stood in front of the crowd who all cheered and waved from behind her.

'Margot, I so wish I could be celebrating with you tonight. I hope you're having the most wonderful time and are looking forward to marrying the man of your dreams next weekend. You've been the best sister a girl could ever hope for and I'm lucky to have you in my life. Because I can't be there with you tonight, I'm celebrating you here with my new friends.' She raised her glass. 'To Margot!'

'To Margot!' everyone cried behind her, raising their glasses.

She blew Margot a kiss and Jude stopped the video. She immediately sent it and crossed her fingers that Margot would send her a reply—a happy reply.

An hour later, just as the party was winding up, her phone vibrated in her pocket: a text from Margot. Her heart picked up speed.

What is your gratitude list today?

Another text pinged.

Top of my list is my message from you. xx

'Everything okay?'

Jude watched her with bright intent and she doubted she could've blinked the tears from her eyes or stopped her smile—not even if there'd been a photographer's camera trained on her. 'From Margot.'

She held out her phone so he could read the text, her breath doing a funny little stutter in her throat when a grin spread across his stern features. Giving a whoop, he picked her up and swung her round, and for the briefest of moments it felt as if everything in her world had aligned.

'Happy?' he demanded, setting her on her feet again.

'Over the moon!' A moment later, she murmured, 'People are staring.' Though they were staring at him, not her—and in bemusement, not disapproval.

'Don't care.'

And why should he? These people, his family, were people he could trust. They'd accept him for who and what he was.

You can trust your family too.

Not like this.

Whose fault is that?

She pushed the thought away. She'd made things right between Margot and her again, which meant they'd be okay again between Cleo and her father. She'd be careful not to create more drama or scandal and everything would be just fine.

She clasped her phone to her chest. 'Thank you, Jude. Not just for this party, but for everything. For helping me save the day.'

'You saved the day yourself, Cleo. I just gave you a place to hide.'

'You came to my rescue more times than I can count. You let me stowaway on your boat.'

'Grudgingly.' He grimaced.

'You whisked me away to the French Riviera when it became clear journalists were on our tails.'

He shrugged, as if that was nothing.

'And then you brought me here because I couldn't relax with all of those darn helicopters.'

He gazed around, his face softening. 'It's good to be back.' He looked more content than she'd seen him.

And, just like that, every atom flooded with awareness: for the strong, lean lines of Jude's body that felt like silken steel beneath her fingertips; for firm lips that could be as gentle as a summer breeze through the fronds of a weeping willow, or as demanding as a surging tide; for the feel of his body moving against hers, as if the fact of them becoming lovers had always been inevitable. As if there were molecules in him and her that otherwise would've always remained dormant.

Dangerous, a voice whispered through her.

'This hasn't been one-sided, Cleo. If it weren't for you...'

His words petered out when he registered her desire and need. She couldn't hide it. Her body pulsed with it, on fire with an urgency she couldn't explain. The darkening of his eyes and the quickening of the pulse at his throat told her he felt the same.

'Party's breaking up.'

His hoarse whisper rasped across her skin. 'Do you think that means it'd be okay if we slipped away?' she whispered.

Taking her hand, he pulled her from the room.

'They're all going to know.' Her heart pounded in her throat. 'That was hardly discreet.'

'I don't care.'

Then she wouldn't either.

The moment they reached their suite, she slammed the

door behind them and backed him up against it. Stretching up on tiptoe, she pressed her lips to the spot where his pulse pounded in his throat, lathing it with her tongue and drinking in the scent of him—all spice, fresh mint and warm musk, a heady combination that made her head spin.

As did the sound of air hissing from his lungs and the touch of his fingers at her waist.

'I wanted to do that all night,' she said, pressing a series of kisses along his jaw towards that beautiful, beguiling mouth.

'Want to know what I've wanted to do?'

He'd eased back a fraction so she'd have to stand higher on tiptoe to reach his lips, but his hands tightened on her waist and she couldn't move. She nodded.

He lifted the hem of her skirt in one motion until it was hitched around her waist, the move shockingly brazen and shockingly seductive. In a flash of movement, he whirled them around so it was her back pressed against the door. His fingers slid beneath the lace of her panties with a wicked intimacy—his fingers unapologetically bold and searching. She gave a shocked moan of need, her head lolling back against the door.

He swore softly in French, making her toes curl. 'I touch you like this...' that finger moved against her with merciless thoroughness that made her legs tremble '...and I'm in danger of losing control.'

'Please...lose...control.' Each word was ground out—a gasp and a plea.

'It's why I've taken to carrying condoms with me wherever we go.' He tore the corner of a foil packet with his teeth.

Cleo had given up speaking, too busy fumbling with his belt and then the zip of his trousers. He sheathed himself in the condom and lifted her. She wrapped her legs around his waist and he entered her in a smooth motion that filled her body, making her mindless, spiralling her to another place— a place of pleasure and delight where they both rode wave upon wave of pleasure that lasted forever.

She came back to herself to find Jude resting his forehead on the door beside her. Her arms were looped round his neck and her legs dangled loosely round his hips. Turning her head, she pressed a kiss to his neck. Very gently, he eased away and let her slide down until her feet touched the floor.

'I think I might've screamed loud enough for them to have heard me back in England.' She'd never realised she could be so vocal.

'I couldn't hear you over the noise I was making.'

He grinned. She grinned.

'Don't worry, Cinderella, the castle walls are thick.'

They made love again. Of course they did.

Afterwards Cleo watched as the light outside the window began to filter into the room while Jude slept beside her. She'd never had such a generous lover. She hadn't known that making love could be this good. But she was starting to feel as if it meant more to her than it should. She could feel herself wanting to plan a future with Jude.

She needed to knock that on the head because it simply wasn't going to happen. He'd warned her that he didn't do long-term. And last night she'd fully reconnected with Margot at last. Margot had finally forgiven her. She couldn't do anything to risk upsetting that balance. Acid burned her stomach—which another disastrous love affair with another high-profile man would absolutely do.

Silently she slid from Jude's bed and made her way to her own room to slide between smooth sheets that felt too crisp and cold.

* * *

'You returned to your own room this morning.'

Jude watched Cleo's face closely as she sipped her tea. The staff brought a pot of tea into the library at ten-thirty every morning. It was where he and Cleo had taken to working. Often an hour or more would go by without them speaking, both immersed in their work—she with her website designs and he writing the third book of his trilogy.

Dammed for so long, the words now flowed with a speed he could barely keep up with. He couldn't explain how, but writing again made him feel strong—gave him the resources to deal with other tougher things.

He couldn't stop thinking about Cleo's suggestion to change the internal structure of Giroux Holdings. He'd started researching what it would involve and had made a list of family members to approach. It had filled him with a new sense of purpose and a new optimism for the future.

Her gaze skittered away from his now. 'I was feeling a bit restless. I didn't want to disturb you.'

His heart sank. It was a lie—or at least not the full truth. He understood it, though. Their love-making had taken on a new edge—had become something deeper, both fiercer and more tender somehow. It had filled him with exhilaration. But, staring at Cleo's face now, he realised the other side of that equation.

'What?'

He blinked to find her frowning at him.

'You've turned grim,' she said.

'I didn't mean to. I just...' Moving from his desk and pouring himself a tea, he forced himself to sit in his usual spot on the sofa beside her, careful to keep some space between them.

'You just...what?'

'I just realised what you're doing. You're trying to create some distance between us, and I can see the wisdom in
that.' Neither of them had made promises. Neither of them
was looking for a relationship.

'Last night we were indiscreet.' The way they'd beaten a
hasty retreat from the party wouldn't have gone unnoticed.
In the cold light of morning, did Cleo regret that? Was she
worried rumours would reach the tabloids? 'I promise you
can trust my family, *and* the staff here. No word of this will
reach outside ears.'

She turned back so fast, tea sloshed in her saucer. 'I trust
you and them.' Setting her teacup onto the coffee table, she
turned to him more fully. 'I love making love with you, Jude,
but we were clear from the beginning about not making any
kind of commitment to one another. We always knew that
our...*amour*...'

His lips twitched at the quaintness of the word on her lips.
She half-smiled too, and he found an odd comfort in that. 'We
always knew our *liaison* had an end date,' he finished for her.

'Yes.'

She'd be returning to England on Friday—in five days'
time, he realised with a jolt. 'You're worried I'll read more
into our affair than I should.' As the words left his mouth,
he wondered if she had every right to worry.

'I want to make sure *I* don't start reading more into it.'

Her hands twisted and it was all he could do not to lean
over and cover them with his own.

'My past has proved that me rushing headlong into things
without thinking is a recipe for disaster.'

And they had rushed headlong into their affair. He didn't
regret it, but she was right: it was time to be sensible. It was
time to remember the boundaries they'd set.

'Now that Margot has forgiven me, I can't afford to do anything to ruin that.'

His jaw clenched. 'You should live your life to please yourself, Cleo, not to make your sister and father happy.'

She reared back, as if he'd slapped her. 'It just so happens that those things are inextricably entwined. And you'd be lying if you said it wasn't the same for you.'

That was true, but it seemed to him that it was Cleo who made all the sacrifices and compromises in her relationship with her family, while Margot and their father made none. But it was none of his business and he had no right to criticise. He nodded. 'You're right.'

'I just want to get my life back on track.' She rolled her eyes. 'And *never* appear on the front page of a newspaper again.'

And being linked with him would mean living her life in the spotlight, which was everything she didn't want.

'Are you angry?'

He stared at her, shocked she could think such a thing. 'No! I'm thinking how right you are and how wise you're being. We didn't make promises for very good reasons.' His chest grew heavy as the weight of those reasons pressed down on him. 'My and Elodie's relationship has started to mend, but the equilibrium is…'

'Delicate?'

Exactly. It'd be cruel to flaunt any sort of romantic happiness in front of her when she was grieving for Matt. Had Elodie witnessed Cleo's and his exit from the party last night? He scanned his memory, sagging when he realised she'd excused herself earlier. But she'd probably hear the speculations of all those who'd been present.

He squared his shoulders. She wouldn't hear any more,

though; he'd make sure of it. He glanced back at Cleo. 'I have so much I need to do, so much to accomplish. It deserves my best efforts.'

She nodded her understanding and drew closer. 'Okay, this is what we're going to do: for the next five days, we're going to be discreet.'

She was gifting him the next five days!

She tapped his chest. '*Seriously* discreet.'

Taking her face in his hands, he kissed her. 'Deal.'

CHAPTER ELEVEN

EVERY DAY CLEO'S departure grew closer, the darker Jude's world became. Was it because it meant the adventure would end? He'd never felt more alive than he had in these last two-and-a-half weeks.

She'd helped him see things so differently. Was he concerned they'd go back to the way they'd been? Was he worried about taking up the mantle as head of the family, or finishing the current book?

It all fell into place for him on Thursday afternoon. He couldn't let Cleo go. He'd fallen in love with her. Despite his best efforts, despite believing love an exercise in deception, disillusion and despair.

The thing was, Cleo had never deceived him. She'd eased the despair of his grief…and she'd turned his disillusion into wonder, and had made him see a world worth fighting for. His scowling and grumpiness had been no match for her teasing, her laughter or her frank confessions. And the thought of her leaving...

Of course she needed to go to her sister's wedding. But then *she had to come back*. Their attraction had taken them both off-guard. Was it out of the realms of possibility that love could take her by surprise as well?

She *liked* him. And the way she made love with him that evening made him dare hope.

Lying in bed afterwards, trailing his hand idly over the soft skin of her back, he wanted this forever. 'Cleo, is it really outside the realms of possibility that after Margot's wedding we couldn't see each other again?'

'What do you mean?'

She looked warm and rumpled and utterly beautiful. 'You and I have always been honest with each other.' He frowned. 'Well, okay, I mightn't have told you who I was immediately.'

'We've always been honest about the things that mattered,' she agreed, sliding her hand into his.

Generous—that was Cleo. He pulled in a breath. 'Which is why I want to be honest with you now.'

Blinking, she sat up, drawing the sheet with her. 'Okay.'

He sat up too. 'I'd like to see you again.'

Something in her face softened. 'Oh, Jude. I've loved the time I've spent with you.'

Loved. She used the word *loved*.

But then she shook her head. 'I don't think that's a good idea.'

Was that because she thought he was toying with her... wasn't serious? 'Would it make any difference if I told you I've fallen in love with you?'

Her jaw dropped. She stared as if she hadn't heard him right.

He rolled his shoulders. 'I didn't mean for it to happen. It wasn't part of my plan. But I have and...' He petered off as he recognised the emotion dawning in her eyes: horror.

Backing away, she scrambled out of bed and thrust her arms into her robe, tying it tightly at her waist before turning to face him. 'You said your heart was safe! You told me you wouldn't fall in love with me!'

'I didn't know I had!' The accusation in her tone stung. 'I realised this afternoon, which is why I'm telling you now.'

She raked both hands through her hair. 'This can't happen, Jude.'

Leaping out of bed, he hauled on a pair of boxers. 'Why not?'

'We had rules!'

'Which we both kept breaking.'

Her gaze caught on his chest and she swallowed.

'Why not?' he repeated. 'I know you want me.' The expression in her eyes assured him of that. 'And I know you like me.'

'Of course I do! But attraction and like aren't...'

She broke off, and he went cold all over. Ice crawled across his scalp. He'd been reading too much into it all— her warmth, her generosity, her honesty—because it meant so much to him. And to imagine his world without her in it was unbearable.

'You do *not* need someone like me in your life, Jude. And neither does your family. Believe me, I am not *"on brand".*' She made quote marks in the air.

What the hell...?

'Once the papers get wind of the story—' she gestured between them '—and things get real, you'd see that too.'

Did she think he'd abandon her?

'And what about *my* family, Jude? My notoriety reflects on them. It impacts their careers. They don't deserve to have their colleagues and friends whispering behind their backs every time my life is splashed across the papers. They deserve better than that. They deserve *better* from me.'

All his wealth and the power of his family name wouldn't be able to prevent the story from hitting the headlines once he and Cleo were linked. It was everything she didn't want; she'd told him that repeatedly. What part of that hadn't he heard and heeded?

'My family deserve me to lay low for a while.' She dragged in a breath. 'They deserve me to be whole and happy for them.'

He rocked back on his heels. He clearly wasn't part of a future where she saw herself as either whole or happy. His mouth tasted of ashes.

Her chin wobbled. 'I'd give a thousand worlds not to have hurt you—'

'I'm sorry I raised the topic,' he cut in. 'I shouldn't have said anything.' He could see that now.

Her knuckles turned white from where they gripped the front of her robe. 'I'm sorry, Jude,' she whispered.

She left, closing his bedroom door softly behind her. It felt as if every light in the world had gone out.

He drove her to the airport the following afternoon. What little conversation they had, they kept practical.

'Has your father organised a car for you at the other end?'

'Yes.'

'I've arranged a contact to take you to the first-class lounge.'

'That's very kind. Thank you.'

Her hands twisted in her lap. She bit her lip and stared out of the window. Her misery washed over him in waves. He should never have burdened her with his declaration last night. If he'd been thinking with any logic at all, he'd have waited until after the wedding—waited until she'd felt secure again. Then he could've orchestrated a meeting and they could've taken it from there. Instead, he'd told her he loved her, and now the guilt at being unable to return his feelings was eating her alive. For God's sake, he knew how beholden she felt to him!

He pulled the car into a space at Departures. 'Cleo, I want you to understand that knowing you has made my life better. I also want you to know that I'm going to be fine.'

She swallowed. 'Of course you are.'

'I'm disappointed, but...' He shrugged. 'I've much to keep me busy.'

She turned to him. 'I can't thank you enough for everything you've done.'

'Then don't. It's been a pleasure.'

Her gaze met his and she nodded, then she gestured out of the window. 'Don't come in with me. It'll be better this way.'

He wanted to argue, but didn't. 'Let me text my contact to say we're here. He'll take you the back ways the media don't know about.' He sent the text. The silence between them stretched. He found his fingers going to his pocket, reaching for her sunglasses as if they were a talisman.

'You know—' he held them up '—you never did tell me what the story was with these.'

She glanced at them and then smiled, truly smiled. His heart started pounding like a wild thing.

'They were my mother's.'

His jaw dropped. Her *mother's*?

'She loved those sunglasses; she took them everywhere. When she died, I asked for them. They've been my most treasured possession ever since.'

He thrust them at her, horror filling his belly. 'You must take them back!' He couldn't deprive her of her mother's sunglasses. He'd have never made that deal if he'd known…

She shook her head. 'She'd have been so proud of me for the deal I made with you, Jude. And that means more to me than anything.' Reaching out, she curled his fingers back around the sunglasses, touching her other hand to her heart. 'I carry my mother with me wherever I go. I don't need a pair of sunglasses to remind me of that, not any more. Keep them. Use them and enjoy them, and remember how you once helped a silly girl out of a pickle—that will make me happy.'

He put them back in his pocket. He'd treasure them forever.

Jude's contact appeared and opened Cleo's door. 'I will be pleased to be of service to any friend of Monsieur Blackwood.'

Cleo smiled her thanks, before holding her hand out to Jude. 'Thank you.'

He curved his fingers round her hand, fixing the feel of her in his mind for the very last time. 'It's been a pleasure knowing you, Cleo.'

He watched her until she disappeared from view, the weight bearing down on his chest growing heavier and heavier.

Elodie took one look at Jude's face when he returned, and she lifted the coffee pot in a silent question. He shook his head.

She set it back down. 'Did Cleo get off without drama?'

'Yes.'

'She must be excited about the wedding.'

'Yes.'

He ached to talk about her. In equal measure he ached not to talk about her. 'Excuse me, Elodie, I have some calls to make.' Turning on his heel, he left the room.

It was just Elodie and him for dinner that evening. Unusual for a Friday night, but there was a glittering black-tie affair in the city that many of the extended clan were attending. Elodie cut into her perfectly cooked chicken breast before glancing across at him. 'When is Cleo to return?'

He kept his gaze on his food. 'She isn't returning, Elodie. Our business here is complete.'

Her cutlery clattered to her plate. 'That's nonsense!'

Elodie's lips had pinched into a tight line and his throat went dry. 'Why?'

'Anyone with eyes in their head can see the two of you have feelings for one another.'

All of this time he'd thought they'd been discreet... He rubbed a hand over his face. 'You must hate me.'

'Hate you? *Why?*' She blinked at whatever she saw in his face. 'Because I lost my love, you are therefore not allowed your love? Is that what you think?' When he remained silent, she slammed her hands on the table. 'Do you think me so ungenerous?'

'No! I just...'

'Did it not occur to you that seeing the people around me fall in love and find happiness might be a form of consolation?'

He closed his eyes and let out a breath. 'I might be in love with Cleo, Elodie, but she's not in love with me.'

Elodie gave an undignified snort. 'You did not see her face when she was telling me what a heroic Galahad you had been, saving her from all the journalists. You did not see how her eyes softened when she said how kind you had been to her.'

'And you didn't see her face when she told me she doesn't want the complication of a relationship with someone as high-profile as me.'

Her eyes narrowed. 'Did she tell you she did not love you?'

'Yes.'

'Did she say those actual words?'

He frowned. She'd certainly implied it.

'Tell me what she said, exactly—because I do not believe she does not love you.'

He told her as much as he had the heart to.

Elodie folded her arms. 'She told you what you needed and she told you what her family needed. She did *not* tell you she didn't love you.'

'That's semantics.'

'She is afraid she cannot fit into our world. She is afraid of letting you down. She is afraid of letting her sister and her father down. She is doing what she thinks is the best thing for everyone.'

She… His frown deepened and his mind raced.

Her panic when he'd said he'd loved her; the expression on her face at the airport; the fact she'd given him her mother's sunglasses: had all that meant something after all?

Wishful thinking.

'It seems to me that Cleo fights for everyone else's happiness.' Elodie glared at him. 'But nobody seems to be fighting for Cleo.'

He shot to his feet, his hands clenching and unclenching. Elodie was right. He hadn't fought for Cleo. He'd made his declaration, she'd panicked and he'd retreated into his shell like a scared little hermit crab. He'd let Cleo walk away without a murmur of protest. He hadn't told her that he loved her again. He hadn't told her that, if she changed her mind, to call him. He hadn't told her he'd be there if she ever needed him.

What he'd told her was that he'd be okay. As if losing her hadn't shattered his world. As if his broken heart was a small thing easily recovered from. Cleo might not love him, but she deserved a man who would fight for her. And, if there was the slightest chance of winning her love, he'd fight with everything he had.

Cleo arrived at the Dorchester under the cover of darkness and was whisked straight up to a suite of rooms her father had organised for the bride and her attendant.

Other than the butler on hand to ensure she had all that she needed, the suite was empty. 'Your things arrived earlier, Ms Milne, and have been unpacked.' She handed her a letter. 'Your sister asked that I give you this.'

Cleo took the letter. 'Thank you.' Where was everyone?

'Dinner has been ordered for you for seven-thirty.'

Would Margot and her father be joining her then?

'If you need anything, please ring.' The butler gestured towards the phone and Cleo managed a polite smile before the other woman left. She felt like a robot. Ever since she'd walked away from Jude, she'd felt like half a person.

It had taken all her strength to force herself out of the car and to walk away from him this afternoon. The real reason she hadn't wanted him to come into the airport with her was that she hadn't been sure her resolve would hold. She had been afraid she'd weaken and tell him she loved him too.

But what had loving her given anyone? Nothing but headaches and heartache. Jude didn't need a mess like her in his life. He'd been through enough. He needed all his energy and resources to take his place as the head of the Giroux family. She swallowed. He'd forget about her soon enough.

Which was just as well, because with her on his arm he'd be nothing more than a laughing stock. He deserved better. He deserved the best.

She rubbed a hand across her chest, trying to ease the ache there. Nor could she let her sister down again. She hungered to make Margot and their father proud of her. And she would! Regardless of what it cost her.

She gritted her teeth. Staring at Hyde Park through the French doors, she rested her shoulder against the door frame and tore open Margot's letter.

Cleo,
Dad and I think it's best if you spend the night in the hotel suite where journalists can't get to you, while I spend the night at the family home. We'll arrive at the hotel at ten a.m. on the dot, as will the hairdressers and make-up artists, along with the seamstress, in case last-minute alterations are necessary.

Do not step foot outside your room. Do you hear me? Do not mess this up for me. If you do—

That last half-sentence had been left unfinished and the words had been crossed out, but they blazed off the page like a threat.

I will see you tomorrow.

It was signed *M*—no love, no kisses, no thank you. Just '*do not mess this up for me*'.

The letter dropped from her nerveless fingers and floated to the floor. 'The seamstress won't be necessary,' she whispered.

* * *

Cleo gazed in the mirror the next morning and hoped the make-up artist was a magician. She'd barely slept a wink, and hadn't touched her food last night or this morning. She looked as lacklustre as she felt.

She practised a smile, and then another one, because the first was so appalling. She *wouldn't* ruin Margot's big day. But a growing sense of disquiet had been building inside her since reading Margot's letter. She'd thought Margot had forgiven her. She'd thought things were right between them again. She'd done everything that Margot had asked of her—*everything*.

There was a slim chance that Margot had turned into a panic-stricken Bridezilla, but the more Cleo thought about it the less likely that seemed. For heaven's sake, Margot had trained as an international lawyer and was embarking on a political career. The one thing Margot *did* have was nerves of steel. And yet Margot continued to avoid her.

Cleo made herself smile in the mirror again and, while the smile was better, the tears that filled her eyes completely ruined the effect.

She forced them down. She suspected she knew why Margot was avoiding her and it had nausea churning in her stomach. She flashed back to New Year's Eve, once again feeling the impact of her fist colliding with Clay's jaw after those dreadful words had left his mouth. If what he'd said hadn't been a pack of lies...

A knock on the door had her straightening. Margot and Dad were ten minutes early. *Smile*, she silently ordered herself as she rushed out of the *en suite* and through the bedroom to fling open the door . 'Margot, I—'

She stopped dead, her mouth working, but not a single syllable emerging.

Jude! Jude stood on the other side of the door, looking grumpy, dishevelled and utterly wonderful and she drank him in with a greedy thirst. His scowl deepened. 'Can I come in?'

Closing a hand round one strong forearm, she hauled him inside, glancing outside the corridor to make sure it was empty before slamming the door shut. Her fingers tingled from where she'd touched him. She had to fight the urge to fling herself into his arms.

'Jude! What are you doing here?'

'I needed to see you. I forgot to ask you something.'

The expression in his eyes turned her insides to mush. She did everything she could to harden her heart. 'You can't stay.'

Oh, God! Margot and Dad would be here any moment. If they found Jude here... Her heart stuttered. They'd think she'd reverted to type. That she'd been partying and drinking. They'd believe the lies the newspapers had printed about her. Their smiles would slip, their mouths would twist, a cynical disillusion would spread across their faces. Worst of all, it would cast a shadow and a stain on Margot's day that could never be erased.

'There's something I need to ask you, Cleo.'

She barely heard him. Her heart fluttered too fast, like the wings of a hummingbird. Everything was unravelling.

Jude's hands curved around her shoulders. 'Cleo, I need to know—'

A knock on the door and Margot's, 'Cleo?' had her wanting to cry.

Jude stared at the door. His eyes widened. 'I thought there would be time before the wedding prep took over.' He kept his voice low. 'The wedding isn't till four o'clock.'

Seizing the front of his shirt, she shook him. 'They can *not* find you here.'

He spread his hands in a gesture that said 'what the hell do you want me to do?'

She pushed him into her bedroom. *'Hide.'*

'Where?'

'The *en suite*, wardrobe, under the bed... I don't care!' Hopefully there'd be a chance to sneak him out when no one was looking.

Another knock came. 'Cleo!' Margot sounded impatient.

'Coming!' She pointed a warning finger at Jude as she pulled the bedroom door closed, then rushed to answer the door. Her father and Margot stood on the threshold, thankfully alone. The army of hairdressers, make-up artists and dressers were yet to arrive.

They both gave her perfunctory kisses on the cheek—no hugs, no warm words.

Why had Jude come?

'I was starting to wonder if you were here.' Margot's ash-blonde hair swung in a shiny curtain as she moved past.

'Of course I'm here. I received my orders and have been following them like a good soldier.' She'd meant to say the words lightly, but they held an edge that made her wince internally.

Margot turned with stricken eyes—as if Cleo had plunged a knife into her heart. Cleo made herself smile and shrug. 'I was in the bathroom, that's all. Now, should I order tea to be sent up? Or maybe you'd like a glass of fizz instead?'

Was it her imagination or did Margot look a little green? *Did you really just order Jude to hide?*

Her father strode to the phone and requested both tea and champagne to be sent up, before settling on one of the sofas.

Cleo couldn't drag her gaze from her sister's. Margot swallowed. 'I trust you had a pleasant night?'

She'd spent fewer more miserable nights in her life. She'd missed Jude with an ache that had made her chest cramp. She'd missed Margot and the fun of the night before the wedding. She'd missed their mother. *Everything* had felt wrong.

'Yes, thank you.'

Margot's and her gazes remained locked. She could tell Margot wanted to break the contact, but couldn't. She recognised some of the emotions churning in the amber brown of her sister's eyes and for a moment she wanted to cry. Clay's ugly words went round and round in her mind.

'Cleo,' Michael Milne started, oblivious to the silent battle going on between his daughters, 'I wanted to say how impressed I am. You've handled yourself extremely well over the last two-and-a-half weeks.'

That had Margot swinging around. 'No thanks to you! I still can't believe you turned her out of the family home.'

Cleo smiled then because she knew in that moment, despite her fears, that she hadn't lost her sister. 'Clay told me you and he had kissed.' The words blurted from her. She wished she'd found a way to say them with more grace, but the air needed to be cleared.

Margot turned back, her pallor making Cleo wince. Their father rose to his feet.

'He put it far more crudely than that—called you something dreadful. And, before I'd even realised it, I'd hit him. Over the years I've heard a lot of bad things said about you, Dad, because of the politician thing, but I'd never heard anyone say anything awful about you, Margot. If you're going to be a politician, I'm going to need to work on that. I can't go around beating up everyone who says something mean.'

Margot's knuckles turned white where she gripped them in front of her. 'Cleo, I—'

'I didn't believe it at first. The penny only dropped because of the way you've continued to avoid me. I—'

'You kissed your sister's boyfriend?' Michael suddenly roared.

'Don't you start!' Cleo rounded on him. 'Margot has always tried to be perfect to make up to the both of us for losing Mum.'

He blinked.

'She looked after me when you closed yourself off, but who looked after her, huh? Not once has she ever rebelled. You've absolutely no right to judge her.'

His jaw slackened.

Grabbing Margot's hands, she squeezed them hard. 'The thing is, I don't care if it *is* true. You could do something a hundred times worse and I'd still forgive you. Look at all I put you through, and yet you still stood by me.'

Margot's face crumpled. 'I'm so sorry, Cleo. *So* sorry. I've never been more ashamed of myself. I—'

A knock sounded: the tea and champagne. Cleo gestured for it to be placed on the sideboard.

What was Jude doing here?

Only when they were alone again did she speak. 'I was never in love with Clay. You knew that.' She frowned. 'Why did you talk me out of breaking up with him?'

'I felt so guilty about what had happened. I blamed myself and that stupid kiss for your changing feelings for him. I was worried I'd wrecked things for you.'

'So you wanted me to give it another chance?'

'I just wanted you to be sure. The thing is, Clay really did love you. I felt a bit sorry for him.'

It was Cleo's turn to blink.

'I think it's why he kissed me—he was searching for comfort from someone he associated with you. It's not really an excuse, but…'

But it was a human thing to do.

Did you really just order Jude to hide?

She glanced at her father and gestured to the tea things. 'Do you want to play Mother?'

He moved across and poured the tea.

'As for me…' Margot stared down at her hands before meeting Cleo's eyes once more. 'I was having one of the worst weeks of my life. A parliamentary paper I'd spent months working on was sent back to the drawing board and the party had decided not to approve my nomination just yet.'

They'd what? 'But—'

'They changed their minds a few days later, but…'

She nodded to let Margot know she understood.

'Worse than that, though, Brett and I had a huge fight. We never fight, and it was unexpectedly fierce.' She grimaced. 'He made his excuses and didn't come to Dad's sixtieth birthday party.'

Ah, so that's why Brett hadn't been there.

'I thought we were over. You and a few of the other girls were talking about what we should do for my hen night and I didn't have the heart to take part, so I drifted off. I found myself alone with Clay in the library. It was obvious he felt a bit left out and…'

She shrugged, the skin at the corners of her eyes drawing tight. 'It was stupid. But for that brief moment we felt like two lost souls and we turned to each other for solace. We sprang apart a moment later, both utterly appalled.'

Cleo's heart burned for her sister, and a little bit for Clay too. Pulling in a breath, she pressed her hands together. 'I need to check—are you sure you want to marry Brett?'

Margot stiffened.

'And, while we're talking so frankly, do you truly want to be a politician or are you doing that to make Dad happy?'

From the corner of her eye, she saw her dad's gaze sharpen.

'Yes, and yes. I told Brett about what had happened between me and Clay. I couldn't lie to him. He was hurt, but was mature enough to point out that we hadn't made any formal vows to each other at that point. He was ridiculously understanding. He still wants to marry me, and he knows I love him.'

Cleo sagged.

'I'm the luckiest woman in the world.' Margot's smile told them she meant it. 'And I do want to be a politician, Cleo. I promise you I do. I want to make a difference, and it feels like the right platform to do that.'

Their father sagged then too.

Cleo clapped her hands. 'Look, we're all adults and it's time to start acting like it. We can't keep playing the same roles we have since Mum died.'

'Agreed,' Margot said.

Her father nodded. She pointed a finger at him. 'You need to be more present.' She turned to Margot. 'You need to stop trying to be perfect. And I—' she slapped a hand on her chest '—need to stop appearing in the papers. I know the tabloids love labelling me a wild child, but I need to stop providing them with fodder!'

Her father frowned. 'But the reason you landed on the front page this time was…due to someone else's bad behaviour.' His frown deepened. 'And the time before that too.'

Margot stared at her. 'And the two times before that it was due to Ewan and… Oh, that pretty boy! What was his name?'

'Austin.' Cleo nodded and swallowed. 'I haven't been a wild child since I was twenty-two. It's just that no one wants to believe it.'

Margot took her hands. 'Then *you* don't need to change anything.'

'Yes, I do,' she said slowly, remembering something Jude had once said. 'I need to forgive myself for past mistakes and stop trying to win everyone's approval. I need to learn to be proud of myself instead.'

Proud of herself? She'd just pushed Jude—a man who'd proven himself a true friend, a man who'd told her *he loved her*—into the bedroom and ordered him to hide, as if he was something she was ashamed of.

Her stomach churned. What kind of person had she become? 'There's something I need to tell you both.' She pressed her hands together. 'Jude,' she called out, 'would you like to come out here?'

CHAPTER TWELVE

JUDE STEPPED INTO the living room, his head spinning from all he'd overheard. The *someone* Clay had taunted Cleo with had been her *sister*?

Yet Cleo had still done Margot's bidding. She had done her utmost to ensure her wedding was everything she wanted. She'd effaced herself and put Margot's needs first. His heart pounded. Cleo loved so hard. If only he could convince her to love him just a little with that big heart of hers.

Cleo took his arm and faced her father and sister. 'This man helped me at his own personal expense when he didn't have to, just because he has a good heart. He went above and beyond.'

She dragged in a breath. 'He turned up here two minutes before you did and I panicked when you knocked, because I thought it might look bad if you found him here. I thought you'd be disappointed in me.'

She glanced up at Jude with burning eyes. 'That was an awful thing to do, Jude. I'm sorry.'

He shrugged. 'Apology accepted.'

'If it wasn't for this man, I'd have been plastered across all the newspapers *again*.'

Margot leapt forward and hugged him. 'Thank you for helping Cleo. I'm so grateful to you.' The warmth in her eyes had him understanding why Cleo loved her so much. She hugged Cleo too. 'I think we've been taking dysfunctional to a whole new level.'

'Nonsense.' Michael cleared his throat. 'This is just normal family…'

Cleo raised an eyebrow. 'Drama?'

'Dynamics?' Margot offered.

'Muddle.' He cleared his throat. 'When people care about each other they can get into the occasional muddle, that's all. And, while we're on the topic of being adults, Cleo, will you please introduce us to this young man?'

Cleo made the introductions.

Michael Milne's lips twisted, but there was a twinkle in his eyes. 'Now, in case you've forgotten, we're supposed to be having a wedding today, and the crew are impatiently waiting downstairs.' He held up his phone. 'I've been holding them off, but they're becoming increasingly frantic.'

Margot clasped Cleo's arm, her eyes going wide. 'I'm getting married!'

Cleo laughed. 'To the man of your dreams, remember?'

Margot's smile could've lit up an entire city block. Jude found himself grinning.

Margot wrung her hands. 'We have to get ready! I want it to be perfect!' She turned to Jude. 'Please come to my wedding.'

If it meant being near Cleo… 'I'd be honoured.'

'Come with me then, young man, and we'll get you sorted.' Michael clapped him on the shoulder.

Glancing back, he found Cleo watching him with eyes the colour of a still sea. Striding back, he squeezed her hand, the scent of pears engulfing him. 'Later,' he promised. He'd wait as long as he had to if there was the slightest chance of winning this woman's heart.

The wedding went without a hitch. The bride glowed while the groom couldn't wipe the grin from his face. Cleo, in a dress of dusky green that highlighted the colour of her eyes, was the picture of propriety.

Michael made a speech about how proud he was of his two daughters, how their happiness was his happiness, which barely left an eye in the room dry. The best man made a speech that had everyone laughing. And Cleo made a speech so heartfelt and sincere, it had a lump lodging in Jude's throat.

The cake was cut. The bridal waltz was danced. Jude's hands clenched as he watched the best man twirl a radiant Cleo across the dance floor. A young woman tapped his arm. 'We haven't been introduced, but Michael sent me over. He implied you'd be eager to dance with Cleo.'

He had?

'And as Cleo is dancing with my husband…'

Excellent.

'Shall we?'

He waltzed a direct path to Cleo. 'We're hoping to cut in.'

Cleo's eyes widened, but she moved into his arms without hesitation. 'Is it *later*?'

He nodded. Holding her so close, their bodies moving in

harmony, had warmth encircling him and he closed his eyes to savour it.

'Why have we not waltzed before?' Cleo murmured, her left hand sliding further round his back so she could press herself closer.

Heat flooded his veins. 'Not much room for waltzing on a narrow boat.' And on the yacht they'd been too busy keeping their distance.

Mischievous eyes met his. 'It'd be fun to try, though.'

Images flooded his mind, making his nostrils flare.

'So...' She eased away a fraction. 'Are you enjoying the wedding?'

The wedding was nothing more than an interruption he had to endure before he could have Cleo to himself again. He hadn't prepared a speech, but...

Margot sidled up beside them. 'I seem to have torn the lace on my dress, Cleo. Can you pin it back up for me?'

Cleo stepped out of his arms with an apologetic wrinkle of her nose. 'Later is going to have to wait for a bit.'

He wanted to howl at the moon. He shrugged instead. 'For you, I'll wait as long as I have to.'

Her lovely lips parted, but then Margot tugged on her arm and Cleo moved away before he could kiss her which, despite the itch of impatience chafing through him, was probably for the best.

Cleo's heart pounded. What was Jude doing here? He'd said he'd wait as long as he had to, but...*why?* She'd already told him they couldn't be together. That had been hours ago. And, true to his word, he was still here—waiting.

And she loved it. *Loved him.* But she needed to fight that because the thought of letting him down at some future date and seeing his love turn to derision, realising she'd made his life worse instead of better... She didn't think she could bear it.

What if you don't let him down?

Yeah, right, and pigs might fly.

She did her best to focus on her bridesmaid duties. Margot and Brett were sent off with cheers and well wishes as they climbed into the white stretch limousine that would take them to a secret location. Cleo clasped her hands beneath her chin as the limousine pulled away. 'It was the most beautiful wedding.'

Her father rested an arm across her shoulders. 'It was a beautiful wedding, and your sister is a very happy woman. And, Cleo, I believe you will be too.'

She blinked when he took her arm and handed her inside a black cab that had drawn up behind the limo. 'Look after my girl, Jude.'

'I will.'

Jude slid in from the other side and her heart hammered, leapt and swooped. Her father pressed a kiss on her cheek, though she barely registered it, her mind too full of the man beside her. 'Give your dear old dad a call tomorrow, huh?' Dragging her gaze from Jude, she nodded.

The door closed, the cab pulled away and piercing blue eyes met hers in the semi-darkness. The breath squeezed from her lungs. She wanted him so much, she ached with it.

Don't focus on that.

'Where are we going?' she managed instead.

'You'll see. It's a surprise.' He threaded his fingers through hers. She stared at their linked hands. She ought to pull hers free...but she didn't.

They drove over Westminster Bridge and through Southwark. She'd assumed they were heading to his apartment. She straightened as the cab wended its way down to the Thames river-front.

Jude squeezed her hand. 'This is where we get out.'

He leapt from the cab and strode round to open her door. She took his hand and stepped out. There was a gate in front of them, but not one that led to an apartment building. 'Jude, where…?'

He led her through the gate and her eyes widened. A ramp led down to the water and the most spectacular… 'Is that a canal boat?' She couldn't call it a narrow boat—there was absolutely *nothing* narrow about it.

'It was the floating Customs and Excise Office. It's been decommissioned and is now a luxury house boat.'

She pulled to a halt. 'We're going on board?'

'I've leased it for a few days.'

He had?

'I thought it might appeal to you.'

It did, but… 'Why?'

'Why what?'

'Why are we here rather than your apartment, which has to be nearby, or my apartment in Fulham? Or in a private room at the Dorchester?' Why had he brought her *here*?

His face settled into familiar stern lines. 'It's *later* and I don't want to be interrupted.'

'But I don't have an overnight case or—'

'Your father had the staff at the hotel pack up your things. They've already been stowed on board.'

Her father had been party to this?

'Come and see.'

That lopsided smile could do the craziest things to a woman's pulse. She let him lead her down the ramp and onto the boat. It was two storeys of absolute luxury. Jude led her up the wooden staircase to an open-plan living room, dining room and kitchen. There was oak furniture, big, comfy sofas and bold art on the walls.

Walking across to the enormous windows, she stared at the view of Tower Bridge. 'This is bigger than my entire apartment!'

'It's something, isn't it?'

The boat rocked gently beneath her feet and she wanted to close her eyes and savour the familiar motion.

'No expense was spared restoring it. It can comfortably accommodate twelve. Sleeping quarters are on the lower deck—four bedrooms and two bathrooms. It puts *Camelot* to shame.'

Not true—she would *always* be grateful to *Camelot*.

'Would you like a cold drink, or something to eat?'

A platter of hors d'oeuvres sat on the table and drinks were chilling in a silver bucket.

'The pantry is stocked.' He started towards the kitchen. 'So if there's something else you'd prefer...'

She couldn't stand it another moment. It was taking all her strength not to stride across and kiss him, or say something she might regret, like *I love you*.

'Jude.' She pressed her hands together. 'You said there was something you needed to ask me.'

He stilled. 'Before we get to that...' He turned and moved back. 'Was Margot the "someone" Clay referred to?'

She couldn't decipher the expression in his eyes. She shrugged and nodded.

'You knew from the first that Margot had betrayed you?'

'No.' She pointed a surprisingly steady finger at him. 'And there are two things to unpick in that sentence. The first is, of course I didn't know. I thought Clay had lied. But when Margot kept avoiding me…' She swallowed. 'It clicked into place when I returned to London last night and found we were staying in different venues.'

He didn't say anything. It made her fidget. 'I had no plans to confront her with it, but the moment she clapped eyes on me…' She winced. 'The guilt was eating her alive. It was better to get it out in the open.'

'It was brave.'

'Nonsense.' She straightened. 'And the other thing you need to understand is that Margot didn't *betray* me. She was desperately unhappy and did a stupid thing. She didn't deliberately set out to hurt me. She didn't think to herself, "what's something I can do to hurt Cleo?"' Blue eyes throbbed into hers. It took everything she had to remain where she stood rather than sway towards him.

'You meant it when you said you'd forgive her something a hundred times worse.'

Of course she'd meant it. Margot was her sister!

He leaned down until they were eye level. 'Your father refused to let you hide out at the family home?'

She huffed out a breath. Where was he going with this? 'Look, I understood his frustration and his impatience. It was a classic case of my past coming back to bite me.'

'This past you continually refer to, Cleo, was over three years ago. Since then you've turned your life around— changed jobs, been sober, been a responsible adult. Your only crime,' he added when she opened her mouth, 'was to date a few untrustworthy jerks.'

She folded her arms. 'Your point being?'

'That you harbour no resentment towards your family for not realising that earlier.'

She folded her arms harder. 'Families can fall into patterns. They came to think of me as the problem child. Don't forget, they were grieving for my mother at the time too. Dad had no idea how to help me. And he's not the kind of man who takes kindly to feeling helpless. Margot just wanted to make everything right for everyone. All of us made mistakes.'

She hitched up her chin. 'It's taken me years to see that, though.' *And a lot of therapy.* 'So, no, I don't feel resentment towards them.'

Jude widened his stance. 'So you don't want them feeling bad about how they've dealt with you in the past? You don't want Margot to keep beating herself up for kissing Clay?'

She gaped at him. How could he even think such a thing?

His face darkened. 'Then why don't you cut yourself the same slack? Why aren't you just as kind to yourself?'

That had her speechless for a moment. 'I…'

'Since I've known you, you've continually beaten yourself up and blamed yourself for putting your family through the wringer. Over the last three years, though, you've done nothing to be ashamed of. So what if you've dated a few bad eggs? We've all done that. Unlike the majority of us, though, your romantic woes were splashed in the newspapers—*not* your fault.'

She didn't know what to say.

'The things you did when you were younger were understandable.'

'It doesn't mean I condone them!'

'When are you going to forgive yourself for them?' His hands slammed onto his hips. 'The way you've forgiven the mistakes your family have made?'

She took a half-step back.

'Earlier today you said you needed to forgive yourself. *When* are you going to do that?'

Her heart hammered. He spread his hands and scowled, but she saw the exhaustion behind it and it had tears pricking her eyes.

'What if I backslide?' she whispered, blinking hard. 'I can't afford to do that. I don't want it for me or my family. Keeping a catalogue of my sins at the forefront of my mind and reminding myself of the damage I did ensures it won't happen. It keeps me on the straight and narrow.'

His face gentled. 'Oh, Cleo.' He reached out as if to touch her, but his hand fell back to his side. Her pulse jumped and jerked. 'What if that mindset is stealing your joy?'

Maybe that was a small price to pay. His eyes narrowed, as if he'd read that thought in her face. 'Do you think Margot will ever kiss another one of your boyfriends?'

'*No.*'

'Do you think your father will ever again refuse you sanctuary?' When she remained silent, he continued, 'So why can't you believe *you* won't make the same mistakes you once did?'

She moistened her lips and frowned. Actually…that was an excellent question.

'You're not an angry teenager any more, Cleo. You now have the strategies you learned in therapy to help you cope. Isn't it time to start trusting yourself?'

Very slowly, she started to nod. The thought of treating anyone she loved the same way she'd been treating herself had her breaking out in a cold sweat. She rubbed a hand across her chest, acknowledging silently that she didn't want a life devoid of joy.

'On Thursday night you told me I didn't need someone like you in my life.'

Her gaze flew back to his. She'd walked away from him. It was the hardest thing she'd ever done. But if she was going to start trusting herself...

'When you said I didn't need someone like you in my life, I know that you meant someone lumbered with your kind of notoriety.'

He was the head of a family with a proud heritage. He was good, kind and honourable. He deserved the best.

'But in my eyes that meant I was being deprived of someone like you—a person who has the most generous heart I've ever had the privilege to meet. It meant being deprived of your kindness and your humour and your teasing—all of which lighten my load. It meant being deprived of seeing the world through your eyes—because your way of seeing it gave me a different perspective, and that helped me find my way forward.'

Tears burnt a hole in her throat.

'On Thursday night you told me what I didn't need in my life and what your family didn't need in their lives, but what you didn't tell me is what you needed in your life, Cleo.'

Tears spilled from her eyes.

'And you didn't say you didn't love me. So the question I came here to ask you today, Cleo, is...do you love me?'

She couldn't speak. Her throat was too thick and her voice had deserted her. But what she could do was nod and throw herself into his arms.

He crushed her to him as if he meant to never let her go. She sobbed incoherently into his shoulder for several long seconds. Lifting her head, she cupped his face. 'I love you, Jude—so much. You're the most amazing man I've ever met—the *best* man. You make my life better, in every way.'

'Cleo.' Her name was a groan from his lips.

'In my mixed-up way, I thought you deserved better than me. I thought I'd just cause chaos in your life and you'd had enough of that. I didn't know…'

His fingers travelled down her cheek. 'What didn't you know?'

'That you feel exactly the same way about me that I feel about you.'

His smile, when it came, was the most beautiful thing she'd ever seen. She suspected her smile was just as radiant.

'I love a good epiphany,' she whispered.

He nodded, his head lowering to hers. Their kiss had stars bursting behind her eyelids.

Lifting her in his arms, Jude lowered them to the sofa, keeping her in his lap. She rested a hand against his cheek. 'Thank you for coming back for me.'

He half-scowled and shrugged lightly. 'I couldn't not come back for you. I fell for you the moment you crashed onto my boat and held a finger to your lips as you hid behind my chair. You've had me in some kind of spell ever since.'

She grinned. 'You were so grumpy.'

'What did you expect? You'd turned my world upside down in under ten seconds flat.'

Her grin widened. 'You were so kind, though you tried to hide it.'

He shook his head, as if still befuddled. 'I went from agreeing to hide you for an hour, to agreeing to drop you further along the canal path, to letting you stay for a week…and then a fortnight.'

Her chest fizzed with so much emotion, she could hardly breathe.

'It should come as no surprise to either one of us that I can now not let you go, that I want you in my life for good—that I want a lifetime with you. You also ought to know that I asked your father for your hand in marriage.'

The edges of the room blurred.

'Not that we need his permission, but I wanted him to know I was serious. I want you to know that too.' He cupped her face. 'You love so fearlessly. You showed me how to love fearlessly too.'

Something too exceptional to be called happiness bubbled up through her. 'I am going to be the best wife you could ever have, Jude. I'm going to make you the happiest man alive.'

He stared at her and then he grinned—*really* grinned. 'Was that a yes?'

She grinned back. 'It's most definitely a yes.'

Could a person have been any happier than she was at that moment? Hooking a hand behind his head, she drew his face down to hers. 'I love you, Jude. I love you with my whole heart. It's all yours.'

Their lips met in a kiss that was both tender and intense, fierce and loving. It was the kind of kiss that lifted her up on a wave of optimism and *joy* that didn't lower her back again—as if her world now was bigger, better...truer.

It was a kiss that she'd remember for the rest of her life...

* * * * *

Fake Fling

Rachael Stewart

Rachael Stewart adores conjuring up stories, from heartwarmingly romantic to wildly erotic. She's been writing since she could put pen to paper—as the stacks of scrawled-on pages in her loft will attest to. A Welsh lass at heart, she now lives in Yorkshire, with her very own hero and three awesome kids—and if she's not tapping out a story, she's wrapped up in one or enjoying the great outdoors. Reach her on Facebook, on X (@rach_b52) or at rachaelstewartauthor.com.

Books by Rachael Stewart

Billionaires for the Rose Sisters

Billionaire's Island Temptation
Consequence of Their Forbidden Night

Claiming the Ferrington Empire

Secrets Behind the Billionaire's Return
The Billionaire Behind the Headlines

How to Win a Monroe

Off-Limits Fling with the Heiress
My Unexpected Christmas Wedding

One Year to Wed

Reluctant Bride's Baby Bombshell

My Year with the Billionaire
Unexpected Family for the Rebel Tycoon

Visit the Author Profile page at millsandboon.com.au.

Dear Reader,

Sleepwalking is a scary thing, right?

For those dreaming and those observing!

Imagine my surprise when I encountered the behavior for the very first time with my husband. Just like Cassie and Hugo, we weren't married then, either... Though I will admit, we were a little more acquainted.

Years later when it happened again, inspiration struck and the idea for a book was born. Cue me now, writing this letter to you!

Cassie and Hugo took me on such a fabulous adventure around Paris, filling my head and heart with all the imagery and romance of the city, and I hope they fill yours with it all, too!

Beaucoup d'amour et profite bien de Paris <3

Rachael x

To all the Dreamers and those that go the
extra-special mile with the sleepwalking,
like those closest to my heart, my hubby,
this one is for you.

xxx

Praise for
Rachael Stewart

"This is a delightful, moving, contemporary romance....
I should warn you that this is the sort of book that
once you start you want to keep turning the pages
until you've read it. It is an enthralling story to escape
into and one that I thoroughly enjoyed reading.
I have no hesitation in highly recommending it."

—*Goodreads* on *Tempted by the Tycoon's Proposal*

CHAPTER ONE

PARIS. THE WITCHING HOUR.

Cassie's favourite time to venture out in recent years. Though she was no witch. No matter how much her ex and his family would like to paint her as such.

She sipped her vodka martini, finding peace in those precious minutes between two and three in the morning while most around her slept.

In the distance, the Eiffel Tower had emitted its final sparkle long enough ago to see the last of the tourists in bed. Its structure a dark silhouette in the inky sky. The avenue of the Champs-Élysées and impressive Arc de Triomphe below flaunted their own muted glow. Equally beautiful in their subtlety, just as reassuring in their solitude too.

'Would you like another, Your Highness?'

Her fingers tightened around the crystal stem of her glass. 'Just Cassie, please, Beni.'

The young waiter bowed his head, his dipped gaze polite.

Every night for the past month Beni had opened the rooftop bar for her after hours and every night he had addressed her like so.

Tomorrow, she would still be a princess. And the day after. And the day after that…well, who knew.

Public opinion was a fickle thing, especially when it was fed by the lions—her ex, the Prince of Sérignone. His royal family, the Duponts. Their loyal staff. The world's press.

They'd all crowned her long before her marriage to the Prince…would they go on crowning her long after she was done?

It had been a month. A month divorced. Two years separated. Four years married. Five by his side. A sixth of her life. A sixth she would sooner forget…if only the world would let her.

There was only so long one could bear the title that reminded her of the fool that she had been. The fool that she had let him take her for. And if she was honest, the fool that she had been long before then, courtesy of her parents and their skilled puppeteering from birth.

But she was done dancing to the tunes of others…it was time to choose her own tune. Her own path. And she couldn't afford for it to be derailed by the vitriol now coming out of Sérignone.

She picked at some invisible lint on her black shift dress as she mentally picked at the remnants of her life. At thirty-three, she'd gone from cherished British socialite to prized princess of a tiny Mediterranean kingdom a thousand kilometres south of where she sat now, as a woman trying to find herself while the world at large tried to keep her pigeonholed.

Though pigeonholed as a beloved princess beat being painted as the scandalous woman the Duponts and their team of spin doctors were trying to turn her into. Spinning the tale of the woman who had *driven* her husband into the arms of his many lovers. By being emotionally unavailable and 'over-familiar' with the household staff. Fuelling rumours that she had taken more than one to her bed, because there could be no smoke without fire…not when it worked in their favour. As it did now. Because, in the Duponts' minds, the Prince could not come out of their divorce smelling of roses while she still did.

One of them had to suffer. And so, it had to be her. Some-one had to be blamed for the shocking behaviour of the Prince, and it made most sense—most royal and socioeco-nomic sense—for that someone to be her.

Didn't matter that she had already suffered enough. *Wit-nessed* enough. That the behaviour they laid at her door, be-longed solely at the Prince's own.

She didn't know what was more galling—to learn that Georges had married her purely for the money, what with the royal reserves in dire need of a cash injection that her father had been all too willing to provide.

Or that she had been naive enough to have believed that she was enough for Georges. That her appeal—her beauty and in-telligence, her charity endeavours and European connections, her ability to converse in several languages and win over the people—had been all Georges could have wanted in a prin-cess. That he had wanted her. That he had, as he had told her and she had so desperately wanted to believe, loved her.

But no, it had been a lie and she had been a joke. A laugh-ingstock to all who were in the know. The *real* know.

Behind closed doors. The palace doors. They'd been laugh-ing at her.

Had her parents been cruel enough to laugh too?

They certainly hadn't been laughing when she'd turned up on their doorstep almost two years ago. Desperate for a place to stay. A place to escape to. A place to feel safe from the speculation and the censure and the pain.

They'd only delivered more of the same and tried to force her to return, because heaven forbid, she'd walk out on the Prince and bring shame to their door...

A frenzied stream of reporters too.

'Your Highness?'

She blinked through the painful haze to find Beni still stood over her, waiting expectantly.

'Apologies, Beni. *Ça va, merci.*'

'You are sure?'

No, she wasn't sure. She wouldn't be sure of much for a long time—how she felt, who she could trust, what was real, what was fake, but as far as her need for a drink went, she was done for the night.

'I think I'll head on down, Beni.' She smothered a yawn—at last, sleep beckoned—and rose from her cushioned haven, the scent of the night lifting with her. Far from natural, the fragrance drifted from the inside out...the hotel's signature scent. Bold and woody, a touch of citrus too. Expensive but heavenly.

She gave him a smile filled with her gratitude. 'Thank you again for this evening.'

'So long as you need the rooftop—' he gave a nod of respect, his brown eyes soft '—it will be here for you.'

If only her own parents had been so generous. She swallowed the tears that she refused to let fall. She'd cried enough over them, and she was done grieving for what she'd never had in the first place. A family. A place to call home. A real one.

'*Bonne nuit*, Beni.'

She tugged the lapels of her jacket around her throat to ward off the chilly autumn breeze now that she wasn't protected by the decorative trees that bordered the roof terrace and stepped away.

How crazy it was to think that once upon a time, she had thought herself in love with a handsome young prince. A real-life prince with a horse and a carriage and a castle to boot.

She gave a choked laugh, mocking herself like all the others, and pressed her fingers to her lips, steadying herself as she checked Beni hadn't noticed.

If he had, he made no show of it as he cleared the table she had used. Her mini sanctum. She didn't have a lot of spaces to hide away in, and whether Beni knew it or not, it really was quite precious. As was the suite she was staying in one floor down. Louis's suite. One of her oldest and dearest friends. One of her *only* friends, if she was honest. Because as she'd swiftly learnt, fame brought out the worst in the best of people; private stories sold in exchange for a price or a royal favour or two.

The crown had cost Cassie her friends, her family, her identity, her financial independence and her freedom, but she was on a mission to take it all back…save for the family and friends. Those that hadn't stuck by her were not worth keeping. But the rest…she'd get there. She would.

She weaved her way through the empty tables and headed for the lift. Too tired to take the stairs. Another good sign that sleep would come easily tonight.

The ornate brass doors welcomed her in, and she stepped inside, stretched out her tired limbs as they closed around her. Breathed in the soothing hotel scent and let it calm her as the lift slid to a gentle stop on her floor and the doors opened.

She walked out, head down as she searched her bag for the

key, when something made her still. A sixth sense, a prickle along her spine—she was used to having her space invaded when she was out and about, the odd stalker or excitable fan getting too close and then security having to intervene. But the hotel was locked down. No one got to this floor without a pass, and at this time of night, there should be no one else around but...

Her lashes lifted, head slow to follow as her mouth fell open, because there, straight ahead, was a man. A very tall, very broad, very *naked* man.

The first thing Hugo became aware of was the cold. The second was a soft ping. The third was a gasp. A very horrified, very feminine gasp!

His eyes flared wide. Every sense now alert as he registered his reflection in the French windows ahead; his nude silhouette against the dimmed lights of the Champs-Élysées far below. And that's when he realised, the ping was an arriving elevator car and the gasp—

Oh, Mon Dieu!

He spun to face the woman who'd stepped out of the lift. Dressed in tailored black to her knees, nude tights, classic heels, she stood as regal as a queen...of the haunting, screaming kind!

Her handbag hit the deck as he watched, her belongings spilling free as she pressed her hands to her ghost-like cheeks and the elevator doors slid closed.

'*Oh, Mon Dieu!*' he repeated aloud, clamping his hands over his front. '*Je suis désolé!*'

Perfectly arched brows disappeared into a sweeping dark fringe, and unthinking, he stepped forward. Her eyes darted down and she stumbled back, one hand blindly reaching for the elevator button. 'Don't come any closer!'

'*Pardonnez-moi!*' He scanned the hallway, wishing that for all it was opulent and timeless, it had something he could readily use as a shield. He discounted the bronze bust on the console table—too weird. The baroque lamp. It was plugged into the wall. The bin. Just, no. And grabbed an ample-sized vase complete with high-rising white foliage, thrusting it before him as he turned to face her again.

'Please.' He spoke English with her, blowing a stray white frond out of his face. His allergies were *not* going to appreciate this up-close encounter. But they had nothing on her and his nakedness. 'I didn't mean to scare you. I live here.'

Cascading brown waves shimmied with her panicked head shake as she batted the button, which seemed to be having no effect whatsoever. Was she even hitting it? He'd be taking *that* up with hotel maintenance come morning...

'I *do*,' he stressed, focusing on more pressing concerns— panicked hotel guest versus his indecent exposure. 'Just here!'

He nudged his head in the direction of his very closed, very *locked* penthouse door.

He swallowed a curse. 'And it appears, I am now locked out.'

She eyed the door, her hand ceasing its attack on the elevator button as she lifted it to the pearls around her neck. Did she think he was going to rob her? A naked robber? Was that a thing?

He shuddered and hurried to explain. 'I know this looks bad. And I'm not making this up. I sleepwalk. And just now, as far as I knew it, I was stepping into a cab, going who knows where with who knows who, when the elevator went ping and you gasped and I came to. I *swear* it.'

The fear in her big round eyes eased a fraction. He couldn't make out their colour in the low light favoured by his hotels at night, only that her perfectly applied makeup accentuated their alluring shape and size...the kind a man could readily lose his mind in.

And yes, he had to be half asleep if *that's* the thought he was entertaining while the chilling draft from the ancient glass continued to assault his very exposed ass.

'Then why haven't I seen you before?' She gifted him the side eye with a hint of fire. *Hallelujah.*

'I've been away on business for the past month. I got back a few hours ago. You can call Vincent on the front desk. He'll confirm it. In fact, *do* call Vincent because I don't have a key on my naked person and I really don't want to terrorise the rest of the building by going down there like this. Terrorising one hotel guest is enough, and as I own the place, it really won't look good for business.'

Her mouth twitched. The pink glossy shape pulling back into one dimpled cheek, a hint of colour creeping in—*Dieu merci!*

'You own the place?'

'This and many others. *Oui.*'

'You are Chevalier of Chevalier Clubs?'

'I know, yes. It's very original. I've heard it all before. '

She laughed softly and *damn* if the sound didn't warm him all the more. He needed more of that.

'I'm just relieved I can trust you to be well behaved while I call in the cavalry, Mr Chevalier.'

'You can call me Hugo. I think we're long past the need for surnames here...'

She didn't comment as she dipped to the floor, not once taking her eyes from his as the elevator doors eased open behind her. He half expected her to scurry back inside and get the hell away while awaiting said cavalry. But she didn't. She swept up her belongings, dropping all but her phone back inside her bag.

He was right about her regal air. Every movement was so carefully poised, the way her knees stayed pressed together, her head remained high, her shoulders held back. There was something about her too. Something familiar…achingly so…

Or was it just the late hour, the hazy remnants of his dream messing with his head? His memories? The warped world between reality and make-believe…because if he'd met her before, surely, he'd have remembered her name at least.

And what was a woman like her doing wandering the halls of the hotel at such a late hour, or early, depending on how one looked at it. Alone too?

She looked like she'd been to dinner, or the theatre, a function perhaps. Her appearance *too* pristine to be doing the walk of shame. Too composed to—

And what are you even doing debating her presence when you're the one stood in the public corridor? Butt! Naked!

He watched as she dialled the front desk, her elegant long fingers making light work of the task before her eyes returned to his. Her gaze thankfully more bemused now as she lifted the phone to her ear and Hugo rocked on his feet. Wondered where to look. As first meetings went, this had to be up there with the most embarrassing, most memorable…

And still, the question remained. There were only two penthouse suites on this floor. His and Louis Cousteau's. And she wasn't Louis's type. Wrong sex for a start.

'Vincent, c'est Cassie…'

Cassie. The name softened her somewhat. Made her more…accessible. He listened as she spoke to his night porter. Her French seeming to come easy, though there was an awkward stumble when she got to the state of his…he cleared his throat…undress.

Hugo pulled his shoulders back as a shiver threatened to roll through him. He couldn't do much about the head-to-toe goose-bumps, though, or the rapidly shrivelling… *Oh, dear.* Throat clearing could be quite habit forming—who knew?

'He's on his way.'

She slotted the phone into her bag and Hugo gave an abrupt nod, which in turn sent the floral fronds right up his nose. He scrunched his face up, battling a sneeze, battling it… battling it—

'A-Achoo!'

She flinched. 'Bless you.'

'I'm sorry!' He turned his head to the side, swallowed another. 'Allergies.'

'Oh, dear, perhaps flowers weren't the best choice of a shield.'

'Short of pulling the lamp out of the wall, I didn't have much choice.'

She looked around too and then stepped forward, shrugging out of her jacket as she went. 'Here.'

Now he was the one taking a back step. 'I couldn't possibly.'

There was no way on earth he was going to put her clothing anywhere near his—

'It's fine.'

She was a stride away, jacket held out, decorative vase the only thing keeping her from getting another eyeful. This time, up close and personal.

Maybe he should install coat stands complete with coats

throughout his hotels for such random eventualities in future…hell, he'd settle for an umbrella!

'I promise not to look…' she said, her eyes meeting his as her delicate little throat gave a delicate little bob '…not again anyway.'

What on earth was she doing?

The only man she'd ever seen naked in all her adult years was her ex, the Prince. But if anyone deserved to wear the title visually, it was this man.

He was a solid wall of muscle. Tall. Broad. Fierce. And she would have said Eastern European, but his accent was all French. Thick and seductive and…and she really should have stopped at one martini.

She turned her head away, eyes averted as her skin prickled and warmed. Every millimetre aware of him being so very close. So very close and so very naked.

'Are you sure?'

She nodded, not trusting her voice.

And as he moved, the air shifted between them. Her senses strained. The soft clink of the vase against the marble ridiculously loud as he returned it to the side. The heat of his fingers sweeping like fire against hers as he took her jacket from her outstretched hands. His scent invaded her nostrils. He'd showered recently. He smelled clean, masculine, and her head…her head was busy visualising far too much. The reflection in the gold elevator doors, distorted, but revealing enough. Especially when her memory was all too willing to fill in the blanks.

'Thank you, Cassie.'

Her lips parted with her breath. To have a stranger address her by name…it had been too long. Louis still called her Cassie. Always had. Always would. They'd been friends long before the crown. But this man…this Hugo Chevalier. She wanted to kiss him. *Not* a good idea.

She opted for a much safer smile, turning back to him as she secured her arms around her middle. 'You're welcome.'

'But now you're cold…'

He gestured with one shoulder as he tied her jacket around his waist, his brow furrowed in concern as he took in her bare arms and tight grip. Her clenched jaw likely too.

'I'm fine.'

She tried to keep her eyes level with his, but this close she could see every exquisite detail of his face…and the man was, well, he was bewitching. Maybe there was something mystical to this whole witching hour after all, because she was losing her ability to think straight.

From his dark cropped hair with the slightest peak that gave him a heart-shaped brow…a kind brow. To his dark eyebrows that arched over eyes that spoke of a strength, a steeliness, but also a sweetness…and how was that even possible? They could be grey or blue. It was hard to tell in the low light of the hall.

He had a kind nose too—straight and smooth. And a mouth that softened into a smile that made her stomach turn to goo. The dark stubble that bracketed his mouth and followed the sharp cut of jaw seemed suave and deliberate. The man *liked* to look good. *Knew* he looked good. Just like Georges. Which should put her on edge.

But how could she be on edge when he was the one naked and locked out, her tiny jacket his only protection…

'I think it looks better on you,' she murmured, a teasing quirk to her lips.

He chuckled, his pecs giving a delightful ripple that had her palms tingling against her arms.

'Once again, I do apologise. I'm sure this is the last thing you wanted to come home to.'

'You're just lucky it's me and not Louis. I don't think he would have been so kind as to offer out any form of a shield.'

'Louis is a friend of yours?'

'*Oui*. He's kindly gifted me his place until I...' Her gaze drifted to the Champs-Élysées beyond the glass as her thoughts drifted to her unpleasant reality and she beat them back. 'Until I can find myself a more permanent home.'

With a career that she had yet to get off the ground...

'Are you looking to stay in Paris?'

She frowned at him. Did he really not recognise her?

At first, she'd been too stunned by his nakedness to think about him recognising her. Then she'd been too caught up in getting him covered up. But with him calling her 'Cassie' and the continued ease? An ease that shouldn't really exist. He was still very much naked, and her jacket wasn't covering all that much. And seriously, those abs and those legs... they looked like they could crack a—

'Cassie?'

Gulp. She tugged her gaze back to his. *'Pardonnez-moi.'* She really wasn't used to such a fine specimen of a man this close and this naked. 'What were you saying?'

His eyes lit with something—something she wasn't all too sure she should be identifying with. 'I was asking if you're looking to stay in Paris?'

'I'm looking to stay in...' she repeated dumbly, wondering if she could stay a whole lot longer if these were the kind of encounters she might experience with the owner of her current abode…which was a wholly inappropriate thought to be having. Once again, she blamed Beni's excellent martinis.

And thank heaven for the ping of the elevator at that precise moment.

She sprang back. 'Vincent!'

Hugo's mouth, a rather deliciously full mouth for a man, quirked to the left and flashed a dimple. 'Funny place that…?'

'I should let you get back to your bed.' She backed up, all the way to Louis's door, scrambling for the key in her handbag. 'I hope your sleep is much more restful from here on out, Mr Chevalier.'

'Wait! Your jacket…'

She waved him away—*oh, God no*—eyes anywhere but on him as she fumbled over the lock. Telling Vincent the situation over the phone was one thing, having Vincent *witness* the ex-Princess of Sérignone in a deserted hallway with the naked hotelier, aka his boss, was something else.

Especially with the flush of colour she was now sporting from the chest up.

The door finally sprang open and she sprang in.

'Goodnight, Mr Chevalier. Sweet dreams!'

Because she was sure to have plenty.

Though perhaps *sweet* was the wrong descriptor for the hot and tangled mess of Cassie's sheets that night…

CHAPTER TWO

THE NEXT MORNING Hugo knocked on Louis's door, rolled his shoulders back and waited.

He was sure she was in. The floorboards in the old building gave enough groans away to indicate that someone was home…and that was without him being extra sensitive to her presence following their impromptu encounter.

He eyed the flowers in one hand, her dry-cleaned jacket in his other. The former, an apology he'd had sourced from his favoured florist early that morning. The latter, hers to return.

He didn't want to leave them on her doorstep like some coward. He didn't want her to think him too embarrassed to say hello. Even if the smallest wriggle in his gut told him there might be some of that going on.

He'd never been so quick to escape Vincent's presence as the night before. Though his concierge had handled his state of undress remarkably well, he wasn't ready to be reminded of it just yet. And though he was sure his concierge hadn't shared the news around his staff, Hugo hadn't done his morning rounds as was his usual way upon his return. He'd simply requested that the bouquet be sent up and left it at that.

Besides, he had more pressing matters to attend to. Like a personal apology to deliver now that he was in full possession of his faculties and his clothing.

The elevator pinged and his cheeks heated as he relived Cassie's arrival… Okay, so the embarrassment was still there. But, *Dieu*, it was hardly ideal meeting anyone for the first time in one's birthday suit. Only your parents should get that privilege, and even then…

The elevator opened and the cleaning trolley emerged with two members of staff. One he recognised, one he didn't. Must be new. He sent a polite smile in their general direction and went back to his business while they went about theirs. Clearing his throat, he knocked again.

This time he heard footsteps on the other side. Slow but coming closer. They paused and his senses came alive, awareness prickling as she eyed him through the peephole. An eternity seemed to pass. Was he going to have to explain his presence through a…*closed door*?

Click. The lock turned. The door eased open a crack and one eye peeked out. Vibrant and green. *Sans* makeup today too.

'Mr Chevalier?' She seemed to breathe his name, the delicate sound doing something weird to his chest and that ring of familiarity upped a notch. 'What are you doing here?'

'Good morning.' He tried for a smile, feeling oddly unnerved. Was it the familiarity or the fact that she wasn't exactly welcoming?

Well, would you be after seeing you *naked?*

'I come bearing a gift as an apology and one freshly laundered jacket.'

He lifted both items into view and a delightful flush filled her cheek. He caught the hint of a smile too.

'You really didn't need to do that.'

'I must confess, *I* didn't. I had my staff do it for me.'

'But you would've missed housekeeping for this morning...'

'There have to be some perks to owning a hotel.'

The door eased a little wider, as did her smile, and his shoulders eased from their surprising position around his ears.

'That is most kind.' She reached out for the jacket and her oversized cream sweater slid down her bare shoulder. She hurried to tug it back up, her blush deepening. 'You really needn't have troubled yourself further.'

She was looking at the flowers as she tucked the jacket to her chin. Eyeing him beneath her lashes as though she was shy. *Was* she shy? Hell, he'd been the naked one, but then maybe she was still *seeing* him naked. *Mon Dieu.*

Until he could bury that image, she would likely keep seeing him so.

'Here, please.' He offered the bouquet of classic cream buds, which she took, her green eyes lighting up as she brought them to her nose.

'Hydrangeas?'

'I put in a special request for a hypoallergenic variety.' He gave her a lopsided grin and cocked his head towards the floral display that had been his protection a few hours ago. 'And I'm now considering that for the health of all my guests, I should have these evil varieties replaced throughout.'

Her eyes danced. 'Hydrangeas certainly would have hidden a lot more.'

She was warming up. And her teasing had him warming from the inside out too, which encouraged him enough to say, 'Can I tempt you to a coffee? There's a barista down the road that the tourists have yet to discover, and I'd love to...'

His invitation trailed off as the colour drained from her face. Had he dropped his pants unawares again, because now she was back to being aghast? Not quite the screaming, Hail Mary affair of the night before, but pale, nonetheless.

'What's wrong?'

And truth was he hadn't *meant* to invite her for coffee. It hadn't been his intention at all when he'd come here. But he didn't feel in any hurry to leave her orbit. Not after the week he'd just endured with his parents in LA. His father had refused to stick to his retirement plan and keep his nose out of the global security business he'd set up forty years ago...a business that would take his dying breath if he let it.

Only, Hugo hadn't thought of his father and his firm since Cassie had stunned him awake.

And today was Saturday, the weekend for most. Not that he had treated it as such in a long time. Especially since he'd rolled his father's business into his ever-expanding list of responsibilities.

But now he was taking a moment to think about it, it was the perfect excuse for a leisurely coffee with a companion who certainly looked like she was enjoying her own chilled-out weekend. Her jumper having resumed its slouched position off one shoulder, her soft grey leggings and fluffy white socks designed for lounging, her hair hanging free and tousled to her waist...

He could feel another throat clearing coming on, and what was that about?

You really need to ask?

'Nothing. I'm—' She licked her lips. 'I'm not dressed to go out.'

'I'm talking coffee, not cocktails at the Ritz.' He was hoping to reassure her, to tease a little too. Surely she had to know how good she looked? Sweet and cute, in a sexy girl-next-door kind of a way. But her smile remained weak.

'I should get these in some water.'

'Of course.'

She eased away from the door and a chill washed over his front. Disappointment wrapped up in that same sense of familiarity—ringing stronger, resonating deeper. But then, he'd walked many a hotel corridor, attended many a black tie affair, met many, many people over the years. Though it was more than how she looked. It was the way she was. The regal air. The shyness. The sweetness and light.

'I'll leave you to get on with your day.'

He turned on his heel and moved off, cursing the disappointed burr to his voice. It wasn't in his nature to guilt trip people. Problem was, he *was* disappointed, and it had taken him by surprise.

'Mr Chevalier...'

He paused, angled his head just enough to say, 'Hugo, please.'

'Would you like to come in for coffee?'

His brows drew together—was she just being kind, polite...?

'I was about to have one myself,' she added as though sensing his hesitation.

'So long as I'm not keeping you from whatever you had planned for today?'

'Not at all. To be honest, it would be nice to have some company.'

His frown lifted. 'You're sure?'

She stepped back to make room for him to enter. 'Though I don't know how well you know Louis or if you've been in here since he took ownership of the apartment, but...'

Her voice trailed away as she let the space speak for itself, which it did, a thousand times over as he crossed the threshold and chuckled. 'I believe one's home should always be a reflection of the occupant's personality, and since this is Louis's and Louis Cousteau is a flamboyant fashion designer, I think it is perfection.'

The twinkle in her eye was worth every eye-watering item adorning the large entrance hall. 'That's one word for it.'

He and Louis's penthouse suites were of a similar size and layout, but there the similarity ended. Statement pieces, whether it be in colour or shape, personality or origin, filled every wall, every space. And if Hugo was honest, it gave him the twinge of a headache, but who was he to judge? He was a minimalist through and through. Everything in his life had been about pleasing others, or at the very least, avoiding offence.

The same could not be said for the great Louis Cousteau.

'You do get used to it after a while.'

She was at the glitter-bedazzled sink, in the equally bedazzled kitchen, filling a vase with water.

'I'm saying nothing.'

She smiled. 'You didn't need to.' Sparkling green eyes went back to the vase as she arranged the flowers within it. 'Louis was never one for toeing a line of any sort.'

'A trait I can admire.'

And he did. That was no lie.

Hugo had grown up in a household at war…whenever his father was at home at any rate. He'd been trying to find the line to toe forever, and then beseeching everyone else to toe it too. He'd been the doting son, the people-pleaser, the peace facilitator in his parents' marriage, where there had always been three according to his mother—her, his father, and the company.

Not any more, though… *Retired*, remember.

If only his father would get the message and leave well alone.

'Is filter coffee, okay?' The hesitation in her voice already had him giving a smile in reassurance—*see*, people-pleaser. Even though he'd long ago left that boy behind, some habits were harder to shift. 'Or I can try and master the machine?'

He looked at the contraption against one wall, too shiny and new to have ever been used. 'A filter is perfect.'

And if he was honest, he liked his coffee by the vat. He might be French—well, Polish if one wanted to go a generation back, but he'd take a giant mug over a measly espresso cup any day of the week.

He entered the living space, leaving her to get the coffee going. He got the impression she didn't entertain often. Which again was strange, considering how she'd appeared the night before. How sophisticated, elegant, and dressed for entertaining.

Or was it that he'd been the complete opposite, so unprepared for company?

No. He didn't think it was that. More that she was used to being waited on. And unaccustomed to entertaining anybody when dressed so casually. But if he was honest, he liked her like this.

Even if she did stand out against the backdrop, her hesitation and muted presence against the garish backdrop a bit like setting a skittish kitten down in a neon nightclub. Maybe he should have invited her round to his place…she'd have fit right in with all the monochrome and he could have taken care of the coffee. Though he'd need to put a few coffees between them and his nakedness before that could happen!

He followed the criss-crossed panels of sun coming through the many French windows and doors to the low-slung coffee table that was scattered with drawing paraphernalia. Pencils, pens, sketches of clothing and accessories…

'Please excuse the mess.'

He turned to find her behind him.

'Louis left it like this?'

The man didn't strike him as the kind to leave stuff just lying around. Chaotic but not messy. Especially when such designs were obviously in their early stages and likely to be considered top secret. His cleaning staff could be trusted but…

She coloured, swept her hair behind her ear. 'No, they're mine.'

'*Yours?* Wow, they're really—' He was about to say *impressive*, but she was already hurrying forward, gathering the sheets into a pile. Did she not want him to see? Was she self-conscious? Or was it as he thought…

'Top secret?'

'What?' She straightened with a laugh, clutching the drawings to her chest. 'Hardly. Not really. They're—they're just some designs I've been working on.'

'Do you work with Louis? Is that how you two know each another?'

'Not officially, no. We've known each other for a long time. We went to school together in London.'

She stacked the papers on a side table shaped like a palm tree and gestured for him to take a seat on the velvet sofa, the colour of which made him wince but the fabric was soft enough. He swung an arm across its back, was about to ask her which school when his gaze landed on the pile of magazines her cleared-away sketches had unveiled.

Or rather, landed on the cover model of the top magazine...

The cover model who then took a seat beside him in the flesh.

'Yes,' she said, and he started. 'That's me.'

No, he couldn't have been so unaware, so sucker-punched by their first encounter that he'd missed...missed...

He blinked and turned to face her, eyes widening and seeing every detail anew. The green eyes. The dark hair. The petite frame. He thought of the recognition that had been nagging at him. The familiarity. The poised elegance with the touch of shyness—something thousands if not millions adored, and others questioned.

Cassie was Cassandra, Princess of Sérignone. *Ex* Princess.

English socialite. A woman of the people. A woman whose recent divorce was the talk of the world's media, and there he'd been...naked...unawares...how stupid she must think him!

'Mr Chevalier?'

Though he hadn't been in his right mind. And it had been dark in the outer hall. And even this morning, he'd been too concerned with making right what he had made wrong. And then she'd been all shy and sweet and...

Princess *Freaking* Cassandra?

He dragged a hand down his face.

'I'm sorry. I didn't realise.'

He contemplated standing. *Dieu*, he contemplated bowing, but it all felt a little late for that.

She gave him a coy smile. *That* smile.

'I know. And I wasn't quite sure how to tell you.'

'I would bow but...'

Her eyes danced, her thoughts travelling all the way to his naked backside and beyond, he was sure...

'So, you're the reason for the extra footfall outside when I arrived home yesterday? I'd assumed we were having an out-of-season flurry of tourists.'

She grimaced. 'Mostly press I'm afraid. I'm sorry.'

'Why are you sorry?'

'For bringing the madness to your door, to your hotel.'

'Considering I brought you my nakedness, I think we can call it even, don't you?'

She gave him a full-on smile. The beam of which made him lose his breath. *Breathtaking*. It was a word he'd heard of, knew of, never had he deemed it fit for another person. A hard run, a spell in the boxing ring, a blast round the Nürburgring. But never about a woman.

And that's when it hit him. The nagging recognition, the stirring in his gut—it wasn't because she was Cassandra, Princess of Sérignone. It was that she reminded him of another woman. Another dark-haired, shy yet teasing woman. She reminded him of Sara. Of his past and his one big mistake.

Ice rushed his veins, goose-bumps prickling against the sleeves of his shirt.

'Your hotel security have been amazing, Mr Chevalier, but I am sorry for the extra work I'm putting them through.'

He swallowed the chilling boulder that had lodged itself in

his chest. 'We're an exclusive hotel, we deal with clients that require extra security all the time. It's their job to handle it.'

'Still…'

She looked hesitant, and he knew his tension had seeped into his words. He cursed the memories for rearing their ugly head. It was ancient history. Over a decade old. He'd not thought of Sara in so long. She had cost him dearly in so many ways. She wasn't just the woman he'd thought himself in love with, she was the woman who'd lost him his father's respect, his first career, almost his life as well as hers…back when he'd been a rookie bodyguard.

A bodyguard who should have known better than to fall in love with his principal.

It's why he kept a tight hold on his emotions now. Especially when it came to people. He didn't depend on them to give him a rush of any kind.

Now he was thirty-six, a billionaire hotelier with a finger in the pie that was his father's global security firm. The biggest lesson he'd learnt was that you couldn't control what others thought or did or felt. They would go the way they wanted. And it was best to disassociate your own happiness, your own feelings, from those of others.

Which left him all the more disturbed now, because he cared about this woman. This woman who was no more than a stranger to him personally, but he'd seen enough in the press to know her life had to be some kind of living hell of late. Her divorce as loud and as messy as a catastrophic world event. He wasn't one for reading the gossip columns, but she often featured in the mainstream headlines. People picking and probing into her personal life like they had every right.

'I'm sorry you're under such attack, but if my hotel and my

staff are helping you to feel safe from their prying presence, then that's as good as any five-star review for me.'

Her eyes warmed with his words. 'Are you going to ask if any of it is true?'

'If any of what is true?'

'I don't know—take your pick. People usually have their favourite headline…corrupting the son of my ex-husband's driver seems to be the latest story.'

'You're confusing me with someone who cares, Cassie.'

To anyone else, his remark may have caused offence. Instead she positively bloomed and, in her warmth, the chill within him eased.

'It really is none of my business, unless of course you would appreciate a friendly ear.'

Her lashes flickered, her green eyes signalling something that he couldn't read but it had the unease returning—the familiarity, the need to protect, the urge to run and stay at the same time.

'Anyway…' He shifted back in his seat, creating an extra inch between them like it would somehow release the weird hold she had over him. 'The extra income from the reporters staying and dining here will be good for business, but if one crosses the line, you only have to say the word and they're out. Though to give them their due, they all seemed rather well-behaved upon my arrival.'

'That's because it was you in their orbit.'

And not her.

She didn't need to say it for him to know that's what she meant. And there was so much in that one statement. So much vehemence, so much power that she had bestowed on them—the press—and so much fear. Just like Sara.

He opened his mouth to reassure, to tell her she was safe in his building, to tell her he'd evict them all, if need be, when she stood. 'I'll get the coffee.'

He doubted the pot would be ready but he got the impression she wanted a breather more than the drink, and so he let her go. It could wait.

And if he was honest, he could do with a breather too.

It wasn't so much that she was royalty—*ex*-royalty. He'd protected royalty. He'd housed royalty. Hell, he'd *dated* the equivalent of royalty. And there came Sara again.

'You know what your problem is, son? You've got a thing for a damsel in distress, and until you can keep a lid on it, you're no use to me...'

His father's decade-old words were in his ear, his disappointed gaze in his head too...didn't matter that it didn't apply now. That his father's grave dismissal had no place in the now.

His career was his own. His money was his own. His life was his own.

But the damsel in distress, was that what this was...? Sara. Cassie. Both damsels of a sort?

He shook off the thought, dismissed it even as it tried to come back at him...history on repeat just in another form.

But if it was a case of history repeating itself, didn't that mean he had a chance to rewrite the ending and come out the hero this time? Could he help Cassie get through this turbulent time in her life and not play himself for a lovesick fool, because this time he wouldn't *be* a lovesick fool.

Cassie brought the tray back into the lounge. She couldn't tell if Hugo Chevalier had a sweet tooth. Her gut told her not. Or rather, his well-toned physique did, but she brought the brass pineapple sugar pot anyway. More because it made her smile.

He started to rise. 'Let me help you with that.'

'No need.' She set the tray down, careful not to spill a drop from the two steaming mugs filled with coffee or the jug of milk. 'Despite the rumours, a princess can manage to serve her own coffee...'

And brush her hair, cleanse her face, clothe herself...*how novel!*

He settled back into his seat. 'Do you have to do that a lot? Justify what you can and can't do, fend off the would-be waiting staff?'

She didn't meet his eye. She already felt like he'd leapt inside her head, read her every thought as she'd had it. Not that there were any staff waiting in the wings here. Not any more.

It didn't stop the learned response though—the slight tension in her spine, an attuned ear, and the tight lip, which she swiftly loosened into a smile for his benefit.

'Once upon a time, in a castle far, far away...' She handed him his mug and he thanked her, his gaze flitting to the exposed skin of her shoulder, and she fought the urge to cover it as her cheeks heated. She was dressed for comfort, not for company. A fact she'd tried to point out when he'd made the joke about the Ritz. But there was being dressed for the Ritz and being dressed like she was. Braless and in her comfiest clothes. Her go-to outfit after a morning's workout, when all she'd planned to do was to block the noise of the world out and let her creative juices take over.

'But not any more?'

'No.' She sank back into the sofa, curled her legs up under her. 'Now I get to make my own coffee. When I want, how I want, and drink it with who I want.'

'And this is a good thing, right? Because from where I'm

sitting, there seems to be some unresolved tension about the whole situation.'

Her eyes shot to his. Had he really just gone there? Outed her and her 'situation' again without a moment's hesitation? She gave a grimace. 'Did it really come across like that?'

'A little.'

'Sorry. I'm not very good at this.'

'Good at what exactly? The coffee. The talking. Or...'

'The company.'

'Am I that hard to be around?' But his eyes danced with the question, the soft curve to his lips telling her he hadn't taken offence, and he didn't mean any.

She laughed, the tension between her shoulder blades easing with every ripple. What was it about this man that made her feel almost normal. 'Not at all. Just...different.'

'Different?'

'To be honest, a coffee date of any kind is a new one on me. Even with Louis it's usually a glitzy affair that revolves around fashion and dogs.'

He cocked a brow. 'Dogs?'

'Oh, yes, he *loves* dogs.'

'I can *try* and talk fashion and dogs if that'll make you feel more comfortable, but I can't make any promises about how riveting it'll be. Or accurate. I can do colour, size, maybe the odd name drop, but that's my lot.'

'I take it you have people who pick out your clothing then, because for one who claims to have little knowledge of fashion, you clearly have an eye for it?'

'Is that a roundabout way of complimenting me on how I dress, Cassie?'

Her cheeks warmed and his eyes dipped, taking in the flush that must have risen up her chest, too. Oh, dear. She was so out of practice and very bad at this. 'It was merely an observation, Mr Chevalier.'

'Now that we're enjoying coffee together, do you think you could drop the Mr? Especially since technically if anyone should be giving anyone a rank, it's me to you.'

Her coffee threatened to escape her mug as she thrust her hand out. 'Please don't!'

He raised that same arrogant brow.

'I've been called *princess* enough to last one lifetime, and I know that probably sounds ungrateful when it's many a young girl's dream but…'

She shuddered. She hadn't meant to, but the chilling memories creeping along her spine were impossible to suppress.

'Let me guess, the reality isn't all it's cracked up to be?'

'No.'

He captured her gaze in his. The warmth, the understanding in his crystal-clear blue eyes choked up her chest and had the words spilling forth before she could stop them, 'It's more prisoner than princess.'

She bit her lip. Shocked at what she'd said. Because she knew full well how that line would be printed in the press. How it would look to the world when shown in black and white and worse still, it would be the truth. Because she *had* said it.

And she didn't know Hugo from Adam. How could she trust him not to spill all when he left here? To sell her story like so many others had before. Her nearest and dearest, people she'd once thought of as friends. 'I shouldn't have said that.'

She clamped her teeth down again so hard she thought she might draw blood, because the truth was, she wanted to talk to him. The urge like an ever-swelling tide within her. She couldn't explain it. She'd had no one for so long. Not even Louis would sit quietly, calmly, and listen like this. Oh, he was a good friend, so long as it was surface level talk. The practical or financial. Designs and creative fun. But this... the deep, emotional, real.

There was just something about Hugo. Something that told her he understood. That he got it.

'It's okay, Cassie. You can trust me.'

He lowered his mug to the table, rested his elbows on his knees as he interlaced his fingers and gave her his full attention.

'I don't make a habit of gossiping, and I certainly don't talk to reporters, and in all honesty, the idea that *you* could go outside and tell the world that you found me wandering one of my hotels in my birthday suit fills *me* with dread.'

A streak of pink marred his cheeks and she found it endearing. Both the blush and the honesty.

'That aside, it would hardly look good for business if I were to go about selling stories on my guests. And in case you need it spelled out, I really don't need the cash or the press attention.'

There was no arrogance, just fact.

'So, if you keep my secrets, I'll keep yours. How does that sound?'

'*Très bien*, Hugo,' she said, and with all her heart, she meant it too. 'I agree.'

CHAPTER THREE

'SO, A PRISONER, you say? How so?'

Though he could take a wild guess. Not so wild if he was to think of Sara and her life as the daughter of a head of state. Her father may have been the figurehead, but the rules and expectations very much applied to her. Governing what she could and couldn't do. Where she could and couldn't go. Who she could and couldn't see. Who she could and couldn't *date*. Him.

'Where do I even start?'

He settled back into the sofa, making clear he had all the time in the world to listen. 'Why not start at the beginning, it's as good a place as any...'

She sipped at her coffee, her mouth twisting around the mug. 'You might regret saying that, Hugo.'

He waved a hand through the air. 'Feel free to remind me later.'

She gave a soft huff, the returning shadows in her green

eyes chasing away the amusement and making him want to close the gap between them. But he also sensed the persistent skittishness about her, the wary kitten-like quality he'd spied earlier.

'If I'm honest, I never had freedom like other kids growing up, so it wasn't like I could miss it. My parents had my life mapped out from birth. Every step was strategic and they played me to their best advantage.'

He gave a slow nod. 'That sounds…'

'Militant?'

'Exhausting.'

She blew out a breath. 'That too. But the palace was different. Every day had a schedule. Breakfast, lunch, dinner. You name it. There was a time for it and someone would produce it. And if you were especially lucky, there'd be a different outfit for each.'

'Where my family comes from in Poland, such abundance would be severely frowned upon.'

'You're from Poland—I thought so.' Her smile made a return. Bright, genuine. 'And I would agree with them all. And I said as much to the King. Who was of course horrified, as was his mother. I was quickly shushed and escorted from the room by Georges and told never to give my opinion in public, or private, again.'

'How lovely.'

'Quite.'

'What are they like? Really?'

'His family?' Her eyes flashed and her nose flared. 'The King is a brute. His wife is a spendthrift. And while the Queen Mother despairs at their behaviour, his son runs amok. If I was to be kind, I would say the King is angry at the world for daring to mock his virility. His wife spends to make up for the abundance of children she so desperately wanted. His mother despairs at her lack of power, and as for Georges, well, the apple doesn't fall far from the tree…after five years of marriage I failed to provide even one heir.'

His gut clenched. 'So, he divorced *you*?'

'God, no. I divorced him. When I realised I was the only one who took our wedding vows seriously.'

His shoulders eased as he released a breath he hadn't noticed he was holding.

'I'd had enough of the real Georges and everyone laughing at me behind closed doors. I think he shares the worst qualities of both his mother and his father, and now he can share those qualities with whomever he chooses, as I no longer need to care because I'm no longer there to witness it.'

Hugo shook his head, unable to understand how she'd been able to bear it for so long and still hold her head as high as she did. All that poise and elegance, she had it in spades. She hadn't lost it. Georges hadn't stolen it. No matter how the palace had tried.

'And so, they sow seeds of twisted dealings and affairs on your part, suggesting it was *your* unfaithful behaviour that led to the breakdown of your marriage? Despite all the stories that have been in the media over the years about him?'

She gave a sad smile. 'I know.'

'But how do you stand it? All the slander being thrown at you.'

'I ignore it as best I can. I made my bed. I knew who he was when I agreed to marry him. I knew of his reputation, but I thought I'd done the unthinkable and reformed the playboy prince. Though even I hadn't known just how much there was to reform when my parents presented our engagement as a fait accompli.'

'But surely you had a choice, you could have said no?'

She gave a tight laugh. 'One does not say no to my parents.'

'Why?'

'I'd lived a life doing what was expected of me and so I did it.' She tilted her head at him. Green eyes probing as they scanned him from top to toe. 'Call it fear, impotence, apathy… I can't imagine someone like you knowing what it means to live like that.'

He shifted under that gaze because he'd felt it all. Once. Feared for his life. Watched the woman he'd believed in walk away, powerless to stop her. And when his father had stripped him of his role in the company, he hadn't cared. He'd only vowed never to feel any of those things again.

'Did you ever rebel, even when you were younger? There must have been times…?'

She caught her lip in her teeth as her eyes drifted to the coffee table. 'When I was seven, my mother bought me a dress to wear to a summer function. I hated it. It itched like crazy, making my skin red raw, and I refused to wear it. She locked me in the basement and left me there in the dark. Told me I could come out when I had the dress on. The party was two days later…'

He waited for the punch line and when nothing came, he realised that was it.

'She came and got you…'

She nodded. 'Yes. Two days later. The staff fed me scraps but she saw to it that my hair was scraped up, my blotchy cheeks were well covered, and I smiled until my face ached.'

He felt the bite of his nails in his palm and flexed his fist. 'Some parenting technique.'

'Mind games were always my mother's way.'

'Dare I ask about your father's?'

'My father was all about the purse strings and the silent treatment. It could have been worse.'

And he'd been thinking worse. Now he felt bad to be relieved!

'I often wondered if it would have been easier if I had had a sister or a brother to love and to share the load a little, but I think that would have made it worse. I would have worried about them too.'

He could believe it.

'And the truth is, I *was* the one who said yes to the marriage. I met the Prince and he—he charmed me. Georges was good at making you believe what he said. He had these dreamy blue eyes and this compelling smile. And I'd been so caught up in his flattery, his attention, his *kindness*. He gave me everything I'd been starved of as a child. While my friends were all craving sweets, chocolate, the kind of treats Mum would never permit, all I'd wanted was love, a kind word, cuddles...' She gave a shaky laugh, her cheeks blooming with colour that killed him now. 'God, I sound pathetic.'

'No. No, you don't. *They* do. Your parents. Georges. His family. The whole lot of them.'

Hell, he wanted to storm the castle and hold them all to account.

'He made me feel special, and I—I was swept up in it all. I thought we were falling in love and so I married him. I believed our own love story. *The English Socialite who had snagged the Playboy Prince.*'

Her green eyes misted over, her thoughts travelling back in time as she relived those early days. 'I didn't realise I was being played for a fool until it was too late. My father had saved the royal reserves with Fairfax money and I was Princess of Sérignone. There was no going back…until I couldn't take it any more.'

He studied her quietly, admiring the strength it must have taken to walk away, to *stay* away. 'And what about your parents now? Where are they?'

'At home in England, last I checked.'

'Have you…'

'Have I spoken to them? Oh, yes, they were my first port of call when I ran from the palace. I'm not sure why I thought they would shelter me, but what choice did I have? A princess doesn't really have many friends they can trust, and I figured they wouldn't want me roaming the streets stirring up ever more trouble…'

'But?'

'My mother tried to talk me into returning—like I said, mind games are her speciality—while my father physically escorted me to his private jet back to Sérignone.'

'Your own father?'

'*Oui.* So you see, I am done with them, Hugo. Since then, the few friends I have left have helped me by giving me places to stay while I build up my portfolio, in the hope that soon, I'll have enough to launch a career in fashion and become financially independent once more. Then I can pay back all those people like Louis who have helped me get here and I can also get back to my charity work that I have missed so much.'

He shook his head. 'I can't believe that you're here, fighting to take your life back and already thinking about giving back to others.'

She gave him a lopsided smile. 'I'm sickening, I know.'

'Is that what Georges would tell you?' Because he wasn't seeing the funny side.

Her eyes widened. 'How did you…?'

'Something tells me that that man and his family tried to stamp out every good thing about you so that it may make him shine that little bit brighter.'

'Funny you say that.'

'How so?'

'Because after our marriage it often occurred to me that it wasn't just the Fairfax money the Duponts were after, but my 'clean' image too. I was a way to mop up the mess that Georges was making with his wild and hedonistic parties. *Now*, if I'd known about *those* at the time of our engagement then I might have been more reluctant to trot down that aisle…'

Hugo didn't think he could take much of the Georges revelation train, or rather, his teeth couldn't. 'Seems to me the Duponts got plenty out of the marriage, and I can see how you were duped, but what I don't understand is what your parents got in return?'

'Status. Royal connections. Another boost for the family tree? I don't know and I don't want to know. Unpacking that only leads to me understanding my true worth to them, and I'm not sure I want to know that. Whereas I do know that I want a fresh start and a clean slate so that I can focus on my future free of them all.'

She gave a smile and, cupping her mug in both hands, she retreated further into the sofa. He knew the mug was giving her the warmth her body lacked. The sofa, the comfort. And he had the deep-rooted urge to provide both.

'And heaven knows there are people in this world who are starving, who don't have a roof over their head, live under threat each day with zero hope of change. People who I want to get my life in order for, so that I can get out there and help.'

She shook her head, her knuckles flashing white. 'People who are truly powerless on their own, and I have no right to say such things about my own experiences.'

'You have every right.'

Because she'd clearly been punishing herself with those same words for heaven knew how long. Since she'd married into royalty or long before then too.

'Now you're just humouring me to be kind.' She gave him another of her shy smiles. A hundred times genuine. He'd bet his life on it.

'I've been called many things in my life, but *kind* isn't one that springs to mind.'

Fierce or *fun*. Depending on the circumstance. *Stubborn* or *obstinate* to use his father's most recent favourite when his retirement had been forced upon him. But, *kind*?

'I don't believe you.' She rested her head against the back of the sofa, not so shy now as her gaze narrowed on him. 'Your eyes are kind.'

'Regardless of what you think of my eyes...' Though her words did warm his voice, his smile '... I always say what I mean, Cassie. As for what you are going through as a person, not as an ex-princess or as a lady of the English aristocracy, but as a person with real feelings, it's a lot under any normal circumstances. Divorce is one of the hardest, most stressful challenges anyone can face...'

'You sound like you're talking from experience.'

'No, not me personally. Though there were times as a kid that I thought maybe my parents would have been better off apart. And even then, the arguments were mainly about Dad not being home enough, so maybe not.' He gave a smile that was so caught up in her present hurt he wasn't sure if it came across as more of a grimace. 'But what I'm trying to say is, at least most of us get to go about our business without the whole world breathing down our necks through a camera lens and forming an ill-informed opinion on it. It stands to reason you're going to have your moments.'

She gave a soft huff. 'I've not been permitted such moments for a long time.'

'And how do you cope with that?'

'I'm not sure I am coping all that well.'

'I don't know, from where I'm sitting you seem to have done remarkably well.'

'What?' She gave a brittle laugh, and he missed the woman of seconds before—the one that thought him kind and looked increasingly relaxed in his presence. 'By spilling my heart out to a total stranger who I met only yesterday?'

'You carry yourself with such grace and poise, I never would have known that the woman who stood before me last night and thought to offer out her jacket was the same woman being hounded by the press, vilified by a royal family, and as you've now explained, ostracised by her own. You are a wonder, Cassie. And if you don't know it, allow me to tell you it is so.'

Her mouth twitched, the warmth once again blooming in her cheeks and her chest and, *Dieu*, was he glad to see it. 'Ah, well, last night you had me distracted.'

He fought the reciprocal warmth in his chest, the cheeky twitch to his own mouth. 'And when you're out in public, I assume you have a team with you to help keep the masses at bay?'

She gave another laugh, this time it sounded more delirious than brittle and it had him worried. Not that he could say why.

'I don't go out.'

'What do you mean, you don't go out?'

'Just what I said.'

'Cassie, everyone goes out at some point.'

'Not me.'

She couldn't be serious. Something inside his chest shrivelled.

'So last night…before you came upon me?'

'I'd been to the rooftop bar for a drink.'

'Alone?'

She nodded.

'Beni is a sweetheart and is kind enough to open it after everyone else has gone to bed.'

'Because that way you don't have to see anyone?'

Again, she nodded, and again he felt this weird shrivelling sensation inside his chest. If he wasn't so traumatised by the whole conversation, he'd be touched that she had taken the time to learn the name of his bar staff.

'Don't get me wrong, sometimes there's the odd person, but in the main, it's just me.'

She smiled. Actually *smiled*. And he wanted to cry. Which was as ridiculous as this whole situation. Ridiculously unfair.

'When you've lived enough days and nights being chased down, Hugo, with no regard for your personal space, you begin to crave those quiet hours while the city sleeps. And the witching hour has kind of become my time to dine. Though I don't really eat as such, more get some fresh air while everyone else is asleep.'

He took up his coffee, needing something to do that wasn't taking her hand and walking her out of here right now…

'How long have you been here for, Cassie?'

'What? Staying at Louis's?'

'Oui.'

'A month.'

'And for that entire time, you haven't left this apartment?'

She gave a subtle shake of her head, as though she could sense the storm brewing within him as he stifled a curse with a sip of his coffee. 'Have you seen the sights, walked the river, been to the Louvre, the parks?'

She was shaking her head at everything, and he was—he was losing his mind at the very idea that she could have been in the city for a whole month and seen nothing. Nothing at all!

'But I am lucky because your hotel is well positioned. I have a view of the Eiffel Tower, Arc de Triomphe and Champs-Élysées depending on where I stand. The balcony is vast, the private plunge pool a delight, and the room service is all-encompassing.'

'But, Cassie!' Her eyes flared and he immediately softened his posture and his words—remembering that for all she was fierce in some ways, she was still that skittish kitten in others, and he couldn't blame her. Living a life being papped 24-7. A life like Sara had led. 'Living inside these four walls day in, day out, is not living.'

'People regularly survive on a whole lot less.'

'Survive, sure. One's sanity, however…?'

'And as we have established, I cannot move for reporters… some days I only have to turn my head in the wrong direction in the presence of the wrong person and someone will make something of it, and that could be as catastrophic as a natural disaster on the world's stage.'

As he had seen for himself. But to know that she had escaped one form of prison only to land herself in another—his Parisian paradise of all places—when she had the City of Love on her doorstep.

To live in it like a prisoner, when her only crime had been marriage to a prince.

A prince whose own reputation was scandalous at best, who'd managed to make her feel ridiculed and laughed at in her own home. *Mon Dieu*, if he ever met the man...

'Do you care what the world thinks that much?'

'It's not a question of care as it is being impossible to ignore. They're like pack animals and I'm their prey. I can't go about my day without being set upon. Though that's probably being unfair to pack animals...'

'But now you're divorced, surely, things will start to ease?'

'When the Duponts stop stirring the pot, perhaps they will. Right now, they need me to lose face so that he may save his. It is far safer for me to keep a low profile while our divorce is so fresh. He needs to find a new bride, someone willing to look past his reputation like I once did, and they will paint the picture they need in order to make the future look how they wish.'

'No matter what damage it does to you?'

'The picture is not yet tainted enough.'

He cursed. The heartless nature of it all too much to take.

'Precisely. And I have my own dreams to consider and protect.' Eyes likes emeralds, glittering and bright, drifted to the drawings she'd set aside. 'While all those girls dreamt of being a princess, I dreamt of one day having my own fashion label.'

He'd warrant she'd dreamt of a lot more than that...before her prince had shattered those dreams, had she wanted mini princes and mini princesses to fill her fairy-tale castle?

And why on earth had his head gone there? Maybe because he could see her as a mother? With the good heart she wore on her sleeve...it must have driven the Prince crazy that she bore that trait so effortlessly, that people flocked to it, trusted it.

'I even had a name…'

He lifted his chin, focused on what she was saying and not the wild assumptions he was making about the man he really would like to put in a ring and go ten rounds with.

'Care to share?'

'Cassie Couture.' She laughed softly. 'I know. I know. It's probably a little cheesy.'

'Only as cheesy as Chevalier Clubs, perhaps.'

They shared a laugh. 'How true.'

'And if it's good enough for Coco Chanel…'

'Ah, life goals!' Her gaze lifted to his. 'As for the dream itself, it still feels out of reach, like the foolish dreams of a foolish child. But maybe, one day…'

'And the drawings?'

'Louis thinks he could test some out on the catwalk next February.'

'Louis? Why not you? Surely with your name, you could secure funding, put yourself out there?'

She nibbled on her lip. 'For now, I'm content hiding out up here, sketching.'

'And letting someone else take the credit?'

'All big names have a team behind them, and we all have to start somewhere. I'm lucky I have someone like Louis willing to take a chance on me.' She was saying the right things, even if they sounded hollow to him. 'Hopefully, soon enough, the press furore will calm, and I'll be able to step outside once more, live my life again.'

'How I wish you were talking metaphorically, but you're not.'

'No.'

'But that's not healthy, can't you see? What about fresh

air? What about everyday things like taking a walk, fetching some groceries, seeing a film, eating out?'

Mon Dieu, the list was endless. His father's firm—*his* now—provided protection for people like her day in, day out for this precise reason. To make sure they lived as normal a life as possible. To make life about saying 'yes' again, within reason. So long as situations were assessed, prepared for, managed.

She smiled. 'You know what I miss most?'

'No.' But he knew it was going to kill him, whatever it was.

'Aside from the charity work, which I truly am desperate to get back to, but I don't want it tainted by all this noise.'

'I think you put too much stock in what the Duponts are throwing about. Your charities will still benefit from your presence regardless.'

'I want the attention to be *on* the charity work. While it's on my personal life, it defeats that.'

He nodded. 'I take your point...so you were saying?'

'You'll think I'm odd.'

'Try me.'

She beamed. 'Running.'

'Running?' He choked over his coffee. Not what he'd expected her to say. Enjoying a drink in a bar uninterrupted. Taking her art to the park. Sketching in a museum or a fashion house where she could feel inspired. Even dress shopping. But *running*?

'Yes. See. I told you.'

'Of all the things...'

She raised her brows, eyes sparking. 'You thought I was going to say clothes shopping, didn't you?'

'In my defence, you'd already said charity work, so...'

He shifted against the fabric of the sofa, willing it to open up and swallow him whole. He'd never considered himself sexist before.

'I apologise.' And swiftly, he went back to the reason he'd landed himself in this mess, 'So, you like to run?'

'I do. And I used to like to run outdoors, even back in Sérignone. The palace grounds were vast enough that I could fit in a five-k run without ever having to venture outside the gates...that was until the rumours became too much for the palace.'

'The rumours?'

'Oh, yes.' She gave a wry smile. 'At which point the King put a stop to my exercise outdoors.'

Hugo clenched his jaw to stifle a curse.

'Apparently a princess in running gear, exerting herself no less, is unacceptable. I was seen as flaunting myself in front of the grounds staff, courting trouble.'

'Meanwhile his son could carry on how he liked?'

'He knew I would listen.'

He clenched his jaw once more and there went a tooth, Hugo was sure of it.

She didn't wait for him to respond, which was lucky, because there were no words Hugo could give that he would deem fit for her ears as her gaze drifted to the French windows. The balcony with its abundance of flowers hanging on to the end of the season, just a sample of what she'd see if she was to hit the vast and varied parks Paris had to offer, not to mention the incredible views along the river Seine.

So much beauty on her doorstep, it was a crime she didn't get to see it. Had she *ever* seen the Seine up close? He didn't dare ask. She'd probably tell him another horror story. And he didn't think his teeth could take any more grinding.

Whether it was the similarity to Sara, the knowledge

of what Cassie had been through, what she was *still* going through at the hands of the Duponts and the press...

'But yes, I love to run. I love to feel the wind against my face, in my hair...it didn't matter what troubles I faced, there was something about the way I could lose myself in the rhythmic rush of it that just worked. Some women choose yoga—' she shrugged '—I choose to run.'

'Then do it.'

Because in that moment, he was one hundred percent determined to see her do it. And as soon as humanly possible.

Her head snapped around, her eyes flaring wide as she looked at him like he was crazy to suggest it. And maybe he was.

'Just like that...get into my kit, my trainers and poof, out the door?'

'It's what millions do every day.'

'Have you been listening to me? I'd barely make it into the hotel lobby without a wall of people forming a human assault course. I'd do myself an injury, if not someone else.'

'What about your witching hour?'

Her eyes flared further, which he wouldn't have believed possible. But then, she really did have the biggest, greenest, most alluring...

'Because that's going to be so safe?'

'You'd be safe with me.'

She gawped at him, a solitary strand of glossy brown hair sticking to her luscious pink lips. 'You can't be serious?'

'Absolutely. And if you don't want to use your security detail, I will bring in—' She pulled a face that gave him pause. 'What's that look about?'

She hesitated.

'Cassie?'

'I don't have a detail.'

'You don't...'

'Do you see any guards hovering, Mr Chevalier?'

No, he hadn't noticed any extra security people hanging about, but then the best always managed to blend into the background. And as she had already said, she didn't venture outside of her room, so it wasn't like she went anywhere to require one. But someone of Cassie's status would have at least one Certified Protection Officer on a permanent basis.

'Obviously, not right now, while we're here, but if we were to venture out...'

'If we were to venture out, I wouldn't suddenly have the funds to pay for one. And yes, before you say it, I am aware of the risks. My continued love-hate relationship with the world, the would-be stalkers and so on. However, I took nothing from Georges in the divorce. We have no children to provide for and so it didn't feel right. And yes, I am more than aware of how foolish many consider that to be, my lawyer was very open on the matter, but I just wanted to be free of the Duponts and any hold they had over me. Yes, that has kind of backfired in the aftermath, but in the long term karma will hopefully be my payback.

'As for my parents, they have to all intents and purposes disowned me, and until I can sell my designs, I am beholden to my friends and your hotel's excellent hospitality and exceptional security. So, I will make do. Can we consider this conversation done?'

Why did Hugo feel like this conversation had been done many times before him? With her lawyer, like she had already said, and Louis too, perhaps.

'We absolutely can.'

'*Bon.*' And then she smiled as she considered him with a tilt of her head. 'You would really take me running?'

'Are you saying I don't look like the type to run?' He feigned insult over his physical ability rather than accept she was questioning the generosity of the offer. Because then he'd have to question it himself. And that would mean examining his own good conscience and whether he was in his right mind to suggest it too. After everything that had happened with Sara—gone *wrong* with Sara— But this was about getting things right this time… With access to his father's firm—*his* firm now, he could make sure they were well protected, and he could give her the freedom she so desperately deserved and needed.

'Because I can assure you, Cassie, I'm quite capable of a five-k run at a decent pace. And further if you really wanted to push it out, but any longer and you'll be hitting the early-morning commuters and I believe that defeats the point.'

'It's not your ability to go the distance that I'm questioning, it's the fact you're offering to run at that ungodly hour.'

He shrugged. 'If we stick to the Seine, it's lit and, aside from the odd stretch of cobbles, perfectly safe.'

'You really are serious…'

'You're awake anyway, so why not?'

'But you're not! Unless you're planning another…'

She coloured, clearly thinking of his naked night-time misadventures.

'I don't plan them. They happen when they happen.'

'Of course, I shouldn't have teased. Forgive me.'

'There's nothing to forgive.' And this time he softened his tone, stripping it of the defensive note she'd clearly picked up on, because it wasn't directed at her. She wasn't the reason he'd been wandering the corridors in such a state.

'They must be quite unsettling for you…to go to sleep in one place and wake up in another.'

'Thankfully they don't happen all that often. It's usually when I'm not sleeping very well to begin with.'

Her brows twitched but she didn't press. Was it a learned response to life in the royal family, her time before with her parents or was she leaving it up to him? Whichever the case, he found himself starting to explain…

'I've only just returned from LA which means I'm still on their time.'

'LA? Business or pleasure?'

He gave a tight laugh. 'Family. Which sort of makes it a hashed attempt at both with a side order of stress.'

'Ah…' She placed her mug down on the coffee table, pulled the sleeves of her jumper over her hands and curled back into the sofa. 'Goes without saying that you have a friendly ear willing to listen if you want to offload some of that?'

He choked on another laugh, because in that moment he realised two things: one, he'd never spoken to anyone about the pressure he was now under, running his hotel empire alongside his father's global security company. Made worse by his father's inability to let the latter go.

And two, he was about to spill it all to Cassie. Not the caricature the press liked to flaunt. Poised, shy, scandalous or otherwise. But the very real, very warm, very attractive brunette, curled up on the sofa beside him. Patiently waiting for him to speak as though she had all the time in the world for it. For him.

And it felt like bliss.

A sensation he'd never quite experienced before… The world and his wife could wait…or rather, the global companies on his shoulders could. And as though summoned, his phone began to ring, and he checked the screen.

It was Eduardo. CEO of Dad's—*his*—security firm.

Eduardo was capable. He'd been his father's number two for twenty years. He could cope for a day. A *Satur*day. He should just ignore it, follow her lead and hide out from the noise.

'Do you need to get that?' she asked.

Did he? He was a few months into his reign. Would it do for Eduardo to report back to Dad—which he would do at some point—that he was deflecting calls?

But you're the boss.

Still, he needed Dad to back off, which he wasn't going to do if he thought Hugo wasn't getting the job done. 'Give me two minutes.'

'So, LA?' Cassie said as he returned to her, his phone tucked away, his smile enigmatic.

'Yes.'

She imagined him, the broad-shouldered man before her with his kind blue eyes and chiselled features, as a son. With a doting mother and a proud father. She could see it so readily. The warm and happy picture painting itself. Could see them all walking down the palm-lined strip of Sunset Boulevard or Rodeo Drive, places she too had been. But she believed her experience to have been so very different.

'My parents—or rather, my mother has decided they should retire out there.'

'Sounds lovely.'

'My mother thinks so.'

'You don't?'

'Oh, I do.'

She frowned. 'So, it's your father who doesn't?'

'My father thinks any home that's not on the same continent as the company headquarters he has been forced to leave behind is anything but lovely.'

'I take it the company headquarters are here?'

'*Oui.*'

'And he likes to keep a toe in?'

'A toe?' He chuckled, the sound deep and throaty as it rippled through his burly frame and did something unidentifiable to her own. Something that felt awfully close to excitement. 'He likes to keep his whole body in.'

'Was he not ready to retire?'

He eased back into the sofa, one arm along its back, one leg hooked over the other by the ankle, everything about him relaxed, though she sensed that, like a panther, he was never far from pouncing should the need arise. She knew he had the physique for it, beneath the crisp dark shirt, the carefully pressed chinos too.

'If I'm brutally honest, I think my mother feared we'd be carrying him out of his company in a box. At first it was getting him out of the field, then it was getting him to simply stop.'

She frowned. 'The field? You make the hospitality industry sound like the military.'

He gave another chuckle. 'Oh, we're not in the same business. Well, we weren't. We are now. Or at least I am.' He paused. Took a breath. 'I'm not making much sense, am I?'

She smiled. 'Perhaps it's your turn to start at the beginning.'

'You're right, I should.' He returned her smile, though it lacked the warmth that had existed moments ago, and she wondered at its cause. Was it his father? The business? Businesses, if they weren't one and the same. And the recent stress he'd eluded too? 'My father's company, now mine since he retired, is in the business of protection—money, data, people—if there's a risk, we protect it.'

'So, you're in leisure *and* protection... How come you ventured into one when your father was in the other?'

'I guess you could say, I carved out my own path.'

There was something about the way he said it. Something that made her want to delve deeper, like a child wanting to ask 'why?' on repeat. And perhaps she would have if he hadn't said, 'but he always intended for me to take on his firm one day, when he felt I was ready.'

'And how old is your father?'

'He celebrated his seventy-fifth birthday while I was in LA.'

'Seventy-fifth!'

'Quite. And I say *celebrated* in the loosest sense of the term. The man does not take kindly to growing old.'

'But growing old is a privilege.'

'Of that he would agree, he just doesn't appreciate the ailments that come with it.'

'Or the retirement?' Because to wait until one was seventy-five to hand over the reins...?

'Or the son who has filled his shoes.'

She stilled, caught off guard by the unexpected bitterness in the man who, up until now, had been the biggest, strongest, cuddliest, and sexiest of teddy bears if such a thing were to exist. 'I'm sure that's not true.'

He fell silent, his gaze shifting to the outdoors as she lost him to his thoughts. Maybe she'd been too quick to paint Hugo's family as picture-perfect. But it was a habit she'd formed long ago. Imagining what everyone else's life was like to avoid having to think about her own.

'I don't know, it's complicated for him.' He gave an awkward shrug. 'To see his son grow stronger as he gets weaker. Especially when things were so much harder for him. Hell, at my age he was fleeing Poland with nothing more than the clothes on his back...' His mouth twisted to the side as he stroked the stubble of his chin, admiration flashing in his eyes. 'And that's another secret I probably shouldn't share, especially when it isn't mine to give...'

'I think we've already established that secrets are safe here.'

She tucked a hand around her legs as his gaze returned to her. Gave him a smile that she hoped would encourage him because she had shared so much of herself, and she hoped he felt secure enough to share a little of himself too. He returned her smile and for a moment, they shared nothing but that look, though she felt it—the connection, the warmth of it. It caught at the air, at her breath, at her pulse...

'My father was part of the Służba Bezpieczeństwa—the SB, Poland's secret police,' he added at her raised brow. 'He didn't agree with Soviet rule, wanted out and he came to Paris. Went into security. It suited his natural talents. He met Mum. Fell in love. They got married. He took her name. And the rest as they say, is history. He built a home and a global security firm that protects everything from data to individuals. He left Poland with nothing. No family, no support. And I guess, I grew up with all of that...'

She frowned. 'But why would that make it hard for him to hand the business over to you now? Surely he can't begrudge what he gave you.'

It didn't make any sense to her. The man should surely be

proud that he had provided for his family and their future. Escaped a life that he hadn't wanted for himself or for his future family. And to see his son take on the mantle of his firm…

'I think it's more that his life made him hard, whereas he perceives me as the opposite.'

'I still don't follow.'

A shadow chased over his face. A shadow she wanted to catch and probe and soothe away. But before she could press, he shifted forward. Gave an awkward laugh. Changing the mood up so entirely she didn't feel she could.

'I'm not sure I do either. I'm rambling.'

'I don't think you are. I'm just trying to piece it together.'

'How did we get to this point again?'

He gave her a lopsided grin that made her stomach flip over. Almost making her forget the sombre mood of seconds before.

'I think you were telling me how you ended up responsible for two global companies in two very different industries.'

'Ah, yes. And I went off on a tangent telling you all about how my father doesn't want to give up what he built, despite building me to give it to…'

'That's quite the conundrum.'

'It is, and so when I went to LA last week, I gifted him a digi-detox for his birthday in the hope that it would gift me some temporary quiet in return.'

She laughed. 'You did *what*?'

'It's one of my most exclusive resorts—a Caribbean haven, cut off from the outside world. No comms, only paradise. A true digital detox for a month. No expense spared. They should have checked in yesterday.'

'And your father was happy to receive such a gift?'

'I'm not sure *happy* was the word I would use, but desperate times call for desperate measures. He needs to find a new way of living, and I'm hoping a month on the island with a life coach and other specialists in their fields will help retrain his brain. And my mother will get a holiday.'

'Is he really that bad?'

'Put it this way, in the three months my father has been retired, he has called me almost daily for an update. Between him and his number two—now my number two, Eduardo, the man who just called—I'm on speed dial. I figured at least this way he's forced to try a new way of living and Mum gets to relax.'

'And you get some peace.'

'One can hope.'

'And no more sleepwalking.'

'That's the dream,' he teased.

'What about Eduardo? What does he make of your father's constant check-ins?'

'Eduardo could run the company with his eyes closed. He knows what he's doing, my father just never left him alone enough.'

'And yet, he is the one ringing you on a Saturday?'

'More out of habit than necessity.'

'I see. And is that a habit you intend to break.'

He paused. 'Perhaps. Right now, my priority is exerting my authority. For forty years my father was the boss. Now I am, and it's important that they know that. My father included.'

She heard the vehemence in that one statement. The fierce sense of ownership. Whether he was trying to prove it to himself or his non-present father or employees, it spoke volumes.

'And you will. And you will do him proud too.'

He gave a grunt.

'But you need to be your own man in the process. Don't

lose yourself in trying to become him. You need to do it your own way.'

She didn't know where the words came from, or why it felt so important that she said them. Perhaps it was the sense that he was battling a vision of the man his father wanted him to be, rather than simply being the man he was…and she knew how that felt. How it felt to be caged by someone else's ideal.

His clear blue eyes narrowed on her. 'You know, for a morning coffee, this got deep pretty quickly.'

'And there was I, thinking we couldn't get much closer than last night's escapade.'

'You're not going to let me forget that, are you?'

She gave him a smile full of the warmth she felt inside. 'It will be nice to get to know you well enough to let you forget, Hugo.' Because she wanted to get to know him better. She wanted to make a friend. A true friend. Not one that was looking for a way into Princess Cassandra's inner circle. But one that she could confide in and who could talk to her in return. 'If you will come for coffee again?'

'I'd like that, Cassie. Very much.'

CHAPTER FOUR

THE NEXT MORNING Hugo was eating his breakfast while reviewing the financial headlines when his phone started to ring. He checked the ID. Mickie. On a Sunday. This early?

His friend rarely saw 8:00 a.m. on a weekday, let alone on a Sunday.

What kind of mischief had his friend got into now?

He swiped the call to answer and prepared himself for the worst. Of course, there was nothing to say Mickie wasn't on the other side of the globe in which case it would be late rather than early for him. And that probably made the potential trouble worse...

'Hugo, my friend, you got something you want to tell me?'

'I don't know that I do, since you're the one calling me?'

Mickie's laugh rumbled down the phone. 'So that's how you're going to play it?'

'Play what?' Hugo put down the toast he was about to bite into. 'It's too early for riddles, Mickie.'

'Come on, don't be coy! Fancy my surprise this morning when I wake up to see you plastered all over the celebrity gossip channels.'

'The *what*?'

'Funny, you sound about as shocked as I was.'

'Is this some joke?' Hugo pressed his forehead into his palm and took a breath. It really was too early for this.

'Skylar, chuck us that remote...' his friend said.

'Skylar?' Hugo repeated. 'Who's...?'

'My date from last night. You didn't think I was the one catching up with the celeb goss, did you?'

Hugo didn't know what to think. Didn't *want* to think for fear of what was happening outside his four walls if Mickie knew all about it and thought it was worthy of this kind of a call.

'Thank you, darl.'

'For what?' Hugo said.

'I wasn't talking to you.'

Clearly, but...

'Get yourself onto Celeb 101, Hugo. Your mug's right there, right now.'

'Celeb 101?'

'Use the TV guide...you'll have it there somewhere. Right next to those 24-7 reality TV channels...'

Like Hugo would know where any of those were either... but on autopilot, he switched on the TV embedded in the wall above his sleek black countertop. Searched the guide with rising trepidation. Especially as his phone started to chime with another incoming call, then another. He eyed the screen. One was Eduardo, another was his PA.

This wasn't good. His skin started to crawl, the hairs on

his neck rising. There was only one reason he could have made that kind of news…one reason only…

'You found it yet?'

Just. He clicked on the channel and the screen filled with a pimped-up news studio starring living, breathing Ken and Barbie lookalikes seated behind a desk. A fuchsia-pink ticker tape ran along the bottom spewing out 'news'. And there, in the top right corner of the screen were photos. Photos of *them*. Cassie and Hugo. Him on her doorstep with the flowers. Her with her naked shoulder, all flushed and—*for the love of…*

'In the two years since her separation from Prince Georges,' the Barbie lookalike was saying, 'speculation has mounted over the breakdown of what was once considered the marriage of the decade if not the century. A real life fairy tale has become a tale of tragedy. People were quick to blame it on the Playboy Prince, his reputation making him an easy target, but with stories surrounding the Princess, friends and ex-lovers selling stories to the tabloids, and now this latest scandal, it really does beg the question, do we truly know who this woman is? We were so quick to adore her, yet here she is jumping from the bed of one man to another, the seal on her divorce barely dry. And who is this man? Our very own Suzie is out in the field to tell us more…'

'Got to hand it to you, man, I didn't know you had it in you.'

He'd forgotten Mickie was on the line. He'd forgotten the world existed. He'd forgotten everything but the woman next door and the impact such a report was going to have on her.

Such a ridiculous report, but a report out in the world all the same. And one with a picture to back it up. A picture he might as well have handed to the greedy mob pounding the pavement outside…

Taken inside *his* hotel, on *his* watch, on *his* floor.
'Merde!'

Cassie hadn't slept. Not properly. She kept tossing and turning, feeling the after-effects of Hugo's presence well into the night. The apartment had never felt so vast and so empty... even with Louis's abundance of ornamental delights.

She'd become accustomed to her own company long ago. Being in her own company amongst others most of all. Loneliness was something she'd learnt to live with rather than bemoan. And normally she would throw her restlessness into her designs or lose herself in the pages of a good book. Always something creative if she could choose.

But she'd been left with this frenetic energy that she just couldn't shift, so here she was on the treadmill, trying her second run of the morning because all else had failed. She increased her speed because a jog wasn't working. Turned the volume on her music up too.

A sprint to Taylor Swift full blast—this *had* to work, surely?

She snatched up her towel from the rail on the treadmill to swipe away the layer of perspiration already thick across her skin. Adjusted her earbuds. Slugged her water. And felt Swift's lyrics to her core as she pounded the rolling road beneath her feet.

For years she'd worked hard to be the woman her family had wanted her to be, eager to please them, eager for a kind word too. Then it had been all about the Prince and *his* family. Trading one impossible mission for another.

She hadn't stopped to think about her own happiness in any of it. She'd been too focused on their happiness equating to her own. Now she'd finally broken free. Finally realised the only person she could truly depend on for her own happiness was herself. And to achieve it, she needed to find herself. Who she was without the noise of the outside world and the constraints she'd lived her life bound by thus far. And she was getting there. Kind of.

So why did she feel all at sea again?

She had no clue and she wasn't hopping off this treadmill until the noise in her brain resembled something more like the quiet she had found of late. The quiet of—

The ring of the apartment's ancient doorbell broke through Swift's triumphant chorus, and she checked the time. Frowned. It was still early. Not that the time made any difference to her surprise. She wasn't expecting anyone.

Room service had already been and gone with her breakfast plates. That day's housekeeping too. It came again, more insistent. She hadn't imagined it.

She hit the pause button and grabbed her towel, headed to the door.

It couldn't be Hugo. It had been a day. Twenty-four hours since their impromptu coffee date. Her eyes caught on the flowers he had brought her, the classic white bouquet blooming bright and beautiful in the hallway. He had no reason to call again so soon. Unless—she smiled helplessly into her towel—he too had found himself in some curious state of limbo since he'd vacated her orbit. How weird that would be.

Weird and kind of wonderful if she was being totally honest with herself.

Careful, Cassie, don't be getting carried away.

Especially over a man like Hugo, who would be so easy to get carried away by…

She was supposed to be focusing on herself and what she wanted from life.

But what if that something was a six-foot-four hunk of male charm?

And that was precisely the kind of want that would land her in trouble. The kind of trouble her ex and the rest of the royal family would use to their advantage and she would do well to avoid. Though who was to say he was interested in her in the same way? She hardly had the best track record when it came to reading others. Case in point!

Love, affection, desire…what did she truly know of it? A bit fat zero.

Hugo had been kind and understanding, that was all, and now she was likely projecting her own feelings onto him. Just as she had done with Georges in those early days.

She caught her reflection in the free-standing gilt-edged mirror at the end of the hall and grimaced. Both at her thoughts and at her flushed state of disarray. Hardly present-able. Unless one was trying out for a sports advertisement, and even then she'd leave a lot to be desired. She lacked the glow of sun exposure for a start.

And here she was, debating her appearance like it was him on the other side of the door, projecting her hopes, when it was probably—

The doorbell rang again, and this time Hugo's urgent cry came with it, 'Cassie!'

Okay, so it *was* him, but his voice…

With a sharp frown, she swiftly unbolted the door and yanked it wide. 'Hugo, what's wrong?'

'Cassie, Dieu merci!'

He grabbed her arms and she stiffened, heat surging to her already scorched core. Tiny, frenzied currents, the likes of which she'd never felt before and barely understood now, zipping through her and spreading fast.

She gawped up at him and he cursed, his hands falling away as he stepped back to give her space.

'*Désolé*. I shouldn't have.'

She closed her mouth, swallowed. What was going on within her? Desire? Is that what this was? The heat, the fire, the need…because Georges had never done this to her. Not with a simple grasp of his hands.

'You *are* okay?' His desperate gaze raked over her. 'Aren't you?'

Answer him…

She nodded, her unease building by the second. Because the words coming out of his mouth suggested something was wrong. Very wrong. And it was pressing back the heat his contact had stirred up, common sense overriding her body as she forced the words through her teeth, 'What's wrong?'

'You don't know?' He dragged a hand down his face. 'You haven't seen the news? How can you—can I come in?'

'So many questions, Hugo.' She gave a shaky laugh, clutched her towel beneath her chin as goose-bumps prickled across her skin. Aware more than ever that she was wearing nothing more than an exercise bra and cropped shorts.

'And I'm not the only one with questions, believe me.'

A trickle ran down her spine, the chill on the rise as she dabbed at her cheeks, which felt fuzzy and faint. 'You're scaring me.'

'I know and I'm sorry, Cassie. But it's best we talk inside.'

She backed up, making enough space for him to enter as he swung the door closed on them both. Though she didn't move from the vestibule. Her stomach rolling too much to put one foot in front of the other.

'What is it?' she said to his back as he made his way into

the living area, scanning the room like one would for danger, checking every nook, every cranny.

'Hugo?'

'I thought you would have seen. I thought you weren't answering because you *had* seen, and you were—I don't know. Despairing. Panicking. Packing!'

He rubbed the back of his head, up and down, eyes chasing over the objects in the room, anywhere but her, and slowly she joined him.

'How could you not have heard the commotion out there?'

He threw a hand towards the balcony and the muted sounds beyond. Granted, there was more noise coming from the street than usual. But she'd long ago stopped listening to what happened outside the four walls she was in. Beyond the conversation she was involved in too. The whispered words of judgement, the gossip, and the snide remarks.

'Hugo,' she said softly, wishing to steady him, because she sensed that whatever this was, it had more to do with her than it did him. And she was used to her own baggage, he didn't need to carry it for her. 'Whatever it is, I am sure it can't be as bad as—'

'Someone saw me come to your room yesterday morning,' he said as he paced up and down. 'They took a photograph and it's everywhere. *We're* everywhere.'

Cassie's heart did a weird little dance, rising part-way up her throat. 'What do you mean, *we're* everywhere?'

Though she knew, of course she knew. She'd been the subject of enough tittle-tattle over the years to know exactly what he meant. But she was stalling. Biding her time while she processed it.

'I'm sorry, Cassie.'

He stilled, his eyes finding hers. She saw the guilt weighing heavy in his crystal-clear blue eyes. Saw the guilt as she also imagined the glee in her ex-husband's face.

'The world thinks we're together. That you and I—' He shook his head. 'I'm sorry. I don't know how this could have happened, and had I known the trouble I would cause you by coming to your room with flowers and—and the kind of headlines it would stir up…'

Slowly she brought her hand back to her chest, steadied herself against the onslaught of what was to come—what was already happening out there. The Duponts wouldn't hang around. They'd be straight on this salacious piece of ammo, using it to elevate Georges's reputation and sully hers.

And all because she'd had the gall to get up and walk away.

'I don't understand how you didn't know.'

Hugo snapped her back into the present, his face blazing with concern and obliterating Georges from her mind.

'My phone is always on Do Not Disturb,' she said, her voice devoid of emotion. Because this wasn't Hugo's fault. This wasn't hers. And this *would* blow over. It was the nature of the beast. She just had to keep it in perspective. 'I don't watch live TV. I don't listen to the radio. Only the people that I care about and want to hear from get through, the rest I mute.'

'But out there, the noise…' He gestured towards the balcony once more…at the commotion outside that suggested there were more vehicles. More press. More people. The hotel would be cursing her name. *He* would be cursing her name. 'I'm sorry, I will sort myself somewhere else to stay as soon as possible. This is the last thing you and your guests need.'

'Oh, no, you won't. You're fine to stay here.'

'But Hugo…'

'I mean it, Cassie. Louis gifted you his home, and I stand by that offer.'

The stubborn set to his jaw, the flash of steel in his blue eyes told her he meant it. 'I'm sorry.'

'You don't need to apologise to me.'

'Oh, I do. Because if they're making something out of this, I'm sure you're not coming off too lightly either. If not in today's news reports, then tomorrow's. Georges and his ego will see to it.'

'I couldn't care less about myself in all of this. It's you I'm worried about. You must have a PR team, a spokesperson you can liaise with to issue a formal response?'

She gave a soft huff. 'A PR team? Because they don't cost the earth.'

'Right. Of course you don't. We can use mine.'

'No, Hugo. There's no point. They'll print what they want to print. You deny it and they'll think there's more to it. And what are you going to say? Tell them the truth of how we met and tackle *that* tale, too? No. It will blow over. They'll tire of it eventually.'

'And in the meantime, what? You sit back and let them rip apart your character?'

He was so fierce. So ready to fight for her honour. And there was something magical and wonderful and surreal about it. No one had ever looked ready to do battle for her. Not ever.

'Sticks and stones, Hugo.'

'No, Cassie.' He shook his head, legs wide, fists on hips. Fighting stance. 'This happened on my watch, in my hotel. I besmirched your character and I need to fix it.'

'This wasn't your fault.'

He raised his hand. 'It doesn't matter that it wasn't my intent. What's done is done and I will not stand by and have them twist the person you are into someone you are not. You don't deserve it.'

Her heart swooned. *Positively* swooned. 'Then what do you suggest?'

'For starters, I'll be speaking to the head of security. It must have been one of the cleaners from the lift. You can't access this floor without the right pass and there was only me, you, and the staff that morning.'

She shook her head. 'I don't want to cause any more trouble, Hugo. My presence has already caused enough. All the extra security, the extra checks, the chaos outside the doors... I'm a headache for everyone concerned.'

'But what they did was wrong—it needs to be investigated and the person responsible held accountable.'

'I'd rather just let it blow over.'

'That out there isn't blowing over any time soon, and in the meantime, what? You're going to hide away even more?'

'If I have to.'

'No, Cassie. You've lived your entire life on hold for others. It's time you started living it for you, and you have the city of Paris on your doorstep to get outside and enjoy.'

She gave a shaky laugh. 'No one could enjoy Paris hounded by that lot.'

'I think it's high time you tried another strategy.'

Her chin lifted, ears and heart pricking with something akin to hope. 'Like what?'

'I think you should give them more not less.'

'What on earth are you talking about?'

'They think you and I are together so let them think that. Let them think that rather than a fling, a brazen hop from one man's bed to another, that this is more than that. Deeper than that. A romantic tryst in the world's most romantic of cities. And while we give them more, I can give you what you deserve. I can give you Paris. I can show you the delights of the city, get you out of these four walls and out into the real world. Let me make up for my part in what has happened and give you something you're long overdue in return.'

'I told you…' She gave a laugh that sounded as deranged as she suddenly felt, because his idea was making her feel all manner of things. Some crazy. Some fabulous. Some wonderfully thrilling. 'It isn't possible. I can't step foot out of this building without a gaggle of reporters and photographers dogging my every step, without drawing the attention of every innocent passer-by too and causing chaos. It isn't pleasant for anyone.'

'And so you've hidden yourself away. But by hiding your face, you've made it a rarity. Don't you see?'

'What choice do I have?'

'You can choose to give them more not less. And soon your face will be a novelty no more. And that rare photo opportunity will be as common as the next among a million of snaps. Granted, they won't all be of your best side, but if you can learn to live with the odd stray bit of snot or lucky bird poo drop…?'

'Hugo…' She shook her head, laughing at the ridiculousness of it all. Because it was ridiculous—*wasn't* it?

'Think about it, Cassie. It's all about supply and demand, give them more and they will demand less. And in the meantime, you get out of these four walls and live in the real world.'

'And the stories they are spreading, what about those?'

'By hiding away you've allowed the rumours to build, fed the gossip and the whispers, let them draw their own conclusions. Why not paint the tale you'd rather have spread? A love story, however short-lived, is far better than the harlot they seem determined to label you as.'

'Not them,' she said through her teeth.

'What was that?'

'I said, not them. Georges and his family. They're the ones who want to paint me as such. I told you—it suits them to make me look bad. He needs a new wife and quickly, with his father...'

She bit her lip. She'd said too much. She may not have any affection for the Duponts, but there were things she was not permitted to divulge. The King's health and her ex-husband's imminent succession to the throne being two of them.

'He will need to find someone to replace me as his wife. Someone willing to look past his behaviour and provide him with an heir too.'

Something she'd been unable to give him and something at the time she'd seen as another of her many failings. Now, of course, she saw it as a blessing, because to have a child caught up in all of this... She shivered and wrapped her arms around her middle, and Hugo's eyes dipped, a crease forming between his brows as his hands flexed at his sides.

'Do you want to change, and we can talk? I can wait here.'

'No, it's fine.'

He nodded, though his frown didn't ease. 'So, you think the Prince might have had a hand in this—this photograph?'

'I don't know. Maybe. Perhaps.'

'I assume he knows you're staying here.'

'There's not a lot the Prince doesn't know about me. He has his *spies* everywhere.'

'Then he will also know this is nonsense.'

'So long as it works in his favour, he doesn't care about whether it is true or not.'

'In which case, we'll make it work in our favour too.'

'I really don't see how we can spin this into a positive for us.'

'Everyone loves a good love story, Cassie.' And then he grinned, and it lit her up from within. 'You of all people should know this.'

And he was right.

Her marriage to the Playboy Prince had been one such adored tale once upon a time.

Which was why their breakup carried such media weight now.

Were ex-princesses permitted a second chance at love?

Even if the first had never been a love story at all…

'But, Hugo, you have two global companies to run. You don't have the time to spend ferrying me around Paris.'

'I will make the time. I will give Eduardo the autonomy to run the company he has been running for long enough anyway. And I will take a long overdue holiday from the hotel group, let Zara, my number two step in. Besides, it will do wonders for business…just think of the headlines… *Cassie Couture and Chevalier Clubs, a match made in heaven*— you couldn't write it better!'

She laughed wholeheartedly now. 'Hugo! I'm not even out there as a designer yet.'

'Not yet you're not. But you will be if I have my way.'

She shook her head, her chill forgotten. In fact, she felt positively balmy. All thanks to him.

'But I am serious, Cassie. Being seen on your arm can only do great things for Chevalier Clubs, so you have nothing to fear for me on a personal or professional level. And, dare I say it, we enjoy each other's company, and it has been a long time since I have taken any kind of holiday, as my latest night-time misadventures prove, so I am long overdue a break too. You will be doing me a favour as much as I you.'

How could she turn down such an offer?

He was handing her the perfect solution to her current nightmare.

A chance to come out with her reputation intact, protect her dream, and get back out into the land of the living...but was it right to bury one falsehood with another?

And what choice do you have? The Prince threw you to the wolves the second you dared to leave. It's time to push back. Play them at their own game.

'What's that look about?'

'I've never been...*bad* before.'

He gave a low chuckle. 'It's not all that bad, Cassie. You're divorced. Very much single. I'm single in case you need that clarified. There's nothing wrong with us dating. Nothing to say we didn't meet here in this very building—which we did by the way—then hit it off and chose to date. Like millions of people do every day.'

'And you're okay pretending be in a relationship with me?'

A curious spark came alive behind his eyes. 'It would be an honour to escort you around Paris as your friend, and if the world wants to read more into that, then so be it. But if, on the other hand, you wanted to present us as more than that or even go as far as to make a formal statement about us dating, I will do that too. Your wish is my command.'

And now she laughed. Because this truly was crazy. And fun. And no matter what he said, it still felt bad. Very, *very* bad.

'But if it makes you laugh like that...' He took her hand

in his and squeezed, the look in his eyes stealing her breath away. 'I refuse to believe there can be any bad in it.'

And maybe Hugo was right.

One thing was for sure, it was time she got back out in the world. As her. The *real* her.

Not Cassandra, Princess of Sérignone.

But as Cassie. Fighting for the life *she* wanted.

Nobody else.

And with a little help from Hugo, her very hot, very capable next-door neighbour and new-found friend, that feat didn't feel so impossible any more.

CHAPTER FIVE

'YOU READY?'

Hugo hadn't known it was possible to nod and shake your head at the same time, but Cassie had just perfected the move. And the sight amplified his guilt.

The similarity to Sara had been disconcerting before... with their public-facing roles, controlling families, lack of freedom. Poised yet shy. Quiet yet teasing. Kind too.

And to find himself in this position again.

With Sara it had been his fault. He'd thought their love worth outing, worth fighting for, and then he'd almost got her killed.

With Cassie, he had taken her already troubled situation and piled on a whole heap more. And Cassie was right, it wasn't his fault, but it didn't make the situation any better.

And he was determined to make it better.

He was determined that this time, he would get it right.

He would see to it that she was okay. That she would come out of this situation better for knowing him. Not worse.

'It's going to be okay.' He took hold of her hand. 'We have the best security detail looking out for us. A path has been cleared and all you have to do is smile and wave.'

'All?' She gave a tremulous smile, touched her free hand to the braid that fell over one shoulder. It looked simple but he'd warrant she'd spent hours making sure she'd perfected the casual look this morning. The pale pink sweater complemented her English rose complexion. The skinny jeans, knee-high boots, tailored coat and beret gave off every bit the Princess on tour vibe, whether she wanted to or not. Because she had a regal air about her that was all natural. Something her family and the Duponts would have bled dry.

'Or you could do the classic?' he said, pushing away the thoughts that would have seen his fingers crushing hers.

'And what's that?'

'Pretend they're all naked.'

She laughed. 'I thought that was a presentation technique.'

He shrugged. 'Whatever works, right? And once we arrive at the Louvre you will only have eyes for the museum and the architecture anyway.'

Vincent stepped forward. 'The car is ready, Monsieur Chevalier, Princess.'

Cassie's hand tensed around his. He knew she hated the title. But he also knew it was going to take time for the world to drop it. She was their beloved princess, whether she wanted to be referred to as such or not. If she could only see that it came from a place of affection rather than being a cold-hearted stereotype.

No matter the names being thrown about, the slander coming out of the palace, and the trouble Prince Georges was determined to stir up following *that* photograph. It would take more to ruin the woman most of the world at large adored.

And Hugo would do his best to see to it that they continued to adore her.

By fulfilling this role for as long as she required it.

He'd done some extra digging into the Prince of Sérignone, and the more he'd learnt, the more his protective instincts had kicked in. The idea that the Prince had once had any claim over her riled him enough. The fact he now dared to ruin her from afar to save his own face...

Hugo fought the tension coiling through him anew. But the deceit it took to behave like so, the duplicity and the cowardice too. The nerve of the man to transfer his own crimes onto her.

'Hugo?' Her soft prompt brought him back to his senses.

'Shall we?' He released her hand to offer out his elbow, and she gave him the coy smile the cameras knew well. The smile he knew to be as genuine as she was because she *was* nervous, but she wasn't backing down. The nod she gave him now devoid of its contradictory shake.

'Let's go.'

They stepped through the revolving door together and the wall of noise instantly upped, threatening to press them back. He'd anticipated it, of course he had, though nothing could have prepared him for the reality. And though he had worked in the field many years ago, this felt different. But then it was different. This was personal.

And for a split second, he was in another country, another place, another time. And there was another woman beside him. A cold sweat broke out across his skin, the world closed in. Cameras were going off. Blending with the shouts.

A gun. A man.

He turned.

Left. Right. Ahead. *Bang!*

'Boss.' It was the driver in his earpiece, grounding him in the present. 'Are you good?'

Focus. Focus.

His people were doing their job; they were keeping the crowd back. The car was straight ahead. Everything was good. They were waiting for Cassie and him to deliver the agreed smile, a wave, and then he ushered her into the car.

'Are you okay?' He didn't waste a second to ask.

'Are you?' She blinked up at him. Concern glittering in a sea of green. The black interior all around and the smell of leather, a reassuring cocoon.

'You think to ask me that?'

'I'm used to this, but you...'

He checked her seat belt was secure before fastening his own. 'I know this scene well enough.'

'They were calling your name as much as mine.'

They were also 'name-calling,' but he didn't feel the need to point that out. Not when she could hear it for herself. And though those names were only few and far between, they were the ones that would've landed the loudest and the hardest.

'Drive on,' he urged their driver, his chest too tight for comfort.

'It wasn't as bad as I feared.'

His eyes snapped to hers. 'No?'

Was she mad? Delirious or on something?

She smiled up at him. 'No. Though you're making me question myself now.'

Yes! He mentally cursed. *Get a hold of yourself. You were the one taking a trip down memory lane. Not her. Dieu Merci.*

'You were exceptional.' He righted his jacket, gave a brusque nod and a smile. 'As calm and as regal as a—'

'Don't say it, please.'

'*Désolé*. You took it in your stride, Cassie. No one will have known that inside you were feeling any different... I'm glad you found it okay.'

'That's because you were there.'

She met his eyes, her own big and wide, her vulnerability genuine and tugging on his heartstrings. Strings he never left exposed. Not since Sara—

And that's why you're freaking out now. And you're supposed to be making her feel better. Not worse.

'You and your team.'

He took her hand in his once more and gave it a squeeze.

'Good, because you're stuck with us for the foreseeable.'

He held her gaze as the vehicle pulled away from the hotel, the camera flashes hammering against the blackout glass and the noise of the reporters muffled by the whirring in his ears. She truly was stunning. Her smile, her eyes, her trust in him...

He had this...didn't he?

He could keep her safe and give her a glimpse of the life she deserved.

And what about you? And your heart? And those strings you never leave exposed?

It was a short drive to the Louvre. Nowhere near long enough to ease the tension that had built throughout his body with the flashback that had come from nowhere. But he forced himself to appear at ease for her sake.

Now he just had to hope all went smoothly, because he sensed that his skittish kitten was only one pit bull away from scurrying back to Louis's and he was determined to see this day through. The first of many outings he had planned if all went well…

As for his own tension, he'd deal with that later. If he had to go ten rounds in the ring with Mickie, he'd do whatever it took to exorcise that demon once again.

And be there for Cassie now.

Cassie had felt the impenetrable shield form around her the moment they had left the hotel.

And for someone who had spent years behind a security detail, indeed being directed by one, this felt different. And she knew that was down to Hugo. Something about this great big bear of a man, with warm eyes and a strong sense of honour, made her feel like nothing could hurt her.

No camera flash or threat from afar. No snide remark or snarky look.

Never had her family or the Prince made her feel quite so invincible.

With her head held high, she walked the grounds and the halls of the Louvre, in awe of its beauty and its art. Its history and its majesty. And it was wonderful. To breathe in the air and the space and be amongst the people too.

They'd even paused and conversed with a few groups. Taken an extended break when Cassie hadn't been able to resist a group of children who had likened Hugo to a real-life superhero. And he'd spent at least twenty minutes 'flexing' his muscles to whatever feat they had devised. Something their teacher had indulged since they were on their lunch break. Though Cassie got the impression it had more to do with Maîtresse's pleasure than the children.

'I think she liked you…'

'Huh?'

'The teacher…are you *blushing* Hugo?'

'Non.'

She paused, forcing him and his team to pause too as she peered up at him. 'Yes, you are.'

'I do not blush.'

She pursed her lips. 'Whatever you say, but for the record, I'm more than happy to share the limelight.'

And he chortled at that, clearly pleased to have her so at ease.

Because she was at ease. Surprisingly so.

She couldn't care that the headlines that morning had been less than kind. That they had smacked of the Prince's skilled spin doctors. She was living in the moment, thanks to him. And the more she thought about his whole idea, the rules of supply and demand, it really did make sense.

'This really is wonderful, Hugo. Truly. Thank you.'

'You're welcome. Now, are you hungry?'

Was she? She hadn't thought about food at all. Her senses were too busy being overloaded by the sights, sounds, and scents of Paris, having spent the last month cooped up in Louis's apartment. But she must be.

It had been many hours since breakfast—a coffee and the smallest dollop of yogurt on fruit had been all she could manage with the nervous churn, courtesy of the headlines.

'I reckon I could eat.'

'That's lucky.'

'Lucky?'

To their left, a grand doorway had been roped off and a liveried footman bowed his head to them both.

She frowned. 'Hugo, what's this?'

'I believe it is the location for dinner.'

'In the Louvre? But the restaurant is back…'

'I thought you might enjoy some privacy for our meal.'

'But I thought the whole point was to give them more and they will demand less?'

'But I'm also a firm believer in balance. There will be a gazillion photos from this morning, Cassie. Now *this* is for you.'

He placed his hand in the small of her back, and she caught the sudden gasp that wanted to escape. It wasn't like his hand was hot. Or that she could feel his palm's heat through her coat, the cashmere of her sweater or the silk of her camisole but she *felt* it.

'This?' The question was more breath than spoken word.

'You'll see...'

He led her through the door that was now being held open to them. A classical tune played softly through some invisible sound system, and inside, the rich red walls created an intimate backdrop for the table that had been lavishly laid out for two with a gold candelabra adorned with white roses at its heart. And to the side, glass cabinets had been rolled in on wheels, each displaying pieces of art.

She sent him a questioning look, unable to form a word.

'When you've worked in the hospitality industry for as long as I have, you build up an extensive contact list...and the odd favour or two.'

'*This* was a favour?'

He didn't reply, only smiled as she made her way over to one of the cabinets. Hand to her throat because she couldn't believe any of this was real. That Hugo had organised this. It was too much. Too sweet. Too thoughtful.

'I arranged for them to be brought from the Prints and Drawings Study Room. They can only be viewed by appointment anyway, and I thought...well, enjoy.'

She looked down and gave a soft chuckle. 'The Gallery of Fashion by Heideloff... You brought these here.'

He came up behind her. 'Not me *personally...*'

She gave him the elbow. 'Funny.'

'Like I already told you, I don't know much about fashion, but a quick search of the Louvre brought up this collection, and I thought since we're here, it might inspire you with your work and...'

He leaned over her shoulder to take a closer look, his warmth, his masculine woody scent enveloping her as he did so. She felt her eyes threaten to close, the desire to savour the moment as ludicrous as it was real.

'Though looking at them now, I can see how foolish *that* was.'

She forced her eyes to widen at his sarcasm, forced herself to take in the beauty of the drawings that were over two hundred years old. 'Hugo! They're of their time, but no less exquisite!'

'Of their time? How you women managed to sit down let alone put one foot in front of the other in all those skirts is beyond me.'

'But look how delicate they are, and who doesn't love a good fan?'

He gave a soft chuckle.

'You laugh, but back then a fan could convey a multitude of secret messages.'

'Right,' he drawled.

'I'm serious! They weren't just a beautiful accessory but a way of communicating with a lover or a would-be suitor...it could be as innocent as declaring your wish to stay friends or as ardent as "I love you".'

She could feel her cheeks warm under his gaze, though

she kept her own fixed on the images beneath the glass. They truly were beautiful.

'Seems dangerously open to interpretation to me. I'm a literal man. You've got to tell me how it is.'

She laughed. 'I'll remember that—*not that we're...*'

She let her words trail away with the background music as her blush deepened further. The effect of his body so close behind her, enough to make her feel like he was a furnace in full flame.

'Monsieur. Madam. Dinner is ready if you are?'

An older gentleman entered the room and she sidestepped away, feeling oddly caught in the act. The act of what she wasn't sure. Only that her blush made her look as guilty as she felt. But to have someone other than Hugo address her as something other than princess...to know that Hugo must have had a word...that he had done all of this for her too. She was walking on air and her smile filled her face.

'Favours go a long way,' Hugo whispered in her ear, his hot breath rushing through her veins as his thoughtfulness continued to warm her heart. 'Henri, it is so good to see you again.' Hugo swung away from her to greet him. His hand-shake and arm clutch the kind one would give an old friend, not an acquaintance delivering on a favour.

'And you, sir. I trust everything is as you wanted.'

'Impeccable, merci.'

She felt the older man's curious gaze drift to her and she kept her gaze lowered. She was giving too much away. For a woman used to locking her true feelings and thoughts in-side, this was definitely too much. But then she wasn't used to someone doing such things for her. Such deep and mean-ingful things. And she felt overwhelmed. Tearful even.

'And you're sure you want us to leave the food to the side?'

'Absolutely, Henri, we will serve ourselves. We have everything we need.'

And they did, because as the two men talked, another two delivered trolleys laden with food and drink. More than she and Hugo could ever hope to consume in their time here.

'All we require now is privacy.'

'And for that you have come to the right place.'

'Thank you, Henri.'

Henri clipped his heels together and bowed. *'Bon appetit, monsieur...madame.'*

'Merci,' she managed to say with a shaky smile.

'Do you want to help yourself while I pour us a drink?' Hugo said, checking the labels on the bottles. 'Would you like some wine or some champagne perhaps?'

'Champagne would be lovely.'

Because it truly would. And, *oh, my,* she simpered on over to the exquisitely arranged trolley. What on earth was wrong with her? She was used to people going overboard to make her feel welcome when she visited establishments. To serve and to lavish her with the best they had to offer, but this was so different to all of that.

Just as Hugo's protection felt different to all that had come before.

'Are you okay?'

She sensed his frown rather than saw it, because for the life of her she couldn't look at him. Not with the tears in her eyes, and the chaotic race of her thoughts and her feelings.

'Of course. This is incredible, Hugo.' She focused on filling her plate with all manner of delicacies, not that she saw a single one. 'I'm just a little overcome, if I'm honest.'

'But you must be used to such attention? I know you're not used to serving yourself dinner but for the rest...'

She spun to face him. 'No, Hugo!' She placed the plate down before she dropped it, her entire body trembling as she shook her head. 'I'm not used to any of this!'

He paled as he straightened from the table—champagne forgotten. 'Cassie?'

'I'm sorry! It's just too sweet. Too thoughtful. Too—just too much! *All* of it. Georges knew my passion for fashion. And that rhymed and it wasn't meant to rhyme.' She gave a laugh that sounded as silly and as stupid and as ungracious as she suddenly felt. 'But never would he have thought to arrange such a private viewing. So intimate and thoughtful and caring. Yet here you are, knowing me what—a few days? Whisking me up in this…all of this?' She lifted an unsteady hand to gesture around her at the beauty of it all, her eyes misting over. 'It is too much and yet it is wonderful, and I am so grateful and I am so sorry because I am not behaving like one who is grateful should.'

He was across the room in a heartbeat. His hands wrapped around hers. His body—tall, strong, and warm—before her. 'Breathe, Cassie. Just breathe.'

She did as he commanded. Took a breath and another. Looked up into his eyes that were calm and steady and sure.

'It's okay. You are okay. Nothing can hurt you here. No one can hurt you here.'

She shook her head. 'I don't know how I can repay you for this—this kindness you have shown me.'

'You insult me by suggesting that such an act requires payment. This has been a pleasure shared, Cassie. To see you leave that hotel room has been all the payment I need.'

'But it is too much, all of this. You know I have no money of my own. Not yet.'

'I care not for your money but your happiness.'

And there was such strength to those words, such warmth to his touch, his hands caressing her own, his body pressed so close to hers that she felt like she could combust on the spot and would still be the most deliriously happy person alive.

'Apologies, Cassie, yet again I overstep.' He broke away from her, so quickly she staggered back. 'Please excuse me.'

She snatched his hand back, eager to reassure. Eager all the more to make him see that this was more on her than it was on him. It was her own insecurity, her own uncertainty about where her head was at, her life and her heart, to know what was and wasn't okay.

Hell, her friends, those people that she could really trust, were few and far between, and he was so new and so dizzying in the way he made her feel, too.

Feelings that, if she was truly honest, she had no experience in understanding or trusting, let alone managing.

Especially when she feared that she was projecting those feelings onto him too.

'There's nothing to excuse...' And leaning up on her tiptoes, she pressed a kiss to his cheek. It was fleeting and barely there and very much driven on impulse. 'Thank you, Hugo. For getting me out of the apartment and for all of this. Georges may bear the title, but as far as fairy tales go, you most definitely befit the role.'

And then she turned away before she said anything more revealing, *did* anything more revealing, and focused on the delicious spread of food to devour rather than the man.

Though, if she were given the freedom of choice, she knew in a heartbeat which would win.

CHAPTER SIX

A FEW DAYS LATER, Hugo knocked on Cassie's door.

He'd called ahead to make sure she was up for a day out. Told her to layer up in outdoor exercise gear and left it at that.

She'd been in the public eye a lot over the past week. Following the success of the Louvre, they'd crammed in plenty—the Palace of Versailles, the Musée d'Orsay, Sacré-Coeur—the list went on and the press were spoilt for choice when it came to pictures and stories. Last night's trip to the opera had been particularly romantic and snap-worthy.

Though today was once again about striking a balance, gifting her Paris and some anonymity in one, and it was either going to be a brilliant surprise or an epic disaster. He couldn't wait to find out which.

The security detail could though. Their faces when he'd told them what they'd be doing…he should have recorded it for his father. That would have made the old man laugh.

Not that his parents knew about Cassie yet, because if

they'd heard, *he* would have heard. And right now, digi-detox land was gifting him more than just a quiet life workwise, it was protecting him from the third degree on a personal level. Because his mother would be all over this, her excitement unbearable.

Almost as unbearable as his father and his work interference.

He was going to have to get ahead of it and tell them the truth *before* his mother got wedding planning. Though he had a few weeks before they were out of digi-prison—his father's choice of name—and that should buy him some time. He could cross that bridge then.

And he'd just tell them the truth. It was a fake relationship to protect a good woman's reputation. Hell, his father might even be proud of him. They were well protected by the firm. And ultimately, Cassie wasn't Sara, so he wasn't about to make a public fool of himself. They would manage the breakup, when it came to it, with dignity on both sides. No harm, no foul. Simple.

Her door opened and she smiled up at him, all tentative and unsure as she finished tying her hair back into a pony-tail. 'Will I do?'

He took a second to steady his heart, another to reply…and even then, he paused to look at her, truly look at her. Taking far too much pleasure in drinking her in, but knowing she wanted his honest opinion.

Was there anything this woman couldn't pull off? She was wearing trainers, socks slouched at the ankles, black leggings, and a sports jacket zipped high to her chin—nothing sexy about it but…

Just tell them the truth, he quoted himself back. *But*

which truth? That this is a fake relationship or that you find her sexy?

'Are you windproof?' he said, ignoring the inner taunt as he mentally waved the platonic flag...though he might as well have waved a red rag to a bull. 'We're not due any rain but without any cloud cover the wind has a bite to it.'

'I'll be good.' She pursed her lips. Green eyes sparkling. 'Thanks, Mum. And that's a compliment by the way, because my mum was all about how we looked and *not* whether we caught our death.'

His cheeks warmed while his heart chilled over the woman he'd now been able to put a face to thanks to one of his late night googling sessions while catching up on some work. Yes, he'd taken some overdue holiday, but there were some things he couldn't just drop last minute, not at his level.

'Of course she was. But just in case, do you have a buff?'

'A what?'

'A neck warmer? Something you can pull up over your face?'

Which would also have the added benefit of concealing her lips from view...lips which seemed to get more alluring and distracting by the day. And how was that even possible?

She unzipped her pocket and pulled out a tube of fleece from her pocket, her smile proud as punch. 'You mean one of these.'

A brusque nod. 'That'll do. Let's go.'

'Wait.' She grabbed his arm as he started to race away, and he had to resist the urge to snatch it back as the connection thrummed through his veins, leaving him craving more of the same. 'Do I need my purse, a drinks bottle, snacks, anything else?'

'Everything else is taken care of.'

She gave him a peculiar look. 'You going to tell me what we're doing?'

'You'll find out soon enough.'

She let him go and closed her door. 'Are you always so mysterious?'

He didn't reply and she hooked her fingers in his as they headed for the elevator. A connection they had come to do so often when in company of late that she obviously did it now, and ordinarily it would be fine. But they weren't in company yet, and there was no one around to put a damper on what she had sent licking along his veins...

'What's that frown for?'

'Huh?'

She was pressing the button for the lift, but her green eyes were very much on him.

'Nothing.'

'Liar. I've not known you very long, Hugo, but I know when you're pensive about something.'

The elevator pinged, launching him back to the discomfort of *that* night and the present moment in one, and he propelled himself inside as soon as the doors slid open, taking her with him.

'Hugo?'

His eyes slid to hers.

Nom de Dieu, she's had enough dishonesty in her life... just give her something.

'If you really must know, I was thinking that I'll have to come clean to my parents about our relationship and the reasons behind it at some point.'

'Oh, goodness, of course.' Her eyes flared up at him. 'I'm sorry I hadn't even considered it. How thoughtless of me!'

'Hey.' He squeezed her hand. 'These are my parents, my

concern, and we don't need to worry about them just yet. They're still enjoying my birthday gift, remember? We have a few weeks' grace.'

'You reckon news isn't going to slip through the resort's net?' She gave a dubious laugh. 'I can't imagine any place on this earth being *that* secure.'

'Depends on how desperate you are to get a fix, I guess.'

'Your father strikes me as the kind to get his hands on a phone at the very least.'

'If he does, the last thing my father will be checking is the celebrity news.'

She gave another laugh. 'True. Though are you sure one of your staff isn't going to let something slip about the boss of the hotel chain? Especially when the father of said boss is a guest…'

'I think that makes them all the more likely to be discreet, don't you?'

'You put a lot of faith in your staff.'

'I do.'

She eyed him from beneath her lashes.

'What's that look about?'

She chewed the corner of her mouth.

'Cassie?'

'Did you find out who took the photo?'

He clenched his jaw. He hadn't wanted her to ask because he hadn't wanted to tell her, but he wouldn't lie. 'Yes.'

'And?'

'It's been dealt with.'

'Hugo, please…?'

'She was a young, single mum. Desperate for the money. She passed all the checks, there was no reason for my team to be concerned. Though we can assure you changes are being made to avoid the same thing happening again.'

'I see.' She fell silent for a moment then, 'Did you report her to the police?'

She sounded sad, forlorn, and his mouth twisted to the side as he thought of the young woman's face, the evidence of drug addiction too obvious to ignore.

'No, Cassie. I did not. Vincent has put her in touch with a women's support group that his wife is involved in. Hopefully getting help that way will set her on a path to a better future.'

She looked up at him, the golden light of the lift sparkling in her emerald depths.

'What's that look about?'

'I'm not sure you want to know.'

'No?'

She shook her head. Her ponytail sashaying down her back and taunting him further.

'Cassie…' It was a low growl and she nipped her lip, eyes still sparkling.

'You really don't, Hugo.'

He reached out and hit the emergency stop button. 'I'll be the judge of that.'

Her eyes flared. 'Hugo! You can't stop the lift.'

'It's my lift, I can do what I like. Now, I gave you the truth, so out with it.'

She lifted her chin, the defiant angle triggering a rush of heat south. 'If you really must know, you give off this Mr Suave Sophisticated Hotelier Tough Guy vibe, but you're as soft as they come, Mr Chevalier. An absolute teddy bear! And you should be out in the suburbs setting up a home with some lovely woman and popping out glorious mini-Chevaliers with hearts as good as their papa's.'

Her finger was pressed into his chest by the time she had finished her little speech. Her cheeks were streaked with the passion of her words and her mouth was parted on her last breath and her eyes held his, fierce and determined.

'Is that so?'

And hell, she could have said anything, done anything and he would have taken it, because in that moment she was glorious, impassioned, and so far removed from the wallflower who had been hiding out in her room that first morning.

'It is so.'

'Monsieur, madame, quel est le problème avec l'ascenseur?'

Hugo looked up at the camera above his head, to where Vincent was likely eyeing them in confusion and gave an apologetic wave.

'Tout va bien, Vincent.'

He sent the lift back on its journey to the basement, where his team were waiting to kit them out with their mode of transport for the day. And counted his lucky stars for the camera keeping watch and his team that would continue to keep watch. All holding him to account that day and every other day, because what he'd been about to do no one should have witnessed.

And his good conscience should not have permitted. He was supposed to be helping Cassie on a journey to a better life, not complicating it.

As for what she'd said, it was so close to what his mother had been begging him for since he'd turned thirty. But as he'd made clear, he had no interest in going there. His relationship with Sara had left him scarred not just physically but emotionally. And whilst the former had healed, the latter not so much. And his mother knew it.

Knew it and still she pressed, wanting him to move on.

To find love, to trust and have a family of his own. But you couldn't simply stitch the heart back together. It didn't just heal.

A strange warmth crept along his arm and he looked down to find Cassie's thumb caressing the back of his hand. A mindless caress that had him clearing his throat. Did she even know she was doing it?

The lift came to a gentle stop at the basement level, and he pulled his hand free, raked it over his hair.

'I hope you had a hearty breakfast,' he said, more for something grounding to say as the elevator doors opened and they stepped out.

'You know exactly what I had—you sent it.'

'But did you eat it?'

'I ate— Oh, my God, Hugo! You're kidding!' She came to a standstill, her hands pressed to her cheeks as she took in the van ahead with the bikes, the bags, all the equipment and his team...

'It's not quite running but you said you missed the wind in your hair, the freedom. I figured this was the next best thing. And with the helmets and the clothing, no one will even know it's us sneaking out of here on the bikes.'

'They'll work it out at some point.'

'Let them. I think we rock the exercise gear, don't you?'

She laughed, her cheeks warming under his gaze that was likely ablaze with far too much appreciation and not enough jest.

'And your team are up for this?'

'They're all up for it, aren't you, guys?'

There were a few grunts, a few smiles, even some boisterous lunges from the back. 'We have an inconspicuous mix of runners, cyclists, and a car. We're good. We'll get to see some sights and so long as the weather holds, we'll have a late picnic in the Bois de Boulogne. Maybe even spot a red squirrel or two.'

Before he could say anything else, her arms were around his neck, and she was squeezing the very air out of him. 'Thank you!'

'Well, we haven't left yet. This could be my craziest idea so far, cycling and picnicking at this time of year in Paris, but I figured it gave you the best chance of beating the foot traffic.'

She dropped back just enough to look into his eyes. 'See! Teddy bear!'

And then she was racing off to get her bike, and his team were all easy smiles and eager to please because nothing was too much trouble when Cassie was in the room. Nothing whatsoever.

The spell she cast over all around her was as effortless as it was unintentional.

No wonder the Prince was behaving like a man still half mad, a man still half possessed by her...

Hugo had breathed the same air for a week and it might as well have been a year for all he felt overrun by her.

She mounted her white-framed bike and tested out its bell, her laugh lighting up his world, and he accepted that he didn't mind being overrun at all. Not if it meant he was going to get it right this time and she was going to walk away happier for having met him.

And what about you? Are you going to walk away happier? Whole?

But this wasn't about him. This was about her.

Cassie not Sara.

And he had this, he reminded himself firmly. This time, he had it, because he wasn't a man being led by his heart but his head. He was in control. And he would do this to make up for the past and fix the future for a woman who had no one else to fight in her corner for her.

Though if he was honest, he could see her fighting for herself very soon.

Cycling around Paris with Hugo made Cassie wonder why she hadn't thought of getting a bike sooner. With the helmets and all the layers, no one recognised them to begin with. The varying modes of transport meant the team as a whole blended in with the general population, and at their core, they just looked like a group of friends taking a ride out.

And it was amazing. To act the tourist, to *be* a tourist. To be able to stop and take photos, rather than be the subject of them. To have a drink and sample the street food, rather than dine at prearranged times and prebooked establishments.

To see and experience the real Pah-ree!

They weaved their way to the Bois de Vincennes—a sprawling expanse of woodland to the east of the city—and from there he told her they would take the Rive Gauche, the left bank of the Seine all the way along to the Bois de Boulogne, another stretch of woodland to the west. Though if she was honest, as she took in the boats floating on the picturesque Lac Daumesnil, she felt the smallest pang of envy.

'Would you like to do that another day?'

She found him looking over his shoulder at her. Was there anything this guy didn't detect? He seemed as skilled as any one of the bodyguards. The way he scanned a fresh room. The way his body somehow managed to be ahead and behind her all at once. The way he seemed to spy a potential problem before the team could fully express it.

There was the feeling of being safe and protected because

of Hugo, and then there was the feeling of being all warm and fuzzy and cherished because of Hugo.

And that's where things got tricky…

'I wasn't expecting so much hesitation after such a smile of longing.'

She gave an abrupt laugh. 'Don't you have a job you need to get back to? You've already taken a week out to show me the city.'

And now she just sounded ungrateful.

She bit her cheek and winced.

'Eduardo is thriving now he's off the Chevalier leash. And Zara, once she picked herself up off the floor, is very grateful to have been entrusted to run things in the hotel group for a while. Your appearance in my life couldn't have come at a better time it would appear.'

'To be considered a blessing when I've been something of a distraction…' She shook her head. 'I never thought I'd hear that one.'

He slowed his bike so that he was alongside her, his piercing blue eyes seeking out hers, which she purposefully kept averted. 'That wasn't what you were thinking about though, so stop trying to distract me and spill.'

'You need to keep your eyes ahead Mr Chevalier, else you'll end up in the lake *today*.'

'Are we back to titles, Princess?'

She winced. He was right. And she knew why she'd done it. She was hiding behind the respectful form of address, using it to create distance between them, which wasn't fair. Not when he had done nothing wrong, and everything right. Not when she was purely protecting herself by pushing him away, inflicting hurt in the process, and that wasn't on.

'Sorry, Hugo. Consider me told.'

'I don't need you told. I just need you to stop it.' He smiled. 'And you don't need to tell me where your head has gone, not if you don't want to. Your private thoughts are your own and I'll respect that.'

She shook her head. 'It's just... Why are you doing this, Hugo?'

'Because I want to.'

He sent her a guarded look that she so desperately wanted to rip apart and understand. Regardless of the privacy he had just granted her. Which she knew was about as unfair as her pushing him away, and still she pressed. 'But why?'

'Because I couldn't bear the thought of you trapped another day inside that apartment with all of this on your doorstep.'

'I would have got out eventually.'

'And that's the problem—*eventually*! Life's too short to live your life like that. Trapped by what you can't control.'

'So, you thought to lure me out?'

'I figured it was high time you had yourself an ally, someone to fight in your corner with you... Is that so bad?'

'No.'

'And I'm afraid it's in my nature. You speak to my mother and I was always one for bringing home the stray and injured when I was a kid. Not that I'm comparing you to the stray and injured,' he hurried to add when she gave a choked laugh. 'But I'm serious...if you ever meet her, she'll likely tell you the tale of the water boatman I tried to save from drowning, not that I knew what he was at the time.'

She frowned. 'Water boatmen. But don't they...?'

'Swim. Yes. I soon learnt as much. Once she got over her fit of the giggles.'

'Oh, Hugo, you really are a—'

'No more teddy bear, please. It's bad enough that my father always accused me of being too soft. And I was four.'

'Yes, and now you're a full-grown man…'

One sexy specimen of a man who she had all these feelings for, and she didn't know what to do with them or whether he felt them too. And that was scaring the hell out of her. Not that she was about to tell him that.

'And you have a company to run and friends you must want to spend time with. A family too. You shouldn't be out here, spending all your spare time with me.'

'I told you, my parents are on their retreat, and yes, I have friends of which you are now one. As for work, a perk of being the boss is that I get to choose when I do it, which is something I've forgotten in recent years. Besides, this is kind of working, getting to see this side of the business that I've not been a part of in so long.'

'But I'm not paying you.'

And what did he mean—*a part of in so long*? Had he worked for his father? And when?

'See it as extra training on their part.'

'And do they need it? The extra training?'

He grinned.

'Hugo?'

'We only employ the best, Cassie.'

And there was her answer…he wasn't boasting, he was simply stating a fact. And she admired him for it. Her gaze swept over every chiselled feature in his stocky frame, which somehow managed to look lithe and athletic as he pedalled beside her.

'I'm sure you do.'

'But the best always leave room for improvement.'

She snorted. 'My father would see that as some kind of ridiculous riddle never to be solved.'

'Impossibly high standards?'

'You could say that.'

'And your mother?'

'You know the saying, if you can't say anything nice, don't say anything at all?'

'*Oui.*'

'I think she makes it her mission in life to live by the opposite.'

'Oh.'

'She's a delight.'

They fell silent as the path narrowed into single file for a stretch before widening once more and he was back alongside her.

'I was thinking about how safe you make me feel, Hugo. Just now,' she blurted before she could chicken out a second time. 'When you asked. It's not just about your team, the security detail, but it's you, how thoughtful you are, how your presence is like this shield that's several times your physical size, and it…it feels good.'

Heat bloomed in her cheeks and she hoped he'd attribute it to the exertion and not the extra kick to her pulse that her confession had triggered. Though maybe it was as simple as what Hugo himself had said. That he *was* her ally. Her champion. That for the first time in her life, she had someone to encourage her to go after what she wanted for a change. And it felt good.

It didn't have to mean she was starting to have *feelings* for him. Messy. Complicated. Feelings. That ran deeper than friendship.

'*Bien.* That makes me happy.'

'You said something just now, something about seeing this side of the business after all this time…does that mean you used to work for your father?' she found herself asking, needing the focus off her, but also wanting to understand what he'd meant. Whether he'd tried it out and walked away at some point. Whether, like her, he'd chosen to break away from the expectations of others.

'I did,' he said after a long pause. 'Many years ago.'

He didn't look at her now, the tension in his jaw telling her he wasn't happy with the change in topic. She wanted to press, but she also wanted the man at ease back.

Ahead, the art deco masterpiece that was the Palais de la Porte Dorée came into view—something she'd only previously glimpsed from the speed of a passing vehicle. She wanted to stop and take a closer look. The National Museum of Immigration History was something that truly interested her, but she also knew that as soon as their helmets came off, the anonymity they were enjoying would swiftly be gone.

The noise of the traffic built as they came to the edge of the park and they slowed to a stop in silence. Took a drink.

'My father is a hard man to please,' he surprised her by saying. 'I had to do more than prove myself before I joined his company. I had to prove myself above and beyond those that he employed, because heaven forbid it looked like he'd given his son a free ride.'

'Would you have had it any other way though? Truthfully'

He gave a soft huff, took another slug from his bottle. 'I would have taken a kind word occasionally, some encouragement… I guess I resented it at the time.'

She frowned. 'The fact that he made you work for it?'

'No, not that. But the fact that he made me feel like nothing I ever did was good enough. Until one day something changed, and he saw me. Congratulated me. Welcomed me in.'

'And let me guess.' She smiled as she thought about how much that must have meant to him, meant to them both. 'By that time, you were better than all the rest?'

He gave a tight chuckle. 'Are you going to break out into song for me?'

'God, no. You never want to hear me sing.'

'I'll be the judge of that.'

'So, what happened?'

His eyes wavered as they stayed connected with hers, shadows chasing behind his eyes that she couldn't read.

'You ready to go again?'

No, she wanted answers. But she could wait until he was ready. He'd gifted her so much of his precious free time, after all.

She nodded, and they eased off. Falling into single file as they hit the busier streets of the city and though the traffic made conversation impossible, she was no less happy. No less grateful too, because she was out in the fresh air, seeing Paris the best way possible thanks to him.

Her teddy bear made of steel...

CHAPTER SEVEN

'ARE YOU WARM ENOUGH?'

The late-afternoon sun hung low in the sky. Its orange glow more visual than effective at keeping off the chill now that they'd swapped the bikes for the picnic rug. And though their spot beside the lake was sheltered from the wind by the trees and the general public by his team, he was starting to question his choice to dine outdoors.

The autumn chill did mean less of an audience though, which also meant less chance of an unwarranted intrusion and therefore more pleasure for her. Or so he would have thought. But she'd fallen unusually quiet through their meal. Her gaze on the lake turning distant. And, yes, Lac Inférieure, with its pretty little island and its rounded monument dedicated to Napoleon III, deserved to be looked at, but he got the impression she wasn't seeing any of it.

'I'm fine.' She snuggled deeper into the blanket he'd wrapped around her, the curve to her cheeks giving him a hint of the smile beneath. 'I'm more than fine. This has been the most perfect of days. Right up there with the Louvre.'

He cocked a brow. 'A day of cycling…many would see that as some kind of torture.'

'You knew I wouldn't though.'

'That's true enough. And yet you seem a little distant now that we're off the bikes…was it too much food? I warned Lucile you ate like a bird.'

Now she was the one cocking a brow as she eased out of the blanket cocoon to give him the full weight of her unimpressed stare. 'A bird?'

'A bird with very discerning taste.'

That earned him a laugh. 'Sorry, old habits and all that. I'm getting better. Moderation is your friend. Mum was all about the slippery slope growing up.'

'Hence the no sweets and chocolate.'

'You remember me saying that?'

'Of course I remember. Hearing someone say they were forbidden treats as a child isn't something you forget in a hurry.'

'So that's why Lucile provided them in abundance.'

'No, Lucile just likes to do her own thing. Just like you're getting to do these days.'

'Well, you can tell her it was delicious, all of it. And I am pleasantly full and very much looking forward to the cycle back so that I can work it all off again.'

'Oh, no, there's no more cycling today. We have a van returning all of this and we're taking a car back so we're free to enjoy this.' He turned to pull a bottle of champagne from the cool box. 'If you're not too cold for it?'

'One can never be too cold for champagne, surely? Especially in Paris, the city of…' She bit her lip, her cheeks flooding with colour.

'You can say it, Cassie.' He eyed her, wondering why she wouldn't. Was it for his benefit? Was she worried he would get the wrong idea? 'It's what we're here for after all.'

'Only we're not.'

And what did he say to that?

She wasn't wrong. But she wasn't right either. Because the whole point of this pretence was to show the world they were in love. But no one was eavesdropping this second, he'd muted the comms. And visually, *he* was right. They were out in the open. On a picnic rug. Sharing champagne. Any passer-by could snap the classic 'love shot'. So why had she felt the need to say it?

'I'm sorry.' She touched a hand to his arm. Gave an apologetic smile. 'You're right. This looks good. Sets the perfect scene. I was just…overthinking.'

He returned her smile. *Overthinking.* That sounded about right. Because he felt like he'd been treading those murky waters too of late. Questioning things too much. The way he felt, too much. The desire, too much.

He popped the cork, the explosive action too in tune with his thoughts, and she gave a small squeal as it overflowed. 'Was it a stubborn one?'

'A little,' he hurried out, clinging to the excuse she had gifted him as he plucked two flutes from the hamper and offered one out to her.

'Thank you.' She wet her lips. 'You're very good at this, you know.'

'Which bit? The cycling or the opening bottles of wine?'

She gave a soft laugh. 'I was thinking more the romancing.'

He filled her glass before seeing to his own—at least she seemed comfortable mentioning the *R* word.

'We have to make it look believable remember…'

'I think you're doing that very well…it's only been a week and the press are lapping it up—lapping *you* up.'

He grinned. 'Sorry. You can't blame a man for wanting to look good in the process, and if my hotels are taking a boost, all the better.'

'Not blaming you at all, though I apologise now if they start interrogating your exes.' The bottle hit the bottom of the hamper slightly harder than he'd intended, but he didn't make a show of it. 'That's something they can't seem to help themselves with.'

'There isn't much of substance to report on I'm afraid.'

She leaned closer, trying to get a better look at him. 'Explain?'

He shrugged. 'There isn't much to explain, I'm your classic bachelor. I date for fun, nothing more.'

Because the really interesting titbit—the bit the press would love to get their hands on—had been well and truly buried by the people with the power and the influence to make it so.

Much like the remnants of his heart.

'And besides…' He forced a smile, refusing to let Sara out of the darkest recesses of his mind and into the moment that up until now had been warm and quite enjoyable. 'They'll be too busy reporting on us. Like I said, they love a good love story as much as they love a bad one.'

She gave a tiny shiver and eased her legs up to her chin as she gestured to the path ahead. 'Well, something tells me one of these walkers will have a snap of this out in the world tomorrow.'

'Tomorrow? Don't you mean in the next thirty seconds.'

'Probably.'

'And so long as we're controlling the narrative, it's all good, right?'

She met his gaze. 'Right.'

'And that feels worthy of a toast, don't you think?'

She smiled, green eyes twinkling with gold much like the Eiffel Tower in the distance. 'To us.'

'To us.'

She clinked her glass to his, and he opened up his blanket to her, offering to share his warmth as well as the perfect camera opportunity.

Sure enough, he could sense a snap in the distance as she snuggled into his side, and he suppressed the twinge of annoyance—he was courting it after all—as much as he suppressed the warmth her body provoked. And focused on what mattered, her and the little bit of her past she had divulged. Because talking about her past sure beat thinking about his...

'So, tell me, was it just your mother's controlling influence or society's in general?'

'Hmm?'

'The eating habits...'

'I don't know. I guess it's easy to blame others when really, the true person to blame is yourself. I should have been stronger. If I wanted the cake, I should have eaten the bloody cake.' She gave a tight laugh, shook her head. 'Yes, my mother watched over me, made sure I was always careful, always knew how many calories were in what. I knew from a very young age that every delicacy came with a price, and hell, the press never let you have a day off. But maybe I shouldn't have cared so much about what they thought in the first place.

And then maybe it wouldn't have hurt so much when they turned their back on me.'

'Your parents never deserved to have you as a daughter.'

'On that, I think they will now agree. After the shame I brought on them…'

He squeezed her into his side, his jaw pulsing. 'They did that to themselves when they backed you into a very public marriage with a man who no more deserved you than they did.'

'Not how they see it.'

'That's their problem, not yours.'

'I guess it is. I guess it's also the difference between you and me. Railroading me into the future they wanted for me is a move they will live to regret, whereas for your father, I can't imagine he will ever regret choosing you to take on his firm.'

Oh, there was a time…

'Do you really want to talk about families when we're in this amazing parkland, red squirrels playing at your feet?'

'Red squirrels. Where?'

He dipped his head to a spot in the distance. Nothing but fallen oak leaves now lay at the base of the trees but there had been a red squirrel not so long ago…it wasn't a complete lie. But she knew.

She nudged him with her elbow, the contact as provocative as the truth tightly packed inside his chest. Just not in the same way. 'Hugo!'

'I made him regret it.' He ground out. 'Once.'

It came out as raw as it still felt. Because *he* regretted it. The pain. The foolish act. The stupidity. He stared at where their glasses almost touched, watched the bubbles rising in the glass, but his head had travelled back. Reliving the past as she searched his face and likely saw it all.

'When?'

'When I worked for him all those years ago… Carving out my own path and going into the leisure industry wasn't entirely by choice, Cassie.'

'No?'

'No.'

She shivered and he pulled her closer. Kissed her hair on autopilot. 'In my defence, I was young. Twenty-four. It was my fifth close protection detail. But even then, I should have known better.'

'What happened?'

'I made a mistake. One I would never be so stupid as to make again, but my father wasn't a man you ever got to disappoint twice. Though when you're in the business of close protection, such a hard rule saves lives.'

'Did someone get hurt? Did you…?'

She looked up and he tucked her back under his chin, unable to look her in the eye as he admitted, 'I got involved with the principal.'

He sensed her tense, her soft gasp barely audible as he eased back on the rug and she came with him.

'Her father was a head of state in a country where culture and custom would prohibit any sort of a relationship between us, and that was before you put my job into the equation…'

He was so grateful that he'd killed the comms with his team before they'd sat down, grateful all the more for the twenty-foot safety perimeter that meant no one could overhear his shameful tale.

He'd thought he was over it. He'd endured the therapy. Relished the recovery.

Yet here he was, retelling the tale over a decade later, and it felt as raw as if it was yesterday. The heartbreak. His father's disappointment. It didn't matter that he was a billion-aire hotelier now, his father's firm under his wing too. He felt transported back to that moment. The twenty-four-year-old son who had broken his father's trust and his own heart in the process. Lost. Susceptible. Weak.

'What was her name?'

Her soft request pulled him back to the present. So typical that Cassie would want to put a name to the face that she didn't know because it mattered to his past.

'Sara.'

'I take it her family weren't very happy when they found out?'

His mouth twisted into a derisive smile, because of course that's where her head would go based on her own experience.

'They had every right to be angry. Cultural and family ex-pectations aside, I was supposed to be protecting her. Love shouldn't have come into it.'

'And did you love her?' she said quietly.

He threw back his drink, but it tasted bitter, unpalatable, or was that just the memory?

'Hugo?'

Answer her.

'I thought I did, at the time.'

'And did she love you?'

'She said she did.'

He took another swig and realised his glass was empty. Reached for the bottle and topped himself up. Went to do the same for her only hers was still full. Not a good sign. He tried to relax. Took a breath. This was ancient history. Dealt with. Though, as he had discovered in the last week alone, it wasn't as buried as he wanted it to be.

His heart too was beating far too close to the surface.

'Then what happened?'

He ground his teeth. He didn't want to go there. But refusing to give it airtime was as bad as admitting it still hurt…

'Her family forced her hand. She made her choice and it wasn't me.'

Whatever she heard in his voice had her hand reaching up to cup his cheek, her palm soft, her green eyes softer still. 'I'm so sorry, Hugo.'

But that wasn't everything, was it? She wouldn't be so sorry when she knew how he had failed Sara. How he had let his heart get in the way of his head.

He was back on that street, Sara's car waiting, door open. The heat suffocating. The look in Sara's eyes all the more so as he caught at her wrist. Desperate. Helpless. Weak. *'Don't go.'*

'Hugo?' Cassie took the glass from his limp fingers, returned to cup his cheeks, her thumbs gently stroking. Her face so close he could see the ring of fire around his pupils. Could see his pain being reflected back at him in the swirling sea of green—and *this* is what love did. *This* is why he never wanted to go back there.

And Cassie was giving him all this compassion when he deserved none.

'It's okay, Hugo.'

He grabbed her wrists, almost threw them down before realising how it would look to a passer-by. How it would feel to her too. An outward sign of rejection that *she* didn't deserve.

'No. It is not.'

'It wasn't your fault.'

'What I did, that was my fault.'

She searched his gaze, unflinching from the pain she could

see there. It was the first time she'd witnessed it within him. Such hurt. So raw and unguarded. He had loved. Hugo had loved. More than she ever had.

And he hadn't denied it either. *'I thought I did, at the time.'*

Though Sara had crushed it. Walked away. Chosen her family over him.

Cassie couldn't imagine it. No matter how hard she tried. Cassie couldn't imagine having the heart of the man before her and choosing anything but that. Though he wouldn't have been the same man...at twenty-four he would have been young, untainted by the world and all the work that would have hardened his shell since. The heartbreak that would have toughened him too.

And she needed that reminder. She needed it now because every day in his company, every day they played out this charade that was their epic love story, she could feel herself getting as lured in as the press. Lured in by him and his kind gestures, his kind smile, his kind heart.

Because it couldn't be so easy as this, could it? After a life of living for others, an adulthood of having her men chosen for her, she couldn't be so lucky as to have landed her own perfect love story right next door. To believe that would truly be naive, wouldn't it?

And she'd almost given herself away too.

It's why she'd blurted out. *'Only we're not.'*

Hugo hadn't needed the reminder. Cassie had.

Her *heart* had.

'By falling in love? I can't see how that's your fault, Hugo.'

He stiffened. 'No,' he ground out. 'But leaving her exposed was.'

The chill ran from him into her and she lowered her palms from his face, rubbed them together. 'I see.'

'No. You don't.'

'Then make me see. Tell me what happened.'

He kept his gaze fixed ahead, but she could see his self-loathing, the sickness in his pallor, and she tucked her hands between her legs, forbade them from moving. He didn't want her touch right now, no matter how much she wanted to give it to him.

'You don't need to tell me, not if you don't want to, but…'

His throat bobbed as he swallowed, his dark lashes flickering over his eyes that were so haunted she prayed that talking about it would in some way release the ghosts from his soul. Ghosts he must have had buried deep for so long.

'I lowered my guard. I was focusing so much on her, fighting with her to see a different future for us that I didn't see the threat until he was upon us. I had my hand around her wrist, I wasn't prepared and when he drew his gun, she was completely exposed. The only thing I could do was throw myself into it.'

She failed to suppress a shiver as it played out in her mind's eye. 'You threw yourself into the path of the bullet?'

'He never should have got that close.'

'But you did what you were trained for,' she whispered.

'Far too late.'

He raised his hand to his shoulder, scratched at the skin beneath, the scar that must exist and Cassie tracked the move. 'If he'd been any further to the left, or if I'd been any slower…'

She felt the tremor that ran through him with his breath. 'But you weren't.'

He shook his head, stressed, 'He *never* should have been able to get that close.'

'But you were there. And you saved her.'

'I took the bullet but—' he choked on thin air '—it was not my finest moment.'

'We all make mistakes, do things we're not proud of, but you were in love—'

'I was a fool.'

He sounded so angry, so hurt, so bitter, and Cassie's heart ached for him. She could think of nothing else to do but to fold into him, moulding her body into every hard ridge of his until the tension gradually seeped from his limbs. So grateful to have him here now. That he hadn't lost his life in the line of duty to the woman who hadn't loved him enough to keep him.

'I'm so sorry, Hugo.'

'I'm not. Like I said, the only time I let my father down was when I was distracted and infatuated. I learned from that mistake, and I've been committed ever since. Proved myself to my father. Made myself into the man I am today. As for the press, you needn't worry about them digging this story up. Sara's family made sure there was nothing to discover. Nothing to ruin their reputation and her marriage potential back then, and I've told no one of it...my family certainly don't speak of it, and those at the firm are under NDAs.'

She lifted her head a little. 'You think I'm worrying about any of that?'

He gave a stilted shrug.

'I'm more concerned that your relationship with Sara has seen you walk away from the possibility of love in your future, Hugo. This is why you don't have a home in the country with those mini-Chevaliers I mentioned, isn't it?'

He stroked the hair away from her face. 'You make that sound so tragic, Cassie.'

'Because it is tragic.'

He gave a choked laugh. 'Love isn't for everyone. *Mon Dieu*, if you saw my parents…it's a miracle they've got to where they have. My mother has the patience of a saint, I'll say that for her. And I'm a better man without it. I don't need someone else to make me feel fulfilled. I don't want to rely on someone else to make me feel whole and happy again, because when you lose that someone, it's like—it's like having your soul ripped out, and you struggle to see the path for the pain of it.'

'I understand why you don't want to rely on love to make you happy again,' she whispered eventually. 'It's not all that different to me spending my life tying my happiness to that of others. My parents, Georges, things you can't control. But… I don't know. To swear oneself off it because you fear losing it again… I'm not sure that's all that healthy either.'

'I never said it was healthy, Cassie. Just that I don't intend to suffer it again.'

And that was her told.

So why did she get the distinct impression her heart wasn't listening…?

CHAPTER EIGHT

Hugo knew Paris like the back of his hand. He'd grown up in the city. Lived and worked in the good and the bad. Spent time as a driver and on the doors of its clubs until his father had deemed him good enough for the family firm. And then, of course, he'd been launched on the path that had led to his independence.

But he'd never seen it like this...like he did through Cassie's eyes.

And for the next two weeks, while balancing his return to work with his mission to show Cassie off to the world and vice versa, he lost himself in her pleasure, her joy as he took her to his favourite spots, some well-known, some less so.

'I can't believe I'm eating ice cream outdoors when it's almost November.'

Her green eyes sparkled up at him as she touched a finger to the corner of her mouth—*always* smiling—and scooped away some imaginary stray dribble of the sweet delight he had coaxed her into buying.

If he was honest, he couldn't believe he was doing it either. On a Monday too, when he should be at work, but he'd taken one look at the blue sky that morning, the amber leaves on the trees lining the Champs-Élysées creating a stunning walkway all the way down to the River Seine, and he'd known where he'd rather be.

And who he'd rather be with.

And he hadn't questioned it. He'd just gone and got her.

Which in itself was a bad sign to add to the ever-growing list of bad signs…

'I can't believe you've never had one of Pierre's ice creams before.'

'If someone had told me croissant infused ice cream existed down the road, I think I would've sneaked out of my room sooner.'

He had to force his jaw to relax. The memory of her hiding away still too recent to ignore. The gossip headlines that morning, or rather a flippant one-liner from the palace spin doctors, even more so. Not that he was about to ruin the moment by giving it any airtime now.

'It's pretty good, isn't it?' He filled his mouth with the creamy goodness and focused on the tasty delight instead.

'Oh, yes,' she murmured, her pleasure obvious as she licked at her own, her eyes rolling back. The red of her jacket working with the flush in her cheeks and the gloss to her lips as she swept up the remnants with her tongue…

Don't look at her tongue.

'And the nutty chocolate sauce,' she was saying, 'it really takes it to another level, don't you—'

'Princess! Hugo!'

Her eyes widened as he stiffened.

'Give us a smile!'

The shout came from across the street, and like an echo more shouts followed in quick succession. Other voices, different people.

'Sourire à la caméra!'

It was inevitable. There wasn't an outing where they flew under the radar for its entirety, but his plan was working. The interruptions *were* less frequent. Less intense. Less intrusive. And less insulting with it, too.

Or was that just wishful thinking on his part?

He searched her face, looking for any sign that the unbridled joy of seconds before was dimming. 'What do you say?'

'Do I have food on my face?'

He cupped her cheek, swiped his thumb along her lower lip, felt her subtle tremor beneath his touch—or was that purely within him? The act driven by the thrill of it, rather than to remove any trace of chocolate or cream.

It was the kind of act they'd been indulging in, playing up to the cameras, fulfilling the role of the loved-up couple with ease. Driving the Prince crazy, if the reports were to be believed, and sweeping the public up in their love story. Winning them over to Cassie's side. As it should be.

The only problem was training his body to calm down, reminding it that this wasn't the real deal—because A, he wasn't in love. And B, he never would be.

Which meant *this*—the sexual attraction—it needed to be caged.

'All gone.'

He wondered if she noticed the husky edge to his voice. Noticed it and knew its cause, like he did. That this pretence, the desire, was no act at all.

But her grin widened, and she leapt up, her eyes flashing with mischief as she caught the tip of his thumb in her mouth. *Mon Dieu.* Never mind the cameras going wild, his entire body surged—heart, mind, and soul—urging him to tug her body to his and kiss her deeply. An act they hadn't been so bold as to share, and it was that deep-rooted desire that had him slipping his arm around her waist and urging her into walking instead.

Because if they were moving, they couldn't be doing all the other things his brain was fervently entertaining...

'You okay?' She leaned into him as she asked, her body readily moulding into his as they fell into an easy step together.

'Better than okay. It's a glorious day. Even the river looks more blue than brown today...which feels like something of a miracle.'

'*Everything* looks and feels a little better when the sun comes out to play.'

He glanced down at her, his brow creasing. 'And are you needing the sun today, Cassie?' Because the wistful note in her voice told him that she did.

Had she seen the same headlines, was she too pondering what her no-good ex would say next. Did he raise it, or did he let it go?

'Are you enjoying your bit of rough, Princess?'

The voice came out of the trees up ahead, but no one stepped forward and he nodded to his team to check it out as he slowed their pace.

'Do you want to comment on the suggestion that Prince Georges was always a little too refined for you, Princess?'

Hugo saw red. His emotions a sprint ahead of where they should ever be, and not in defence of himself. He couldn't

care what the guy said about him. He was lowering Cassie
to Hugo's level. And hell, he could say what he liked about
Hugo but Cassie…

She tugged on his arm. Her steady hand holding him back
when he would have launched forward as the smug-faced
journo peered out from between the trees.

'I beg your pardon?' Cassie stepped forward, her hand still
on Hugo's arm urging him to hold his ground. Was his skittish kitten finding her claws?

His team in the wings looked to him and he silently gestured for them to hold their position. They were close enough
to move if she needed them, but she wanted to handle this,
and he wanted to give her that opportunity.

The man came out of the trees. Dark, shaggy hair. Leath-
ers. A motorbike just behind for a quick exit should he need
it. Phone ready to snap a pic. 'I said…'

'Oh, I heard you.' She gave her classic coy smile, a lick of
her ice cream as she eyed him up and down. 'I just needed a
better visual to do this…'

And then she stuck her cone, ice cream and all, right on
the end of his nose.

So swift the man had no time to dodge it.

So surprising all the man could do was gawp back at her
like some frozen human snowman.

'What can I say? Georges was probably right. I always
did have a more playful side to me, and now I'm all about
having fun with my man. Life is for living, after all. Don't
you agree, Hugo?'

She turned and beamed at him.

'I think I need to go and buy you another ice cream, *mon
petit chaton.*'

She wrinkled her nose. 'Did you just call me…?'

'My little kitten, *oui*.'

She hooked her arm back in his. 'Care to explain?'

'Later.'

She gave him a sparkling smile before turning to throw over her shoulder, 'Oh, and, Mr Reporter Sir, I hate having to waste anything, so please be a good soul and lick as much of that up as you can. It truly is delicious.'

And then she practically skipped Hugo back to Pierre's.

'Are you going to explain the kitten reference?' she asked as he handed her a replacement ice cream.

He chuckled. 'To be clear, to call one *mon petit chaton* is a common endearment in France so you shouldn't take offence.'

'I wasn't.'

He cleared his throat as he thought back to that first morning in Louis's apartment, when he hadn't known who she was...

'And...?'

'It was something that sprang to mind when I saw you standing in the middle of Louis's apartment that first morning.'

'The morning of the photograph?'

He nodded. The story that had triggered all the rest. 'You were wearing that oversized cream sweater, grey leggings, soft and muted against the garish backdrop. Sweet, but skittish too. Wary of me, I guess. Why I was there? Could I be trusted?'

'I suppose I was.'

'And all around you was this chaos and colour and it made me think of a kitten being set down in a noisy neon nightclub. And then you talked about how you were hiding out, and it reinforced that view.' He swept her hair behind her ear, scanned her face as he saw how far she had come to be the woman before him now. '*Mon petit chaton*, hiding from the world, but not any more. My little kitten has found her claws.'

'Hugo…' She wet her lips, her eyes glistening up at him. 'I don't know what to say.'

'Well don't cry.'

'I'm not. I think that's possibly one of the nicest things anyone has ever said to me.'

'And yet, you're crying.'

She shook her head, blinked the tears away. 'I'm not. I'm—I am angry though.'

'I told you, it's a compliment.'

'Not at you! At the reporter for insinuating what he did.'

'Which bit?'

'That you were unrefined.'

'You took that from what he said?'

'Well, the suggestion was there.'

He gave a low chuckle. 'I really couldn't care less what he said about me.'

'Tomorrow's headlines might make you think otherwise.'

'Something tells me that reporter got what was coming to him, I think the reports will swing very much in your favour.'

'You reckon?'

He grinned, his admiration for her swelling out of his control as he caught another stray hair before it found its way into her mouth with her ice cream. 'Hell yeah, you were incredible.'

She stepped closer, so close her chest brushed his front. 'You truly think so?'

He hooked his hands into the rear pockets of her jeans. She felt good. So very good.

'Cassie, I have seen some fierce take-downs in my career, but that is up there with one of my all-time favourites.'

She laughed, though it sounded strained to his ears, strained with the same kind of heat that was working its way through him. 'Now I know you're exaggerating.'

'I swear on my mother's life. Just remind me never to get on your bad side. Like I said, *mon petit chaton* has found her claws.'

She placed said claw over his shoulder. 'I still can't be-lieve that's how you saw me—*see* me, even.' She bared her teeth and gave a playful little *'raa'* that made him laugh… made him feel more than just the flutter of amusement too. 'But have no fear, I don't plan on wasting Pierre's amazing ice cream a second time around, even if it's on your delight-ful nose… I will share it though.'

Then she licked her ice cream right beneath his nose before lifting it over his shoulder and kissing him. Whether it was for the benefit of more hovering reporters or for her or for him, he had no clue. And he had no good sense left to question it, or prevent it, because he was lost to it. The touch of her lips against his, the taste of the ice cream and her, a delight like no other. And it was heaven and hell in one.

Heaven because it was sheer bliss, and hell because it wasn't enough. And he wasn't sure it could ever be enough. And he shouldn't be doing it. Taking what she was offering, but he was.

Whether it was fake or not. He was rolling with it. Roll-ing with it and revelling in it. His hands forking into her hair, deep and hungry. The growl low in his throat, fierce and unrestrained. Because he was finally giving it free rein, the desire that he'd been suppressing for so long. It was vi-brating through him. Taking over every part of him, until he realised it wasn't just within him, it was against him, in his pocket between them—his phone!

Bzzzz…bzzzz…bzzzz…

He squeezed his eyes closed, swore he heard her whimper, felt her claws along with the drip of her ice cream down his neck.

Bzzzz…bzzzz…bzzzz…

He cursed and she fell back with what sounded like a sob come laugh. 'Maybe you should get it.'

She pressed her fingers to her lips, her other hand outstretched with the dripping ice cream as she kept her gaze low. *Mon Dieu*, she looked thoroughly kissed. Hair mussed, lips swollen, cheeks pink. He wanted to toss the ice cream, drag her back to the apartment, forget the world and why this wasn't real. Why this couldn't *be* real.

He tugged the phone from his pocket as it cut off, cursing the unknown caller for the unwelcome interruption.

Unwelcome? You should be grateful for the reality check!

He raked an unsteady hand over his hair. Took a breath. And another as he stared at the screen and anchored himself in the present. Who she was. What this was. Why he couldn't pick up where they'd left off.

'Do you need to call them back?' she asked, and he could hear the hesitation in her voice, the uncertainty that their kiss had put there. That *he* had put there. Though she had kissed him, that much was certain. But he hadn't had to kiss her back.

'Unknown number. I'm sure they'll leave a message if it's important.'

She nodded but they remained at some weird kind of impasse. Neither knowing how to press Play again…how to resume…not back in each other's arms though, that was for sure.

Maybe he needed to get back into a steady routine. There

was something to be said for the reassuring monotony of the daily grind. Less emotion, less hormonal churn, and more making money and decisions with clear thought and logic.

None of which he had when she was around, not any more. And that was a problem. A big Sara-style problem.

Bigger even. Because he was supposed to be older, wiser, and better than the mistakes of old. His phone gave the solitary buzz of an answerphone message, and like a lifeline now he pulled it out. Nodded to one of his team to step in.

'I'll just check what this is,' he said to Cassie.

'Sure.'

He walked a few strides away and dialled his answerphone, surprised when his father's gruff voice came down the line.

'Call me back, Hugo.'

Ice ran down his spine. Was it Mum? Was she sick? Had something happened?

He immediately dialled the number and his father picked up in one.

A stream of Polish flew at him, so rapid even Hugo struggled to piece it together, but he'd caught enough. Princess. Cassandra. Sara. *Imbecyl*—much like the French *imbécile*. So much for his parents being blissfully unaware in digi-detox land.

'Father, stop.'

'Don't you tell me to stop. I knew we shouldn't have left. I *knew* I couldn't trust you to manage things with me so far away.'

Hugo's chest grew tight with every word. 'It is not what you think.'

'How? How can it not be how I think? When your mother learns of this—'

'She doesn't know?'

That was something at least…

'No. Thanks to this *ridiculous* place she's in cloud cuckoo land.'

'Which is where you should be—not the cuckoo—' Hugo broke off with a curse. This was coming out all wrong. Why did his father always get to him like this?

'Did you honestly think I wouldn't find out?'

'And how did you? You're not supposed to have any contact with the outside world.'

'I abide by my own rules, son. You of all people should know that.'

Hugo raked a hand over his hair, gripped the back of his neck. He'd suspected as much. Hell, even Cassie had warned him his father might do as much. But again, he'd been too distracted by the same to do something about it before now.

'Eduardo says you have a team on her 24-7.'

He huffed. 'Eduardo needs to remember who he works for now.'

'Don't change the subject.'

'I'm not. My CEO should be more concerned with running the company than telling tales to my father, who should no longer be getting involved.'

'When those tales pertain to mistakes my son is making in his personal life which could affect his work life, it's my business to know. I thought you'd learnt your lesson with that disastrous affair. Sara and your silly infatuation almost got you both killed. Or has time made you forget?'

'No, Father. And I don't need the reminder now. This is not the same.'

'Then you best enlighten me because from where I'm sitting, it is precisely the same. She is a client and you are—'

'That is *not* how this is.'

'In what way is it any different?'

Hugo blew out a breath. 'Because we are friends and what you're seeing is all for show, Father. I'm helping her out of a difficult situation.' And then he added because he couldn't help himself. 'But even if we were in a relationship, this is nothing like what happened with Sara. I *run* the company now. I'm not in the field. I'm not running the protection detail. I'm being protected right alongside her. And I trust my team. Just as you trusted them. And now, I need you to trust me.'

The line fell silent. Nothing but the sounds of Paris on Hugo's side of the world and the early-morning wildlife in the Caribbean.

'Please, Father, I promise you, I have it all under control.' *Only you don't...*

'For the first time in your life, can you just trust me?'

His father grunted. And then he was gone. And Hugo had no idea whether that was a yes or a no. Much like his entire life.

But he knew one thing for sure, he needed to get it under control. His feelings for Cassie and the entire situation and prove to his father once again that he had this.

And prove it to himself while he was at it.

'Everything okay?'

Because Cassie knew it wasn't.

The moment they had kissed, her world had tilted and failed to right itself again.

Cassie now knew how it felt to be wanted by Hugo. Not the kind of want that was make-believe. Projected or otherwise. The kind that she could confuse because he had been so kind and understanding towards her. Because he cared for her.

No. He'd *wanted* her. She'd seen it in his eyes when he'd

called her his *mon petit chaton*. She'd heard it in his growl as he'd kissed her. Felt it in his hands as he'd forked them through her hair. Felt it in his body as he'd pressed against her. And she'd wanted him too.

But she'd also sensed the fight in him. The way he'd pulled away and withdrawn.

The phone call gifting him a get out that she had permitted him to take.

And now the wall was well and truly up and he wasn't meeting her eye.

'Hugo?'

'Oui.' He pocketed his phone, then his hands. 'But something's come up and I need to get back and pack. I have to fly out to New York for a few days.'

'Oh.'

And she really didn't like the way her heart sank at the thought.

'I have some business to take care of out there.'

Of course he did, he had a life with responsibilities. Just because he'd *chosen* to spend most of his free time with her of late didn't change that. But now it felt like he was running. From the kiss. From her.

'When will you be back?'

'I'm not sure. Friday maybe? It depends how it goes.'

She nodded. Tugged the collar of her jacket high around her neck, wishing they hadn't bought the replacement ice cream as her stomach threatened to throw it back up. 'I'll miss you.'

And why on earth had she said that?

His eyes caught on hers. For the briefest second their gazes locked, and then he turned away but took her hand as though softening the move. Gave her fingers a squeeze. 'I'm sure your designs will benefit from the extra attention you'll be able to give them without me around to distract you.'

She interlocked her fingers in his. Cherished the connection as she focused on the conversation rather than the weird dance of her heart that was telling her plenty if she dared to listen.

'You're right. If Louis is to unveil them on the catwalk next February, I need to have them ready soon.'

'Still not up for going it alone then?'

She laughed. 'Not yet I'm not. Our little love story may have worked wonders, but I don't think it's worked that kind of magic yet.'

'Our love story has nothing to do with it, Cassie. I'm talking about you and your designs. I've seen them, remember—they're incredible and the world will think so too.'

'And as you so rightly pointed out, you know nothing of fashion so…'

'But Louis does, and he wants them *so*…'

She gave a small smile as she considered what he was saying…while also acknowledging that he was probably saying it to distract her from whatever else was going on inside his head, and between them too.

Was she reading too much into it? She'd kissed him…had he just been going along with it for her sake, for the cameras, for the role?

Or had she gone too far? Crossed a line in kissing him so brazenly? Maybe she should just ask him outright? Or maybe she was overthinking the whole lot, and it really was work taking him away and she was just being paranoid?

Because the real problem came down to what was going on within her. Her own feelings that she was struggling to contain.

So maybe his work emergency was actually a blessing in disguise.

Some space after all the time they'd spent together. A chance to be herself, the new and energised and fierce her. On her own two feet. Alone. And she'd be perfectly fine and perfectly happy without him.

Because she didn't *need* Hugo. She wasn't *in love* with Hugo.

She cared for him. He was a wonderful human being who'd given her so much joy. Saved her from herself and her self-imposed little prison.

She was indebted to him—that was all.

Nothing more.

Absolutely not.

And she'd prove it.

CHAPTER NINE

CASSIE WAS HUNCHED over the coffee table in Louis's living room, a frenetic energy flowing through her fingers and onto the page. The scratch of pencil on paper as soothing as the classical tune she had playing in the background. The tune similar to what had been playing at the Louvre the first time they'd dined together. When he'd had those cute fashion plates brought in for her eyes only.

Had that really only been five weeks ago?

She felt like so much had changed since then. She had changed. Life had changed.

It was half two in the morning. Her witching hour. A time she hadn't needed. Not since Hugo. But in the past week, she'd found herself getting up again...

He'd said he'd be away for a few days, but it had been almost two weeks since she'd seen him. They'd exchanged messages. Mainly him making sure she was okay and that his team were looking after her. Safe topics.

And what exactly is safe *supposed to mean?*

She nipped her lip and went back to her drawing. More focused. More frenzied. Even though her hand and back protested. She lost herself in the beauty of what she could create and control. And her creativity was soaring, her designs were taking shape. She was almost ready to share them with Louis, who'd been messaging daily for an update. Which made her think of Hugo again and his parting words, to think about going it alone. That Louis's eagerness meant the world would be eager too.

But it was still early days. Even with the great strides she'd made to stand apart from her royal identity, standing beside another man was hardly standing alone...but the idea of standing up there without Hugo?

The pencil fell from her grasp and she shivered as she pulled the sleeves of her robe into her hands and curled back into the sofa. She wasn't cold because she feared going it alone.

She was cold because she didn't want to think of life without Hugo in it.

And *that* scared her.

The problem was, she knew it was an act for him. The fake dating, the playing up to the camera. She knew he cared for her as a friend, but the rest—the loving touches, caresses, gestures—they were all part of the act. Though that kiss... Her fingers fluttered to her mouth that burned with the memory of it...her heart fluttering too.

Because her heart had been fooled.

And her heart wanted to carry on being fooled because it had fallen for the man who had cared enough to coax her out. Who had cared enough to save her from herself.

And when he touched her, when he looked at her, when he

made her smile and laugh and feel special in all the ways he did, planning days out that meant so much to her…activities that not even her husband or her parents would have thought to do, would have understood her *well enough* to do…it felt like more. She *felt* so much more.

And she missed him. *God.* She *missed* him.

Waking up each morning knowing he was so far away, that he wouldn't be calling by that day, or the next… She blew out a breath and stood. Walked to the window and gazed out over the darkened city.

How different it now felt having walked it many times with Hugo. Hugo and his team. But that couldn't be her life forever. At some point she was going to have to move out, take her own path on her own two feet.

That was the deal. That was what she'd wanted more than anything when she'd first fled the palace. Louis had come to her aid with the apartment, and then Hugo had come to her aid in ways she'd never have had the means or the gumption to pursue. Not in the short term when everything had been so fresh and raw.

She had so much to be grateful for, so why did it feel like something was now missing in her goal for the future?

A gentle knock—knuckles against wood—made her jump. She turned from the glass to squint down the darkened hallway. It came again, slightly louder, but very definite. Someone was at her door. At this time of night?

But who would call now unless it was an emergency, and even then, they'd use the bell or pound a lot harder…? She padded towards it, tightening her robe.

A loud whisper came next. 'Cassie?'

Hugo!

She raced the final few steps, unbolted the door, and threw

it open. Would have thrown herself into his arms too if she hadn't had the last-minute foresight to realise that would be unwise. Unless she wanted him to know *exactly* how she felt about him.

'What are you doing here? I thought you were still in New York.'

'I was. I just got back.'

'Like—' she waved a loose finger and swore her heart was about to soar right up out of her chest '—*just* this minute got back.'

'Oui.'

'And you're knocking on my door *because*…?'

He raised his arms out like it was obvious and she eyed him up and down. He was a sight for sore eyes. Even in joggers and a training top.

'Because in the last month we have done many things, apart from the one thing I told you I would do that first morning we had coffee.'

She frowned. 'Remind me…'

Maybe she was losing her mind. Maybe she'd fallen asleep sketching, and this was some weird, Hugo-starved dream.

'A run! It's your witching hour. And I could hear you moving about in there, so I figured, why not?'

Her face broke into a grin. 'You're serious?'

'I've dressed for the occasion, haven't I? You, however…' His eyes dipped, dipped and heated, and heaven help her, she felt the flush creeping up her chest as he cleared his throat and clapped his hands together. 'Right! I'll give you five minutes to get changed because that gown isn't conducive to any form of exercise.'

'Are you—'

'Shoo-shoo!' He took her by the shoulders and turned her around. 'I'll be right here when you're ready.'

And then he closed the door on her, and she was alone once more. Only this time he was on the other side of it, and she was laughing and shaking and completely abuzz with him.

Hugo was here and he was taking her running.

At two-thirty in the morning!

Was there anything this man wouldn't do for her?

He won't love you, so don't be getting any funny ideas!

She dismissed the sarcastic retort—*hell*, what did she care? Her parents hadn't loved her. Georges certainly hadn't loved her. What was another man to add to the list?

But Hugo was different and therein lay the problem.

He was worth loving.

And, breathe.

Watching Cassie run was extraordinary.

Or was it the act of running with her that was extraordinary? Because Hugo didn't feel tired. He felt fired up. Exhilarated.

He hadn't slept since the previous night in New York and, granted, it was only nine in the evening stateside. *She* was the one who should be tired.

But then he'd barely slept the last two weeks away. His sleep was disturbed, and he'd found himself back on the sleepwalk train. Troubled by his own unease. The past and the present colliding. Worry over how he'd left things. Worry over the future. Over what he wanted. What he didn't want. Worry that her ex would cross the line. That another hack of a journalist would. There was the slightest niggle that one would uncover his past too, and the idea that his tainted past could ruin her…he couldn't bear that.

It didn't matter that she'd shown how strong she was either, he'd still worried.

So, the second he'd heard her footfall on the other side of the wall, he'd been racking his brain for an excuse to see her. To see for himself that she was okay because the reports from his team simply wouldn't do.

Running and her witching hour had been a spark of desperate inspiration.

But now they were out in the cool night air, he was loving every second.

All the more so, because she was.

Her entire body encased in black Lycra, she was a powerhouse. A petite, lithe powerhouse. Her hair was tied back in a ponytail, her face half hidden by a cap, but her eyes shone out, glittering into the night as she turned to him and grinned.

'This is immense!'

They were crossing the Pont Neuf, the Seine flowing black beneath them, the starry sky above, and if he had to choose a perfect moment in his life, he might have chosen this one. 'I'm not going to lie. It is surprisingly awesome.'

She laughed. The sound giddy and light and nowhere near as breathless as it should be. 'Epic!'

'But you know we do need to turn back if you want to avoid the early-morning risers?'

'I know.' She gave him what could only be described as a cheeky look. 'You want to race?'

'Back to the hotel? It's almost five kilometres!'

'And?' She broke stride to give him a light elbow. 'You chicken?'

'Am *I* chicken?'

She nodded, eyes goading him beneath the rim of her cap. 'You're on!'

And like that, they were off. Any thought of gifting her a head start forgotten as he realised this woman didn't need it. What was she powered by? Moonlight? The reflective details on her kit taunting him further as they flashed him all the way.

By the time they reached their hotel, he swore he'd got a PB along with a rather unpleasant stitch. He cursed as he came to a halt in the outer courtyard, clutched his side as he struggled to suck in a breath. 'You're dangerous!'

'You can't come to an abrupt stop, it's not good for your heart.' She pulled on his arm, her eyes dazzling in the warm glow of the hotel's lighting. 'We'll take the stairs up. You can jog it off.'

He stared up at her. 'Jog it off?'

She nodded. 'Yup.'

'Did you just "*yup*" me?'

'I guess I did.'

He shook his head, hands on knees. 'Who are you and what have you done with my Cassie?'

'I've got claws now, remember?'

She perfected her cat pose, claws and all, before spinning on her heel and jogging inside, ponytail swinging.

'I've created a monster,' he murmured, pushing up to standing with a laugh. 'Never mind a cat.'

Not that he was complaining. Not in the slightest. He followed her on through to the lobby and to the stairwell. There was one thing to be said for jogging up the stairs behind her, he had the most amazing view of her in Lycra. And, *Dieu*, that did not help. Not one bit. It stopped him thinking about his stitch though.

Probably because his blood was rushing elsewhere.

Two weeks apart was supposed to have dulled this.

Made it go away.

Made it containable.

All it had done was made it explosive.

And if he didn't get out of her orbit like now, he was going to do something profoundly stupid, the kind of stupid his father had cautioned him against, the kind of stupid that had made him run two weeks ago...

'Drink?'

'Huh?'

She had her hand on the door to Louis's apartment. 'I make a mean post-workout smoothie?'

The last thing you need is a smoothie...

Though he found himself saying, 'Sure.'

He followed her in and she stripped off her jacket. Underneath she wore nothing but an exercise bra with her leggings. *Gulp.* She pulled her cap off and tossed it aside, her ponytail swinging free down her back as she set about mixing stuff together in a blender. 'Water?'

'Please.'

At least it was supposed to have been a please. Instead, it sounded like someone was strangling a cat and the look she sent him as she pulled open the fridge said she thought so too.

She tossed him a bottle, which by some miracle he managed to catch, and he twisted off the cap, took a long slug. Wiped his mouth. 'Cheers.'

She set the blender going and the noise was about as loud as his pulse in his ears. She set two tumblers on the side with straws and drummed her nails while she waited for the blender to finish.

Was she as edgy as him? She wasn't looking at him and the way those nails were working against Louis's psychedelic marble, the way every exposed muscle of her torso looked clenched... *Dieu*, he wanted her.

Wanted her more than he could ever remember wanting anything in his life. More than he'd wanted the family firm in his twenties. More than he'd wanted to make his first million. More than he wanted to taste the ice cream on her lips a fortnight ago. And that kiss...

The blender finished its incessant thrum, and she let out a sudden breath, her head snapping up. She'd been lost in her thoughts, too. Had she gone to the same place? Unlikely, but the slash of heat still in her cheeks, across her collarbone...

She reached for the jug and poured the luminescent liquid into the awaiting glasses.

'It tastes better than it looks, I promise.'

She stepped up to him, glasses in hand and as her eyes lifted to his, the world stilled.

Because he knew in that moment that nothing could taste better than her.

That he wanted to *taste* nothing but her.

And that he needed to get the hell away from her.

Now.

'I'm sorry, Cassie, this was a bad idea.'

'The drink?'

But he was already turning away and walking, and she was right on his tail. Drinks forgotten on the side as she grabbed his arm to pull him back. 'Did I do something wrong?'

'No, no, of course not. You could never do anything wrong. I'm sorry, I just...' He turned to face her and she was so close, her body virtually pressed up against him, and they were so hot and sweaty from their run. Everything was in some heightened overdrive. Now wasn't the time to make any crazy decisions or cross any rational lines when there was no press corps to excuse it.

'Then what is it?'

She reached up. Her palm soft against his cheek. Her brow furrowed with concern. But there was something else in her green eyes. Something so akin to the fire in his gut, and *hell*, he wanted to act on it.

He cursed under his breath, and her luscious mouth quirked to one side. 'You do have a filthy mouth at times, Hugo.'

'If you could read my mind, you'd say I had a filthy one of those too.'

Her eyes flared, the fire he had glimpsed turning into a full-on blaze. 'What are you saying?'

'What do you think I'm saying?'

Her delicate throat bobbed, her eyes raking over his face as her fingers trembled against his cheek. 'Don't tease me.'

'*Me?* Tease *you*? When you're the one standing before me in nothing more than a bra and skintight pants?' His voice was raw—raw with a need that had been building for weeks! And *Dieu*, he wasn't a monk!

Two weeks without sight of her in the flesh! Oh, he'd seen plenty in the press. Plenty enough to tease him and drive him half mad. Plenty of dated coy shots with the Prince too. And he wasn't a jealous man. He *wasn't*.

'Then why aren't you kissing me?'

'Because I don't believe in taking what I want without express permission.'

'I am granting you permission, Hugo. Right here…' She pressed her body up against him, hooked her hands around his neck. 'Right now.'

And then she kissed him, and this time, he quit thinking. He quit every sense that wasn't all about her and took all that she was offering because consequences were tomorrow's concern.

Or today's, depending on how one looked at it.

Only he wasn't looking, he was living in the moment and loving every second.

Cassie was no virgin.

The Prince may have gone elsewhere for fun but he'd done his 'duty' by her. And that was just it. He'd always made it feel like a duty. Like it was all about producing an heir and never about desire. Never about lust. Fire. *This!*

And Cassie *was* on fire. Her entire body combusting with an explosive passion that she couldn't contain. She'd known her feelings for Hugo were growing out of her control but this…this raging heat in her bloodstream, this tension coiling through her body, this liquid heat pooling in her abdomen… She was kind of…scared.

'Hugo,' she panted, clawing at his chest through his T-shirt as she tore her mouth from his so that she could stare up at him, wide-eyed and dazed.

'Yes?'

'This is…'

'Crazy. Insane. Ill-advised.'

She gave a choked laugh. 'Yes!'

'You want me to stop, because I will.'

'No! Hell no.'

'Dieu Merci!'

She tugged him back to her kiss, marvelling at the way their mouths fit so perfectly together. The way his tongue teased and tangled with her own. Georges had never kissed her like this. With such passion, such intensity. Like he wanted all of her and more.

He walked her back into some hard surface, and she felt it rock. Heard something fragile rattle and he flicked a hand out to catch whatever it was without breaking tempo or the exploration of his kiss.

'Though we should take this to the bedroom before something hits the deck that shouldn't...'

She nodded and twisted in his arms, leading him down the corridor and into her room without pausing to turn on the lights. She was in too much of a hurry. Too scared that to pause would snuff out whatever this was building between them because *this* was what she had read about in books.

This was what she had seen on the TV.

This was what she had started to think was the stuff of make-believe...but was it possible that it was real after all?

Real and she could have it. With Hugo.

He spun her into his arms and she tore his T-shirt over his head before his mouth claimed hers once more. To be able to touch the body she had seen that first night, the broad shoulders, the chiselled pecs, the hard ridge of every ab...

She sighed into his mouth and he nipped her lip. 'Did you just sigh at me?'

'Maybe.'

'Sighing after sex is okay, but before?'

'I'm sorry, but your body is wholly satisfying.'

'I'll show you satisfying.'

And with that, he threw her back on the bed and stalked towards her.

'Wait!' She thrust out a hand and he paused, his cocked brow just visible in the light being cast from the outer hall.

'I'm all—' she wriggled against the sheets '—sweaty.'

'Believe me, you're going to be more sweaty by the time I'm finished with you, *mon petit chaton*.'

She wanted to laugh. She wanted to cry. She wanted to thank the heavens for bringing her this man, because Georges would *never* have stood for 'sweaty her'. He'd have marched her to the shower, but Hugo, he was her *real* prince.

'In that case...' She relaxed, ran her teeth over her bottom lip as she thought of all that lay ahead. 'Come get me.'

Come get me? Have you heard yourself? And what about after, when he has your heart too? Because there can be no coming back from this!

The bed shifted with Hugo's weight and then he was beside her, his eyes level with hers, his hand in her hair and all her worries evaporated in the heat of his kiss.

Because everything felt right. So right and perfect.

Because Hugo made her *feel* just right and perfect just the way she was.

CHAPTER TEN

IF THE WEEKS prior to Hugo's leaving for New York had been incredible, the week following his return could be deemed nothing short of revelatory. And Cassie wasn't just referring to the orgasms, of which there had been many.

All to varying degrees of exemplariness.

Which was a word, right? Because it was Hugo all over when it came to being a lover. Attentive, thorough, going above and beyond.

Now she understood what a true climax was and there was only one problem with that discovery—it made them quite addictive. It made the *whole* act quite addictive.

And she was starting to feel like the harlot the Duponts would love to paint her as.

But it didn't count if you craved them all with the same man over and over, did it?

Though she digressed, because what she was really talking about was the *L* word itself and all the wondrous feelings that came with it.

There was no proving the opposite any more.

She was wholeheartedly and unequivocally in love with Hugo, and it was joyous.

She had gone her whole life without love, and finally she knew what it felt like to truly love another, and she was starting to hope that he felt the same. Because how could it be like this and not be reciprocated? How could *he* be like this and not feel it too?

'What's that grin about?'

He offered her a spoonful of Pierre's ice cream as he asked, the black and white movie they were watching playing over his features as they lay in her bed late one night…

It turned out Pierre's ice cream wasn't just perfect for a sunny Parisian autumnal day but the perfect post-make-out dish too.

'I was just thinking that you've turned me into a bit of a harlot.'

He chuckled. 'I think that technically a harlot has sex with multiple people for money, whereas you only do it with one man for Pierre's ice cream.'

'I was thinking that too.'

'So, you admit it, you do only have me for the ice cream?'

'Guilty as charged.'

'Why you…' In seconds he had the bowl shoved aside and he was upon her, tickling her ribs until she was laughing uncontrollably.

'Hugo, stop! Stop!'

'Not until you—'

And then he froze. Her body fenced in by his thighs as he

rose above her, ears attuned to the outside world. 'Do you hear that?'

'What?'

And then she heard it. The rumble of people in the outer hall.

His phone started to ring and he sprang off the bed, reaching for it as he tugged on his lounge pants. Her mouth dry despite the recent ice cream, she eyed him, naked from the waist up. Would she ever be immune to him? She hoped not.

'Oui?' He blurted into his phone and his frown sharpened. *'Quoi?'*

His eyes launched to hers and she tensed—was he grey or was it the movie?

Please let it be the movie.

Are you okay? she mouthed, pushing herself to sitting.

The smallest shake of his head.

'Je viens.' He hung up the phone. 'I have to go.'

'Now?'

It was like *déjà vu.* Two weeks ago, the same thing had happened. The same wall had gone up. Work again? Or something else? But it was late, a Sunday too.

Though his companies were global, operating 24-7. She got that, but still.

'My parents are here.'

'Your *parents*?' She launched out of the bed, swept a hand over her wild hair. 'Oh, my God!'

'Exactly.'

She covered her mouth and stared at him. His parents. They were *here*? Across the hall? Right *now*? The parents of the man that she…that she *loved*. That was huge. A big deal. She swallowed.

She wanted to meet them. But not in her—not in her *un-*

derwear. She'd dress first. But how did she broach that without broaching the real question of what they were. Him and her. For real. Not pretend. Because one couldn't meet the parents without first knowing how they would be introduced.

Because yes, they'd spent a week wrapped up in one another. To the outside world, nothing had changed, but behind closed doors *everything* had changed.

The problem was, neither of them had spoken of it. There'd been no heart-to-heart. Because she hadn't wanted to rock the boat. Too scared that she would push him away. Ruin whatever this was between them when it was too new, too fragile.

'Do they know about us?' she asked instead.

'I told my father we had an arrangement.'

'Oh.' Her heart gave a little shiver. That was news to her. And an arrangement wasn't a lie. It had been…in the beginning. 'When?'

He raked a hand over his hair, blew out a breath. 'A fortnight or so ago. The news got through to him so he called me, and I explained we were doing it for show.'

'You didn't say.'

'I didn't think I needed to. I wasn't expecting them to just turn up like this.'

'What are you going to tell them now?'

'Damned if I know, but I best go.'

She winced as her nails bit into her palms and he started for the door. 'Wait!'

He paused, angling his head just enough to eye her.

'Can I—? Do you want me to come too?'

'I don't think that's a good idea.'

'What about tomorrow?' She tried for a smile, though inside she could feel herself wilting. 'Perhaps we could take them for breakfast together somewhere?'

She could see the muscle working in his jaw—he didn't like the idea. Not one bit.

'Maybe. Let me just get the lay of the land first, yeah? See what's going on.'

She fought to keep her smile in place. 'Sure.'

He went to move off again.

'Hugo?'

He stopped.

'Aren't you forgetting something?'

She picked his T-shirt up off the floor, where she'd carelessly tossed it only an hour ago, when life had felt so very different, so very perfect. How was that possible? She wanted to bury her face in it and breathe in his scent. Relive that moment and the man he'd been then, to suppress the tears that wanted to fall now. Instead, she lifted her chin and handed it over.

'Thanks.'

And for a world-stilling moment she feared he would leave without a kiss goodbye. And when he bowed his head and swept his lips against her cheek for the briefest most heart-stealing kiss, she almost wished he had.

'*Bonne nuit*, Cassie.'

'Goodnight, Hugo.'

She gripped her middle, holding herself back when she wanted to race after him and confess all. Knowing that now wasn't the time. He needed to see his parents. He needed to deal with that challenge alone. Then they could face the next one together—their future and what it looked like.

Because she knew what she wanted.

The question was, did Hugo want it too?

'Maman. Papa. What are you doing here?'

'Hugo! Is that any way to greet your parents?' His mother

hurried up to him, cheeks glowing from her time in the sun, but it was her eyes that truly sparkled. She looked joyous as they exchanged air kisses before she cupped his cheeks to take a closer look at his face. Her intense scrutiny heightened his nerves. 'How could you not tell me?'

'Tell you what?'

She smiled wide, patted his chest as she swirled away and took the drink his father now held out for her. In the time it had taken for Hugo to cross the hall and enter his home, his father had been let in by his team and made himself at home in the bar because, of course, he had. *What's yours is mine and mine is mine*, would be his father's motto forever.

'What's going on?'

'What do you think is going on, son? Your mother has discovered the news and was too excited to stay in paradise. She *had* to come and see it for herself.' His father raised his own glass in false cheer. 'Did you not want to bring the Princess with you?'

If looks could kill...

'Don't look so cross with your father, Hugo. It was my idea we turn up unannounced. I wanted to surprise you.'

He dragged his gaze back to his mother. 'Surprise me, why?'

Now she looked sheepish. 'I know you had us on that blissful retreat all these weeks, so I understand that you may not have wanted to break the rules to share your news, but something of this magnitude, darling. Don't you think you could have at least let a note slip in, given us just a little hint at your happiness.'

'My happiness?'

His eyes flitted to his father. Had he not told his mother

the truth? Was that a sparkle in his father's eye, and to what end? Was he playing some kind of game with him?

'Father hasn't told you?'

'Told me what?'

'I figured this was your mess, son. You could be the one to explain it.'

'Mess? What do you mean? Will you two stop behaving like children and just explain.'

Hugo strode up to the bar and poured himself the same drink—like father like son. Only they weren't. They were chalk and cheese. And that was part of the problem. Why he was such a disappointment. Hugo wore his heart on his sleeve far too much for dear old dad. And he wasn't about to do it now.

'We're not in a relationship. Dad should have told you.'

Yet you were making love with her not an hour ago.

'I've been helping her out of a bad situation with her ex.'

And helping her into a new one with you.

'It's all an act for the cameras.'

An act that's been getting ever more real behind closed doors.

He threw back the drink with a wince.

'And you knew this and you didn't tell me, Antoni!' His mother rounded on his father.

'Don't blame me, Mary. I was on the retreat with you, remember.'

'But you knew all along!'

'I didn't know before he embarked on this whole debacle. If I had, I would have had something to say about it.'

His mother sank onto the edge of the sofa as she seemed to fizzle out before Hugo's eyes, and he scratched at his chest, the same sensation happening within him. And he felt his father's gaze on him, observing it all.

'Can you give us a second, Mary?'

His father's tone brooked no argument, and that's when Hugo knew, the real reason they were here was yet to come. His mother may think they were here because she wanted to be. Because she wanted to have it out with her son, the relationship she believed he'd been keeping a secret from her and to meet the woman she'd hoped had brought him happiness. But his father...

Slowly she got to her feet.

'The guest room is made up, Maman. You'll have all you need in there. I'll come and see you shortly.'

She looked so deflated, and he wanted to take it all back. The secret and the lies. He wanted to promise her the world with Cassie at the very top. Because hell, in a perfect world where he could have everything he wanted he would have that. Of course he would.

But a perfect world did not exist. Not for people like him. He'd believed in it once, and look where it had got him.

'We need to talk,' his father said as soon as his mother was out of earshot.

'Yeah, I got that.'

'It's about Sara.'

'I got that too.'

'I don't think you do, son.'

His knuckles flashed white around the glass, his eyes barely lifting from the drink as his father handed him his phone with a draft press article already active. There was the woman from his past, only she was very much in the present. She looked the same. Her warm caramel eyes, rich dark hair, alluring smile...

And there was his every flaw printed in black and white. Everything he had done wrong. His mistakes laid bare. The bodyguard who'd put his heart before his head and almost got her killed. Crossed a line when on duty. An absolute embarrassment. Brought shame on the company, on his family, and on hers.

'You need to bury this before it buries you and brings shame on her.'

He swallowed. Nodded.

And then he saw the profile shot of the reporter who had written the article. Frozen human snowman himself. How he must have loved getting his hands on this story. He shoved the phone back at his father. It didn't matter who had found the story, or how old a tale it was, it would be today's news tomorrow.

'Has Mum seen this?'

'Not yet. A friend gave me an advance read, but it'll be everywhere come tomorrow. Sara's family won't be happy.'

'It reads like it *came* from her family. A way to get their own back now that it won't affect them.'

'Perhaps.'

'I'll deal with it.'

'I'm sure you will. And what about the Princess?'

'Her name's Cassie.'

'Princess Cassandra. Cassie. They are one and the same.'

'They're really not.'

He could sense the curiosity in his father's gaze and avoided his eye. 'She goes by Cassie. And I'll talk to her.'

'I meant, what about this relationship you have going on? How long do you plan on keeping this up now this is soon to be out there? If it really is as fake as you say it is…'

He gripped the back of his neck with a curse. What a mess! What an absolute mess!

So tell him it's not. Tell him things are different now. That it's real. You can't, can you? Because the idea terrifies you.

He'd been so happy in their bubble of the past week.

Refusing to put a label on what they were now.

Refusing to think on what came next.

'She hardly needs this kind of a scandal following her about, Hugo.'

'Are you referring to me as some kind of an albatross around her neck, Father?'

'If the shoe fits. People like the Princess—*like* Cassie.' He changed it up with the look Hugo sent him, his brown eyes softening with what could even be interpreted as compassion. 'Like Sara, they come from another walk of life, son, and the sooner she goes back to it the sooner you can go back to yours. Before you get embroiled in her further... I've seen the way you look at her.'

'You haven't been here to see us together.'

'The photos are telling enough.'

'You don't know what you're—'

His father cut him off with the arch of a brow, and Hugo's chest tightened around the rest of his denial, the rest of his lie, because ultimately, his father was right. Cassie did come from another walk of life, just as Sara had. And she would return to that life and she would launch her career in fashion. She would forget about him and she wouldn't just survive, she would shine.

And if he thought life without Sara had hurt, life without Cassie...?

'Can we not do this now, please?'

'All those years I tried to make you more like me, harder,

emotionally closed off,' his father said over him, 'but you had too much of your mother in you. When Sara came along, I knew she was trouble from day one. I saw what was happening and let it run its course, hoping it would teach you a lesson and I almost lost you in the process. This time I won't be so stupid. Don't be so foolish, son. Women like them, they're trouble. Why can't you find someone steady, someone home worthy, someone like—'

'Someone like me?'

'Mary!'

They both turned to find his mother stood in the hallway looking about ready to scream blue murder. 'So that is how you see me, Antoni?'

Oh, Dieu, here goes...

In a moment of madness, he thought about returning to Cassie. To escape the fight and find solace with her. But in mere hours the press would be pounding the streets outside, and his age-old wound would be tomorrow's tittle-tattle.

How did he even begin to bury it?

He didn't know, but he had to try.

Cassie barely slept a wink.

Funny how one could sleep alone for months, but a week with another and your body suddenly depended on that person to be there.

When her phone rang at the crack of dawn, she was grateful for the interruption. Grateful all the more to hear Louis's excited chatter on the other end offering to pay her for the designs she had finally sent over. A collaboration to get the name Cassie Couture out into the world—yes, please.

It was what she needed. What she'd wanted for so long. Only it landed...flat.

'You are happy—*oui*?'

'*Oui*, Louis. *Oui*.'

'You do not sound it? What is wrong, Cassie? I can… maybe offer you some more money. Is it not enough? Let me see. What about—'

'No, Louis. It's fine. Honest. More than fine. I promise.'

'Then what is it? Is it that Hugo? I bet it is! He is a big man. A beast! I am coming home tomorrow. I will sort him out!'

She gave a hitched laugh. 'No—No, Hugo is fine. We are fine.'

'I don't believe you. Don't lie to me.'

'Louis, behave. All is good. I will see you tomorrow.'

'*Oui, bien*. And then I will see you for myself and we will celebrate. Champagne! *Ciao*, darling.'

'*Ciao*.'

She hung up, a sad smile on her lips. She didn't even have the energy for a morning run. Instead, she got dressed and took her coffee out onto the balcony, watched the sun rise and Paris wake up. Surprised when the doorbell rang not long after.

Her heart did a little jig. It was too early for Housekeeping and her heart did what it always did now—it sprang to Hugo.

She peered through the peephole to find an older woman on the other side. Dark hair to her shoulders, same heart-shaped brow, same blue eyes—Hugo's mother!

She eased open the door, trying to second-guess if this was a good sign or a bad sign. Could Hugo have sent her? And if he had, that would most definitely be good, wouldn't it?

'*Bonjour*, I hope you don't mind me calling by.' Her French accent was thick, her eyes and smile both warm and welcoming. 'But since my son was so rude as to keep you a secret for over a month, I thought I would introduce myself. I'm Hugo's mother.' She held out her hand, which Cassie took, and she gently covered Cassie's with her other. 'Mary Chevalier.'

'It's a pleasure to meet you, Mrs Chevalier. I'm Cassie.'

'So I hear.' Her smile widened as she released her. 'And you can call me Mary. Can I tempt you to breakfast, Cassie?'

'Erm…sure.' She stepped back. 'Would you like to come in?'

'I thought we might go out.'

'Out?' Cassie gulped. 'Just me and you?'

'Oui.'

'Does Hugo know?' She looked across the hall at his very closed door and Mary nipped her lip, leaning in conspiratorially.

'I won't tell if you won't.'

Cassie gave a nervous laugh. She couldn't help it. Now she understood where Hugo got his playful spirit from.

And what could it hurt, really? Though what did his mother know, exactly? Had Hugo told her the truth about them… were they fake…were they real…?

The problem was, not even Cassie knew the answer to that. Not from the all-important man himself.

But this was a chance to get to know more about Hugo. Hugo from before she knew him. Hugo from his mum's perspective. And if she knew more, maybe she could find a way to make this into more for him too.

'Let me get my purse…'

Hugo woke to laughter.

The kind of laughter that had no place in his penthouse. Two women. His mother and—*Cassie?*

He shot out of bed, following the ruckus into the kitchen,

and there they were. The two thick as thieves, wearing aprons and smiles and an abundance of good cheer.

'What in the love of—?'

'Ah, Hugo!' His mother swept towards him and clamped her flour-covered hands on his cheeks as she kissed him. '*Bonjour!* Cassie and I are making your favourite!'

'My *what*?'

'Madeleines, of course!'

'Madeleines?' he repeated.

'Yes, French madeleines.' His father put down the newspaper he was reading at the table before the window and eyed him over his glasses. 'It's good of you to join us.'

Hugo ran his hands over his hair. Had he walked into some strange parallel universe, because this could not be his life today?

And then he heard it, the frenzy outside. The press. It was like the day after the night before. Or rather, the day after the flower photo had broken. Only now it wasn't him with flowers on her doorstep that had sparked the uprising, it was his decade-old failing. Almost getting a woman killed. So much for spending half the night awake, calling in favours and doing what he could to smother it.

But this laughter, this chaos in his kitchen, it was all about distracting him from it. Pretending it wasn't happening. It had to be.

And Cassie was here. Smothering herself in his shame when she should be distancing herself, getting as far away from him as she could.

He shook his head. The pounding within not thanking him for the gesture.

'Maman. Papa. Can you give us a moment, *please*?'

'I think it better you give *us* a moment, because we don't

want to let the little madeleines burn.' His mother gave him a wink. A wink!

And he reached for Cassie's hand, pulling her from the room without looking at her because if he looked at her, all cute and homely in her apron, with flour on her cheeks, in her hair—*gah!*

He was going to surrender on the spot.

Too much emotion trying to overrun his good sense, and then where would he be?

Out of control of his life and lost to it. Just like he'd been all those years ago. His life in pieces with no way of knowing how to pull it back together again.

'You shouldn't be here.' He closed his bedroom door and stalked to the window, looked down over the Champs-Élysées and the hovering journalists demanding their ounce of blood, *his* blood this time, and yanked the shutters closed.

'Why?'

'You must have seen the reports?'

'You mean the stuff about Sara?'

She said it like it was nothing. How could she say it like it was *nothing*? 'Yes!'

She walked towards him and he backed away. 'It's okay, Hugo. It'll all blow over soon enough. It'll be yesterday's news. They'll print something else and the world will forget and—'

'But *I* won't. I won't forget what I did.' He pounded his chest with his fist, spat the words out. '*I* won't forget how it felt.'

She covered his palm with her hand, and he flinched away as though burnt. 'Don't. Don't touch me.'

'But Hugo, you—'

'*Please*, Cassie!' Because she was killing him. *It* was killing him. This feeling. Crushing him inside. Suffocating him. The same feeling as back then, only it cut so much deeper now. 'You need to stay away from me. You deserve someone who won't bring this to your door. *You* deserve more. *You* deserve better.'

'Don't do that. Don't stick me on some pedestal like my parents did, telling me who I should or shouldn't be seen with. Who is considered good enough for me. *I* choose those things. And I choose you.'

He shook his head so viciously he thought he might be sick. Or was that just the rolling in his gut.

'I don't care what the press says any more, Hugo. I don't care what the world says. The only person I care about is you.'

He pressed his palms to his temples, pushing out her words. Because she couldn't mean them. She only thought she did because she had spent her whole life being treated so badly. So starved of love and affection that to have known it through him these past few weeks, she now felt him worthy of it in return. But he *wasn't* worthy of it. And she would see that once she got out in the world and experienced it properly. Once he freed her of the hold he had inadvertently cast over her.

'I can't do this any longer, Cassie.'

'Do what?'

He threw a hand towards the kitchen—at the baking and his mother's presence, all mixed up in Cassie's. All homely and sweet and nice. 'Live this lie.'

'Which lie? The fake relationship to the press or the real one we have…'

He shook his head, trying to cut her off, and she gave a shaky laugh and wrapped her arms around her middle.

'Because I know you told your parents it was fake too.

But your mother took me for breakfast this morning, and she made it pretty clear that she thinks it's quite real and—'

'No, Cassie!'

Hugo stared back at her, the tortured look in his blue eyes crushing her with his words.

'No, Cassie?' she repeated softly. 'What do you mean, "no"?'

Though she knew, could already feel the chasm so vast between them.

'So, it's over,' she said, when he failed to speak. 'Whatever this was, it's over. You and me. This?'

Still nothing. Barely a flicker of his dark lashes over eyes that still raged a storm.

'Fine.' She lifted her chin, stood tall as if she owned her feelings and wanted him to know them too. That way there could be no confusion between fact and fiction when she was gone. 'But since we're done with the lies, Hugo, here's my truth—I love you.'

He blanched, and she wanted to choke on her own heart.

'Yes, I know you don't want to hear it, but tough. I do. You have given me so much. You have shown me how to live and to love and for that I will always be grateful to you.'

He'd gone so very pale, his eyes so very vacant. She pleaded with him to say something, anything, but…nothing.

'As for going forward, I'm moving out. Louis is coming back tomorrow, so you won't need to see me every day either. You can count your blessings there too.'

Still, nothing.

'Goodbye, Hugo.'

And she walked before her legs refused to function and

she crumbled at his feet. Because she refused to let him see how broken she truly was.

She would be okay. She had her future. She had Cassie Couture. She had her whole life ahead of her. Her dreams were coming true.

Even if Hugo wasn't to be a part of them any more, it was better to have loved and lost than never to have loved at all.

And she truly believed that, having known it now, pain and all.

CHAPTER ELEVEN

Three days later

'IF YOU HADN'T made him feel so worthless growing up, maybe he'd feel worthy of her now.'

'And if you hadn't made him feel so soft, maybe he would have been man enough to fight for her.'

Hugo gawped at his parents, who had made themselves right at home on his sofa.

'Will you two just stop, please. This isn't helping.'

'Well, if you'd been honest with me about how you felt, son.'

'You didn't give him the chance to be honest, Antoni. You were too busy throwing Sara back at him!'

'*I* messed this up, Maman. Me! Nobody else!'

Now his parents gawped at *him* and he dropped his gaze to the note in his hand, fighting the reflex that would have seen it crumpled and creased. Scarcely able to believe the words on the card that had accompanied the bouquet of classic cream hydrangeas now on his coffee table.

He would think it some twisted joke of the paparazzi if he didn't know Cassie's elegant scrawl as well as his own handwriting, having pored over enough of her detailed fashion designs...

My darling Hugo,
I am sorry for what has come to pass.
   It was never my intention to hurt you, nor to fall in love with you.
   The press are my cross to bear, and what was printed in your name will pain me for ever. Because, as Wellington once said of Napoleon, you are worth forty thousand men—to my mind, you are worth all the men in the world. Because I have never met one such as you.
My heart is yours.
Always and for ever.
Cassie xxx

He strode up to the window, stared out over the streets of Paris, wondering which one was lucky enough to offer up a home to her now. Because to write the note by hand at the local florist he'd used himself all those weeks ago, meant she had to be in the city somewhere...only where?

He wanted to throw open the French windows and call her name from the rooftops, beg her to come home.

'This was my mistake and now I need to fix it,' he said, his breath misting up the chilled pane of glass. But how did he fix it when he didn't know where she was?

Louis was refusing to speak to him, so there wasn't a chance in hell he'd give away her location.

He pressed his fist against the window, gritted his teeth.

How could he have been so stupid as to let her walk away? The one woman he had come to love with his all. The one woman who had chosen to love him with her all, and he had thrown it back in her face. Rejected it. All because he had deemed himself unworthy of it. How stupid could he be?

What he would give to be able to rewind to that night or that morning, he didn't care which, and make it right. Tell her the truth. Tell her that he loved her. That he'd always love her and only her.

'You know she has Lyon's security working for her.'

Hugo's ears pricked at his father's less than subtle comment. 'Lyon?'

'*Tak*. She asked me if I could recommend a close protection firm...after giving me what for.'

He turned his head. 'She gave you what for?'

'A bit like your mother's doing now. Some nonsense about not telling you I was proud of you enough. That if I'd loved you a bit more, then maybe you'd have accepted her love rather than thrown it back in her face.'

He huffed and his mother gasped. 'You didn't tell me that, Antoni.'

'Yes, well, it was hardly my finest moment to share.' His father cleared his throat and squeezed his mother's hand before getting to his feet and crossing the room. 'And it wasn't nonsense at all. She was right. And I'm sorry for that, son. Because I wish it wasn't the case. You're not me, and neither should I have tried to make you so. You always used this first.'

He touched his hand to Hugo's chest. The contact as surprising as the compassion in his father's brown gaze. So he hadn't imagined its presence the other day either but...his father, compassionate?

'Are you—are you *crying*, Father?'

'No. Absolutely not.'

'You could have fooled me.'

'But I am concerned about Cassie's well-being.'

'Why?' he blurted, all teasing forgotten as worry for her overtook all else. 'Why would you say that?'

'Because she's taken to running along the river at some ungodly hour in the morning like she's got some kind of death wish.'

Hugo's mouth quirked.

'I can't imagine why anyone in their right mind would do such a thing, but she's out there with a team every night like clockwork. Lyon is quite amused by it all and I told him in no uncertain terms he should quit laughing and talk some sense into her.'

'We used to go together.'

'You are joking.'

'No!' He grasped his father by his arms and planted a smacker on his cheek. 'Thank you, Papa!'

'What for?' he chortled.

'For giving me an idea.'

'You're not going to accost her at that time of night on the Seine? Surely?'

'It's our thing.'

His father eyed him dubiously. 'That's some *thing*.'

It really was, and it was all he needed...he hoped.

The witching hour wasn't the same without Hugo. It didn't stop Cassie trying to find its magic though. The peace, the rush, the joyous feeling between night and day when she could run and let go...or at least try and let go of the stress that plagued her through the day and wouldn't let her sleep at night.

That is, thoughts of Hugo and her love for him and the conversation that she knew could have gone better if she'd perhaps given him a little more time to adjust to his parents' homecoming. Hadn't ambushed him with his mother. Hadn't dumped the *L* word on him.

She toyed with going back. Every night she ran a loop that took her past the Avenue des Champs-Élysées and every night she chickened out. Failing to find her peace, the rush, the magic, and her Hugo, all at the same time.

Because of course he didn't love her. How could he? She'd spent her life trying to earn the love of her parents, then the Prince. Why would Hugo be any different?

Because he is different, came the honest answer.

He was kind. He was good. He was honourable.

And she was glad she had met him, even if she had lost her heart to him and feared she would never feel quite whole again.

And she was glad she had sent him an apology too, because he hadn't deserved all that bad press over an isolated incident that had happened so long ago. Maybe if she'd read the articles, given them the time of day, she might have understood why they had cut so deep. But she hadn't wanted to. She hadn't wanted to justify a single word they had printed by dedicating a single second of screen time to them.

But she'd made herself read them in the aftermath. Having witnessed his torment, his self-loathing, his pain. She'd made herself read every word and had hated the journalist as much as she had hated herself for provoking him enough to go to the lengths it must have taken to uncover such a story. And she had hated the world for making it okay to print such words about the man she loved. Words that had cut open a wound that had barely healed, forcing her to leave him bleeding and in pain.

His reputation torn to shreds. His masculinity. His pride. His father's disappointment. His love lost. Not to mention the news spreading within his security company. How it must feel to know that he would have rookies reading the article, learning of his mistakes... All thanks to her.

'Ma'am, you need to slow down. There's someone up ahead.'

Jody, one of her close protection detail, came up alongside her and nodded to a guy as he rounded the exit of the Pont Neuf bridge. Cassie's heart fluttered in her chest. Recognising his broad frame before her eyes did.

'Hugo?'

'Ma'am?'

'It's Hugo!'

And she wasn't slowing down, she was speeding up. Racing towards him, because she knew, knew with every beat of her pulse that it was Hugo. Her Hugo. And there could be only one reason he would be here at this time of night...

'Ma'am!' Jody hurried after her, but Cassie was sprinting and so was Hugo.

'Cassie!'

'It's okay, Jody! It's Hugo! I know him! I know him!'

They came together in a collision of bodies, the air forced from her lungs as his arms closed around her and he hugged her to his chest. 'Cassie!'

He breathed her name into her hair, his voice as pained as the grip around her.

'What are you doing here, Hugo?'

'I had to see you.'

She prised herself back enough to look up at his face, his eyes glittering in the lamplight. Lines of worry creased up his brow, bracketed his mouth—the man had aged a decade in a week and still looked like the sexiest man to walk the earth.

'Is everything okay?'

'*No*. Nothing is okay.'

'Let me guess, you're not sleeping very well again?'

'Hardly a wink.'

'So you've come to hijack my witching hour?'

'If you'll let me.'

'Is this to escape your parents?'

He choked on a laugh, his big strong hands lifting to cup her face as his eyes searched hers in wonder. 'No. For once it is not my parents. Though I'm having a tough time getting rid of them.'

'Then…'

'It is you, Cassie.' He took a ragged breath that vibrated through her too as he kept her ever close. 'It's this pain I now have inside of me because I was fool enough to let you walk away.'

'Then why did you? Why hurt us both so much?'

'Because I refused to accept your love. That for all you said you loved me, I refused to accept I could be worthy of it. But the truth is, I am too selfish to let you go, which probably means I'm even more unworthy of it.'

He gave another choked laugh, his fingers trembling against her face.

'What are you saying, Hugo?'

He lifted the rim of her cap to ease it off her head and the cool night air teased along her skin.

'I'm saying many things. I'm saying I let my fear of getting hurt a second time around get in the way of us. I'm saying I refused to accept the truth of what was there all along. I'm saying my mother was right. I'm saying you were right. I'm saying this is real, Cassie. I am saying that I love you. With all my heart, I love you.'

She blinked up at him, her heart racing a million miles a second. 'You do?'

'I think I loved you the moment you came to my naked rescue. Loved you all the more when you stuck that ice cream cone on that jerk's nose. And I will continue loving you all the more if you can forgive me for being too foolish to accept it and hurting you in the process. I can't *bear* that I hurt you.'

'Oh, Hugo!' Tears filled her eyes, her throat, and she launched herself up, kissed him with all the love she felt inside. 'I'm sorry too. So very sorry. I never meant to hurt you. I never meant for all that stuff with Sara to get dredged up. I never—'

He kissed her deep, unrelenting, fierce. Lifting her off the ground as he pressed her body to his. 'You don't need to apologise,' he growled against her lips. 'That wasn't you. That was them. And I choose to no longer care too. My past is my past. It's a part of me and I can't change that.'

'And I'm not so sure you should… I kind of like the man you are.'

'You "kind of *like*" or do you still…?' He cocked one sexy brow.

'Oh, Hugo,' she crooned 'Are you fishing?'

'It's three in the morning, Cassie, give a man a break?'

She ducked his arms and backed into the middle of the bridge, her arms and smile wide as she twirled on the spot, glossy ponytail swinging out. *Écoute, Paris! J'aime Hugo Chevalier de tout mon cœur!'*

He chucked, ingraining the exquisite sight on his soul. 'Was that loud enough for you?'

'You're going to get us arrested,' he teased as he walked up to her.

'Well, I mean it, Hugo. I love you with all of my heart.'

'And I love you, *mon petit chaton*.'

And then he tugged her to him and kissed her, and Cassie knew that this was it.

This was her love story. This was her man. It had taken thirty-three years and a wrong turn, but love and all its wondrous feelings was real. And it was worth waiting for.

EPILOGUE

September, two years later,
Paris Fashion Week

ROUNDING OFF FASHION'S 'Big Four', with the final week in Paris, was a dream come true for Cassie. Her label was out there amongst the world's biggest names in global fashion, and hearing the ripple of adulation and applause from the audience made up of fashion editors, writers, buyers, stylists, influencers, celebrities—*all* the people she needed to impress—was as joyous as exiting the Louvre on the arm of the man she loved. Her husband.

And she wasn't just exiting on the red carpet, she was walking on air because she had a piece of news to share with the man who had helped to make those dreams come true.

'Cassie! Hugo! Can we get a smile?'

He paused beside her, looking so very sexy in black tie. 'What do you say?'

She pulled her shimmering silver train to one side so that she could turn and smile up at him, remembering a time many moons ago. 'Do I have food on my face?'

He returned her smile, his eyes as wistful as hers as he cupped her cheek and swiped his thumb along her lower lip. All the love in the world shining in his gaze and she couldn't wait to tell him. Was surprised he couldn't read her confession in her gaze.

'Do you think they'll get bored of that move?'

'Never. I told you, as much as they love to play the viper, they're just a bunch of old romantics who love a good love story.'

'Love story,' she said with him.

'Exactly.'

She kissed his thumb. 'I love you.'

'I love you too.'

The cameras went crazy—flashes going off, reporters cooing. Not that she was paying any attention to them—she was all about her man and the love overflowing within her.

'Shall we go home?'

'I thought you'd never ask.'

She led him to their awaiting car, pausing just long enough to say goodbye to all those that needed to be thanked. Good wishes exchanged. Promises to call. Meetings to be arranged passed to her very attentive PA.

He chuckled as soon as they were strapped into the rear seat of their limo, the privacy glass between them and the driver giving them the quiet they so desperately desired. 'Thought we'd never be free.'

She scooted into his side. 'But we're worth the wait, right?'

'We're always worth the wait, *mon petit chaton*.'

She smiled. 'When I said "we" I wasn't referring to you

and me... I was referring to—' she took his hand and pressed it against her tummy '—all of us. Another, even littler kitten.'

He tensed and his breath caught. 'Cassie! You're not. We're not.'

She nodded and peeped up at him. 'We're pregnant. I found out this morning, but with everything happening and we hadn't a moment to—'

He stole her explanation with his kiss, his elation in every impassioned sweep of his mouth against hers. When finally, he came up for air, his crystal-blue eyes glistened down at her.

'I never thought I could be happier than the day you told me you loved me. You've just proved me wrong.'

'In that case, our child proved us both wrong, because I feel the exact same way.'

'Just wait until my mother finds out.'

'Your mother? It's your father who keeps nagging about grandchildren.'

He gave a soft huff as he swept her hair back from her face and searched her gaze, his own filled with wonder. 'I can't believe he is the same man. Retirement has been the making of him.'

'Or maybe it's just softened him, giving him the chance to indulge that side of him that was always there.'

'And for that I'm glad.'

'Me too. You have a good relationship.'

'We do now. As do you.'

Her smile quivered about her lips. 'Thank heaven. I'm blessed to have that with both of your parents.'

'They feel lucky to have you too. A daughter they're very proud of.'

He'd guessed where her head was at. Thinking of what she didn't have with her own blood, but she'd come to terms

FAKE FLING

with that long ago, and she wasn't going to shed any more tears over them. She'd reached out once, with news of her engagement to Hugo, and they'd made their 'disappointment' clear. She wasn't a punchbag, willing to go back for more.

If they wanted to change their attitude and come to her, they knew where to find her. And they could bring their apology with them.

But she wouldn't hold her breath.

She didn't need them. She was happy with the people whose happiness truly mattered to her. With those she loved and who loved her in return. Who valued her happiness as she did theirs. Her family. Hugo, his parents, and their little baby Chevalier.

* * * * *

Keep reading for an excerpt of
River Wild
by B.J. Daniels,
out now!

CHAPTER ONE

HE HAD THE nightmare again last night. The faceless woman, her mouth opening and closing, the primal sounds a deafening shriek, his fear and pain visceral. He knew it wasn't real, just a bad dream, yet he couldn't wake up, as hard as he tried. It was like being caught in an eddy on the river, his fear rising as his thoughts whirled, and the current took him out deeper with only one clear thought. *This time, you're going to die.*

"Still having the nightmares, Stuart?" the psychiatrist asked as she looked up from the notes she'd been taking.

"Nope," Sheriff Stuart Layton said with a shake of his head. He adjusted his Stetson balanced on his crossed knee and lied. He'd been coming here once a month since the "incident," as they called it, seven months ago. As an officer of the law who'd fired his weapon, killing a person in the line of duty, he had been required to have counseling until it was determined he could still do his job.

"How would you say you're dealing with the trauma of the incident?" she asked, pen poised above the paper.

His near-death *incident* was being attacked by a knife-wielding woman who'd left scars over his arms and torso, and even worse, invisible wounds that made him question his sanity—let alone why he was fighting so hard to keep his job.

Seeing that the doctor was waiting for a reply, he shrugged and said, "As well as can be expected. Life goes on. I have a job to do." She didn't like his comment, he noticed at once. "Keeping busy helps. I just had a kidnapping case, a thirteen-year-old." He didn't add that ultimately, he hadn't saved the girl himself. He certainly couldn't take credit for that. He had saved one life, though, and had done his job to the best of his ability, which he didn't feel was saying much.

"Do you ever question that you might be in the wrong profession?" the doctor asked.

He almost laughed out loud. When he fought his way out of the same recurring nightmare at three in the morning, he told himself he was done. He couldn't do this anymore. But with daylight, he could breathe again, forcing the darkness and his fear back for another day on the job—the only job he knew.

His father had been the sheriff before him. He'd grown up with the law living in his house. Going to the police academy out of high school had made sense after living in the small, isolated town of Powder Crossing, Montana, where there weren't a lot of opportunities. When his father retired, Stuart had stepped into the position that no one else really wanted. It seemed like a no-brainer.

"Who wouldn't question going into law enforcement?" he said, more to himself than to the doctor. His strict, distant father had used his silver star like a shield, a stoic, hard-nosed hero. Because of that, Stuart had thought he knew what he was getting into. He'd been wrong. "You start off thinking it's a higher calling only to realize that it's really just a thankless job—one that can get you killed. Pull over the wrong car, try to break up a domestic argument, step out of your office and look down the barrel of a loaded gun in the hand of someone with a grudge against you."

He saw her expression and cursed himself. He'd said too much. This wasn't the way he wanted to go out, failing his psych evaluation. All he'd had to do was get through this last required session of six. It didn't matter that he'd decided he had no business being sheriff anymore. He just needed her to sign off and let him hang up his star and gun on his own terms. Now he feared that he'd blown it.

"Given all of that, why have you stayed?"

He'd been too honest, so why stop now? "Because it's what I do to the best of my ability." Growing up, Stuart had wanted to be just like his father. Now that he had a better idea of who his father really had been, he feared that he had become him.

"Have you been depressed?"

She thought he was merely depressed? "Everyone gets down sometimes," he said, reminded of those nights alone in the house he'd grown up in, thinking about his life as he cleaned his gun. But then there were the nights when Bailey McKenna would stop by at all hours and, fool that he was, he would happily open his door to her, knowing the danger.

He'd definitely been down in the dumps before she'd started coming by. Often, he was depressed after she left hours later, the two of them having talked over a beer or two. Only talking. That's all they ever did, sitting out on the porch when it was warm. Otherwise curled up at each end of the couch while a fire crackled in the woodstove in the corner. He knew she wanted something from him, but he had no idea what. He'd just known that whatever it was, it could get him killed.

"Is there anything that might keep you from continuing to do your job, Stuart?"

Boy howdy, he thought. The last woman he'd gotten involved with had tried to kill him, nearly had. *So, yes, doctor, I have the unfortunate habit of getting tangled up with dangerous women.* It wasn't like he didn't know that Bailey was damaged, and yet she drew him like gawkers to a car crash. But how could he admit to the doctor that Bailey McKenna might prove to be the most dangerous of them all, yet he'd never wanted any woman more in his life?

"Actually," he said to the psychiatrist, "I think this introspection has been good for me. I see things more clearly. Maybe I'm maturing. It's possible, isn't it?"

She smiled, and he saw in her smile that she was going to sign his paperwork. He smiled back, pretending he wasn't worried about anything, not his future, not his growing feelings for Bailey. The last time he saw her, she'd been running scared, confirming what he'd already suspected. Bailey McKenna was in trouble up to her pretty little neck.

He feared what he was going to do about that, especially since things had been too quiet in the Powder River Basin. It gave him an eerie feeling he couldn't shake, like the lull before the storm. As he headed home, the signed psych evaluation form folded into his shirt pocket, it felt as if the storm clouds were already gathering for what would be one hell of a maelstrom.

This time, you're going to die.

BAILEY MCKENNA HADN'T realized it was so late. She looked up from her laptop, surprised to find that some of the library's lights had already been turned off, leaving pockets of darkness. She loved libraries, their smell, their solitude, the silence as heavy as the books lining the walls. And it wasn't just the libraries that she loved. She loved the books that opened doors into other worlds, cracked open other people's lives and shed a blinding and often insightful light on them.

Libraries and books had saved her growing up. Now they still provided her a place to escape. She always found a corner on the least used floor and settled in for hours.

Tonight, though, she'd stayed too long, and now she feared she might have gotten locked in. Closing her laptop, she gathered her things into the large bag she carried everywhere. She didn't let the bag or laptop out of her sight, not after all the months, years that she'd been working on her secret project.

It didn't matter that she'd backed up everything on the cloud. She didn't trust it. She needed to hold her project close. If anyone found out about it, they would try to stop her. She feared it might already be too late.

As she reached the third-floor stairs, she stopped to peer down. Darkness creeped up the steps from the pitch blackness below. What if she was locked in? It wouldn't be the first time she'd slept in a library since she started this. But lately, she'd felt as if she wasn't safe anywhere. She couldn't shake the feeling that she was always being watched. For all she knew, she had been followed here tonight. If so, they understood what she'd been up to.

The real boogeyman was who scared her the most. *He* was out there, had been for a long time. It was just a matter of time before he came for her again. That's why she'd been working desperately to find him before then. As her heart rate kicked up, she told herself she still had time. He'd waited this long. Why would he make his move now?

Starting down the stairs, though, she wasn't so sure about that. She stopped on a step to listen. The quiet she usually loved now felt ominous. She couldn't shake the feeling that while the library appeared empty, she wasn't alone.

On the second-floor landing, she turned the corner, then moved fast down the stairs, eager to reach street level. If she'd been accidentally locked in, she would call the emergency number. Someone would come get her out before long. But with each step, she found herself getting more nervous.

At the first floor, she had started toward the front of the huge building when she heard a scuffling sound, shoe soles moving across the library floor. She'd been right. She wasn't alone. She stopped again, listening even as her hand snaked into her bag for her pepper spray.

She'd been carrying the spray since being attacked outside the Wild Horse Bar in Powder Crossing. Her attacker had tried to take her bag with her computer in it. She'd fought him and gotten the bag away from him. Unfortunately, it had been too dark that night to see his face. He'd worn a hoodie and had run away when the female bartender had stuck her head out the door to see what was going on.

Bailey hadn't realized that she'd been screaming before that. Maybe the attacker just wanted money from her purse, also in her bag. Our maybe he'd wanted her laptop with what she'd been working on. She'd told herself it had been random since no one knew what she'd been up to, but she feared she was wrong.

She heard the scuffling sound again as she moved cautiously toward the front of the library. Maybe she'd been wrong and they weren't closed yet. Which meant the doors would still be open. Or maybe she was only hearing the janitor cleaning after hours.

Bailey rushed to the front door and hit it, expecting it to fly open. Instead, alarms began to go off. She leaned against the glass, clutching her can of pepper spray, expecting whoever she'd heard in the building to appear. If it had been the janitor or a librarian working late, they would come to see what was going on, right? But no one appeared from the darkness inside.

Instead, a police car roared up, siren and lights flashing. She stood, her back to the door, and stared into the darkness. It wasn't *Him*. Not here, not like this. No, but someone knew. She was no longer safe anywhere.

AFTER SHE'D BEEN QUESTIONED, scolded and made the subject of a police report—procedure, she was told—the young deputy offered to walk her to her car. Her answer surprised her.

"Please," she said, a quaver in her voice. She felt vulnerable, something she hated. But she wasn't sure at this moment that she was capable of taking care of herself. She'd had a scare tonight in the library. She hadn't been alone. The library had closed, but hadn't she heard someone else in the building? Where had they gone? Maybe more importantly, where were they now?

The back door opened onto the parking area—now empty except for her car. As she and the cop walked along the side of the building to the back, she saw her SUV sitting like an island in the middle of the blacktop sea. Beyond it were darkness and shadows that seemed to grow and fade with the passing traffic along 6th Street.

"You sure you're all right?" the deputy asked as she slowed, her eyes darting around the parking area—and the night beyond. She could only nod, knowing whoever it was hadn't left. They were somewhere in the dark, waiting for her. Her heart raced. What if it was *Him*? What if he was through waiting? But why now?

She and the officer continued toward her car. Her ears were tuned for the sound of a heel scraping over blacktop. She wasn't even sure the deputy would be able to protect her if the man attacked. Hurriedly she fumbled in her bag for her keys.

For a moment, she panicked. What if the cop left her before she found her keys? Her fingers trembled as she felt warm metal and pulled the keys from her bag—only to fumble and immediately drop them. They fell into the shadowy darkness at her feet, making a ringing sound as they struck the blacktop. For a moment she felt so helpless, so alone, so afraid that she thought she would start to cry and not be able to stop.

"Let me do that," the deputy said, scooping up her keys and opening her SUV's door. The overhead light came on inside it. She saw him look into the back before he handed over her keys.

She took them, fighting to pull herself together. This wasn't her. She was a fighter; it was the only reason she was still alive.

But lately, she'd been feeling as if she was constantly being watched—like now. Watched and followed. If she was right, *He* could be here watching her. Which meant he'd followed her to the library. He'd wanted her to know he was there. He wanted her to be afraid so he could watch her fear grow until he made his move.

Clutching the keys in her fist, she tried not to stop searching the darkness at the edge of the parking lot as she slid behind the wheel.

"You sure you're up to driving?" the deputy asked, studying her in the dim light spilling out of her vehicle.

"I'll be fine," she said, hoping it was true. "I'll stop and get some coffee and a bite to eat. I haven't had anything since breakfast. I'm a little shaky."

He took her answer at face value. "All right then, drive safely." For a moment, he studied her again as if he wanted to say more. Instead, he nodded and stepped back to close her door firmly. For a moment, their gazes met through the glass. She tried a smile as she reached to start the motor. "I'll be fine," she said as the engine throbbed to life. The deputy seemed to hesitate before he turned his back and walked away.

The moment she'd driven out of the semidarkness of the parking lot and caught her first stoplight, she saw it—something small and white stuck under her driver's side windshield wiper.

Her pulse jumped, her gaze flying up to the rearview mirror. She expected to see a face, smell sweat, feel something close around her throat. But there was no one hiding in the back of her vehicle. The officer had checked. Still, she felt jumpy.

Bailey drove a few blocks before she found a busy fast-food restaurant with a well-lit parking lot. She pulled in and, leaving the engine running, jumped out to lift the wiper and free what she now saw was a piece of paper folded tightly.

She didn't unfold it until she was back safely behind the

wheel, the doors all locked. Logic argued that it could be an advertising flyer stuffed under the wiper at any time while she was in the library.

Or it could be what she knew in her heart. The note had been left for her by the person who'd been hiding in the library, watching her.

Carefully unfolding the paper, her hands began to shake as she held up the note to the light. The words were written in a hurried scrawl. *You got lucky tonight. Won't next time.*

She balled it up and lowered her window, ready to throw it out. But she was a Montanan raised by Holden McKenna. You didn't litter. She threw the note to the floorboard.

Cars pulled into the drive-through. Others sped past behind her on the street. There seemed to be people everywhere. Life going on around her, *without* her. Her sudden desperation to get to Powder Crossing verged on panic. All she could think about was getting home. Home. Too bad she no longer felt safe on the ranch that had always been her home. Too bad she didn't feel safe anywhere but one place—the last place she should go.

Pulling out on the street at the first break in the traffic, she checked her rearview mirror again but saw only dozens of headlights. *He* could be in any of the vehicles behind her. The stoplight changed. The driver behind her honked and she hit the gas, telling herself not to look back. But how could she do that? She'd been looking back for twelve years. She couldn't stop now.

SHERIFF STUART LAYTON didn't hear about what had happened at the Billings Public Library until the next morning when the police report crossed his desk via computer. He'd been updated because the woman in question was a local.

Bailey McKenna of Powder Crossing, Montana, was released with only a warning after setting off after-hours alarms at the library. She claimed she'd been listening to music on her headphones and hadn't heard the announcement that the library was closing.

"Well, that explains my visitor last night," Stuart said to himself with a shake of his head. Actually, it had been late when Bailey had shown up at his door. He hadn't known what had happened—just that something had the moment he saw her face in his porch light. He'd been sound asleep when he'd been dragged abruptly awake by her knock. He'd scrubbed his eyes with the heels of his hands, taken off guard not by seeing her at any hour of the night, but by seeing her this upset.

Wordlessly he'd motioned her in. It was too close to daylight for beer. Yet too early for coffee. Still caught in the remnants of one of his nightmares, he'd been taken by surprise when she'd thrown herself into his arms.

He'd held her for a few moments before she'd quickly pulled away. Having grown up with Bailey in the small ranch community, he could count on one hand the times he'd seen her scared. Mad? That was another story. She'd always come out fighting, usually more than capable of taking care of herself.

"Bailey," he'd said, startled and worried. It wasn't like her to throw herself into his arms, though he'd dreamed of her doing just that. She had to know how he felt about her. Terrified, yet tempted by her. It's why, he figured, she kept him at arm's length. But seeing her this scared... "What's going on?"

She'd stepped back, shaking her head as tears swam in

her blue eyes. "I'm fine." Her voice had cracked. "I'm just really tired. Everything is going to be fine." She'd taken another step back, widening the distance between them. For the first time, she'd seemed to notice that all he was wearing was his jeans, his chest bare, his scars showing.

"Let me put something on," he said, uncomfortable around people without a long-sleeved shirt or jacket covering the remnants of the "incident."

"Don't leave." He'd started toward his bedroom, but then stopped, afraid she'd go back out into the darkness, afraid that whatever had her scared was waiting for her there.

He'd suspected there might be a man, a love affair gone wrong, though he couldn't remember seeing her with anyone. If she'd been dating, the gossip would have stretched across the Powder River Basin with lightning speed. He hadn't heard a thing about her and a man. To most people she was a mystery, apparently friendless, coming and going at all hours of the night, alone and secretive.

Turning back, he'd looked at her, so pretty and yet always so skittish. He'd desperately wanted her to open up to him and let him in. But he'd seen that wasn't happening, not then, maybe not ever.

"I just need..." She'd looked around as if almost surprised that she'd come there and didn't remember why she had. She looked exhausted and lost, and it broke his heart. He'd desperately wanted to comfort her but had known instinctively that wasn't why she'd come to him.

He'd pointed to the spare bedroom. "Get some rest. You're safe here. Stay for breakfast."

Her eyes had filled again with tears. "Thank you."

He'd shrugged and padded back to his own bed. He'd only had a few hours before he needed to get up and go to work. He'd thought he wouldn't be able to get back to sleep knowing she was just in the next room, but he'd been wrong. After he'd heard the creak of the bed in the next room as she'd lain down on it, he'd slept hard, awakened by his alarm.

When he'd gotten up, no surprise, Bailey had been gone. There was a slight impression in the mattress where she'd slept on one side of the spare bed. But other than that, there was no sign that she'd stopped by, let alone stayed long.

Sitting in his office now with a mug of hot coffee, he wondered what she'd been doing so late at the Billings library that she'd gotten locked in. At least now he had some idea why she'd come by his place last night and maybe why she'd stayed. But he couldn't imagine that was why she'd been so scared.

Remembering the fear in her eyes only made his concern for her escalate. What was it she'd said? *I'm fine. I'm just really tired. Everything is going to be fine.*

He had no idea what she'd been talking about. But he had a bad feeling it wasn't going to be fine any more than he suspected she did.

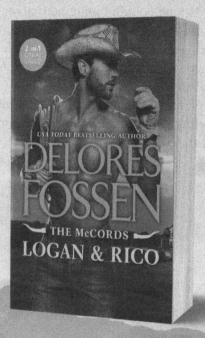